Praise for Gun Brooke

Course of Action

"A glimpse into that fantasy world of celebrity and high rollers...the relationship between Carolyn and Annelie is well worth the trip."
– *Midwest Book Review*

"Gun Brooke's international debut of the romance *Course of Action* is a winner. I could not put this book down. It is tension-filled and fast paced...a wonderful romance from a first time published author. Where have you been hiding, Gun Brooke? I, for one, would like to see more romances from this author." – *JustAboutWrite*

Protector of the Realm

"Gun Brooke has fashioned an enticing love story filled with electrifying conflicts to get this reader's heart racing. The action progresses from the rapid-fire battles to a possible romance beginning with a forced marriage. While the author sets it up as a marriage of convenience, we are not fooled because the tension is present between Rae and Kellen instantly. Using the characters' thoughts, the reader is treated to a promise of eventual passion. But *Protector of the Realm* doesn't give away anything too early, keeping the reader completely engrossed throughout." – *JustAboutWrite*

"Brooke is an amazing author and has written in other genres. Never have I read a book where I started at the top of the page and don't know what will happen two paragraphs later. She keeps the excitement going, and the pages turning. In a century when marriage is recognized between two adults and gender is not an issue, Brooke shows that love and romance and passion can grow. Likewise, she reveals to us the soft vulnerable side of these two strong, battle-hearty women." – *Friends & Family Magazine*

Coffee Sonata

"Each of these characters is intriguing, attractive and likeable, but they are heartbreaking, too, as the reader soon learns when their pasts and their deeply buried secrets are slowly and methodically revealed. Brooke does not give the reader predictable plot points, but builds a fascinating set of subplots and surprises around the romances. On top of this, we are treated to some very erotic scenes too. The author develops two romances within the book, and the story floats effortlessly back and forth between the two." – *JustAboutWrite*

Visit us at www.boldstrokesbooks.com

REBEL'S QUEST

SUPREME
CONSTELLATIONS
BOOK TWO

by

Gun Brooke

2007

REBEL'S QUEST
SUPREME CONSTELLATIONS BOOK TWO

ISBN 1-933110-67-8
ISBN 978-1-933110-67-7

THIS TRADE PAPERBACK IS PUBLISHED BY
BOLD STROKES BOOKS, INC.,
NEW YORK, USA

FIRST EDITION, FEBRUARY 2007

CREDITS
EDITORS: SHELLEY THRASHER AND J. BARRE GREYSTONE
PRODUCTION DESIGN: J. BARRE GREYSTONE
COVER IMAGE: TOBIAS BRENNER (http://www.tobiasbrenner.de/)
COVER DESIGN: SHERI (graphicartist2020@hotmail.com)

By the Author

ROMANCES

COURSE OF ACTION

COFFEE SONATA

SCIENCE FICTION

PROTECTOR OF THE REALM
SUPREME CONSTELLATIONS BOOK ONE

Acknowledgments

I had the help of my great beta reading team, to begin with: Pol, USA, helped me understand the concept of war and supplied tactical advice. Lisa, Sweden, gave me lots of eye-opening comments and contributed to the logical outcome of my plotline. Georgi, Scotland, commented and helped with language and character development. Ruth, Scotland, grammar, style, logical gaps—she found most of them! Jay, Canada, read and commented on plotline and character development. Sami, South Africa, also read and commented on plotline and characterization.

Of course, there are more people who helped, cared, and showed their pride in my efforts; Mom, Lotta, Elon, Malin, Henrik, and one individual who also did his best to prevent me from focusing and physically got between me and the laptop – Jarmo the Wonder-Dog!

Radclyffe, my publisher, who believes in me and continues to take a chance on a Swedish writer. Dr. Shelley Thrasher, my editor and friend, who makes the editing process fun and educational. You are the best! Tobias Brenner, artist, and Sheri, graphic artist – your work is amazing and you make the cover look so great. J. Barre Greystone, copy editor, thank you for the Argus eyes and hard work. Connie Ward, publicist, always enthusiastic and ready to help. Lori A, who creates the BSB newsletters and the "baseball cards" of the books for promotion – you're a wiz! All the people associated with BSB, who work tirelessly at promoting and reviewing the books, and also, my readers, without whom I'd work in a vacuum. Thank you, from the bottom of my heart to each and every one of you.

DEDICATION

To all those who selflessly serve, protect, and fight for
the protection and safe-keeping of others. To my family
and friends that inspire me and help me persevere—
nobody ever accomplishes anything in their life alone.

PROLOGUE

S and blasted Roshan O'Landha's face and crept into every
crevice, every wrinkle. Squeezing her eyes closed behind her
night-vision visor, she tried to soothe the stabbing pain the bright light
from an unexpected explosion caused. It reverberated throughout the
chain of mountains around her, booming until her ears rang.

"Get down and stay down!" Roshan yelled into her communicator
and prayed her team was all right. She pressed a different button with
her thumb, using her call sign. "Paladin to base camp. What's your
status?"

Jubinor's unmistakable voice, intermixed with loud coughing,
emerged through the static. "We've got fighters down and I'm missing
one, Paladin. Trying to get an update now."

"I copy. Standing by." Roshan tore off her visor and moved behind
a pile of debris as she squinted through the whirling sand. She wheezed,
then tried to clear her throat when she inhaled fine dust.

Suddenly she heard an all-too-familiar sound and rapidly flipped a
switch on her communicator. Her voice insistent, she manually overrode
any conversations going on at the moment. "All frequencies! We've got
incoming! Take cover!"

Roshan jerked her chin strap tighter and rolled to her right into
a shallow trench she knew should be there. She landed with a thud in
the apparently not-so-shallow ditch, and the air gushed from her lungs
on impact. Roshan was on her back and couldn't take her eyes off the
missiles as they approached, deceptively looking like pretty falling
stars.

"Damn it!" she whispered as she watched the missiles rain on
their positions. She tore at her radio and switched to another channel.
"Paladin to base camp. We need ARA now! What the hell are you
people doing back there?"

"This is base, Paladin. Counterfire has commenced." The young man responsible for the Automatic Response Artillery sounded urgent. "They fired missiles from Ganath, undetectable by sensors. We had no way of knowing where to—"

"Well, they're here now, so—" The ground shook and tossed the communicator from Roshan's hand. She clawed through the whirling debris for it but couldn't find it. Trying to open her eyes, she quickly closed them again when the sand battered them.

Explosions, on the ground and above her, hurt her eardrums. Roshan rolled into a position that provided better protection and covered her body as she let the shielding vest take most of the onslaught of debris. As the trash and the continued explosions pounded at her, all she could think about were the other members of her team. They were trapped at coordinates due south of hers, which meant they were farther away from this barrage of missiles and plasma-nodes now blasting into the ground.

They have to be all right. There's no other option. Roshan repeated her mantra continuously. Debris hit her helmet with a nauseatingly cracking sound, and she moved her neck carefully, relieved to find that the noise hadn't come from any broken vertebrae.

As another missile hit nearby, the ground shook, and Roshan felt the heat as a ball of fire expanded from the plasma charge. "Damn Onotharians! Damn them all!" The hatred in her voice didn't scare her. She had lived with this hate for so long, nourished it until it had become second nature, as it had for so many of her generation. It was better to fight back than to surrender. *Giving them hell is what we live for. Payback.*

Finally Roshan managed to pull her visor down to cover part of her face. She was tired. Twelve days in the field on emergency rations and recycled fluids, combined with sporadic fighting, had taken their toll. Roshan rose onto her knees and scanned the area. She couldn't use the infrared as long as explosions filled the sky, since it could blind her permanently. Dragging herself forward she felt with her hands to make sure she was following the trench. The luminescent compass strapped to her left arm above her chronometer wasn't working because of the charges' magnetism.

Roshan thought she heard something through the noise and stopped crawling. Pulling out a scanner, she set it to monitor her closest surroundings but found no sign of life. She paused and her blood ran cold. No sign of life? As far as she could determine, two of her team members should be within reach. At least her most junior team member, whom she always made sure stayed close during missions.

Roshan huddled over the scanner cradled in her lap as she rebooted it. When it went online again, it showed the same. No life signs. She wanted to toss the offending piece of technology as far as she could, but she forced herself to pocket it and resumed crawling due south.

A zinging sound from the night sky made her look up involuntarily and spot a distinct light traveling at an unimaginable speed. Not sure what kind of weapon this was, Roshan again threw herself headlong into the ditch. *"H'rea deasav'h!"* She didn't even have time to warn anyone over the comm link.

Deep, resonant thunder permeated the ground and air and rumbled toward her. *Twelve days in hell. Twenty-five years of my life. For this.* Roshan closed her eyes and grew more certain she might not survive. *A trap. A damn ambush instead of the breakthrough we expected.* Roshan braced herself for the impact of the detonation. *What's left, anyway? I've lost so many. Parents, friends, comrades…and, all those years ago, her.* A short moment before the shock wave hit, everything went white and erased the image of beautiful amber eyes. After that, all she knew was complete darkness.

CHAPTER ONE

I'm not using that thing." Roshan scoffed at the thin metal cane in Doc's hand. "Isn't it enough that my unexplained three-week absence will raise a bunch of questions? If my Onotharian contacts see me with a cane, after their successful ambush against the resistance, they're bound to be suspicious."

"But your ankle hasn't quite healed," Doc objected. "If you're not careful, you may walk with a permanent limp."

Roshan gestured impatiently toward her friend and comrade-in-arms. "Doc, listen to me. I have to get back to the capital. I can't limp, and I certainly can't use a cane. I have to appear as if I've just come back to Ganath from the Desamea asteroid belt. The Onotharians know I have my stockpile up there. My foreman created a disaster that needed my personal attention before the mission…and for all he knows I may have been captured, or worse."

Doc shook his head. "All I can do is advise you on what's medically sound. Do what you need to do, but please, stay off that foot as much as possible. And no personal combat training."

Roshan knew from the expression in Doc's eyes not to push any further. Rising from the gurney she reached for her jacket. "Thanks," she murmured, her thoughts already elsewhere. Time was a luxury she didn't possess. She had too much to do. "I'll do my best. I…" Roshan stopped in midstep and half smiled at him. "…owe you one."

"How do you figure that, Paladin?" Doc shook his head. "You were the one who dragged half of the members in the Gedor cell back to safety."

Roshan's chest constricted with a quick, sharp stab of pain. "That doesn't count. They were just inexperienced kids."

"Yeah, not like us veterans, are they?"

"They're nothing more than trainees who think they're invincible. I hate using anyone younger than eighteen on these operations. Their inexperience and immaturity…it's just wrong."

Doc shook his head. "There isn't much of a recruiting pool left to choose from. Let's face it, everyone is either dead, captured, or off planet."

"Maybe, but I don't have to like it. Well, enough of this. Got to go. Thanks, Doc." Roshan nodded briskly and was out the door before her face could give her away.

Roshan had been amazed to find herself still alive when she regained consciousness after that last major blast that had knocked her unconscious. The scene she had come across still haunted her. Five young resistance fighters, two boys and three girls, had all been badly wounded, and their remaining companions were dead because they'd strayed into the enemy's kill zone.

From her vantage point Roshan had watched them try to take cover but without a clue where to go. Every move they made seemed to be a mistake. Logic told her to hold her position, but she couldn't stand to watch the slaughter. She had transmitted her position to base camp and given a spot report to her team. Yanking off her pack and anything else that might weigh her down, she hid the equipment in the building she was about to abandon.

Roshan had dashed toward the wounded, taking cover wherever she could. Once on the ground she gathered the scattered resistance fighters and directed those who could still move to a bombed-out bridge north of their position. It had taken her three trips to drag the ones who couldn't walk, one at a time. As she pulled the last one to safety, Roshan had lost her luck. An incoming barrage threw her several feet, nearly dislocating her hip and damaging her right ankle.

Roshan had still managed to crawl to the bridge, pulling one of the youths with her. There she rendered what assistance she could as they huddled together until the incoming fire ceased, allowing her team to find them.

Roshan rubbed her hip absentmindedly. She needed to forget the ordeal. Doc was right; their pool of recruits was limited. It was the price of this damn war.

"I *still* don't have to like it," she growled to herself as she settled behind the wheel of the hovercraft parked outside the aluminum-carbide cubicle that housed the small clinic. Her cell staged their operations from this site within a deep ravine, located among the Merealian Mountains. The mountains, which stretched from just north of Ganath toward the Davost peninsula, were well protected from the Onotharians' sensors because of the mineral-rich bedrock. When not on a mission, most of the 120 men and women of all ages who were part of the group led unassuming lives in the shadow of the Onotharian occupation, except for herself.

Roshan punched in a few commands, and her two-seat hovercraft hummed to life and rose a meter above the ground. It was time to resume her role as Roshan O'Landha, wealthy business tycoon, and as much as it exasperated her to move among the rich and worriless, Roshan knew her double life was unavoidable, especially now, if she wanted to be able to contact the Gantharians' new allies.

She jumped off the hovercraft without thinking and cursed under her breath when a searing pain shot through her right side. *Damn, I have to remember to be more careful.*

Roshan pushed the door to her cubicle open and looked at the deep blue trousers and blue-black coat that hung there. "Very well," she muttered, and began unbuttoning her coveralls. "Time to go."

❖

"Ms. M'Aldovar! Wait!" a young male voice called from behind her. Andreia M'Aldovar slowed to a stroll to let her assistant, Rix M'Isitor, catch up with her. The young man was the oldest son of Dixmon M'Isitor, the Onotharian leader on Gantharat. He was eager to please her and, she suspected, quite infatuated with the fact that he worked for the most famous person on Gantharat, even when you counted his parents.

"Yes, Rix?" Andreia stopped when she saw the data-filer in his hand. It was blinking blue, which indicated a critical data update.

"Ms. M'Aldovar, there's a last-minute amendment to today's agenda. We received the situation report on last week's arrests."

"Then bring me up to speed." Andreia motioned with her free hand for Rix to continue.

"Three more shipments of rebels from the southern hemisphere have left for Kovos Asteroid Prison, ma'am."

"ETA?"

"They should be on schedule, only an hour or so from now." M'Isitor checked his chronometer. "Perhaps a slight delay since...er... they're fully loaded."

"Thanks for the update."

"No problem, ma'am. I figured you needed it for the meeting."

"That was very astute of you. Well, I must be off if I'm going to make it on time." Andreia dismissed M'Isitor and headed for the vast hallways of the governmental administration building.

Located in the center of Ganath, the building was constructed mostly of alu-carbon and transparent aluminium, except for the spectacular portico that adorned the front entrance. The columns of the portico were made from the rare D'Tosorian silver-marble that the Onotharians had obtained illegally via the black market that operated in deep space between merchants and pirates. She found it telling that the Onotharians would take their smuggled goods and display them so blatantly, since D'Tosoria was located well within Supreme Constellations space and strongly endorsed the partial trading embargo the SC Council had levied against Onotharat. The tall columns supported an impressive transparent aluminum ceiling that gave the structure a dramatic, airy ambiance.

As Andreia tipped her head back and looked up at the blue sky that engulfed them in a bright light, she saw a familiar face on one of the many open ledges. *Mother. Wonderful.* Andreia entered the building and used the senior staff's express lift to reach the third floor.

Her waist-long black hair in a perfect, intricate pile on the top of her head, Le'Tinia M'Aldovar walked toward her daughter with her arms outstretched. Her familiar scent, a delicate Ornamor flower perfume, engulfed Andreia as the stunning woman embraced her. Though petite, Le'Tinia was forceful. Her amber eyes under straight black eyebrows could easily pierce an adversary, leaving him devastated and crushed. She smiled, showing white, slightly pointed teeth. "*Henshes,* Andreia. It's been too long."

"Yes, it has." Andreia kissed her mother's cheeks repeatedly, the customary Onotharian greeting between children and parents.

"Hurry. We're waiting for you, dearest." Le'Tinia pulled discreetly at Andreia's arm.

Andreia bet they were. The GCDL, the Gantharian Community

Data Line system, didn't issue statements of conduct regarding their politics without their favorite spokesperson. Andreia had quickly progressed from being a mere decorative representative to helping the Onotharian citizens woo their Gantharian subjects; she had also emerged years ago as a forceful liaison between the Onotharian homeworld, six light-years away, and the Onotharian interim government on Gantharat. Born on this planet to Onotharian parents, Andreia was the perfect choice, according to her mother. To drive the point home, the data line constantly referred to her as an Onotharian daughter of Gantharat. A blessed mix that, combined with her strong convictions, had placed her in the eye of the storm.

"As you say, it's been a while. How was Onos, Mother?"

"Ah, too crowded and too polluted. We saw a few good performances in the ValaVala Concert Foyer, but living among the musically gifted Gantharians tends to spoil your taste forever." Le'Tinia placed an arm around her daughter's shoulders. "Then I get the news that you've been rock climbing. Isn't that a sport for the young and newly rich? Hardly anything a future president of Gantharat can afford to do, is it?"

"I have to stay in shape, Mother." Andreia was used to her mother's tirades, and nothing she could say would stop Le'Tinia. It saved time to simply nod and pretend to agree, rather than argue every little detail.

"Yes, of course you do. But there are other ways, *henshes*."

The Onotharian term of endearment hung between them as they approached the largest of the six offices occupied by the top men and women in the Onotharian interim government. Andreia knew that her mother probably considered herself the most loving of parents, but her parents' actions and demands had too often proved the opposite, so she couldn't buy into the bright smiles they graced her with in public.

"Ms. M'Aldovar. The chairman wants you to sit on her right, ma'am. This way, please." A young Onotharian woman guided Andreia past the high-ranking members of the interim Gantharian government, which included her father, who sat on one side of an oval table. At the far end, a woman in her late nineties rose to greet Andreia, sending everyone else around the table to their feet. "Ms. M'Aldovar."

"Chairman M'Ocresta. It is an honor." Andreia was still trying to grasp the fact that Villia M'Ocresta, one of the fifteen members of the House of Creators, had arrived on Gantharat without anyone telling her. Andreia refrained from sending her mother an ironic glance, knowing full well that her mother expected it and would triumph later. "I hope you had a pleasant and uneventful journey from our beloved homeworld." The words nearly choked her, but, accustomed to effortlessly delivering untruths, Andreia smiled proudly as she gestured toward the others present. "I'm sure you've received a warm welcome. If I'm not mistaken, this is your first visit to this part of the Empire, isn't it?"

The deceptively fragile-looking woman, her hair still black as the night and her complexion nearly flawless despite her age, nodded regally. "Indeed it is. Recent events have made it safe enough for me to travel to Gantharat. I received intelligence regarding your military's and the Onotharian Empire Clandestine Service's successful countermeasures toward the rebels. Very impressive, Ms. M'Aldovar. I commend you for your work."

"Thank you." Andreia used every ounce of her professionalism and her well-trained voice to sound forceful and self-confident. "We are proud of the dutiful men and women who risk their lives for their homeworld."

"We are, most assuredly."

Chairman M'Ocresta sat down and motioned for the others to follow suit. "I don't have to tell you that even as we continue to make progress and enjoy our victories over these worthless scoundrels here on Gantharat, they continue to make political mischief for us elsewhere. As I am sure you are aware, negotiations with the Supreme Constellations have ceased because of the O'Dal woman and that child."

"Yes, Chairman, I am monitoring the situation and know of its possible ramifications."

"Good. This unpleasantness is about to lead us to war with the Supreme Constellations—something I find undesirable at this time. It annoys me that this planet and its insignificant inhabitants have embarrassed us so publicly. My patience for such things is running out. This occupation has cost us dearly. Now it has drawn the Constellations' attention. I am well aware of the incident that killed your son, Valax," she said, glancing at Andreia's father, who looked uncomfortable and shifted nervously in his chair. Twenty years older than his wife, he was still a handsome man. Tall and skinny, with sharp features and thin lips, he resembled a predatory bird with his bent nose and golden eyes.

"Madam Chairman, it was a tragic incident that we could not have anticipated," Valax said. "As for the Gantharians, they are a proud, resourceful people, and we knew when we conquered this world it would take time."

"Proud? Resourceful? Noble words for such criminals. Cunning, deceitful, and destructive would be more appropriate. As for it taking time, I would think twenty-five years was more than sufficient. Finally, I must say, Valax, failing to anticipate a move on the SC's part was rather poor for a strategic thinker such as you. Once Ambassador M'Ekar behaved so recklessly in his clumsy attempt to commandeer that boy who pretends to be Gantharian royalty, what did you think they would do? Nothing?" Chairman M'Ocresta huffed. "They never sit idly by—and the cost of this folly? Your son, our ability to negotiate, and public humiliation." She paused and emphasized, "I tell you, time is running out."

"What are your orders, Madam Chairman?"

"Now that you've finally incarcerated most of their senior resistance leaders, Valax, I want them broken immediately so we can end this foolishness. I want this planet to submit to our will, our ways, once and for all," the chairman repeated, and let her almost-yellow eyes settle on each face around the table before continuing. "No more second chances. If Gantharat had not been rich in valuable natural resources and an abundant labor force, I would have recommended to the Emperor that we destroy every living being on it. If this situation does not resolve itself quickly, I may still make that recommendation."

Andreia's heart hammered. She could hardly believe her own ears. *Is she serious? After we've practically raped and plundered this planet, using its people as our workforce, she wants to kill off the cheap labor?* Andreia dug her blunt nails into the data-filer in her hands. This surprise meeting proved to be harder on her self-restraint than she'd anticipated. She could see the keen intellect and callous assessment in M'Ocresta's eyes as she sat casually rolling the Garmawood pearls of her necklace between her fingers.

"I don't believe that will be necessary, Madam Chairman," Andreia said, keeping her voice cool and unaffected. "As you yourself have noted, we have captured a large majority of the traitors. The ones that remain at large are inconsequential. They are less resourceful, more like mindless children that we can mold to our will with the right types of propaganda and incentives."

"I have noticed your recent successes, Andreia. They are the only bright points I've seen in recent times," M'Ocresta stated. "So you think we can mend the rift between us and the Constellations?"

"I do. It was unfortunate that the SC spies obtained sensitive materials from the O'Dals' farm, but if we launch a successful information campaign, we can discredit the find as well as the boy's heredity. As for Kellen O'Dal's claim about him and the occupation, we must do the same. If we overreact, her story gains credence, which we must avoid. I say let the SC pay us a visit. We have nothing to hide. All they will find are obedient children loyal to Onotharat," Andreia heard herself say, accompanied by sharp intakes of breath from the others around the table. No one ever contradicted the chairman.

"An interesting take on the matter," M'Ocresta agreed calmly, and smiled. "I've always appreciated your candor, Andreia. You remind me of myself in my youth," she said, and patted her data-filer. "Words are your weapons and you wield them well to keep the Gantharians at bay. Doubtless this method of yours helped us capture the rebels. A useful talent that I may apply with the SC. I will think about what you have said." Villia M'Ocresta gracefully rose from the chair. "In the meantime would you care to join me in an early evening meal with representatives of the Commercial Lobby and their president?"

"Certainly, Chairman M'Ocresta," Andreia replied. "I'd be delighted."

"Very well. I'll see you in…" M'Ocresta turned to her assistant, who checked his chronometer. "Ninety minutes then. I believe we're meeting at the president's residence. Do you know where it is?"

"Yes, Madam Chairman." The reply came out curt and almost rude, but Andreia didn't care. The invitation helped make this day one of her worst so far.

"Until then." M'Ocresta left the room, her entourage in tow. Most of the others followed, leaving Andreia alone with her parents and the provisional Prime Minister of Gantharat.

"What were you thinking?" Le'Tinia scolded. "Do you know how close you came to irreversibly offending the most influential and powerful woman on Onotharat?"

"This isn't like you," Valax added, his voice a fraction softer, but with the same absent look in his eyes that he'd had ever since Andreia was young.

"I got invited to her dinner with the Commercial Lobby, didn't I?" Andreia said, tired of her parents' criticism, their disdain for her when they were alone. At least they weren't glorifying her brother, yet.

"I never saw Trax almost drop the ball as you did this morning." Le'Tinia grabbed her briefcase so forcefully she nearly jerked the handle off.

"Me? I did what I had to. Has it dawned on you that the chairman is probably here because of what my illustrious brother did, or hadn't that thought crossed your mind? He was the fool that allowed the SC spies to get away with sensitive documents and was killed in the process."

Suddenly furious and sick of their attitude, she swiveled and glared at them. "I've always done everything you've asked of me—personally, politically, and patriotically. You can't fault me for anything! I succeeded in keeping the chairman, whom I didn't know was going to be here, by the way, from firing you and killing the inhabitants of this world. Not a bad day's work, I might add, and not only that, she's pleased enough to ask me to dinner."

"You don't need to bring up Trax's unfortunate accident."

"I didn't, the chairman did." Andreia stared incredulously at her mother. "Really, Mother, only you would call the idiotic idea of going toe-to-toe with a Protector of the Realm an accident." She gestured dismissively. "You forget, Mother, it was just another of his foolish acts. He had only himself to blame, and you know it."

"Don't address your mother this way…" Her father seemed to have awakened and now towered over Andreia, who was shorter than most Onotharians. "Your brother made a heroic, if ill-advised, decision, and his death broke your mother's heart."

"I don't want to fight," Andreia sighed, well acquainted with how her parents could rant on and on if she didn't back off. "I have things to do before dinner."

"Your old friend will be there, won't she?"

Thank you, Mother. So nice of you to remind me. "Yes, I assume so. She *is* the president of the Commercial Lobby, after all, and the dinner is being held at her house." It was hard not to sound contemptuous.

"I insist that you take your bodyguards." Le'Tinia suddenly became a concerned parent. "After all, some seventy-five percent of the members of the Lobby are Gantharians. You're popular with most of them, despite things, but after the latest raids against the resistance, you just never know. The word's out and it's bound to affect the general opinion of our cause. The guards must keep you safe."

Andreia agreed with her mother for once. A brewing hatred had flared again after the Onotharian military and their Clandestine Service had so brutally attacked the rebels. "Yes, Mother. I will."

As Andreia said good-by, she no longer thought about her own physical safety, but focused on the unnerving fact that she was about to be in the same room with *her* once again. She had successfully avoided being on the same premises as Roshan O'Landha for the last few years, but had known that sooner or later they were bound to meet face to face.

Andreia just wished that it didn't have to happen like this, on Roshan's turf. *You're right, Mother. She hates me, and I don't feel safe at all.*

CHAPTER TWO

Roshan looked out the window of the living room, the one room used only for entertaining, and saw the hovercraft arrive in her courtyard. She watched with detachment as the three long, sleek black vehicles settled down outside the front door. Her housing staff would greet the guests and guide them to the impressive room where she would be courteous, with just the right amount of formality expected from a Gantharian when dealing with her homeworld's occupiers.

She'd done this before, but never with such dignitaries. Chairman M'Ocresta's presence on Gantharat was the leading story in the Onotharian-controlled media, and Roshan had contacted her superior officers in the resistance cell to discuss how she should proceed. They didn't have enough time to alert Boyoda, the code name for the enigmatic resistance leader who rarely made a personal appearance.

Roshan thought about the mysterious person who'd helped them succeed in many dangerous missions by providing accurate and timely intel. Boyoda's information had saved Roshan's life on more than one occasion when there had seemed to be no way out. Whether providing blueprints of official structures or vessels, crew manifests, or top-secret schedules for guards at military installations, Boyoda seemed to sit on a treasure trove. Roshan knew her cell superiors praised and admired their leader, though they'd never met the person behind the suggestive code name. The boyoda was also the symbol of the royal family of Gantharat, the O'Saral Royales.

However, Boyoda hadn't warned them of the Onotharians' recent brutal attack that had resulted in the capture of Roshan's commanding officer, Berentar, a former commander in the broken Gantharian army. He'd fought the Onotharians for more than two years, before the military surrendered and became a token installation to give the Gantharians a false impression of control. Berentar and Roshan had joined the same resistance cell within weeks of each other and developed an easygoing friendship and a mutual trust. As his second-in-command, Roshan knew most of what went on within the resistance, but she was still not privy to all the information, which suited her fine. She was a resistance fighter, a soldier, and could not be bothered with the political machinery. Seething at the thought of the Onotharians' disastrous offensive, Roshan was sure the resistance had been compromised; there was no other explanation.

The thought of Berentar still missing from their last mission, probably incarcerated, perhaps even dead, made Roshan swallow back the taste of acidic anger. On her way back home to Ganath, she'd talked on a secure line with Jubinor, her next in command, several times, desperate for updates on her cell members, and when the casualties rose every time he contacted her, her anger and determination climbed with them.

So many of their senior officers, the seasoned and most experienced ones, were missing. Reports came in that they had been captured and rounded up at base camps all around the northern hemisphere. After that, there was no word as yet as to what had happened to them, but Roshan could guess. She envisioned the gruesome asteroid prisons and curled her fingers into tight fists.

"The Onotharian Chairman M'Ocresta, ma'am." The soothing voice of Wellter, her butler, interrupted her dark thoughts.

"Chairman M'Ocresta, welcome," Roshan greeted, and forced detached friendliness into her tone. "This is such an honor. My fellow board members will be here in just a few minutes. I wanted to welcome you in private. I hope you don't mind."

"Of course not, President O'Landha." Villia M'Ocresta seemed just as forceful as her reputation suggested. She placed both hands on Roshan's upper arms in the customary Onotharian greeting. "It is a most impressive and beautiful structure. A lovely home."

"Thank you—"

"Ms. Andreia M'Aldovar, ma'am."

What? Roshan's head snapped up.

"I took the liberty of asking Ms. M'Aldovar to join us," M'Ocresta said with a sly smile. "Gantharat is her homeworld, after all, and I thought I could use a guide."

Roshan was certain that her racing heart drowned out every other sound. She hadn't seen Andreia for more than five years, at least not like this. She wore a deep red suit, with a long flowing wool-lace jacket interwoven with sparkling threads. The golden highlights made her amber eyes glitter, and if it hadn't been for their present company, or the fact that Andreia was working for the enemy, Roshan would have been able to admit how stunning her former friend was.

"Andreia. What a…surprise." It was impossible to be more than barely polite.

"Thank you, Roshan. I know this was last minute, but I couldn't pass up an opportunity to spend time with our esteemed chairman."

"*Naturally.*" *You're drawn to everyone with power like a besa-bee to a honey pot, aren't you?* To Roshan, it was little wonder that Andreia now held the powerful position of envoy to the Gantharian people. Presumably, they might consider trusting her, as she was born on Gantharat, almost one of them. *And I know just how much of a traitor that makes you.*

The shuffling sound of many feet in the hallway announced the arrival of the rest of the Commercial Lobby members, and Roshan glued a cordial smile on her face as she swept by both the chairman and Andreia to greet her peers. As she reached the doorway she stopped briefly and glanced back over her shoulder. Andreia was watching her with an odd, indescribable expression, and for a second, Roshan saw not the mature woman holding Gantharat's future in her hands, but the young medical student from twenty-five years ago that she had once loved. Forty-five was still fairly young, but the years had washed away Roshan's idealistic nature, and she wondered if this was the case for Andreia as well.

I never told you how I felt then, and we have even more secrets between us now. Roshan knew Andreia had other reasons for her presence here than to merely bask in the chairman's glory. She could only guess whether Andreia was curious or perhaps suspicious, but she would do everything in her power to find out. The lives of her comrades depended on it.

❖

Andreia was painfully aware of how Roshan was ignoring her and focusing solely on Chairman M'Ocresta as she entertained the table with an anecdote from one of her journeys. No question about it,

Andreia thought, with her high cheekbones, dark blue eyes, and curvy lips, Roshan was stunning. *Just like I remember, but more mature and more...weary?*

Not quite sure why she'd bothered to notice something so personal, Andreia wondered about the dark circles under Roshan's eyes, curious about why her former friend looked so fatigued. When they placed their napkins on the table and rose to stroll over to the fireplace in the rustic salon, Andreia thought she detected a slight stiffness in Roshan's gait, but she could be mistaken.

Roshan turned and faced her before Andreia had time to avert her eyes. They had kept their distance since their initial polite greeting. Roshan hadn't engaged her in conversation, and Andreia knew better than to push. Angry at this blatant contempt from someone who'd made a fortune from trading with Onotharians, Andreia harnessed her bitterness and barely smiled. She knew this reaction would irritate Roshan more than a display of disgruntlement.

The chairman sat down on the large, plush couch in front of the fireplace and gestured for Andreia to join her. But before Andreia had a chance to comply, Roshan placed a strong hand on her shoulder. "If I may borrow Ms. M'Aldovar, Chairman?"

"By all means. Join me later, Andreia?"

"Certainly, ma'am." Andreia hadn't suggested that the chairman use her first name in this casual manner, but it was obviously good for her image. Doubtless Roshan and the other Gantharians present would think that Andreia was close to the chairman and had her ear.

Andreia followed Roshan to the far wall, away from the others, where Roshan stood with her back to the crowd of lobbyists that surrounded the chairman and her entourage. "Care to tell me what's going on? Why you're here?" Roshan sounded harsh.

"I'm accompanying our chairman, of course," Andreia answered calmly. "I realize that you're not happy to have me in your home, but I'm sure you'll benefit from socializing with an Onotharian chairman who sits on more power than I'll ever know. Surely you can tolerate me for a while?"

Roshan impatiently gestured, palm down. "This is personal and you know it. I'm tired of playing diplomatic games whenever we run into each other—"

"Please. It's not as if I'm at your doorstep regularly. I haven't been this close to you in ages." Andreia was proud of how patronizing she managed to sound, but a small part of her wished she could step out of her professional role and talk to Roshan like she used to. The futility of such thoughts annoyed her, and she pursed her lips, unable to hide her frustration. That her presence bothered Roshan exasperated her, but she stifled a deal-with-it comment and merely smiled again. Roshan and most of her peers in the Commercial Lobby made a lot of money from collaborating with the Onotharians.

"You know what I mean!" Obviously Roshan was tired. She probably worked very hard multiplying her wealth. Andreia had never heard rumors that the famous business tycoon Roshan O'Landha partied the nights away, so she voted for her first guess. Work. Roshan had always been extremely conscientious when they'd studied medicine together, always prepared to a fault for exams, a trait which contradicted her then easy-going, almost laid-back, nature. Andreia had been just as serious, but perhaps not quite as dedicated to the prospect of becoming a surgeon, and now...*Everyone says I'm popular among the people, but truth be told, I'm one of the most hated women on the planet.*

"Yes, I know what you mean. Honestly, the chairman sprang this on me at the last minute. I had other plans, but as you can imagine, nothing short of a life-or-death matter would have saved me from this trip." She forced a grin, even if it almost hurt her lips to seem amicable toward her former friend. "You know, the advanced Onotharian medical scanners would have deemed me a liar anyway if I'd tried to fake the Hazsortian flu or something."

Roshan clearly didn't find her remark funny. "I wouldn't know. No Gantharian knows of such elaborate medical procedures."

Damn. "Sorry. Bad joke." Andreia's mood shifted toward that gray state of depression that had plagued her more often lately. It mixed with confusion over Roshan's high and mighty speech that suggested, against better judgment, that she was loyal to her homeworld. "I'm sorry," Andreia said again, before she forced herself to resume the part she played in this mess. "As long as the situation on this planet is so volatile—"

"Volatile?" Roshan stepped closer, her chest almost touching Andreia's. "That's an understatement..." She quieted for a moment.

"It's damn hard to conduct business when you people can't keep the peace." Roshan folded her arms in front of her, brushing against Andreia.

The unexpected touch set off a spark that seared through Andreia. Shocked at her own reaction she had to force herself not to step back. "We both know it's for peacekeeping—" she began, careful to keep her voice low.

"Peacekeeping?" Roshan raised her voice, thundering so loud that Andreia saw everyone around the chairman stare at them. Hoping to calm the waves, Andreia grasped Roshan's upper arms, surprised by her wiry muscles.

"They hear you," Andreia murmured. "Calm down."

"Damn it." Roshan's eyes glittered like blue icicles as she jerked back and shook off Andreia's hands. "You just don't know when to quit. You never did."

The words stung deeper than Andreia would've thought possible. She had opened her mouth to speak when a voice at her side interrupted them.

"Everything all right, Ms. M'Aldovar?" One of the members of the Commercial Lobby approached them. "Can I help?" He looked worriedly back and forth between the two women.

Andreia knew that the mere thought of anyone offending her or any member of the Onotharian interim government practically guaranteed a death sentence, and she didn't want to jeopardize anyone. Over the years, the OECS had imprisoned several Gantharians for perceived arrogance and insults against her. Her objections had mattered very little in the long run, and it pained her that people were still incarcerated in the asteroid prisons for actions that weren't really a crime.

She shook the thought of those men and women off and focused on Roshan, who glared at her as she addressed the concerned man. "Everything's fine, thank you. Ms. O'Landha is an old friend from my university days."

Andreia watched Roshan stop breathing momentarily at this revelation. During the years of the occupation, neither of them had acknowledged their former friendship in front of others.

"Really, ma'am? What an extraordinary coincidence. I had no idea you were…old friends." His doubtful look spoke volumes; he was obviously trying to gauge their sincerity.

"Acquaintances, really," Roshan said with a rigid smile. "Many moons have circled our planet since then."

"So true," the man said with a cordial bow of his head. "But you couldn't tell that from looking at two such lovely ladies."

Andreia wanted to groan aloud at the farce. "Thank you," she managed.

Roshan smoothed her silk jacket and gestured toward the couch. "Why don't we join the chairman? What can I get you to drink? We just imported some wonderful Imidestrian wine that we're about to introduce on a global scale."

Amazed at how quickly Roshan recuperated from her rage and mentally comparing her to an unstable plasma-charge, Andreia pasted on a polite smile and returned to the others on the couches in front of the fire.

"Is anything wrong?" Chairman M'Ocresta asked with a frown.

"No, ma'am," Roshan said, and sat down gracefully next to her honored guest. "Ms. M'Aldovar and I don't share the same opinion of how the Gantharian market should be run and distributed. A domestic issue—only a matter of negotiations."

"Really. Well, then, let me make an impromptu and informal toast." Villia M'Ocresta raised her glass in a ceremonial elliptic movement. "To...domestic bliss and successful negotiations."

"May your wish come true." Andreia held her breath as she raised her glass. She was almost nervous to meet Roshan's eyes while she murmured the correct response and swallowed a mouthful of the sweet Imidestrian wine. To her surprise, Roshan raised her glass as well and sipped. Andreia wondered whether Roshan could relate to the chairman's toast, or if the deceptively frost-layered tycoon had something else up her sleeve. All Andreia knew was that she intended to keep an eye on Roshan from now on. She didn't trust her.

CHAPTER THREE

Roshan watched the hovercraft lift off and remained at the window in the marble hallway until the last of them had passed the outer perimeter of her property. Small golden and blue lights disappeared into the foggy night, and Roshan breathed deeply, relieved that she didn't have to pretend anymore tonight.

She grimaced at the pain in her ankle and felt like massaging the back of her neck.

"Lights out." Roshan switched off everything but the emergency lighting via voice-command. *Andreia M'Aldovar.* To host the woman who'd gutted her emotionally and committed the ultimate betrayal twenty-five years ago had clearly been dangerous. Roshan had forgotten her closely guarded self-control for only a few seconds, but enough for her to risk everything. *What an idiotic thing to do!*

To complicate matters, Andreia looked stunningly beautiful, even if her twenty-some years in the public eye had taken their toll. No doubt, Andreia, as many of her peers, had access to the best beauty spas in Ganath. Some things hadn't changed. Andreia's dark, golden eyes were still able to drill into Roshan and create havoc. Always serious, but also undeniably intense, Andreia obviously knew the impact she had on other people.

Roshan climbed the stairs toward her bedroom. She knew she'd find the same weary, slightly lined face that she'd seen just this morning staring back at her in the mirror. To her surprise, her eyes were clear and steadfast, and her skin quite flushed. A certain fire burned in her eyes, and the muscles in her jaws flexed as Roshan immediately thought back to how Andreia had looked at her. Her dark eyes, with glittering amber speckles, had been almost disdainful, which surprised Roshan. She had no idea what Andreia's opinion of her was, and she shouldn't care.

Andreia was enmeshed with the ultimate powers on Gantharat, and many times Roshan had thought about rekindling and cultivating a relationship with her. However, for some reason, just thinking about acting appreciative around Andreia nauseated her. *It's easier to risk my neck in battle than to play act around Andreia M'Aldovar and her damn family.*

More than anything, Roshan hated the role Andreia's brother Trax had played within the OECS. His units were little more than hit squads that preyed on the Gantharian citizens. They tried to intimidate people and help the Onotharians rule by fear. They conducted very little actual espionage, and when they did, the people involved suffered intensely. Roshan knew personally of at least twenty families, whole generations, that the OECS had eradicated.

When the rumors began surfacing that Kellen O'Dal had returned briefly to Gantharat, for reasons unknown, the same rumors told the story of how she'd fought and killed Trax M'Aldovar in a Gan'thet fight.

Roshan's hatred for the OECS was so profound that she would have given anything to witness that fight; however, another part of her ached for Andreia. When they were young women at the university, Andreia had idolized her brother, but Roshan had considered Trax a sociopath even then. Roshan wondered how Andreia had taken the news of her brother's death. Had she mourned him with her usual stoic resolve and rationalized it as a price worth paying for Onotharian future success?

Disrobing, Roshan took a quick hydro shower, to conserve energy. Gantharat had an abundant supply of water but scant power, which kept most people from using the more modern ionic-resonance cleansing. Roshan could afford it, but since her fellow Gantharians couldn't, she hated to treat herself to such luxuries. Besides, having hot water run down her back after a stressful ordeal relaxed her.

Checking her chronometer, Roshan grabbed a large towel and hurried toward the dressing room next to her spacious bedroom. She stopped and listened, making sure nobody was within earshot, then pressed a button hidden behind a clothes rack. Her fingerprint and her DNA disengaged the auto-lock and polarity of a holographic wall behind the rack. A small room that served as an office as well as a walk-in closet appeared, displaying coveralls, technical equipment, an array of weapons, ammunition, and a small lab.

Roshan tossed her towel onto an already-cluttered chair and pulled on mesh-reinforced underwear and, on top of those, dark gray coveralls. Her hands flew over her pockets as she stashed her standard-issue equipment and concealable weapons in them. The resistance was not as well equipped these days as it had been shortly after the occupation began. Times had changed, and the Onotharians sat on seemingly endless wealth, always bringing the very best and latest technology to their battles. The resistance had no such means, and Roshan was often infuriated that she had to make do with antiquated equipment. *As if we're not already outnumbered.*

She secured a laser knife to her calf before lowering her pant leg, tugging her combat boots on. Fastening the boot straps, she listened absentmindedly as the locks clicked into place. Roshan grabbed a black fire retardant hood and slipped it on over her head, ensuring she covered every strand, which otherwise would shine in the light of the twin moons. The tight helmet usually fit her perfectly, and she was surprised to find she had to adjust the chin strap. *Have I lost more weight? Damn, that's bad.*

Truth be told, she was exhausted. Her ankle burned, and her mind still reeled from the onslaught of emotions during the evening. She reached into a drawer and pulled out a tube. Taking two pills, Roshan considered for a second, then popped one more pill, just to be sure. Tonight would be stressful since she had to get to the rendezvous point just north of Ganath at the appointed time. She had pushed herself hard since she got back from the disastrous battle three weeks ago, south of the Merealian Mountains, but she couldn't slow down, not just yet.

She made sure the wall closed behind her before she punched commands into a computer console, sending an elevator up through the floor. Made of transparent aluminum, it would take her down into a long tunnel lit by winding phosphorous tube-light, a corridor that stretched for miles, branching out in six directions under her house. Never taking anything for granted, Roshan scanned the tunnel with a remote sensor located in the elevator. When she received an all-clear tone, she set the elevator to descend.

As she stepped out into the tunnel, Roshan heard only the soft hum from the light fixtures. However, she vividly recalled the evening she'd run into two Onotharian guards who'd found the tunnel's exit. She shuddered at the memory of how she'd had to deal with them and fought the urge to wipe her hands. Instead she adjusted her back-strap security carrier and walked over to a small cart. As soon as she sat down on the narrow saddle, the vehicle came to life and hovered a few centimeters above the ground.

Roshan's ankle ached, as did her head, but she shrugged off her pain. It was finally time to take action, and she was full of anticipation regarding tonight's meeting. A sprained ankle wasn't going to keep her from playing a part in the ongoing battle. She'd been through worse.

❖

Andreia was about ready to call it a day and return home to her apartment in the Onotharian Leadership Compound. Standing at her office window, she could see it in the distance, an impressive two-hundred-and-fifty-floor structure, heavily guarded by force fields and patrolling assault craft. The resistance had tried to destroy the military installations at the far end of the compound numerous times, but so far, nobody had been able to even make a dent in the composite-mixed, concrete-reinforced fortress.

It was like a city of its own within the Gantharian capital, its base covering ten blocks in each direction. It contained every possible type of store, and the residential area hosted Onotharian dignitaries, high-ranking senior military members, and wealthy Onotharians who no longer felt safe residing on their Gantharian property. Andreia had always wondered why they felt that way, since the Gantharian resistance never went after soft targets.

Instead, they attacked military installations and interfered with the Onotharian governmental process, even used self-proclaimed embargos that had thrown some Onotharian merchants out of business, but the Onotharian minority rarely suffered any collateral damage unless they brought it upon themselves.

Andreia walked down to the lobby, stepped into the hovercraft always at her disposal, and asked the chauffeur to take her to her apartment. She had more work to do, but it had nothing to do with her official duties.

The technically enhanced hovercraft hummed louder as it rose above street level and entered the air-corridor that would take them to the two-hundred-and-tenth floor where she lived. Normally, Gantharian hovercraft didn't run higher than two meters above the ground, but the Onotharian version had flight capability.

The hovercraft flew through the automatic scanning procedure, and a stark green light filled the cabin. The two-tone signal sounded, which cleared Andreia's identity, and the vehicle jerked slightly as it docked at the door of the airlock leading into her apartment.

"Thank you. I won't need you until tomorrow morning." Andreia nodded briskly at the chauffeur. "Good night."

"Good night, ma'am."

After the door opened with a faint hiss, Andreia stepped into her airlock. The inside door slid open as the outer closed, and she entered, grateful to be home, even if it would be a while before she could relax.

"Music. Selection, Andreia-Two-Four."

Soft music, with suggestive drums and the haunting tone of a flute made from the rare penamera trees that grew on the plains of the southern hemisphere, filled the apartment. The sound system, consisting of echo-panels installed throughout the walls, ensured that Andreia could hear her selection everywhere. It also served an additional purpose, as Andreia opened her briefcase and pulled out a small rectangular device. She walked from room to room and furtively scanned each one, pretending to examine her live plants, always careful of the OECS's paranoid surveillance even of the Onotharat Empire's most distinguished citizens. Andreia knew a wry smile played on her lips when a thought struck her, and she wondered if the OECS even monitored the twelve chairmen.

Thinking of the visiting chairman sent Andreia's thoughts to her hostess for the evening. Roshan O'Landha. Once her friend, now not her enemy exactly, she was someone Andreia could never call her friend again, ever. No matter what the Gantharian people believed, Andreia loved her home planet passionately, having been born into this lush, green world forty-seven years ago. Being Onotharian in this society back then had posed no problem; on the contrary, the Gantharians had considered the Onotharians an asset, and the two races had worked and lived side by side for more than fifty years.

Her older brother by two years, Trax had grown up with a different attitude toward his home planet. Often, he'd accuse their parents of robbing him of his rightful opportunities by emigrating to Gantharat two years before he was born. As a child, he'd spoken about moving back to the overpopulated Onotharian system. Le'Tinia had assured Trax that his future would hold glorious moments and that he'd have ample opportunity to lead a successful, influential life on Gantharat. Trax hadn't believed her but, nevertheless, decided to go into law enforcement after graduation.

Andreia heard the scanner buzz and relaxed marginally now that she knew her apartment was not bugged. She put the scanner back under the handle in her briefcase, where it merely looked like a locking mechanism.

Andreia was astonished, as always, that Roshan, despite her family history, had found it so easy to collaborate on all levels with the Onotharians. Her trading company thrived, and she traveled both globally and intergalactically, making sure her wealth increased at a steady pace every lunar year. How could she have misjudged Roshan to this extent? Certain that her friend would be filled with lust for revenge after her mother's death and her father's incarceration, Andreia had studied the reports from the OECS that painted a completely different picture.

At the beginning of the occupation, Roshan had taken over an abandoned company when a distant relative was killed during the first violent month of fighting and restructured the firm to fit her needs. Soon she had attained a seat in the Commercial Lobby and won the trust of many Onotharians. The Gantharians regarded her with disappointment and even open hatred at times. Still, Roshan's connections and the power that came with her vast wealth seemed to discourage any serious attempts on her life and property.

Collaborator. The ugly word hung between Andreia and the image of a younger, more relaxed and fun-filled Roshan, sharing a desk with her during their lab sessions at medical school. Their mutual passion for healing and helping people in pain and need had bonded them. "And she was stunningly beautiful," Andreia murmured to herself as she removed her clothes. Ten seconds later, ionic-resonance set on maximum frequency, inaudible to humanoid ears, had cleansed her body and hair. She pressed a button as she stepped out of the shower stall, and a discreet puff of her special perfume sprayed her.

When Andreia punched a command into barely visible markings on the mirror in her bathroom, it swung open, and she pulled out a case of makeup. Unlike her normal palette, which was gold, orange, and blue, these colors were black, gray, brown, and green. She began to paint her face with a brush: black circles around her eyes, brown to mask her lips, green to hide the olive tint in her cheeks. She'd be wearing her hood, where only her eyes, mouth, and lips showed. And, granted, the light would be muted, but she could afford no risks.

Her curly hair wasn't easy to tame; it flowed around her shoulders in a shiny cloud, and she had to tie it down with a silicon ribbon to lock it securely in place.

Dressed entirely in black, she wore a long-sleeved silk shirt, snug trousers, and a weapon harness under a wind-sealed tight jacket. Andreia tugged a thin helmet over the hood, to protect her head, before donning a small oxygen mask. A night-visor would also serve to protect her eyes from the wind.

"Lights out. End music."

The apartment became dark and quiet, and she waited exactly five minutes before she moved toward the airlock. She didn't use the command to open the door, which would have sent a signal to her hovercraft chauffeur that she needed him. She had long ago overridden that command, and now when she manually attached a suction device and pushed, the door still registered as closed on the security detail's monitors. At least she hoped so. When doing this, she always held her breath for a while, waiting for the alarm klaxons to blare.

Nothing announced her actions, so Andreia inhaled deeply and closed the door behind her. Now for the more tricky part, she placed the suction device on the outer door, bracing herself for the strong wind this far up.

Cold air and a fine rain hit her face like a thousand needles, and Andreia was profoundly grateful that she wore the visor. She pressed her lips together to protect them as the wind howled and tugged at her like a wild animal trying to coax its prey out of its den. Andreia reached into her jacket and found a small, semicircular fastening device. Preparing to press the button underneath it, she stepped out the half-open door, fumbled for a narrow maintenance ladder, and clung to a narrow pipe on her left as she moved the suction device to the outside of the door and pulled it shut.

She was about to loosen the suction device and place it in her pocket when a strong gust of wind snatched her and nearly ripped her from the structure. As she clung to the pipe she slammed the suction device into the wall next to it and pressed the button, the device holding her just as her feet slipped on the wet bar on which she stood.

She hung sideways in the strong wind for a few moments, trying to regain her footing. The rain made it nearly impossible, and Andreia groaned as yet another strong gust slammed her body against the door.

"For stars and skies," she muttered through clenched teeth. "I don't have time for this!" She detested having to resort to low-tech solutions, but this was the only way to leave the building undetected, especially at night. Because Onotharian technicians were about to install biosignature-scanners everywhere, it would soon become impossible to escape even this way.

Andreia forced her body to slide to the right and pressed her forehead hard against the cold, wet surface. Her left foot found the bar again, and this time, she stood steady enough to let go with one hand and reach into her jacket. Pulling out the semicircular object, she placed it against the pipe, pressed the button underneath it, and engaged the magnetic lock. She tested its strength, and, pleased with its grip, she placed her hands loosely around the pipe. "Thank you, Gods of Gantharat. Keep me safe so I can do my duty," she whispered and blinked rapidly three times. After the night-vision feature in the visor switched on, she placed the suction device in her pocket.

"Here we go." As she kicked off and removed her feet from the bar, her body plummeted straight down, the filament-wire enabling her to descend at a steady pace. The small object she'd attached near her door was programmed to deliver her safely on the ground, so unless more wind gusts sent her sideways, she'd land in a dark, remote corner of the building, on the opposite side of the heavily guarded entrance.

Almost at street level, Andreia bent her legs and landed softly, then disengaged the filament-wire and attached it to the wall. Unless someone knew where to look, he would never see the hair-strand thin wire.

Andreia scanned the area carefully through her night-vision visor. No one in sight. Time to go.

CHAPTER FOUR

Roshan pushed the hoverbike to the side, into the shadow of a deserted-looking warehouse. From its appearance no one would guess the technology hidden inside. Warning signs cautioned potentially curious people that the old plant surrounding the warehouse was contaminated and trespassers would meet with certain death.

The tunnel that originated at Roshan's estate had taken her halfway to the warehouse, and at the end of it she kept a fast two-seat hoverbike. When she was out on these missions, she used mostly back alleys and small dirt roads, to attract as little attention as possible.

Now she locked her bike, pulled an old, coarsely woven blanket from a bag attached to the back of the sleek, leather-like saddle, and covered it. Roshan headed toward the rear of the structure where she pressed her palm against a sensor, hidden under a panel next to the door. A muted purple light scanned her palm print, as well as her heart rate, blood pressure, and blood-oxygen level. Nobody could mutilate a resistance fighter, then use a severed hand to gain access. Only a living, breathing, unstressed person who was in the system could get in. If a resistance member was coerced, and forced to place their hand on the sensor, the scanner would pick up on the elevated heart rate and blood pressure, and alert security to investigate. It had happened only five or six times over the years, and so far no Onotharian agent had gained access that way.

Roshan remembered when she was a rookie how an Onotharian agent had infiltrated one of the other Ganath-based cells and nearly managed to uncover not only their headquarters, but also the identity of several resistance fighters. Eight cell members died while taking the Onotharian agent out. Roshan had never forgotten the incident and was always suspicious of newcomers. An Onotharian with access to dermal regenerators could easily mask as a Gantharian, however, there *was* a way to ensure the true nature of fellow rebels. Though a simple blood sample wasn't enough, since the Onotharians knew how to make their blood look blue, a scientist of the former Tamanor Laboratories had developed a way to genetically distinguish between the two races.

"Member four-four-alpha-epsilon-four," a synthetic voice droned, and the door clicked open. Roshan entered and followed a long, dark corridor into the inner, vaultlike mission rooms. She remembered how, as a young, idealistic foot soldier, still reeling from her mother's death and her father's incarceration, she had entered the headquarters for the first time. It had seemed as abandoned then as it did now, but she knew surveillance equipment covered every square meter of the premises, and camouflaged guards prevented surprise visits.

The corridors, still blackened by a past fire, smelled stale and uninviting, and to an untrained eye, nobody had set foot in the old warehouse in decades. Roshan had been utterly unimpressed the first time she'd been here, more than twenty years ago.

The first sign that all might not be as it seemed came about twenty meters into the corridor when it made a ninety-degree turn and revealed a cagelike construction. Roshan stepped inside without hesitation and didn't even blink when a gate slammed shut just behind her. A scanner flickered its shimmering green light over her, and then the gate in front of her opened, revealing an ordinary wooden door.

Roshan pushed it open and entered a room that buzzed with activity. Elaborate equipment aided the men and women who kept track of all the resistance cells planetwide. Each resistance cell worked independently, and only two or three members of the cell, which usually consisted of 50 to 120 or so rebels, knew how to contact other cells for larger missions.

The previous mission, during which many of the senior officers had been incarcerated or killed, had sent the entire organization into shock. Not once during the occupation had the Onotharians had such a success, and Roshan knew that soon people would start to point fingers and look for traitors within the organization. She shook her head as she put her gloves into her jacket pockets. It wasn't that easy. The surgical precision of the massive attacks suggested that a traitor or two hadn't caused this failure, especially since traitors were rare.

"Ma'am," a young man said, "we're glad you're all right."

He saluted her, and she returned the greeting and looked him over.

"You all right too? Base camp took some heavy fire."

"I'm fine. Two of my friends got singed, but they're going to make it. They're still in the mountain hospital."

"I'm glad they'll be okay. Am I late or—"

"The meeting of the resistance leaders is postponed fifteen minutes, so you're on time, ma'am." The young man, known to Roshan only by his call sign, looked over at a countertop located at the far wall of the room. "I think someone made new *yasyam* tea, if you'd like some?"

"Thanks. No, continue what you were doing. I can get it myself." Roshan patted him on the shoulder and continued among the busy staff. She saw a couple of new, young faces and realized that several of the ones who used to man these stations were probably among the missing. Anger churned in her stomach, and she had to will her hands not to shake when she poured the tea. She stirred some sweet honey into it, thinking it might help offset her fatigue.

Sipping the hot beverage, Roshan nodded at Jubinor, who was talking emphatically with another man across the room. Roshan was grateful that Jubinor had made it from their mountain camp in time for the meeting. He hadn't been physically injured during the Onotharian raid; instead he'd suffered a severe emotional trauma when his life-partner, Berentar, was reported missing in action. It was obvious to Roshan, who knew him well, that Jubinor was balancing on a knife's edge at the moment.

"Paladin!" a dark female voice exclaimed from behind.

Relieved beyond words, Roshan turned around and placed her mug on the counter. "Ma'am," she sighed. "Thank the stars you're okay. The last I heard, you were missing." Roshan had honestly thought she'd never see the senior officer standing before her again. Temmer O'Gavvian was an old friend of her parents, which was the only reason Roshan knew her real name. Temmer led a small cell of medical personnel that Roshan had seen save lives countless times.

"Rumor had it you'd be out of commission for a while yet. What brings you back already?" Temmer regarded Roshan under an inquisitively raised eyebrow. "Ah, don't tell me. You've heard the latest from the SC."

"They're coming. They have to." Roshan didn't like how much her words sounded like a mantra, rather than words of conviction. "Ever since the Protector of the Realm returned to show the Onotharians that she's not going to let anything happen to our prince, or to us, we've had new hope."

Temmer's look grew weary. "As much as I'd like to believe that, I can't help being skeptical, Paladin. Guess I've seen too much of humanoid frailty and to what levels we can stoop…if pressured."

"But that's also when we rise to the occasion," Roshan insisted. She wasn't about to give in to doubts at this point. "I truly believe this is the beginning of the end. It has to be, because I don't think our defenses can hold up much longer."

"Kellen O'Dal is a remarkable woman, and I remember her, not to mention Bondar O'Dal, her father, very well." Temmer leaned her hip against the counter and reached for a mug. "She took our prince to safety and managed to get the ear of the Supreme Constellations Council and, more importantly, their leading orator. I actually met Councilman Thorosac during my travels before the war. He was a young man, but even then a man of vision and convincing political ambitions. I'm not surprised that he's advanced so far within the SC, or that he managed to unite the Council after Prince Armeo's speech. Did you see the recording?"

A majority of the resistance fighters had seen the images of and heard the prince's speech to the Council. Roshan had stared at Kellen, her former cell member, and Commodore Rae Jacelon, of the SC, her new wife. Roshan, overwhelmed, had felt tears stream down her face, something she rarely allowed. So certain that the entire family of the O'Saral Royale had been hunted down and killed, she'd been amazed to watch this child, a handsome, dark-haired boy with his Onotharian father's colors and his Gantharian mother's dark blue eyes and royal poise.

For the first time, she hadn't felt as if her mother had died in vain while carrying out her duties as a colonel of the palace guards. Two lunar months into the occupation, the Onotharians had overpowered Jin-Jin O'Landha and the guards under her command inside the palace gates. Jin-Jin had held them off until the situation became unbearable. In the cellars of the palace, Jin-Jin and a handful of rebels had tried to defend the royal family despite overwhelming odds and certain death.

After three lunar months, Roshan and her father, together with the rest of the Gantharian population, had finally learned what had happened. Roshan couldn't remember if she cried, but she would never forget her father's look of grief.

"Yes, I heard the speech," Roshan answered, and pulled herself together.

"I think you're right when it comes to the impact of Prince Armeo's speech," Temmer said after sipping her tea. "Judging from the number of propaganda radio broadcasts we've had the last few weeks, I'd say the Onotharians are very concerned."

Roshan had started to agree when a double door behind two columns opened. Resistance leaders, fewer than there should've been, began to enter and sit down. The many empty chairs spoke for themselves, and Roshan exchanged grim looks with the other rebels. *Where are they? Dead, all of them? Prisoners?*

Vespes, the joint cell leader of Ganath and the most senior-ranking officer in the building, remained standing by the large view screen in front of them. Not quite powered up yet, it glimmered in nuances of blue behind the tall, white-haired man, creating a ghost-like appearance. "Fellow rebels, members of the resistance," he began in a traditional way, "it's with mixed feelings we gather today. So many of our comrades have fallen or are missing in action, yet we're on a threshold of new times, with new hope on the horizon."

Horizon? Roshan wanted to elbow the superior officer, make him sound more positive, more optimistic. They didn't need to hear that it was as far away as the horizon. *We need to hear that it's just around the corner, damn it!*

"We have to plan. We need to proceed meticulously and carefully. This window of opportunity, the promise of help from the Supreme Constellations, brings hope, but we must be realistic," Vespes continued.

Roshan was sure every man or woman present had had realism shoved down their throats every bloody day since the occupation began. She found it increasingly difficult to keep quiet, but bit down hard on the tip of her tongue. A glance in Temmer's direction also helped her remain quiet. Temmer shook her head almost imperceptibly and pulled her eyebrows together. Roshan couldn't tell if Temmer was as impatient with Vespes's choice of words as she was or was suggesting Roshan keep her cool.

"This is a rare moment. Some of you have been present during these special occasions, but most of you haven't. Our leader, Boyoda, will join us via vision broadcast, thanks to some of our resistance technicians who risked their lives in space to repair the malfunctioning satellite."

Roshan knew he was talking about her special space team, of whom she was very proud. Without them, none of this could take place. *I hope Boyoda appreciates this fact—and that he has more guts and initiative than Vespes.* Part of her refused to be impressed that she'd see the elusive Boyoda, as mythical as the majestic bird that had given its name, *boyoda,* to their resistance leader and its image to the O'Saral Royales' crest. Many times, Roshan, Jubinor, and Doc had half joked that perhaps Boyoda wasn't a real person at all. And now he was going to appear. Roshan squinted against the flickering blue light on the screen. *Come on, boss. We can sure use some of your magical sense of what's going to happen.*

The screen crackled with static and the image went black. Roshan held her breath until a lean figure appeared. Simultaneously, the inner mission room darkened and the audience was lit up from behind, to ensure everyone's confidentiality by obscuring their faces.

After five seconds of more static noise, the still form on the screen spoke. A voice, slightly distorted by a two-way scrambler, which made it sound faintly metallic, addressed them. "Fellow Gantharians, members of the resistance. I am Boyoda."

❖

Andreia counted the blurred outlines of twenty-eight senior members of the Ganath local resistance present at HQ. Visual and audio signals were deliberately distorted to conceal identities. All data was encrypted, and two of the young officers had developed a program that allowed for constant frequency hopping. So far, much to the Onotharians' frustration, the rebels' communications had never been compromised. This was a point of pride among the resistance since communications of any type not regulated by the occupiers were strictly prohibited.

As Boyoda, she knew no individual names or faces, other than those of the five men and women operating the small, underground facility she broadcast from. Her engineering officer, whom she only knew as Ily, was her best-kept secret. Andreia relied on Ily's ability to create technical solutions designed to keep her true identity hidden. It had taken her more than five years to find, and trust, the people she now worked with, and she knew they would give their lives to protect her. In fact, one of their predecessors already had.

She swallowed quickly, eager to sound certain and in charge, even if her jaw muscles tightened at the thought of what had happened to the other twenty-four, not to mention the more than six thousand rebels rounded up planetwide.

She knew that her actions as a double agent had helped so many missions be successful over the years, but she also took every failed mission personally.

"Vespes here, Boyoda. What are the total numbers? Do you know yet?"

Andreia didn't have to ask what he meant. "The last I heard, we're missing more than six thousand members. Entire cells have been destroyed. We haven't found out how many have been killed or incarcerated, but I'm sure I'll have more intel in the next few days."

"Where do we go from here?" Vespes continued.

"We can't sit around and wait for numbers. They're expecting us to go into hiding. I say we attack." A low hum distorted the voice of the person who sat next to Vespes, but it was clearly female.

"And your call sign?" Andreia asked, leaning forward toward the screen. She knew her own voice was scrambled to a higher degree. It was imperative nobody even knew her gender.

"Paladin."

Andreia nodded slowly. She had heard this call sign before, countless times, in fact. Paladin was one of the senior officers who had been part of the resistance as long as Andreia herself. The woman was a legend, whose fearless raids had generated her quite a fan club within the resistance, and Andreia had to concede that Paladin deserved it. "I heard you were injured and treated in one of the Merealian camps."

"I was. I've recovered. What's our next operation?"

Andreia pulled out a small computer console and attached it to a secure station beside her chair. After docking it and logging on, she pulled up a bulleted list. "You know the Supreme Constellations is arming for a confrontation with the Onotharians. In fact, my intel shows it's already begun at the SC border. Onotharians took a squadron of ships, allegedly to try and free Ambassador M'Ekar, but to no avail. When SC rattles their weapons, even our occupiers notice."

"They'll get here, but we may lose a lot of good people while we wait. Time's running out if we want to intercept any prison transports." Paladin spoke urgently.

"I'm aware of this." Andreia knew the woman bordered on insolence, but recent events made her reaction excusable. "However, to execute an operation without adequate planning and preparation is risky, with a high probability for failure. At this point in the war, failure is not an option. I've developed two courses of action. Whichever one we choose will require surgical precision. Collateral damage must be kept to a minimum. I want as little bloodshed as possible."

"Perhaps it's this method, this almost *pacifist* approach, that's caused our conflict to last for almost three decades!" another voice, male and raspy through the scrambler, exclaimed.

Andreia saw the contours of the resistance member's profiles as they turned to look at the man who had just spoken.

"You're out of order, Jubinor," Vespes admonished.

"The Onotharians are a callous, uncaring people, with greedy, calculating minds. They don't do anything unless it benefits them. We should use their tactics. Speak to them in a language they understand!" Jubinor objected.

Paladin rose, and Andreia watched her put her hands on her hips. "At what cost? Do these people, the callous, greedy, and calculating Onotharians, sound like anyone you'd like to emulate?"

"I've fought for the resistance for more than twenty years!" Jubinor spat.

"So have I!" The two figures, outlined by the indirect light, approached each other. The woman placed both hands on Jubinor's arms. "We will *not* compromise our values."

Andreia's throat constricted and she had to swallow repeatedly. So much hatred for her race, for her, if they knew who she was. In fact, many Gantharian-born Onotharians loved this world and its people. They were as much victims as the indigenous people.

"Take your seats," Andreia said, and fought to keep her voice under control. "We don't have time for an internal squabble.

"Both Jubinor and Paladin have valid points. We need to change our tactics without compromising our values, and it's time to move things up a notch. We're low on manpower, and our window to carry out any type of rescue operation is extremely small. Review the data that will arrive in code on your console, Vespes, and decide which one best meets our needs. At that point we will begin deliberate planning and operations. Decide quickly. The window of opportunity will commence in sixteen lunar cycles."

"Understood. When can we meet again and confer about details?"

"Once you have made your decision, contact me through our regular channel. Because we are operating on such a tight schedule I'll need a liaison, someone I can call on a secure channel. An experienced senior officer who can expedite the necessary plans and preparations that will be needed."

"I agree. Paladin is our most seasoned member, apart from myself."

Something about this suggestion disturbed Andreia, either the woman's posture or her strong, unbending tone of voice. "Very well. Paladin, outfit yourself with a Class 1 transmitter and use encryption mega-five. I'll contact you tomorrow evening, and we'll change channel encryption according to protocol."

"Yes, Boyoda." Paladin obviously had herself under control again. "Will I rendezvous with you at some point?"

Andreia forced herself not to flinch. She knew the group of resistance leaders could see her much more clearly than she could see them. "I doubt if we'll need to meet in person, at least not at first. We're in a vulnerable situation, much more so now, with the latest raids." Andreia refused to let the rush of guilt flood her when she thought about how she'd failed to deter the covert Onotharian operation. "However, when the Supreme Constellations becomes involved, we may have to."

Paladin seemed to be lean and muscular. As tall as the man next to her, she resolutely folded her arms in front of her. "Very well, ma'am. I'll wait to hear from you."

"Good. Now, we have another issue. For the first time since the occupation, an Onotharian chairman is visiting Gantharat." Andreia paused, examining the cell members' posture for signs of surprise. The men and women in the first row of seats didn't move, but the ones sitting in the back turned toward each other, as if astonished.

"I heard Chairman M'Ocresta is here," Paladin replied. "A rare opportunity."

Andreia nodded, her voice solemn. "It is. We'll talk more about this later."

"What can't you talk about in front of the capital's senior officers?" Jubinor interrupted. "I don't appreciate being kept in the dark."

"Jubinor!" Paladin growled. "You surprise me. The reasons should be obvious."

Andreia agreed. Jubinor's shortsighted outburst could signal that he was cracking under pressure.

"Jubinor," Andreia now said as she rose to her feet. "Surely you appreciate why we have to be so careful. If my identity becomes known, you'll fumble in the dark, and *then* you'll have to fight the same dirty way as the Onotharians do, harming innocent and defenseless people."

The man sat down, seeming less disgruntled. Paladin also took her seat, crossing her legs.

"Fine, you'll receive my transmission to the main computer before morning. I'll be here for a few more hours, working. In the meantime, we need to come up with contingency plans, covering every possible eventuality, if we hope to save our captured comrades."

"Yes, ma'am. We'll get right to it," Vespes said, and rose. Bowing deeply, he spoke the traditional words. "Boyoda, well met again."

"Well met, Vespes," Andreia replied. She turned her attention to the tall Gantharian woman next to him. "Paladin, until later, then."

"I'll be available throughout the night, ma'am."

"Boyoda out."

Sweat poured down Andreia's neck under the black hood as she punched in the command to shut off the view screen. She knew she had to wear the hood until she got home, but she'd love to tear it off and unbraid her hair that itched so badly. The tight-fitting head covering was all that kept her from risking complete exposure, which would lead to utter failure. She was far too well known and, she surmised, hated, to let anyone see her face. Still, this new working relationship with Paladin might change that. Soon she'd have to trust her, a respected member of the resistance, with her secret, and Andreia shuddered at the thought. This cloak-and-dagger routine had become second nature over the years, and the mere thought of revealing herself to anyone made her skin prickle.

She swung her chair around to face her desk. "Desk light on, point-nine illumination." She began to pull up reports and other documents on her computer, proud of how she, with Ily's help, had managed to outfit her Onotharian state-of-the-art piece of technology with enough Gantharian seals to ensure that the resistance could decode the messages. The resistance worked with far less advanced equipment, having progressed almost not at all during the twenty-five years of occupation. Andreia loathed how the people she considered her countrymen suffered under the oppression of the people whose blood ran through her veins.

If she could only figure out how to mobilize the Gantharians, to ready them for the war the Supreme Constellations was about to engage in for their sake. Andreia scrutinized several documents before she saw a possibility. Energized, she straightened her back and leaned closer to her computer screen. Daring? That was putting it mildly. Doable? Perhaps. Worth a try? Definitely.

CHAPTER FIVE

R oshan attached the Class 1 transmitter to her belt and pulled her jacket down to cover it. Boyoda hadn't called yet, and Roshan had to return home before dawn. Traveling these roads during the day was too risky.

"So you're the chosen one," a voice said behind Roshan as she put her gloves on.

Roshan glanced over her shoulder at Temmer. "Seems like it."

"I couldn't help but notice that Vespes skipped my presence when he volunteered you. I've been a member of the senior staff longer than you, after all."

Roshan didn't know how to tell Temmer that Vespes probably considered her too old, and perhaps too indecisive. Her skill as a medical planner was indisputable, but her tactical skill in combat wasn't as astute. Perhaps Temmer's brilliance only soared when she thought about saving lives.

"True, but only by a few lunar cycles," Roshan agreed. "Vespes nominated the person he felt was best for the job. And you know my allegiance is rock solid."

Temmer frowned. "You seem tired and a bit...off, after the last turn of events, though. Sure you're up for this? Boyoda's bound to ask you to do magic."

"Then that's what I'll do." Roshan injected dead certainty into her voice. She knew when to sound self-assured, and this was one of those times.

"Fine, then." Temmer turned her palms up.

A muted beep from the transmitter at Roshan's belt interrupted them. "Excuse me." As Roshan walked away, she peeled her right glove off and pressed a button on the transmitter, engaging the inserted earpiece. Made of 95% human membranes, it wouldn't show up on scanners when she entered secure buildings. "Paladin."

"Boyoda. I need your input. Vespes just contacted with me with his decision on which course of action we're going to proceed with." Boyoda's voice sounded scrambled and low-pitched over the audio link. "I've come up with some initial planning factors and estimates that need to be fleshed out. This mission will take some ingenuity and, of course, will be dangerous."

"What's new," Roshan said. "Everything I've done in the resistance has been dangerous, more or less."

"More, rather than less, Paladin, I'm sure." Boyoda was quiet for a while. "I need to transmit these documents, and they're for your eyes only. I'll encode them, but after you've read them thoroughly, destroy them."

"Affirmative, Boyoda."

"Excellent. Class 1 transmitters have a memory chip, if I'm not mistaken."

"No, you're correct, Boyoda." Roshan thought she detected a trace of fatigue, or was it resignation, in Boyoda's voice. Pressing a command into the transmitter, she continued. "Ready to accept the document."

"Transmission in progress."

A blue beam that glowed around the device on Roshan's belt confirmed that data was downloading. She'd have the computer read it back to her on the way home, then delete it completely. "Is that all for tonight, Boyoda? I need to get home before sunrise."

"So do I. Contact me tomorrow evening with your response."

"Understood. Paladin out." Roshan tucked her jacket down around the transmitter and made sure her small computer was safely stored in her inner breast pocket. The computer automatically connected to the mesh-wiring in her garments, which interfaced with her transmitter and earpiece. She then headed toward her hoverbike.

Mounting the bike, she powered the engines and sped through empty back alleys and deserted country roads, the early morning air was crisp around her. She was tired, but eager to examine Boyoda's documents. It was extraordinary to work directly with the mythical leader of the resistance. Over the years, the Gantharians had progressed from simply admiring her to worshipping her as a major hero. Roshan knew Boyoda had to have extraordinary insight into the Onotharians' business and tactics, as well as an extraordinary tactical sense that helped the Gantharians mastermind their assaults against military installations.

Roshan turned a corner, tired and lost in thought, and was relieved to see that the small dark road was empty. It led to one of the well-hidden entrances to her labyrinth of tunnels, but she was debating if she should take the hoverbike across the fields to save time, when a sudden movement to her right caught her attention. Roshan slowed down and stopped as three sleek hovercraft pulled out from the trees farther down the alley. They faced her and seemed to wait for her to approach them. Roshan scanned the area and saw two hoverbikes similar to her own pull up on her left.

"Damn," she muttered. She'd taken this dark road many times, and this was the first time she'd met this many vehicles. They had to be Onotharians, since the Gantharian population usually couldn't afford bikes like these. She didn't hesitate any longer. Pulling the handlebars to the left, she forced her bike to turn quickly in a narrow circle. It almost stalled, but she knew exactly how to handle the auxiliary thrusters that the technicians at the mountain camp had equipped it with.

Roshan turned the right handle farther and sped just above the field where the resistance against the uneven surface turned the ride slightly jerky, but she gritted her teeth and pushed on. A glance in the rearview monitor showed the five vehicles careening after her at a maddening speed. Roshan knew she had to lure her pursuers far away from the tunnel's entrance. If they found it, it wouldn't take a genius to figure out the truth.

She thought fast and knew she had only one way out of this, the small path through the dense forest at the outskirts of the village. Riding a hoverbike through the dense growth in daylight was hazardous enough, and at night it was close to impossible. Still, it was her only chance to shake the Onotharians and leave them guessing as to whom they'd tried to intercept.

Twigs and branches reached for her, tangled with her arms, and almost yanked her off the track. At this speed, any careless maneuver could make her hit a tree trunk head-on. A dark shadow appeared only a short distance ahead, and Roshan ducked just in time to feel the large branch smack the top of her helmet. The hoverbike wobbled precariously underneath her for a few seconds before she managed to straighten it up.

Beams of piercing light cut the darkness like laser-scalpels, followed by a loud noise of falling trees and an unmistakable smell of burning wood.

"*H'rea deasav'h!*" Roshan cursed through stiff lips. *They're using laser-pulse weapons to clear a path.* It was unsettling how much they wanted to catch her. An eerie thought struck Roshan as she took yet another hairpin turn. What if they knew who she was? Was there a traitor among the ones who were captured during the massive Onotharian raid?

Roshan glimpsed a set of three small white stones arranged in a clear triangle, bit the tip of her tongue, and adjusted her speed to exactly 70 *uhras* before setting the speed control to automatic. She waited until she passed a tree with a ring of fluorescent green paint on the trunk, then shut her headlights off.

As she slapped a button on the left side of her helmet, the visor switched to night-vision mode. Liquid crystals picked up any residual light in the forest and amplified it until she could see everything in a green shimmer. Roshan gripped the handlebars and tossed her hoverbike to the left, only to repeat the move ten seconds later. Her heart beat fast in a steady rhythm as she listened for any sound of her pursuers.

Seemingly out of nowhere, a hoverbike appeared on her left. Roshan curled her fingers harder around the handles and struggled not to accelerate. She had to drive exactly 70 *uhras* and not deviate from her track. Even at this speed, the risk of a crash was great. She'd practiced this strategy numerous times and knew that if she changed anything, she'd collide with one of the massive trunks. She'd based her autopilot settings on these training sessions and prayed the short-range scanner she'd installed a few years ago picked up on debris that might have fallen into her path since her last run.

The five pursuers were probably agents of the Onotharian Empire Clandestine Service, the OECS. She'd had numerous run-ins with them, and this attempt was hopefully just one in a long line of failures on their part.

People shouted behind her, but the hovercraft roared so loudly she couldn't make out any words. She was surprised that nobody had taken a shot at her, or the bike, yet. A grinding, screeching sound next to her made Roshan snap her head to the left, just in time to watch the OECS agent next to her do a somersault with his hoverbike and twirl headfirst into a large tree trunk. She sped away from the crash site with the sound of the agent's neck breaking, like a dry hempen twig echoing in her mind. However, she forgot about it when an explosion from the plasma-charged hoverbike emitted a pressure wave that made her bike wobble.

Roshan noticed the grim fate of their associate didn't slow down the others. They were approximately thirty seconds behind her, and she had no way of knowing if they wore night-vision eyewear, but it was more than likely. When it came to the Onotharian Empire's pride, their Clandestine Service, they spared no expense. *They have all the best toys.* Roshan pressed her lips together and breathed evenly through her nose to calm down.

She allowed her body to relax and follow the movements of the bike. Knowing this situation could get ugly fast, Roshan pulled a laser-pulse hand weapon from the front side pocket of the bike. It fit snugly in her hand and magnetically locked into place against the palm of her glove. She still squeezed the weapon hard in her hand, afraid to drop it, and the familiar buzz of the small reactor inside the handle reassured her.

Small branches kept hitting her arms and helmet, beating an uneven tattoo. Roshan saw a glimmering red light blink among her instruments and checked the sensors. Two of her pursuers, riding smaller, sleeker bikes, were closing in on her, and she couldn't help but be impressed by their breakneck speed. Obviously the Onotharians' far superior technology made it possible for them to travel safely in the dark at these insane velocities. Thinking quickly, Roshan clenched her weapon and began to shift on the narrow saddle. She knew she took a big risk, but if she didn't do something, they'd be within firing range in a few seconds.

Gripping the handlebar with her left hand, Roshan turned her torso and raised her right arm. Right behind her the closest Onotharian was a bike's length away. Roshan's blood turned to ice as she pressed the sensor and opened fire. The blinding light of the plasma beam cut through the dark forest. The beam had found its mark hitting the OECS agent in the chest, and for an unfathomable moment it looked as if it hadn't even bothered him.

Suddenly his bike seemed possessed by ganyas from the afterlife. It wildly spiraled upward, only to somersault, throwing its now limp rider high into the air toward her before it lost momentum and landed some distance behind her speeding bike. As far as Roshan could see, he didn't move at all.

Roshan scanned for the other rider. She spotted him on a parallel course and was ready to fire when another, much larger branch hit her left shoulder. The bike compensated for the rapid change in weight distribution, but still leaned precariously as Roshan fought to regain her balance and control.

The rider, still on a parallel course, but closer now, had his weapon pointed at her, and she knew she'd get only one chance. Roshan fired and blinked against the piercing light of her plasma-pulse charge. She couldn't make out the contours of the person, but instead she felt her bike jerk, and a new light told her she'd missed and that her enemy now fired at her.

Furious, she cursed, and her anger gave her much-needed strength. She knew she wouldn't survive another round from the pursuer. Taking aim, she fired again. The Onotharian's bike exploded and, to Roshan's surprise, took one more bike with it. The impact of the second explosion thrust her forward, and she had no more strength to hold on.

All she could think of as she whirled through the air was to hang on to her weapon.

❖

Andreia stood in the shadows of her building and watched the back entrances. It was almost dawn, and she was bone tired after her long day. The evening's ordeal at Roshan's estate made her feel choked, and exposing herself via a personal appearance, no matter how cloaked and daggered, always increased her discomfort.

Roshan had looked unexpectedly weary, though the dark circles under her eyes were barely distinguishable under the skin product intended to hide them. Her white-blond hair had been perfectly coiffed in a way expected of the Commercial Lobby's leading lady. Andreia found it amazing that, despite the long years gone by, Roshan was still such a striking woman.

The area behind the compound was almost empty, except for a

few shuttles docked at the fifth floor. This was probably as good as it would get.

Andreia slid along the wall over to a dark console, then attached the near-invisible filament to her belt. Tapping a sensor on her belt buckle, she felt a jerk as the wire pulled her up. She closed her eyes against the wind and didn't open them until she reached her floor. Andreia kicked off with her feet and swung over to her door, which opened as soon as her belt buckle neared the secret sensor in the panel.

Inside, Andreia yanked off the hood with a sigh of relief. One more assignment carried out without getting caught. She could only guess what her own people would do to her, the ultimate traitor, if they found out. She had experienced some close calls over the years, but so much rode on her success right now. She was sure the Supreme Constellations would come, and soon. Unless the resistance was prepared, a lot more people would die.

After removing her clothes, she tossed them into the recycling unit, where they entered the buffer memory and converted into energy, ready to be programmed into anything but a covert operations outfit.

The hydro shower felt like pure luxury, and she closed her eyes as the massaging stream of water flowed down her body. It was a delight to feel sweat and grime leave her skin, and after the automatic dispensers distributed shampoo and soap over her head and her body, she massaged them in as if she was rubbing her cloaked persona off.

After the shower, she punched in a command, and the body-dryer did its job within ten seconds. Her hair was curlier than she liked it, and she made a face as she brushed it before braiding it. She suddenly remembered how, on several occasions, Roshan's soft hands had performed this task. They'd shared a dorm room at the University of Ganath for almost two lunar years. Good friends, bordering on something more, they'd never had the opportunity to explore the possibilities because the occupation tore them apart.

Jin-Jin O'Landha, Roshan's strong, almost regal mother, had fought the Onotharians valiantly, and it had torn Andreia's heart out to learn months later of her death. By then, Roshan had already withdrawn from her. Her hatred for all Onotharians had been strong enough to almost touch.

Roshan quit medical school, as did Andreia; her family had pressured her to join the "movement," their euphemism for the atrocities their race committed, which had left her few options.

As Andreia pulled back the covers and sat on the bed, memories of the last decades flooded her. It had taken her almost a year to join the resistance as a covert informer, and after five, her detailed and accurate intel had paved the way for her to assume command, albeit from a distance and with Ily and Bondar O'Dal as her only confidants. After Bondar was ambushed and killed in action sixteen lunar years ago, Ily alone remained by her side, together with two assistants.

In the meantime, Roshan, who'd lashed out at Andreia so vehemently when the war began, sold out to the Onotharians, an act which Andreia couldn't understand and never forgave. *We killed your mother, whom you idolized.* As for Roshan's father…Andreia shuddered. She didn't want to remember what had happened to Roshan's father a few years later.

A sound rattled against her dresser across the room, and she flinched. The Class 1 transmitter buzzed repeatedly as Andreia hurried to it, her mind reeling. This couldn't be good news.

Uncertain if someone was attempting to compromise her identity, Andreia pressed the switch to respond. "Yes."

Unintelligible sounds came from the transmitter, and at first Andreia thought the voice scrambler was malfunctioning.

"…under attack!"

"Who is this?"

"Paladin to Boyoda. Come in. I ran into an ambush. I am under attack!"

❖

Andreia's mind whirled as she tried to wrap her brain around what Paladin just said.

"Are you injured?"

"Yes. I fell off my bike and lost my firearm. I can't contact anyone else. Four OECS agents are down, and I can't see the last one."

"Do you have *any* weapons to hold off the assailant?"

Static drowned out Paladin's first words. "…laser-blade, that's all. Damn!" More noise and a loud thud. "These are my coordinates. Request backup." The transmitter beeped twice, and a string of numbers showed in the display. "I've found an opening to an old yellow-topaz mine. The minerals protect me, but I can't transmit in there…" More unintelligible words came through the static. "I can play hide and seek with this guy for a while, but with my injury I'm in trouble."

Andreia thought quickly. She couldn't transmit anything to the leaders from her private quarters without risking exposure. And they couldn't afford to lose Paladin or, worse, have her alive in enemy hands, to be interrogated. Andreia knew the OECS's methods well, and they sickened her.

"Stand by, Paladin." Andreia decided not to waste any time. Using the map setting on the large view screen in her bedroom, she punched in the coordinates. Paladin was trapped in the dense forest north of Ganath.

"I'm on the move again." Paladin sounded out of breath. "I hear him behind me, but he's still on his bike, and as long as I stay low... Your guess is as good as mine. Will you be able to send backup?"

"I'll take care of this. Don't engage the enemy unless as a last resort."

"Affirmative."

Andreia thought she heard both relief and concern in Paladin's voice.

"I'll contact you shortly. Boyoda out."

As adrenalin sent tremors through her arms and into her hands, Andreia curled her fingers into tight fists for a few seconds to stop her body's reaction. She had very rarely gone on missions in the field. Usually she delivered the information the resistance needed to operate— and to survive. On the rare occasions she'd been involved with large operations, playing a tactical role, she'd used derma-regenerators and fusers to alter her appearance, but it was still risky. And now, she had no time for high-tech solutions. If they were to succeed in their mission to rescue the captured rebels, she had to extract Paladin.

In a flurry of activity, Andreia made her decision, not allowing herself to consider that this might be the ultimate mistake. Something in Paladin's garbled voice had struck a chord and spun her into action.

She donned her exercise outfit and a leather-like, black jacket. Grabbing a back-strap security carrier, she opened a hidden compartment under her nightstand and pulled out two small handguns and four plasma-grenades; two ultraviolet lights completed her equipment. She then rushed into the bathroom where she grabbed the small med-kit box just inside the door and put that into the bag as well.

Andreia shouldered the back-strap, and, at the far end of her living room area, she pressed the button for the express-lift and waited, tapping her foot. Inside it a few seconds later, she checked her chronometer and realized dawn would break in less than half an hour. Another reason not to use her filament-wire exit. She would be seen, and if anyone came looking for her, having openly left the building would make her absence seem less suspicious.

She passed security in the lobby and waved, determined to look carefree. "Good morning." She beamed at the tall, brawny Onotharian by the door. "How are you today? I thought I'd make use of my insomnia and work out. Anyone else in the gym?"

"No, ma'am," the guard said and stood at attention, looking overwhelmed. "Nobody else has entered."

"Fine. I like having it to myself." Andreia hoped the hint hit home.

"Very well, ma'am. Should I make sure you're not disturbed?"

"Would you? That'd be great." Andreia smiled at him again, knowing full well what effect she could have on a person. "Thanks."

Striding across the lobby she entered a corridor that led to one of the many large exercise areas and sprinted through the hall toward the exit that led into the lower underground floors where she kept her four hovercraft. As she ran down the stairs, so no one could hear an express elevator moving, Andreia pulled the hood of her jacket forward and donned sunshades to cover her hair and face. Finally on the level that held her vehicles, she pressed her left thumb onto the console beneath the handlebars of her favorite—a sleek, one-seated hoverbike. It came alive with a low, distinct hum.

Andreia knew her next hurdle was to pass the guard at the garage exit. She'd seldom gone off on her own the last few years, constantly accompanied by bodyguards, attachés, promotion planners, and her personal assistant. Now, despite the drastic circumstances, she was exhilarated to be self-sufficient.

She was relieved to see that the guard, half-asleep in his booth, barely looked up as she pulled into the dark street. She knew the only way out at night was the north gate, which wasn't as heavily guarded as the others since it bordered on a vast Onotharians-only residential area. Not many Gantharians entered this area, certainly not at this hour.

"Hold on, Paladin," Andreia murmured to herself as she accelerated and felt the powerful machine tremble between her legs. "Just hold on."

❖

Plasma-pulse fire seared the tree trunk behind Roshan, and she rolled behind a large rock as singed wood rained over her. Grateful for the helmet and the protective suit that covered every inch of her body, Roshan huddled, ready to dive into another evasive maneuver if her attacker fired again. It had been more than half an hour since she'd talked to Boyoda, and Roshan knew her time, and luck, were running out.

Roshan hadn't known what to expect when she'd called Boyoda for help. When she'd landed painfully on her left side next to some dense shrubbery, her regular communicator had been smashed. Flat on the ground behind a large tree, she'd tried it several times before she realized it was dead and that her only contact with the outside world was the Class 1 transmitter. Roshan also knew that if Boyoda didn't send someone to help her in time, she'd have to destroy the transmitter to ensure that the information stored in its memory didn't fall into enemy hands.

The sound of her pursuer's hoverbike was closer, and Roshan feared whatever help Boyoda sent would arrive too late. She clasped the laser-knife in her right hand. She was good at hand-to-hand combat and had often spearheaded the units that moved in on Onotharian military installations. Still, it disgusted her to have to resort to such measures. At night, the faces of some of the people she'd killed haunted her. Young Onotharian men and women, whose duties as guards clashed with the resistance's goals, walked in her dreams and made sure she never forgot the price they'd paid or her guilt for ending their lives. Roshan squeezed her eyes shut. *This isn't the time for regrets. Focus, damn it!*

The sudden surge in the hoverbike engine put Roshan on alert. Sweat poured down between her breasts as she crawled backward, her eyes locked on the undergrowth west of her. Expecting her assailant to come charging through it, laser-pulse weapon ablaze, Roshan slid under the dense fern bushes to the right and hid. Her heart thudded like ancient skin drums in her ears. She had to be prepared if he spotted her.

The knife was heavy in her hand. *Remember to breathe.*

With a deep roar, the bushes divided and produced a hoverbike—without its driver. Roshan stared as the vehicle slowly somersaulted, only to slam into the tree she'd just left in a cloud of sparkling debris. The propulsion system erupted, and Roshan curled into a ball to protect herself from the blast. The sound nearly tore her eardrums, and Roshan lay still, rocking slowly, until only an echo remained.

"Paladin!" a voice called from afar. "Paladin?"

"Here," Roshan croaked, trying to clear her lungs of dust. "Paladin here." She coughed repeatedly.

"I'm on my way. Are you injured?"

Was the voice female? Roshan grimaced. "I have no clue," she huffed. She didn't. Her entire body ached, and her ears still rang, but otherwise she was oddly numb. Her already injured foot should've burned since she'd landed on it after being tossed off the bike. "I'm all right." She was. She was still alive. *Stars, I'm getting too old for this.*

Another hoverbike entered the small clearing, and Roshan stared up at the sleek, state-of-the-art revelation. Black and shiny, it looked like a live entity, barely skimming the ground.

The driver jumped off and bent over her, as she stared up at her rescuer through the night-vision visor. Tinted in green, and illuminated from behind by the rising sun, the person seemed overwhelming.

"How are you doing?" a female voice asked, muffled by a scarf that covered everything but her eyes.

"I'll live." Roshan coughed and tried to not inhale too much of the dust. "You were just in time." She glanced suspiciously at the stranger. How could she be sure of this individual's true allegiance? For all she knew, this could be a sixth OECS agent masking as her savior. "Who sent you? How did you find me?"

"Can you stand up?" The stranger tugged at Roshan's arm. "We don't have much time. I imagine the OECS will miss these fellows sooner rather than later. They won't be too happy that we've incinerated half of them and crushed the others. Come on!"

"Answer my question." Roshan rose unsteadily and grimaced as her ankle swelled inside her combat boot. "I'm not going anywhere with you until you do." The knife was still in her hand. Heavy. All set.

Gesturing impatiently with her chin, the woman placed both hands on her hips. She was much shorter than Roshan had first thought, perhaps because of her powerful persona. "Very well. Boyoda sent me. I have the coordinates." She rattled off the numbers Roshan had sent to the rebel leader. "Don't worry. I'm not an Onotharian spy."

Something in the stranger's voice, now less husky than Roshan remembered, puzzled her. She flipped up her visor and blinked as the day's first sunbeams almost blinded her. "Well, you know my call sign. What's yours?"

No reply. The woman's widening dark amber eyes scrutinized Roshan's face, and her narrow pupils grew until they seemed to fill the irises completely.

"*H'rea deasav'h,*" the woman cursed. "It's...impossible."

Roshan knew this woman recognized her, and the knowledge robbed her of all oxygen. She slowly raised her knife and felt it vibrate and hum. "You know me."

"Yes. Or...I used to."

That voice. Roshan tried to think away the huskiness. Flashbacks engulfed her, but she still couldn't make a connection. "Perhaps you should remove your scarf so we can be on equal ground."

The woman folded her arms and stared down at her boots. Somehow it registered with Roshan that her rescuer wore blue and black tights and a hooded jacket, unconventional clothes for a rescue mission, and not very warm. Nothing about this operation seemed done by the book.

After the woman lowered her scarf, she pushed off her hood. "I wasn't going to tell Paladin the whole truth. But since I know you, or thought I did..." She removed her hand, and the rising sun illuminated her face. "All call signs aside, you know me as—"

"Andreia." Roshan stared in disbelief, finding it difficult to draw the next breath. "Andreia?" *What the hell's going on?* She looked pale, with the exception of two red spots on her cheeks, and her expression was completely different than when she represented the occupiers and spoke the language of an enemy.

"Yes. And I'm sure you have a lot of questions, but we have to get out of here." Andreia jerked Roshan's arm as she mounted her hoverbike. "It'll be a snug fit, but climb aboard. They're probably just minutes away."

Startled out of her shock, Roshan jumped on the bike behind Andreia. "Let's go."

Andreia took the first two curves carefully until they emerged onto the wider path that Roshan had followed before. It was easier to maneuver in the daylight, but their increased speed made branches and twigs almost derail them. Roshan had to cling to Andreia's waist to stay on the bike, and being glued to her rescuer was oddly disturbing. Andreia felt firm, well trained, yet soft. *Where the hell is my mind going? This doesn't change the fact that I've hated her for so long.*

"Anything on sensors?" Roshan yelled.

"Nothing. Wait. Yes. Ten minutes from here, four hovercraft heading this way. Hold on!" Their hovercraft skidded sideways for a moment before it accelerated.

"All right!" Roshan leaned forward to shout against the wind. "When you clear the trees, take a right and drive through the low bushes toward the east section of my estate. The gate's located at the far end of the wall. Once inside, we'll be fine. Hurry, and they'll lose us on sensors."

Something dawned on Roshan. *For skies and stars...It's really her. How can she possibly be here...and now she knows my identity. Gods of Gantharat, I screwed up tonight!*

"Pull the ultraviolet lights out of my carrier." Andreia let go with one hand and gestured toward her back.

Roshan opened the small, flat bag and was delighted to see the weapons. Tucking her knife inside her coveralls she pulled out a plasma-pulse handgun and two thin silver-glass tubes. Now that she understood better, she had to hand it to Andreia for her quick thinking. The ultra-violet light, filled with ionized sensor-scramblers, would hide them from the enemy and help them escape. However, Andreia and Roshan wouldn't be able to use their instruments either.

The first silver-glass tube broke easily and engulfed them in a cloud that was invisible to them, but tasted like ionized particles. Roshan knew these things existed, and the resistance had even got their hands on a few, but primarily the Onotharians had been using them to make life difficult for the rebels.

"Hold on, bushes up ahead!" Andreia shouted.

The hoverbike tore through the bushes, and Roshan couldn't hold back a moan when thin branches whipped her legs. She told herself this was why she was clinging so tight.

CHAPTER SIX

A ndreia drove along the well-kept garden paths up to the main
house on the O'Landha estate and parked in front of the two-
story mansion. Originally built two hundred years earlier, of red marble,
it and its tall windows glimmered in the light of the rising sun.

Roshan stepped off the bike first, and Andreia automatically
steadied her when she stumbled. "You're injured."

"I am fine." Roshan emphasized every syllable.

"And stubborn as usual. Here." Andreia stood next to Roshan.
"Lean on me so we can get you inside. We need to take a look at your—"

"*We* don't need to look at anything. *You* need to explain what the
hell's going on, and how you knew I was in trouble and where I was."
There was poison in Roshan's voice, and Andreia realized not much
had changed. At least not yet.

"All right, enough of that right now," she commanded with a calm
resilience that seemed to surprise Roshan.

When they were younger, Roshan had been the dominant one.
Her blue eyes sparkling with mischief, she'd taken Andreia on hikes
and other wildlife adventures. While on breaks from medical school,
Andreia, usually serious and withdrawn, had found an unexpected
serenity in watching the sun set over the Merealian Mountains with
her friend. Before she met Roshan, her whole life had revolved around
her family, her domineering mother the hub. Everything centered on
serious matters, and the family focused on future personal success.
Andreia loved her parents, and adored her brother, but they shared little
laughter and rarely had time for games or fun.

Now Andreia saw no trace of the fun-loving, exuberant young
woman she had once known. Instead, as Roshan pulled her helmet off,
Andreia noticed sharp lines between her eyebrows and a wary hardness
radiating from her brilliant blue eyes.

"Let's go inside. I need to sit down. I've been up all night also, two nights, actually, and I'm not seventeen anymore," Andreia continued. "Come on." She slipped her shoulder under Roshan's arm and knew that she accepted it with reluctance. Still, the physical closeness was strangely familiar, and Andreia remembered doing the same thing once when Roshan had slipped off a fallen tree trunk in the woods and hurt her hip.

Inside, Roshan directed Andreia to the library, where she closed the doors after them. "You can let go now. I'm fine." Despite her words, Roshan limped badly as she moved to one of the red leather-mix couches. "Sit down and start talking, Andreia."

"Why don't you ask specific questions," Andreia sighed. "It'll obviously take a while to convince you that I'm here to help, and we don't have much time because I have to get back. So, what do you want to know?"

Roshan pushed her fingers through her hair with jerky, angry movements. "How do you know Boyoda?"

Andreia scrambled to find the right words, still shell-shocked to find that Paladin was the same woman she'd despised for so long, and decided to be blunt. If Roshan was anything like the no-nonsense girl she was a long time ago, there was no other way. "*I* am Boyoda. I've been part of the same organization as you for the last twenty-three years."

Roshan blinked. "What?"

"I couldn't be more surprised than you. I was convinced that you'd fight the Onotharians to the death, so when you collaborated with them, and made a lot of money too, I...despised you for it. I hated that we weren't on the same side." Andreia's throat hurt. Old feelings surfaced, and she recognized her immense disappointment in Roshan's actions, her perceived treachery. "And now I find out, almost by accident, that *you* are Paladin. A folk hero. A legend."

"If you're who you say you are, you're beyond a folk hero," Roshan murmured and leaned forward, her elbows on her knees. "You're a damn myth. Some people even debate if Boyoda really exists, or if our most heroic and beloved champion is made up of several individuals." Roshan grimaced and rubbed her temples. "Somehow, it all makes sense. You have access to all that information that we need so badly to turn this ongoing war around. You've given us valuable intel, last-minute sometimes, but always accurate, and you've saved operations doomed to fail. But even if this makes sense in a weird way, can you prove that you're Boyoda?"

Andreia thought quickly. "Yes. Do you agree that you saw Boyoda at the view-screen conference last night?"

"Yes." Roshan looked reluctant as she nodded slowly.

"Then you know I watched Jubinor have a fit over our cardinal rule about avoiding soft targets at all costs. He wanted blood to avenge the missing rebels."

Roshan's face changed so gradually that the transformation was hard to trace.

"Andreia…How can this be?" she whispered huskily. "You're Onotharian. You're an undercover agent working for us, for their enemy."

"I'm working for peace between our people, for sovereignty for my home planet, which happens to be Gantharat." Andreia knew her voice showed no mercy and too much emotion, but couldn't relent. "I don't wish the Onotharian people any harm, but the butchers and dictators that starve Gantharat and rape its resources in the name of the Onotharian Empire…I want to see them punished. Remember, they're also the ones that depleted the Onotharian Empire, a situation that created this whole mess to begin with. I hate them!"

"Does that include your parents?"

Andreia almost doubled over at the unexpectedly cruel question, though she caught herself in time and managed to remain unfazed. "Yes. My parents overstepped the boundaries of criminal neglect and political megalomania years ago. I always thought I could never harm them, but after this latest atrocity, when only a handful of people at the top knew about the raid, I can no longer overlook their methods. I can't prove it yet, but I'm certain my mother used her contacts with the OECS and helped plan the surprise attacks. It has her signature, trust me."

"So that's why they were so successful. They kept you in the dark." Roshan raised an eyebrow. "More raids like that, and they'll start to put the puzzle together. They'll realize that they were successful only when you weren't in the loop."

Roshan's words echoed Andreia's worst fears. Lately, she'd felt as if she was operating on borrowed time. "Yes." Suddenly hot and a little nauseous, Andreia pulled off her jacket. "That's my conclusion too," she said quietly. "But we have this chance to do something, and even if we weren't supposed to meet in person, now we have. We need to forget our personal differences and work together to get the information to the right people."

"You look as pale as I feel. Why don't we eat something while we plan?"

"Food sounds good." Andreia watched Roshan reach over the backrest of the couch and press something. "It'll have to be quick, though. Besides, you need someone to look at that injury."

Roshan alerted her butler to arrange a light breakfast for them.

Andreia allowed a few moments to pass. "I have questions too."

"I bet you do."

It wasn't exactly an invitation, but Andreia didn't allow the standoffish tone to discourage her. "You've done a good job with your smoke screens, Roshan. And you've risked a lot by passing yourself off as a collaborator. How have you used all the money you've made from your government contracts?"

She could see that her question angered Roshan, but she wanted her former friend to drop her shields quickly. It was easier to reach an unsettled Roshan, if she hadn't changed.

"What I couldn't launder to use for our quest, I used to expand the business, so no one would be suspicious." Her eyes, now piercing blue slits, flashed with rage as she hissed, "Are you suggesting I used any of it for personal gain?"

"No."

"I have enough scars to prove my allegiance." Roshan sounded both upset and exhausted. "You, with all your privileges, wouldn't know what it's like for the Gantharians who suffer every single day."

"You're talking to me, Roshan," Andreia reminded her mildly. "And I do know, more than you realize, how our people suffer. I also know how often you've risked your life. But my assignments to collect documents and transfer them to the rebel leaders have been just as dangerous. If the truth about me was revealed—" Andreia interrupted herself at the blue-tinted paleness in Roshan's cheeks. "You okay?"

"Damn it, Andreia." Roshan's voice sounded hollow. "That'd be high treason, punishable by death by starvation. Their favorite trick."

"That's why we have to stick to our images as Onotharian-friendly, cooperating women of power." Andreia stopped talking as the butler arrived with a small trolley. She couldn't take her eyes off the stricken expression on Roshan's face. *Does my fate actually matter to her? I'm sure she's only concerned about losing the advantage Boyoda gave the resistance.*

"Thank you, Wellter," Roshan said. "We'll help ourselves."

As Wellter nodded and left the room, Andreia surmised he was used to his employer coming and going at odd hours, even looking as disheveled as she did. It was hard to hide anything from a loyal servant. Andreia remembered Wellter from her girlhood. He was obviously beyond loyal to Roshan, just as he'd been to her parents.

"Do you think we have a chance to make this relationship, I mean working relationship, viable?" Andreia bit the inside of her lip at how she stuttered. Trying to cover up, she reached for a hand sanitizer sitting on the trolley and let the blue beam clean her hands.

Roshan used it as well before she poured Yasyam tea, not seeming to notice Andreia's discomfort, or not caring. "We have to. We have to get our senior officers back, or we'll lose the fight before the Supreme Constellations gets here."

Andreia sipped her tea and followed Roshan's strong, slender hands. A little scarred, they moved with certainty across the tray she pulled from the trolley and placed on the low table between them. Fruit, besa-bee honey bread, cheese, and hot porridge; it looked wonderful, but Andreia's stomach was in a knot.

"Listen." Roshan bit into a piece of honey bread and chewed with a thoughtful expression. "I've met several of the top people in the resistance face to face, globally speaking, and know some of their real names. They've kept my secret also. Without the experience of these senior rebels, the young, new recruits don't have a chance."

"I know you haven't had time to examine the documents I sent you," Andreia said, "but you may have some suggestions already."

Dangerous blue sparks shot from Roshan's eyes before she spoke. "As a matter of fact, I have. It's been on my mind the last few days, ever since I got back from—" She stopped herself.

"The mission from hell." Andreia said.

"Exactly." Roshan nodded. "I watched the transmission from the Supreme Constellations regarding the miraculous news of our young prince. Obviously, Kellen O'Dal has powerful connections within the

SC. If I can get word to her, maybe she can bring reinforcements. Or something!" Roshan flung a hand in the air, a gesture so familiar it took Andreia's breath away.

Suddenly she saw the younger Roshan, with white-blond wavy hair down to her waist, arguing with their professors, her eyes alight with intelligence and a thirst for knowledge. She'd gesture emphatically when she was trying to get her point across, and for a moment Andreia saw the same fire again in Roshan. She kept her hair short-cropped now, which was surprisingly attractive and accentuated her high cheekbones and high forehead. She had a strong face, despite her war weariness and something Andreia interpreted as perpetual pain, or even guilt. *Am I kidding myself when I think I can read her face after so many years? But once I knew it as well as I know my own.*

"Or something," Andreia mused, nibbling a piece of fruit. "Do it. We need every possible advantage. I've sent you data for this lunar month's patrol patterns. You should be able to use it when you make a plan."

"So I'm supposed to do this alone? What happened to working together?" Roshan sounded disdainful, but a tinge of disappointment in her voice gave her away.

Andreia's heart picked up speed. *Is she genuinely concerned about me, now that she knows the truth? Or is it too late for any kind of friendship?* "I want daily updates on your progress, several if possible. I do need to be back doing my job, though. I'm on a tight schedule with very little time for frills. What I do for the resistance, I do at night." Andreia stood abruptly. "Get some painkillers. Preferably more treatment than that. You seem to be in agony."

"I am—"

"—fine. I know. But you have to function at peak efficiency. You have to be able to throw yourself into battle at a moment's notice. You can't do that the way you look now."

"I could take you down any day, Andreia," Roshan said sardonically, with her typical expression, eyebrow raised. "Wounded or not."

"But I'm not the enemy. You may think you're made of steel, but you're not. If you need any medical supplies or equipment, I can arrange it."

A sudden shadow of vulnerability flickered over Roshan's sculpted features. "Thank you."

"Anything, Roshan. All you have to do is ask."

Roshan's lips parted, and she seemed to hold her breath for a moment. Then her face hardened again, and she donned the blasé mask Andreia had seen so many times over the years. "Thank you, but as I said, I'm fine."

"Okay. I'll see myself out." Andreia pulled her jacket on as she strode through the hallway to the front door. Wellter was standing by to escort her down the stairs.

"Thank you for bringing her home, ma'am," he said.

"She's a friend." *She was, anyway.*

"She needs a friend, so I'm glad to hear that."

"Ms. O'Landha is injured," Andreia said spontaneously. "It's pretty bad, I think. Please, make sure she sees a doctor."

"I will do my best."

Wellter's thin features didn't give anything away, but Andreia thought she saw a hint of warmth in his eyes. She guessed that was as much as anybody could promise around the strong-willed Roshan.

After tying her scarf on and pulling up her hood, she mounted her bike. As she engaged the propulsion system and sped down the same garden path she'd arrived on, Andreia thought of her former friend. Her tenacity had probably kept her alive all these years.

Andreia decided to use the official roads back to Ganath. She was less likely to run into scattered OECS forces looking for the rebel who had taken out their assault team. Andreia sighed as she let the hoverbike charge down the thoroughfare. All she wanted was to get back home and stretch out on her bed for a few hours before her mother called and briefed her about today's business.

Andreia hunched over the handlebars, exhausted. Last night's events had overwhelmed her, and she had so many questions and thoughts running through her mind that she deliberately shut them all off. Only Roshan's profound surprise when she realized the truth lingered.

CHAPTER SEVEN

R ae, we need to talk."
Admiral Rae Jacelon looked up from her computer. The sight of the tall, blond woman standing in the doorway, dressed in a Supreme Constellations Fleet uniform with the provisional insignia of an ensign on her collar, made her shiver.

"You sound serious. Is something wrong?" Rae gestured for her wife to sit down in the chair across from her. "Is it Armeo?" she asked, alarmed.

"No. Armeo's fine. I talked to him an hour ago." Kellen, ramrod straight as usual, sat down with a dangerous litheness that Rae knew could combust if unleashed.

"Then what is it?"

"I've received a message…through rather unconventional channels."

"Yes?" Rae pushed the computer console out of the way and sipped her Cormanian coffee. As it spread through her system, she felt rejuvenated.

"My presence is requested…on Gantharat." Kellen held up her hands, palms up. "Please, Rae, listen to me—"

"On Gantharat? There's a price on your head!" Rae slammed her mug down on the desk. "Whose *request* is it?"

"When I was active in the resistance, I belonged to the same cell that my father did before me. One of my senior officers has managed to send me a subspace message, via a chain of beacons that her space team just deployed."

"Who's this woman?"

"Her call sign is Paladin."

"All right." Rae tried to calm the surge of acid in her throat. "And what exactly does she want from you?"

"She sent bad news. Very bad. Apparently the Onotharians have captured most of the senior rebels in the resistance. As we speak, they're arranging to send the ones that survived to the Kovos asteroid. Once there, they'll 'disappear' and we won't be able to get to them."

"How many?" Rae asked in a low voice.

"Approximately 6,000 globally." Kellen pressed her palms together and stuck them between her knees.

Rae knew this meant Kellen was more than upset. "And where do you fit into all this?"

"They seem to think I'm well connected within the Supreme Constellations space. Most people on Gantharat know about Armeo and that the SC is mobilizing." Kellen took a deep breath. "Paladin was responsible for bringing my father's body home. She didn't have to do that, and it was dangerous for her to expose herself. We've saved each other's lives many times."

"Do you know this woman's real name?" Rae fought to remain calm. "Darling, you can't just drop everything and go off half-cocked."

"No, I don't know her true identity. But she's a comrade in arms, and I can't sit idly by when the Onotharians are about to destroy that many people in prisons such as Kovos and Vaksses.

"Kovos is a hellish place, and hardly anyone returns alive. Released prisoners describe long tunnels leading into deep dungeons. Because it has no guards inside to maintain order, every man, woman, or even *child* has to defend himself. Apparently only the fittest survive, because food is scarce, in fact nonexistent for those condemned to death by starvation."

"I know. I've been briefed." A few months earlier, when Kellen had faced possible extradition, Rae had, with increasing outrage, studied one report after another detailing the inhumane conditions and the cowardly way the Onotharians treated their prisoners. Now, Kellen's eyes burned with a piercing light, and her pale features were tense with harnessed emotions.

"Kovos is the final destination. When the Onotharians initially capture a group of rebels, they keep the ones that they think they can successfully interrogate in places like the Vaksses asteroid prison, which has high-tech, top-level security.

"So if Kovos is hellish in itself, Vaksses is all about torture and coercion. You know why I have to act. They need help *now.* Not in two months when the SC has debated and discussed every miniscule detail."

Rae knew Kellen was right. Her wife's blue eyes shimmered, and for Rae, it was still a wondrous mystery that she was married to this extraordinary woman—and that Kellen loved her with such abandon.

A Protector of the Realm, destined from birth to guard the life of the O'Saral Royales, Kellen knew how to fight for the ones in her care. She had shown Rae the O'Dal family tree in a leather-bound book, which they'd manage to rescue, along with documents clearly incriminating the Onotharian Empire. For hundreds of years, the O'Dals had guarded the royal family of Gantharat, the O'Saral Royales.

Marrying her had made Rae a Protector by default, a role she'd dutifully, and gladly, taken on. She loved Armeo, the boy in their care who was the only surviving royal family member, the Prince of Gantharat, as if he were her own son. He was tutored at her parents' estate in Europa, together with his two best friends, and seemed to thrive, though Rae knew he missed her and Kellen, as they did him.

They hadn't been able to visit him for four weeks, and Rae suspected their separation was taking a toll on Kellen. The last few months had been hectic, and with Rae's promotion to admiral, the responsibility for the mobilization weighed heavily on her shoulders.

Rae's father, Admiral Ewan Jacelon, was ultimately in charge of the impending war, and her mother, Dahlia, an illustrious diplomat, worked long days trying to pave the way by persuading other neighboring worlds to join the SC in the fight against Onotharian oppression.

And now this... "Darling, have you thought about the fact that you'd be leaving Armeo behind. Again?"

Kellen winced visibly at Rae's words.

"I'm sorry," Rae said and reached out. When Kellen didn't respond, she knew that her hasty words had stung deeply. "I really am sorry."

As Kellen slowly clasped Rae's hand and held it tight, Rae felt the tremors from her beloved reverberate through her arm. Kellen was obviously torn, and Rae realized how pulled she must be between her desire to help the resistance and her wish to return to Earth, to Armeo.

"I don't want to leave Armeo, or you. But this is about the people of my homeworld. I can make a difference, if I'm allowed to go. And if I succeed, this might pave the way for Armeo...his future as heir to the throne. *That* is my concern, and my business. You know that."

"I know. But…you'd go alone?" Rae stared at her. "Granted you're a formidable fighter, Kellen, but—"

"Not alone. I'd want to take a small strike force—pilots, a marine unit, and a seasoned tactical officer. This would be a covert operation, but I realize it has to go through official channels. And meet with your approval."

Rae rose from her chair and rounded the desk. Sitting down on the corner of it, she slowly swung one leg back and forth, her eyes following her shiny leather-mix boot. "You've really thought this through. How long have you known about it?"

"Since this morning. I wanted to consider my options before I consulted you."

"I see." Rae looked up at Kellen, searching for any doubt in her luminescent eyes. "And do you have any special people in mind?"

"Yes. Lieutenant Commander D'Artansis and Commander Grey. They've been to Gantharat, they're experienced…and I trust them."

"They're our friends," Rae concluded. "Anyone else?"

"I realize that you can't go." Kellen seemed to slump for a second, then squared her shoulders and returned Rae's gaze with apparent confidence. "I'd have preferred to see this mission through under your command."

"Do you have specific plans drawn up already?" Rae asked, but didn't comment on the impossibility of Kellen's last wish.

"Yes, but they're fairly rudimentary. I need more intel from Paladin before I commit to any specific plan. Right now, I'm devising several backup options in case I need to change our course of action."

"You speak of this as if it's a done deal," Rae reminded Kellen. "I haven't approved anything. Yet."

Kellen leaned forward and placed her hands, her fingers laced, on Rae's knee. "This is about doing the right thing. I can't allow my world to lose their most loyal heroes. They've sacrificed almost everything, risked their lives over and over, to take a stand against Onotharat."

She spoke in a low, urgent voice that Rae hadn't heard her use in a long time, not since Kellen had sat across from her after being captured and her ship towed to the Gamma VI space station. Rae remembered the defiant Gantharian with blue tears of fury streaming down her face, and her heart ached.

"I can't promise anything, Kellen," Rae said, struggling to keep the dread out of her voice. "Give me all the information you have and an overview of the plans you're prepared to set in motion."

"Yes, ma'am." There was nothing sarcastic in Kellen's response. This was business and had very little, and yet everything, to do with their marriage. "I'll have it ready for you in an hour."

"Good. Include a request for vessels with the new drive we installed."

The Fleet had made good use of the last months by copying the propulsion system of the Onotharian ships they held in custody. Now they could fly faster than tachyon-mass drive, which was prohibited because it polluted space, and a ship could reach the Gantharat System in one week, instead of three.

Kellen rose. "Thank you."

"You're welcome. See you later."

After Kellen nodded and left, Rae walked to the window, drinking from her keep-hot mug. Vast fields billowed around the Cormanian capital, and the fact that she was on the eighty-fourth floor made it possible to see the curve of the horizon all the way to the ocean. This breathtakingly beautiful planet contained protected areas that normally would have tickled her imagination.

They had moved here from the Gamma VI space station, where Rae had been the commanding officer before her promotion, and now resided in the Supreme Constellations' headquarters on Corma, not far from the SC border, but inside the protective ring of space stations.

At the moment, her life consisted of planning and preparing for war; she worked on tactics all day and processed them all night in her dreams. *Sometimes I feel trapped, as if this is all I'll ever be. A warrior.*

Rae forced her thoughts to return to the people she couldn't do without. Kellen and Armeo. Not even the threat of a protracted war could cast a shadow on her feelings for them. Kellen had made it possible for her to open her heart to others as well: her parents, with whom she'd had a complicated relationship; their friends Leanne D'Artansis and Owena Grey; and the man who held his hand over them politically, Councilman Thorosac. Rae was finally able to show how much she cared for them all.

However, Kellen's latest plans might alter everything, and possibly not for the better.

❖

Roshan sat among her peers in the Commercial Lobby, listening to a speech honoring its oldest, most esteemed member. An elderly woman, at the impressive age of 145, was retiring as CEO for her global conglomerate, and they had gathered to honor her and to welcome her successor, her granddaughter.

"She's too young. She won't last once she has to deal with the Onotharians."

Roshan heard the ironic whisper behind her and at first let it go. However, the Commercial Lobby needed to work as a unit and had no room for internal ridicule or disdain.

"Actually," Roshan stated mildly, in a low tone, but with underlying authority, "Cimilia O'Tarra is not only one of the most promising industrial leaders of our time, but she's run most of the business for the last two years. Perhaps you weren't aware of that?"

Her sarcastic words had the desired effect when the two men slammed their jaws shut and looked as if they'd just tasted something sour.

"We should count ourselves happy that the Commercial Lobby is getting such a resourceful person," Roshan added, unable to resist twisting the knife. A few of the older patriarchs still frowned upon female leaders, but they were a dying breed. *If they knew what my night job is, they'd faint.* Roshan bit down on the inside of her cheek, her usual method of preventing further scathing comments, and turned forward again.

It was certainly hard to focus on her day job. Just this morning, she'd received a coded message from her space team that Kellen O'Dal had acknowledged her message and would respond within twelve hours. However, two transports were due to ship prisoners to the Kovos asteroid, which meant they had rapidly processed the resistance fighters at the assemblage camps such as Vaksses.

Roshan knew Andreia did what she could to delay such a move. Roshan was in contact with her twice a day, using the Class 1 transmitter, which she now kept in a hidden pocket in her silver-silk tank top. A woven net of sensor-deflecting material kept it invisible to most scanners and sensors.

The meeting finally ended, and after a brief lunch, Roshan excused herself and left to return to her office. Her chauffeur waited in her expensive hovercraft. With a familiar tinge of embarrassment, Roshan sank down in the plush backseat. She closed her eyes for a moment and thought of how this vehicle would seem from a poor Gantharian farmer's point of view.

Suddenly a faint vibration hummed against her skin through the tank top, and Roshan's eyes snapped open. Reaching inside her shirt, she tapped the transmitter, and at the same time, she pressed a sensor, making sure the wall between her and the driver was closed.

She engaged her transmitter and earpiece by voice recognition. "Paladin."

"Boyoda."

A five-second-long vibration showed the transmitter accepted their voice patterns. Andreia had suggested they take this extra precaution, since they needed to identify each other unequivocally.

"I hope everything's okay," Andreia said, her voice cheerful and clear.

"Yes. I'm still waiting to hear something from Kellen. I'm cautiously optimistic."

"Good. I have faith in your powers of persuasion."

Roshan shook her head. *Was that a joke?* "Completely unfounded, but thanks just the same."

"I'm not calling to nag you, though," Andreia continued, now speaking quickly and slightly out of breath. Roshan could hear from the quick clattering noise of high heels against marble in the background that she was on the move. "Just hear me out, okay?"

"Very well."

"I need a date for tonight."

What? Roshan couldn't possibly respond coherently.

"Yes. Well." Andreia continued and cleared her voice. "It's an important function, a farewell celebration at the palace for Chairman M'Ocresta."

"And?"

"And, since we're Onotharian-friendly in the public eye, we could attend major events like tonight together and make people think we're friends." Roshan heard a deep intake of breath. "What do you think?"

It was logical. In fact, Roshan wondered why she hadn't thought of it after she'd found out who Boyoda was. *Self-preservation. How can I spend time with her just for show? What if I forget to act and instead react?* "I think it's a good idea," Roshan heard herself say. "We can communicate even easier, not to mention more safely."

"Yes. Can you meet me there in two hours? I'll send a hovercraft for you—"

"No need. I'll be there. I'll even arrive in style. How's that?"

Andreia made a choking sound. "Okay. Good. I'll look forward to it. Boyoda out."

Roshan stared unseeingly at the vast structures that made up the center of Ganath. Did Andreia really look forward to seeing her, or was that just a piece of her false persona? Who was she really? She had sounded sincere, but... Roshan shrugged inwardly and slipped into her familiar, almost comforting, cynical frame of mind.

Roshan sat motionless as the hovercraft pushed through the dense traffic on the way back to her office. She kept a good portion of her sizable wardrobe there, for occasions like these. Trying not to think of the young Andreia and how she had more or less had to drag the shy girl out on the town, Roshan sat back as memories flooded her. They'd grown so close, and been torn apart emotionally with such violence, Roshan felt now as if a deep-sea tidal wave had closed over her head. She closed her eyes and held her breath, trying to keep from drowning in unexpected and unwanted feelings.

CHAPTER EIGHT

A ndreia checked her reflection a second time. Being seen with Roshan would attract even more attention than usual, and it was important to look her absolute best. She knew the public wondered why, at her age, she hadn't entered a union with anyone. Most Onotharians married early in life, in their late twenties at least. The fact that she seldom became involved with anyone romantically would make this date even more interesting. Her parents had tried to push her into the arms of several eligible people over the years, both male and female. However, Andreia's double life didn't allow anything but casual relationships, one or two nights at the most, which she found utterly dissatisfying. Sometimes she shed reluctant tears to know that she was destined for solitude as long as she led the life of Boyoda, and eventually she stopped trying for a "normal" life.

Andreia reached for a long, silver-spun caftan and pulled it over her deep red fairy-silk tunic and black pants. They were supposed to fit her as if she'd been poured into them, but felt a bit too tight, and Andreia wondered if she'd gained weight again. Andreia shook her head as if that would clear it and reset her frame of mind. She fastened the transmitter inside her dress and made sure it was operational, then inserted the tiny earpiece. She took every precaution these days.

After braiding a red and silver ribbon into her unruly hair, she fastened it in at the nape of her neck. She had enhanced her eyes with crème-kohl, a black, smooth makeup paste that enhanced and glimmered on her skin, and accentuated the amber in her irises. Once her eyes had shown every emotion as if she'd shouted them from the rooftops. She'd practiced for years before she could make them become blank and indifferent.

Tonight, she needed the opposite. She was going to spend the evening in Roshan's company, and anyone watching them needed to be convinced that they meant something to each other. *How hard will it be to pretend?* Andreia tapped her foot, annoyed at her lack of focus, and decided she was done.

A green shimmer and a high-pitched tone announced an incoming call on the large view screen in the bedroom.

"Receive call," Andreia commanded.

The image of her mother appeared. "*Henshes*, are you ready to leave soon? I still think it would be better if we arrived as a family."

"I told you, Mother, I have plans."

"You haven't told me what those plans are. We always do things like this together. Why this sudden change?"

"I have a date." Andreia regretted her words as soon as they left her lips.

"A date?" Le'Tinia jumped on the statement like a stinger-lizard. "With whom?"

Gods of Gantharat. "Roshan O'Landha."

Le'Tinia's mouth formed a perfect "o." "Impressive," she acknowledged, nodding slowly. "O'Landha has created quite an empire for herself. You could do worse. Is this a rekindling of your old friendship? I'm surprised, since I assumed you two had a major falling-out."

"We did, but it was all a…misunderstanding."

"Which you settled when you saw her recently?"

Andreia deliberately arranged her facial muscles in a sweet smile. "Yes, Mother. Now, you don't want me to be late, do you?"

"Of course not. Run along." Le'Tinia looked smug, which worried Andreia. "I can see a future in this, *henshes*. Don't worry about a thing."

"Mother, don't interfere—"

"There, there. Run along." Le'Tinia logged off.

With simmering anger at the way her mother addressed her— patronizing and implying that she needed guidance even at this age— Andreia forced herself to breathe evenly. In her mother's eyes, she'd never been more than a useful decoration, and it hurt, even if she knew her own capabilities and strengths.

She entered the airlock and closed the door behind her. The view screen showed the docked hovercraft waiting outside, and Andreia pressed a button to open the outer hatch. Climbing into the enhanced hovercraft, she sat down and willed her shoulders to relax. Soon she'd be on Roshan's arm, and they'd spend the evening together for the first time in twenty-five years.

The last time they'd been together, before the animosity between them erupted, they'd borrowed a boat and gone to the Three Wishes Lakes. Roshan had tried to convince Andreia of the magic of the lakes: if a person let the water close over her head and stayed under as long as possible, her true love and soul mate would find her.

Andreia had laughed, but complied just to make Roshan happy. They held hands and let themselves fall backward, off the edge of the boat, and into the water. It was cool, but refreshing, and it wasn't hard to hold her breath for quite a while. When Andreia surfaced, the first thing she saw in the faint light of the boat's small lantern was Roshan's broad smile and the tenderness shining from her eyes. Water streamed down her bold face, and her waist-long hair lay like wet wings down her back. Beauty was too vague a word for how Roshan had looked that moonlit evening.

It was the closest they'd come to kissing each other. *And how I regretted over the years that I didn't kiss her at least once.*

She sat in silence, leaned her head against the backrest, and allowed herself to dream. This was how she coped. When her responsibilities became too much, and the demands from the interim government and her parents overwhelmed her, she withdrew and let her imagination soar. On occasion she used the holographic imagizer, connected to a sensory device to block out everything but the brief euphoric pleasure it gave her.

"The Palace's main entrance, ma'am," the driver announced, startling Andreia out of her thoughts.

"Thank you. I'll page you in a few hours."

"Very good, ma'am."

Andreia exited the hovercraft and looked around the area below the wide marble stairs. Elegantly dressed men and women strolled to the tall double doors. Several of them nodded toward Andreia, and she quickly returned their smiles while searching for Roshan.

"Andreia!" a resonant voice said from behind, making her jump.

"Roshan!" Andreia turned around and caught her breath. "You look...wonderful." It was true. Roshan wore a black, tailored long-tail jacket over slate gray pants tucked into knee-high, black boots. A crisp white shirt lightened the ensemble. Something red at Roshan's neck caught Andreia's attention. "That's beautiful. An amazing piece of jewelry."

"It's a Merealian ruby that I inherited from Mother. She always said it would be mine one day, since the queen gave it to her when I was born."

Andreia was amazed at Roshan's candid words. She knew Roshan had grown up idolizing her parents, and it hadn't surprised anyone when Roshan decided to follow in her human father's footsteps by becoming a physician.

Andreia had met Roshan's parents many times, often mesmerized at how close-knit the O'Landhas were. Mikael O'Landha, who had taken his wife's surname when they married, had been so proud of his family. A gentle, low-key man, he'd spoken of his travels and told how he, as a young, new doctor, had worked at a remote terra-forming colony on a small planet on the outskirts of the Supreme Constellations.

There he met Jin-Jin when her parents' ship landed to make repairs while on their way back to Gantharat. Completely smitten, he'd arranged for another physician to replace him, and when the new doctor arrived, he'd been ready to follow Jin-Jin to Gantharat.

"Is everything all right?" Roshan frowned. "You seem... preoccupied."

"I'm fine. Let's go inside." Andreia placed her hand in the crease of Roshan's arm.

"All right."

As they ascended the stairs together, Andreia could feel the looks other people gave them. "Seems we're the center of attention. This might work out a little too well."

"Yes. We're not supposed to steal the chairman's thunder," Roshan agreed, a little smile playing at the corners of her mouth. "But, all in a good cause, right?"

"Naturally."

They entered the vast hallway, decorated in Onotharian colors: emerald green and pale yellow. The Onotharian crest, two mythical water dragons encircled by a golden bank with ancient markings, hung from the gallery. Beneath it, Dixmon M'Isitor, the leader of Gantharat's interim government, stood with his wife, and to the left of them, Chairman M'Ocresta stood, perfectly poised. Dressed entirely in black, she looked impressive, despite her diminutive size.

"Here we go," Roshan murmured as they approached their hosts.

"Andreia, you're beautiful!" M'Isitor exclaimed, and kissed her forehead.

Annoyed that M'Isitor acted like a loving uncle in front of all the people present at the historical function, Andreia merely smiled. She felt Roshan squeeze her hand closer against her body, as if to help her stay focused.

"Thank you, *Dixmon*," Andreia replied, deliberately using his first name to point out that they were equals.

Roshan greeted the hosts and the chairman in the traditional Gantharian way, with her hand on her chest and an elegant bow of her upper body.

"Dixmon, Casta, you know of Roshan O'Landha—"

"Oh, Ms. O'Landha needs no introduction," Casta M'Isitor gushed, and reached both hands toward Roshan. She was a tall, curvaceous woman with blue-black hair assembled in an elaborate hairdo. Excessive makeup emphasized her almost animalistic aura. Andreia knew people referred to Casta as one of the most beautiful Onotharian women alive, but she disagreed, put off by Casta's overzealous personality.

"Your reputation precedes you, Roshan," Casta continued, and obviously didn't care about etiquette at functions like these, calling her guest by her first name. "I've admired you for quite some time. I've actually paged your office on several occasions to invite you to my organization's meetings. We had our annual conference a little more than two weeks ago, but your assistant kept saying you weren't available."

Andreia looked at Roshan, who in turn didn't so much as blink.

"I've been on many off-planet business trips lately, Mrs. M'Isitor. I have to sample the merchandise before I bring it back to our homeworld."

It was obvious that Roshan wouldn't exchange any favors with Casta and her organizations, which Andreia knew were mostly about raising money for Dixmon's campaigns back home on Onotharat.

Though the Gantharians didn't have a say regarding who decided their fate, the Onotharians voted every six years for who sat in the most powerful positions, except for the chairmen, whom the current government appointed for life when a chair was available, which occurred only when one of them passed away. Andreia smirked inwardly. Quite a few of the chairmen had suffered wrongful deaths over the last centuries, since it was the only way to get rid of someone you regretted voting in. The practice also kept the chairmen in check, to a degree, since too-controversial politics was the same as a death sentence. And no matter how odd it sounded, this system made it possible for the Onotharians to call themselves a democracy.

"Well, perhaps next month then, Ms. O'Landha."

At least Casta could take a hint. She sounded quite subdued and wouldn't meet Roshan's eyes. Andreia knew the feeling. She half expected Roshan to drill those icicle eyes into her at any given moment.

"Ms. O'Landha. Ms. M'Aldovar. A pleasure to see you again."

"Well met, Chairman. The pleasure is all on our side." Andreia was almost grateful to have Villia M'Ocresta interrupt the awkward chat. "We're sad to see you depart so soon."

"I have urgent business to take care of. I leave for my vessel tonight, but we won't break orbit until tomorrow."

"I hope you have a serene and peaceful voyage," Roshan said.

"Thank you. I hope so. I'm getting too old to travel, I fear." Clear, dark eyes, not looking old at all, contradicted M'Ocresta's words.

"I disagree," Andreia dutifully remarked. "You're by no means old, Chairman. Merely wise." She wondered if she had spread the honey-cream too thick. Another squeeze on her hand told her this might be the case.

M'Ocresta seemed to swallow it, though. "Thank you. Most kind. Perhaps I'll see you inside? And you as well, Ms. O'Landha?"

"We'd like an opportunity to chat with you, ma'am," Roshan said, the low purr in her voice not wasted on the older woman. "We can all learn from your example."

They walked over to the entrance of the ballroom, out of earshot, and Andreia had to laugh when they both drew a deep breath.

"Too much of that, and I'd break out in a rash." Roshan smirked with night-demons dancing in her eyes. "And if it hadn't been for the fact that all the people around us were listening in, I wouldn't have been able to pull it off. Disgusting."

"Yes, that's my sorry existence," Andreia said, and made a wry face. "Disgusting is right. I'm well trained in flattering the right people, and it gets easier with time. I'm sure you've had to do the same."

"Yes, and I hate it. Throw me into battle any time."

People gathered around them, and soon food was spread out on the tables lining the floor. Andreia and Roshan circled the room with thermo-glass plates in their hands, neither of them very hungry, but they gave the impression of eating.

Several times, people were so interested in their presence, they literally bumped into them. Eventually, after two Onotharian politicians crowded her, Andreia stumbled backward right into Roshan, only barely avoiding falling in her thin-sole boots. By then, Roshan had obviously had enough. Taking the plate out of Andreia's hands, she handed it to a servant.

"This is ridiculous. They're obviously expecting us to perform, so why not? Let's give them something to see."

Breathless and confused, Andreia watched Roshan walk over to the head servant standing just inside the ballroom doors. They exchanged a quick word, and Roshan pressed something into his hand so fast that Andreia wasn't sure if she actually saw it happen. *She's bribing the servants? Oh, for stars and skies!*

Classical music began streaming from its sources up under the tiered ceiling, five meters up. It was the customary Onotharian First Dance, meant as an honor to the couple opening the dance at distinguished social functions. Roshan crossed the floor in long strides, and Andreia wasn't sure she liked the look on her face. She seemed determined and—spiteful?

"We can't," Andreia murmured. "There are protocols... regulations—"

"And what did I always say about regulations and protocols?" Roshan asked.

"If not break them, then at least bend them." *How could I forget that?*

"That's right. May I have this dance, *veiled rose?*"

The unexpected use of their secret anagram, *love desire,* not to mention the teasing tone of voice, made Andreia stumble on her words. She hadn't heard the phrase for so long, for obvious reasons, and now... "Mother will have a fit. The M'Isitors will hate me. Very well. Let's dance, then."

Andreia tried to sound casual, but nothing could have prepared her for what she felt when Roshan clasped her waist and began to walk backward. When they'd cleared the crowd of people and Andreia felt cool marble change into wooden flooring, Roshan's steps turned into dance steps, moving Andreia flawlessly around the floor.

Andreia put one hand on Roshan's right shoulder and the other one on top of Roshan's left hand on her waist. Long steps swept them into the center of the floor, and the greater their distance from their audience, the further from Andreia's mind they drifted.

Instead all she knew was Roshan's familiar scent of soap and musk. *It hasn't changed.* The dance dictated Roshan hold her at a certain distance, but for some reason Andreia found herself barely a hand's width from Roshan's chest. *Perhaps she's also reminded of other dances like this?*

Andreia looked up at Roshan, who gazed at her with an obvious darkness in her eyes. Roshan also seemed paler, and her grip tightened with every new step. Eventually her grip around Andreia's waist bordered on painful, making her pull closer as she tried to ease it. "Ro?" The old nickname was over her lips before she realized it.

"Hm?" Roshan blinked and looked down at Andreia with smoldering eyes, now also a bit dazed and less dark.

"You're hurting me," Andreia whispered. More couples followed their example, and she didn't want anyone to overhear them.

"What? Oh, Gods, I'm sorry." Roshan almost let go completely, and only Andreia's determination to keep dancing kept her from losing her grip on her dance partner.

"Don't worry. I'm okay."

"You are?" Roshan danced away toward a remote corner, away from the food-covered tables. "Of course you are."

Andreia closed her eyes for a moment and relaxed. "Yes, and I think we've established ourselves not only as a couple of sorts, but a gutsy, slightly stupid pair, who don't give a damn about etiquette." She frowned. "Perhaps they'll blame it on our 'newfound attraction' and make excuses for us."

"I was acting in haste again, wasn't I?" Roshan sighed. Her eyes, wide and cautious, found Andreia's. "Newfound attraction?"

"From their perspective, of course." Andreia spoke quickly. "Some things never change. You always were the wild one, Ro."

"And you were always the one keeping me in check. In a manner of speaking."

"I was?" Andreia remembered sometimes feeling like the perpetual killjoy. Roshan would go on her crazy spur-of-the-moment adventures, and Andreia would reluctantly tag along, dreading the potential outcome, but refusing to abandon Roshan.

"You always looked out for me." Roshan sounded almost surprised at her own words. "You tried to talk me out of my more insane ideas, and the times you couldn't, you went with me, even with the risk of getting caught hanging over your head. And your fear of displeasing your parents."

"More so, annoying Trax," Andreia added.

Roshan's face became solemn at the mention of Andreia's brother. "Yeah, that handsome, sociopath of a brother of yours. No wonder you were afraid of him."

"I was not!" Anger filled Andreia, and she pulled back as she tried to hide it. "He wasn't an average person in anything he did, and as much I would've liked to see him choose another career…" She clasped Roshan's hand tightly, inadvertently betraying her rage.

"Joining the OECS was hardly a mere *career move*." Roshan's voice sank to a low, hissing murmur. "It was a political decision and, given their methods, a way to fulfill sadistic tendencies."

"Well, it should please you that my brother paid for his faults with his life!" Andreia struggled to keep her voice low and out of earshot.

"I don't mean that. But if your people hadn't attacked my homeworld—"

"You forget. *Our* people. *Our* homeworld." Andreia's fingers were ice-cold, and she realized Roshan must feel the chill. They still had opposing opinions, despite their mutual goal, and Trax's political stance, assuming that death and destruction were an acceptable means to an end, had reignited the animosity between them.

"Yes, so you say." Roshan was obviously not about to give in.

Andreia glanced around, relieved to see that nobody appeared to have overheard. This was too careless. "Let's don't ruin this chance to make people think we have a relationship." Andreia squeezed Roshan's fingertips. "We can't allow ourselves to get personal."

Roshan remained rigid against Andreia for a moment, then relented. "You're right. You usually are."

Surprised, Andreia knew her features softened. "Thank you. I know that's not easy for you to say."

"It isn't." Roshan glanced at the crowd. "Is it just me, or are they dancing closer to us?"

"I think they are. Perhaps they're trying to get the scoop on why we're here together."

"Then let's give them something to make it worth their while." Roshan smiled faintly. "We can call it a...diversion."

Andreia didn't know what to expect. "Diversion? What are you talking about?

Roshan pulled her closer and tipped Andreia's head back. "This." She leaned down and brushed her lips against Andreia's forehead. "And this..." she murmured, and pulled Andreia close, body to body, as they kept dancing.

"Oh, for stars and skies," Andreia whispered. "What are you doing?" Roshan's lips were like velvet against her skin, and Andreia leaned involuntarily into the caress. Still, such behavior wasn't only madness; it was also highly inappropriate at a function such as this. Right then, her parents passed them, and to Andreia's surprise, her mother smiled and winked at her. *Oh, please. She thinks I'm playing Roshan. H'rea deasav'h!*

"Diversion," Roshan breathed. "And a way for them to think we're being unconventional because we're in the process of rekindling our relationship. You know, pheromones."

"Pheromones! Now that's presumptuous. And besides, they don't know if we have anything to rekindle!" Gasping, Andreia resented being so defenseless against Roshan's caresses. "Who'd remember anything so insignificant?" She knew she sounded scornful, but it was the only way she could manage not to give in to her stampeding heart and breathlessness.

"Oh, they've been gathering information about the two of us ever since we entered the ballroom. Your parents have their channels, and so does the chairman. They've obtained more than one report throughout the evening, unless my knowledge of Onotharian perfection fails me."

"You're probably right," Andreia said, reluctantly. "But it doesn't mean it's a good idea to let anyone think we've rekindled anything. Especially since there's nothing to revive!"

Roshan looked down at her with smoky blue eyes in the muted light on the dance floor. "You say that with such conviction. So our friendship meant nothing to you? I should've known. You dropped me and what we had…could've had very quickly, after the invasion. Guess I didn't fit your plans to become a local hero, did I?"

"Of course we were friends!" Andreia could hardly believe her ears. "We were best friends, even. How can you question that?"

"Twenty-five years of damn hard work with my 'best friend' nowhere in sight says I can."

"I worked every bit as hard as you, risking just as much, during that time. I was busy!"

"I know. Your lovers were reported in the media with tedious punctuality."

Andreia knew she paled and her hands grew even colder. "Exaggerations. For appearance," she muttered, suddenly numb.

Roshan stared at her with frosty eyes for a moment; perhaps there was something in her expression, because Roshan's face mellowed marginally. "Maybe. I have no way of knowing, do I?"

"You have my word." Andreia stared up at Roshan as their feet moved automatically with the music.

"But how much is your word worth?" Roshan said. "Trusting you could be the very last thing I do."

❖

Roshan looked down at the dark beauty before her. Andreia's eyes glimmered gold and amber, and Roshan realized her words hadn't helped mend fences.

"You have some nerve," Andreia said slowly. "First you insult me, only to question my honor."

"You don't understand—"

"Oh, but I do. I understand that as long as I'm useful for your quest, your cause, you can force yourself to be in my presence. You don't see this as *our* cause at all, do you?"

"I'm not used to sharing my comings and goings with anyone." Roshan's lips felt rigid, and she hated how stiff she sounded. *Where did my ease go?* She only knew she lost it at the sight of Andreia, in the light of her golden eyes.

"Well, get used to it fast." Andreia pulled back from Roshan's strong grip. "You're not calling the shots here, remember. I am."

The truth was bitter medicine, but at the same time, Roshan felt oddly relieved. *Perhaps it's a good thing, not to be alone in this.* "I know." She still had to force the words across her tongue.

The music quieted, and Andreia seemed eager to step out of Roshan's arms. "I need something to drink."

"Allow me." Following protocol, Roshan guided her dance partner off the floor by offering her arm. Andreia took it, but let go as soon as possible. She walked up to the bar at the far end of the ballroom with Roshan in tow.

"Black Reyera wine, please." Andreia told the woman serving them.

"Yes, ma'am."

"Thank you." Andreia took the glass and sipped it immediately. "Oh, mm. Very nice." She turned to Roshan. "Want some?"

"No, thanks." Roshan watched Andreia shrug and take another sip. The wine moistened Andreia's lips, and a sudden hot, dark feeling weighed in Roshan's abdomen. Furious at how Andreia affected her, Roshan focused on the people around them, nodding to a few familiar faces. The women were all dressed expensively and displayed rare jewelry, which made Roshan grind her teeth, since the indigenous people could have bought a year's supply of medicine for an entire family for the price of one of their bracelets.

As fashion dictated, the women's blouses and caftans were transparent, with just enough opacity to maintain a modicum of modesty. Casta M'Isitor pushed the limits by wearing a white see-through dress that deceptively covered her front all the way up to her neck, only to plunge down to her buttocks in the back, revealing an abundance of olive-tinted skin. Once Roshan would have considered such a display sexy, but now, especially taking into consideration *whose* back was revealed, it left her indifferent. *Am I too old, or just too picky?*

Just then, as Andreia was drinking from a crystal glass someone bumped into her from behind, making her spill a few drops on her chin. She licked them away quickly, and Roshan stopped breathing momentarily at the sight of Andreia's pink tongue running several times across full, deep red lips. *Damn! Perhaps not too old, after all.*

Andreia glanced up, half smiling. "Making a mess again. Sorry about that." She brushed a drop of wine off her chin with her fingertips.

"She bumped into you. Not your fault." Roshan heard how short she sounded and forced a smile again. It certainly wasn't Andreia's fault that she looked so beautiful when she smiled. Unless Roshan was imagining things, Andreia smiled very differently at her in private than the way she beamed during video transmissions, intent on enticing an entire nation.

The smile faded from Andreia's lips, and her face hardened as she paled. "We have to go, Roshan. Trouble."

Roshan didn't question anything at this point. "Okay, let's say good-bye. What's our excuse?"

"You're sick."

"What?" Roshan felt her eyebrows rise.

"You have a bad headache." Andreia waved her hand impatiently. "So look sick."

Grinding her teeth again, Roshan wondered why Andreia couldn't be the one who played sick. After another look from Andreia, she complied as they reached the head table where Chairman M'Ocresta sat with the M'Isitors.

"Chairman M'Ocresta, Dixmon, Mrs. M'Isitor, we need to leave early. We're sorry and don't want to insult the chairman." Andreia spoke softly, with a worried look on her face as she glanced in Roshan's direction.

Playing her part, Roshan sighed and made her breath tremble. "I apologize, ma'am," she whispered and steadied herself against the table. "I know this is rude."

"So this is why you two were clinging to each other?" Casta M'Isitor huffed. She was obviously displeased with their conduct.

"I thought she was going to faint, ma'am," Andreia said, completely ignoring the sarcasm and acting as if Casta had merely stated a fact.

"Really."

Roshan thought this was a perfect opportunity to end the discussion, so she bit her lip and made a gross sound, as if on the verge of throwing up. Casta looked at her with disgust written over her sharp features. "Sorry," Roshan muttered and burped. "Something I ate earlier, I'm sure." She reached out and leaned heavily against Andreia.

"Get her home," Dixmon said hastily. "You're obviously not feeling well, Ms. O'Landha. We'll visit another time."

"Thank you." Roshan kept up the pretence until they were outside, away from the eyes and ears of the Onotharian leadership.

❖

Andreia looked at Roshan with reluctant appreciation. "You're quite an actress. I guess leading a double life for so long makes fooling others second nature." She squeezed a sensor on a device in her pocket as she spoke, to call her driver.

"You sounded so subservient in there, talking to M'Ocresta and the M'Isitors. I almost forgot you were acting. Now," she glanced sharply at Andreia, "what's going on?"

"I'm wearing an earpiece. I always do." Andreia motioned for Roshan to follow her down the wide palace steps to the courtyard. "I had a Code Omega." It was the second most severe of the resistance alerts.

"It must be bad."

"Not a lot of details yet, but it's about our captured rebels. They're moving them out, starting tonight."

"What? That's insane. The prisons can't be ready yet—" Roshan interrupted herself, "unless they completed them before they attacked us. Damn! And that doesn't give us much time. I'm still waiting for Kellen O'Dal's response. I don't know if the SC will help us." Roshan's eyes turned to ice blue slits, as they'd always done when she focused hard. "And if they do, and act immediately, it'll take them a few weeks to arrive, at least."

Andreia's chauffeur pulled up. "We need to get out of here. You should contact what's left of your cell. We don't have time for another Boyoda transmission, so we'll have to play the cards we have left."

Roshan followed her to the hovercraft door as it hissed open. "I'll head for the mountains within an hour. Contact me when you know more. I'll be wearing my earpiece."

"Okay."

Roshan hesitated as if she meant to say something more.

"Yes?" Andreia prodded.

"Be careful." The words came out slightly strangled, and the look on Roshan's face did nothing to soften them.

"I will," Andreia said. "And you too. I ca—we can't afford to lose you."

With a brisk nod, Roshan retreated. Andreia closed the door and leaned back in her seat. "The Government Building. I'm in a hurry."

The hovercraft rose and the driver eased into the emergency air corridor, above the allotted lanes. She had to get there quickly and think of a reason to examine official documents at this hour.

Her excuses grew thinner with every situation. Andreia closed her eyes tightly, feeling like she was living on borrowed time. Any action could be her last, if she was found out.

CHAPTER NINE

Kellen O'Dal stood at attention as her wife and commanding officer, Rae, strode along the lines of provisional officers. More than forty new officers in the Supreme Constellations Fleet had taken the last, and most advanced, course in protocols and regulations, and had also been successfully trained in combat. Now they were about to receive their additional insignias, as well as their assignments.

The levels of the training had been high from a civilian point of view, but for Kellen, they'd been easy. Her trainer in combat skills had claimed that she should've trained him, instead, and she'd struggled only when it came to protocol and regulations. Some of the rules made no sense to her, and she felt they would only hamper a mission. Still, she had to get her clearance and the go-ahead from the Fleet, or she wouldn't be able to participate in her homeworld's liberation.

Rae now stopped in front of her, her blue-gray eyes shining with obvious pride. "Ensign Kellen O'Dal, you are hereby commissioned to lieutenant commander, and your assignment will be under the direct command of...Admiral Ewan Jacelon."

Kellen opened her mouth, stunned, having expected to remain under Rae's command as she had since she accepted the rank of ensign. "Ma'am," she merely said and nodded, her hands strictly by her sides. "Thank you, ma'am."

Rae pinned the insignia on her lapels. "Admiral Jacelon has generously agreed to loan you to my unit, so you will remain on Corma for now, awaiting your first mission."

Relieved, but still mystified, Kellen smiled faintly. "Yes, ma'am."

"Congratulations, Lieutenant Commander O'Dal." Rae moved on to the woman next to Kellen.

Kellen wondered if Ewan had agreed to assign her to his unit instead of Rae's, even if it was only on paper, to forestall any whispers of nepotism. She knew both the Jacelons were very by-the-book, and that they very rarely bent the rules. Rae had once told her that if you stuck to every little rule and protocol, and always kept your wits when it came to the minor things, you could occasionally get away with bending the big ones. Put that way, it made sense, though Kellen preferred the direct, timesaving approach.

Once the last soldiers had their insignias fastened to their lapels, Rae stepped back. "I am proud to see you all so eager to do your duty as we face war with the Onotharian Empire. They are formidable opponents, but the Supreme Constellations will prevail. We have something the Onotharians haven't possessed in decades, if ever. They are a rigid and controlling race, and we in the SC, as a unification of planets, have learned to be more diverse, more humane. This, I'm certain, will be our strength and their downfall."

Kellen hoped Rae was right. Her wife had an unbending faith in her homeworld and the SC Fleet specifically. Kellen wasn't easily impressed, but what she'd seen so far showed her she'd been right to bring Armeo to the SC. As much as she wanted everything to move along faster, the SC war machinery and the way the SC Fleet operated, was impressive. She had watched her wife coordinate with the marine unit generals, negotiate with diplomats from the less-advanced planets, and press the diplomatic corps until Rae's mother, one of the top diplomats within the SC, had everything she needed, including a fleet of six ships in which she journeyed safely back and forth between planets.

"Dismissed."

Rae's crisp voice interrupted Kellen's thoughts, and she relaxed marginally as her peers scattered over the quay area and returned to their temporary quarters. Kellen was about to join them when Rae hurried toward her. "Kellen. Come with me." Rae rushed past her, her facial expression entirely different from only moments ago.

"What have you heard?" Kellen asked.

"We have a conference with Councilman Thorosac. Things are happening fast. I sent him a subspace message through mother and asked for advice, but had no idea it would attract so much attention."

"You're talking about the Gantharat resistance."

"Yes. Apparently, Thorosac feels strongly about this sort of thing."

"You mean resistance movements?"

"Yes. He was once a renegade commander on Colonial 6, before they broke free from the Imidestrian government." Rae pushed her wrist against a sensor, and they entered a long, bedrock-encased tunnel that led to an underground compound where Kellen had previously been allowed access to only the first two subterranean floors.

"And now he wants to help?"

"Let's just say, I pray he's going to help pave the way for a full-scale mission to intercept the prison transports. We have to prevent the Onotharians from killing all these people. The last report I received entailed...perfectly horrific details regarding the asteroid prisons. They're so overpopulated that the current prison transports may be the last straw."

At the end of the tunnel was an elevator, which they hurriedly entered. "Level minus fourteen. Jacelon. Voice mark. Code alpha, alpha, one, six, one."

"Do I have a higher security clearance now?" Kellen stood calmly at Rae's side as the elevator doors opened and they boarded. It didn't even tremble as it took them deep into the bedrock recesses.

"Yes. Father took care of that. He and Thorosac made it possible for us to give you this commission, and also for us to keep working together and still not be directly in the same chain of command. Officially you serve directly under Admiral Ewan Jacelon, and you'll act as his liaison while carrying out your duties."

"So, I report only to him." Kellen stopped talking as the elevator reached the fourteenth level. The doors opened to a metal-plated corridor that seemed to reach endlessly into the bedrock. Immediately outside the elevator, a black elliptical alloy gate hummed.

"Just step through it." Rae smiled. "It'll be all right."

Kellen made a wry face and walked through the gate, which, she surmised, was a detector of sorts, and as she moved, the frequency of the humming changed. Rae followed her and pointed at the fourth door down the corridor. "Over here." It opened and a man poked his head out.

"Admiral," he said, and beamed. "We're ready for you and the... lieutenant commander." He obviously remembered Kellen's brand-new rank just in time.

"Thank you, Ensign." Rae nodded toward the young Cormanian and motioned for Kellen to enter.

Kellen was surprised by the vast array of technological equipment and ongoing security surveillance that hid behind the simple door. Lit up only by the instruments and view screens, the room was at least five times as large as the mission room onboard the Gamma VI space station. She estimated the current crew consisted of a hundred individuals.

The ensign guided them to a small transparent cube hosting a large view screen and two computer consoles. "There you go, ma'am. Councilman Thorosac is ready for you. Just boot the view screen." He closed the door behind them, and crystals within the aluminum changed their polarity, rendering the walls completely opaque.

After they sat down Rae touched a sensor, turning on the view screen. A SC emblem twirled for a few seconds, and the image of two men came into view.

"Councilman Thorosac. Admiral Jacelon, this is a surprise." If Rae was taken aback by her father's unexpected presence, her voice didn't give anything away. She laced her fingers, out of view of the video transmitter, tightly together. Kellen wanted to place her hand over the familiar gesture that indicated Rae's edginess, but knew better. Rae and her father had begun to get along better after Rae had nearly lost her life on Gantharat shortly after marrying Kellen, but there was still tension between them, especially when it came to professional issues. Kellen knew her wife well enough to suspect that Rae thought her father was present to check up on her.

"Admiral Jacelon. Lieutenant Commander O'Dal. Congratulations on your recent promotions. It's good to see you again." Thorosac nodded briefly. Distinguished, and a handsome man of Imidestrian/Cormanian descent, he watched them calmly with silvery gray eyes.

"Councilman, likewise."

"Ewan and I have reached an agreement," Thorosac said. "We have to act quickly if we are to rescue the majority of the captured resistance fighters. Our victory, once we go planetside full force, depends on the collaboration of the Gantharian people, as well as the resistance. The Onotharians will make sure they outnumber us, so we must conduct this operation with all the cunning and skill we can muster."

"So, do I take it we have the go-ahead for Kellen's plan?" Rae asked, and pulled out a handheld computer. After tapping in a few commands she placed it next to the console. "I'm transmitting the updated version to your personal console now."

"Thank you. Yes, we've gone over Commander O'Dal's strategy. The plan is sound, though a bit daring," Admiral Jacelon said. "You need more troops to go with you. You also need more air support, and more assault craft, to arrive on schedule and with your team intact."

"How do you suggest we mitigate the risk of failure, sir?" Kellen knew it was time she began asking the questions. After all, it was *her* plan. *Her* mission.

"One destroyer. The 2nd MSB."

"The second Marine Space Battalion?" Rae looked up from the plans displayed on the computer console. "We'll need them. I can tell you've given this a lot of thought, Father."

"I have. This mission is a huge undertaking, and you need a specialized unit. You don't have any margin for error. The destroyer can easily accommodate the three hundred marines, and you can still handpick the remaining fifty or so—"

"Wait." Rae leaned forward, her voice almost an octave lower. "Does this mean the mission's been approved, I mean, officially?"

"Yes."

"And my special request?" Rae continued, her voice unwavering.

"What request?" Kellen asked. She noticed something in Rae's demeanor that balanced between hopeful and apprehensive. "Rae?"

"Yes." Ewan Jacelon nodded solemnly. "As much as we need you here, we briefed a close circle of military advisors, and they consider this a golden opportunity for a senior officer to personally ascertain the situation. *In situ*, so to speak."

"Rae?" Kellen repeated. She had given up hope that Rae would be able to join her, actually never counted on it to begin with. Flashbacks of Rae lying unconscious on the ground amidst the ruins that were once Kellen's home flickered through her mind. Bloodstained, pale, and clinging to life, Rae had almost paid the ultimate price. *How can I ask her to do it again?* Kellen wanted to touch Rae's hand, but the presence of the admiral and the councilman prevented such familiarity. Rae was as by the book as her father, if not more so, and emotional displays while on duty were not welcome.

"Kellen. I thought you'd be pleased." Rae directed her clear, firm gaze toward Kellen.

"I am." Kellen's tongue felt stiff and uncooperative. "Of course I am."

Rae didn't look convinced, but let it go. "Good, then." She turned her attention toward the view screen. "Will I find the details of our orders in my computer?"

"Naturally," Admiral Jacelon said. "I've enclosed the tactical data. According to my estimates," he checked his chronometer, "you leave in less than five hours. You will use the latest model of the Fleet's destroyer, outfitted with the enhanced Onotharian propulsion system. The SC Fleet Physics Laboratories call it SLMD, superluminal mass drive. Unless there's a snag, the destroyer will reach Gantharat in five days."

"Five! Impressive. I was told a week." Rae lit up. "Has it been tested yet? Or…ah, don't tell me. We'll be doing the honors."

"It's safe enough for you to be the test crew on a longer trip. It's also outfitted with a new, superior transmitter for data and audio. You should have no problems communicating with Gamma VI, using our arrays. Commodore de Vies is the commanding officer there now."

"Alex? I did wonder where he'd take command," Rae said.

Kellen had spoken with Alex's wife Gayle only a few days ago, and even she had had no idea where her husband would end up. Alex and Gayle were two of their best friends, and Kellen knew Gayle worried, even if she was an "expert" when it came to dealing with her husband's position, as she put it.

"We're grateful. We have a better window of opportunity to assist the resistance." Kellen felt her blue blood rush through her veins with more energy than she'd had in weeks. Perhaps this was their break, their chance to get the upper hand. An element of surprise.

"There's a lot riding on the successful outcome of your mission," Thorosac said. His eyes looked tired, if only for a moment, and Kellen guessed his workdays were as long as theirs had been lately. "We have faith in you, Admiral, and Commander O'Dal has proven on several occasions she's a force to be reckoned with. I'm on my way to the court ship *Dalathea*, but Ewan will keep me apprised of your progress."

"Thank you, Councilman, for your trust in us." Rae paused and her features softened. "Marco, how's Ayanita doing?"

Kellen knew the councilman's wife had battled the yezetosha, a cancerous disease that plagued certain families from Ayanita's homeworld, Imidestria.

A brief smile flickered over Thorosac's lips. "She's doing quite well, Rae. She's in remission once again and working around the clock, as I know you do as well." Ayanita worked for the Imidestrian government as a political advisor.

"Yes. These are busy times." Rae glanced at her father. "Admiral. I trust you're well. I spoke with Mother two nights ago."

"She told me. I'll be going home in a few days."

"And Armeo?" Kellen couldn't stop herself from asking. She missed the boy, the son of her heart, so much.

Admiral Jacelon's gaze mellowed. "Armeo's fine. He's staying with Gayle de Vries and her daughter while your mother is on a mission onboard the court-ship *Dalathea.*"

"Seems we're all tremendously busy," Council Thorosac said with a kind look in his eyes.

This was an understatement. Kellen couldn't remember when she and Rae had shared a quiet evening in each other's company, or when they'd made love. Most evenings they'd go home to their temporary quarters, stumble through the shower, and tumble directly into bed, falling asleep immediately. Only in the middle of the night, around 0300-0400 hours, did Rae routinely wake up and curl around Kellen. Kellen had begun to wake up shortly before Rae, readying herself for the strong arms pulling her close. Kellen would relax in Rae's embrace, while trying to convey all her love. She loved her wife, even more now than when she'd discovered the true nature of her feelings a few months ago. Would it ever be possible for them to live more normal lives? A disturbing inner voice warned that this perhaps counted as normal life for a Jacelon.

"Admiral, you said I could handpick whoever I wanted for this assignment," Rae said. "I want Commander Grey and Lieutenant Commander D'Artansis."

"I'll send out an express order, and we'll see." Ewan Jacelon seemed to hesitate for a moment, then leaned closer. "Rae, Kellen...this may well be the opening shot for the war. Once you're planetside and have made contact with the resistance, that's it."

"Seems we're the head of the arrow, then," Rae said with a wry smile.

Kellen could see how the metaphor fit. "It's not my first time in such a position," she said. "It's not an enviable situation, but we'll prevail."

"May the stars guide you well," Ewan said. "I'll get back in touch before you deploy."

Rae closed the comm link after saying good-bye and sat in silence for a few moments, a silence Kellen was reluctant to break. "It won't be easy." Rae had a very familiar look on her face. Her eyes a winter gray and her mouth a mere line, she regarded Kellen solemnly. "Your thoughts?"

"I'm aware of the hurdles, but also confident in my—our strategy. Paladin sent more information, which reached me yesterday, and once I add that to the plan, which I can do en route, our chances will improve."

"You sound more positive than you usually do. You're usually the more realistic, almost pessimistic, of the two of us."

"Don't confuse my confidence with unwarranted optimism." Kellen tried a smile. "And you and I have proved ourselves before. Armeo calls us a winning team."

Rae's expression softened. "He does? Clever young man, our boy." She looked around them, as if to make sure of something. Leaning in, she brushed her lips across Kellen's. "We just have a few hours to get ready. At least we'll be sharing quarters onboard the destroyer."

Kellen was filled with a profound desire for the woman she'd married. She allowed her hands to frame Rae's face for a brief moment, knowing full well that it might be a long time before they had any sort of privacy once the madness of mobilizing their ship and crew began.

"I love you, Rae," she whispered, her heart overflowing. "I'm so proud, and very grateful, that you're heading up this mission."

"Me too." Rae kissed her again. "So how about we unfasten the strut locks and get going, darling?"

Kellen returned the embrace and their lips met again. "Yes," she agreed after letting go of Rae, "how do you say? The show must resume?"

Rae blinked, then laughed. "Go on, Kellen. The show must go on."

"Ah." Kellen appreciated the smile on Rae's face. "No difference."

"You're so right, Lieutenant Commander." Rae rose and switched the walls back to transparent. "Let's get out of here."

As they headed to the elevator, Kellen felt herself slip into her professional persona as a SC Fleet officer. It was remarkable how easy it was, like putting on a cloak. Fortunately, when challenged, she could easily toss it off and become the personality she was born into, a "Protector of the Realm" and Gan'thet master with only one objective—to protect the one in her care at all costs.

CHAPTER TEN

Roshan stepped off her hovercraft and looked around the seemingly deserted mountain camp. She didn't see anyone, but knew that at least ten pairs of eyes followed her every movement through night-vision visors.

Crossing the dusty plane between the many low, camouflaged structures, Roshan kept her sidearm ready. She'd developed this habit when a small rogue Onotharian unit had taken out half the guards. They'd moved the camp several times since then, but this site had stayed uncompromised for more than two lunar years. Roshan reached the command central building and tapped on the door. A sound behind her made her pivot and raise her small plasma weapon with both hands.

"Good evening, ma'am," a young man said nervously. "Am I late? I was at my brother's wedding."

"Timis," Roshan sighed. "Don't ever sneak up on me like that again. It could be the last thing you ever do."

"Yes, ma'am. I mean, no. Ma'am."

Roshan couldn't suppress a smile at her newest resistance cell member. He was as young as they came these days, even younger than she was when she joined, seemingly a lifetime ago.

She tapped the door frame again. "Everyone asleep in there?"

"Name?" a gruff voice said from inside.

"Paladin." Roshan pushed the door open. "Get out of bed too early, Jubinor?"

"Hm. Any earlier and it'd still be last night." Jubinor watched Timis pass them quickly and join his teammates by the far wall. "Damn. Were we ever that young?"

"Once." *Way back during innocent times.* Roshan looked at the chronometer on the wall of the mission room. She'd left Andreia only two hours earlier and headed for her estate, hoping to hear from Andreia by now, since she was fumbling in the dark. Still, she had a lot to do while waiting for the information she needed to take action. "Everyone here?"

"Yes, Paladin." Jubinor's voice sank an octave. "Everyone except—"

"I know, Jubinor. I'm expecting a transmission any minute with information on how to proceed." Roshan lowered her voice. "We'll get Berentar and the others back."

"Good. I'll get the team ready." Though only a muscle twitching to the left of his thin lips indicated Jubinor's feelings, Roshan knew him well enough to read the distress in his eyes. She also saw dead-set determination and realized he was with her, no matter what circumstances they faced.

"I'll be in my office." Roshan walked into the small cubicle she'd shared with Berentar until the last raid. After she logged onto the computer and made sure the Class 1 communicator was set to receive Andreia's call instantly, the signal beeped in her ear. "Paladin."

"Boyoda."

"I'm alone, mountainside."

"Good. I have information to send you." Andreia sounded matter-of-fact, but Roshan still held her breath for a few seconds. "Go ahead."

"Transmitting."

The communicator buzzed as data streamed into its memory. "It's working fine," Roshan said. "Are you...all right, Boyoda?"

"I'm fine."

Too brief. The voice scrambler couldn't hide that Andreia spoke in little more than a whisper. What the hell was going on at Andreia's end? "Glad to hear it. Will you monitor us, or are we flying solo on this one?"

"I have to get out of here. I'm pushing it as it is."

"Are you in danger?" Roshan couldn't keep the worry from showing in her voice. "Damn it—"

"I said I'm fine. Transmission is finished. I'll get back to you later. Go ahead with the mission. Boyoda out."

The signal broke and Roshan grabbed the communicator, relieved to find the transmission was complete. She docked it with the computer console on her desk and waited for it to upload the information. "Come on!" she muttered, impatient and on edge. "What the hell has she found and why did it take her so long?"

The computer beeped twice, and as the screen filled with information, Roshan read with increasing dread. "Damn, Andreia, where did you go to find *this*?"

❖

The dark, empty corridors were eerie, and Andreia sprinted toward the back door. Still wearing her dinner outfit, she balanced precariously on high-heel boots and half expected to nosedive to the floor the next time she had to round a corner. Andreia heard heavy steps behind her, feet clad in Onotharian combat boots, which sounded like at least two individuals. Glass doors with gold-imprinted names flashed by as she rounded another corner.

"Halt! Identify yourself!"

The command boomed through the empty building and, if anything, made Andreia run faster. If they caught her, the game would be over. She couldn't explain being at headquarters, at least not for breaking into her father's office and his computer. Because she was a public figure, the Onotharians would make an example of her punishment. *And who knows if I'd crack under interrogation? I know what they can, and will, do.*

Fear, not for herself, but for the people who relied on her, fueled her efforts. Andreia's lungs burned from lack of oxygen, but she couldn't afford to slow down. Sliding, she turned a corner and reached the back door. She tugged at it, only to find it locked. "Of course. They've called a lockdown," she murmured. *"H'rea deasav'h!"* She couldn't use her identification code to open it without exposing herself. Glancing around, she tried not to panic at the sound of the approaching guards and spotted a console in a niche next to the door. Wires led up the wall and disappeared into a narrow hatch. A chance—slim, but her only option, propelled her into action.

Andreia used the massive brass door handles for leverage as she pulled herself up by the thick wires. Still gasping for air, she gasped inaudibly when her left foot slipped and she nearly fell. When she found new footing, her lungs burned from trying to breathe as quietly as possible. Sweaty, her hands slipped when she pulled herself up.

Eventually Andreia stood leaning toward the wires, outstretched in a forty-five degree angle, parallel to the wall, with both feet on the door handles. Carefully, she let go with one hand, balancing with all of her strength on her other arm. If her feet slipped now, she wouldn't have time to make another attempt.

The steps were closer now. Andreia looked at the hatch, trying to judge on which side the hinges were located, but she had no more time. Desperate, she pushed her right arm up, slamming it into the hatch. Nothing. Her palm throbbed from the impact. Andreia tried again, ignoring the pain, and this time the hatch yielded and flipped up into the ventilation duct with a thud.

The guards were only seconds away, and Andreia knew her time was up. Desperate, she threw herself forward, pushing with all the strength she had left in her legs. The thin metal trim sliced into her palms, but she ground her teeth and refused to let go. While she still had momentum, she pushed up harder. If she failed, she would suffer an agony much worse than the pain in her hands.

Andreia ducked into the hatch and kicked one last time; the guards were almost there. When she rolled to the right and pushed at the hatch, it closed with a faint clunk, which she hoped was too quiet to alert them. She knew they carried scanners, but perhaps the thick metal encasing the ventilation shaft would throw them off for a while.

Squinting, Andreia examined her hands. Two deep cuts across her palms bled profusely. She hoped she hadn't bled all over the trim and given herself away.

Andreia removed the belt to her caftan and managed to tear it in two and tie it around her hands, using her teeth to pull the knots tight. She heard the guards rustle around beneath her, calling out orders. Apparently they assumed she'd fled through the doors, because the sound of their steps faded, and she realized she had a new, and definitely improved, chance to escape.

Getting on her hands and knees she began to crawl. She had no idea where the ventilation duct led, but knew this was her best option. Angry at herself for the chances she'd taken tonight, putting herself in such danger, Andreia crept at an even pace and tried to make as little noise as possible. The shaft smelled of stale dust, and a steady stream of air quickly covered her in a thin layer of white and gray particles. She groaned at the escalating pain in her hands, since having to lean on them exacerbated the agony.

Andreia wasn't sure how long she'd been in the tight space, crawling, sometimes worming her way through it. She passed several hatches, every ten, fifteen meters, but she was afraid to try them, certain that the guards had figured out by now how she'd eluded them.

The ventilation shaft took a ninety-degree turn, then ended, blocked by a thin grid. Andreia crawled up to it, ready to scuttle backward at the slightest sign of trouble. She heard no movement below her, in what looked like a storage room for an assorted collection of technical devices. She pushed at the grid, found it swung open effortlessly, and managed to turn around inside the shaft and push herself out, feet first. Landing on the floor on bent knees, she stood still, holding her breath as she tried to gauge if somebody had heard her.

When she detected nothing but silence, Andreia made a quick inventory of the room, but found nothing to use as a weapon. She looked down at herself and realized she couldn't even try to leave the Onotharian headquarters like this. Her clothes dusty, bloodstained, and torn, she looked more like a choloz mine worker than the most famous Onotharian on the planet. Quelling her small panic at the thought of being trapped, she spied what looked like a closet at the far end of the room. She rushed forward and opened it, and her heart pounded when she saw fabric. Long white workers' coveralls, at least twenty of them, hung in front of her. She stopped herself from touching them with her bloodied hands, knowing she'd leave tell-tale signs. A new search of the closet produced thin-linen gloves, which she pulled on before removing the smallest coveralls from the hanger. Pulling them on, she found that they fit fairly well, and when she put her boots back on, the additional height helped shorten the coveralls' long legs.

Caps, similar to the coveralls, sat on a shelf, and she tucked her hair, which was in complete disarray, into one of them as she put it on. There was no mirror, but Andreia knew nobody would mistake a worker dressed in white for Andreia M'Aldovar.

But how would she be able to sign out as herself when leaving. Granted, the guards rarely halted anyone using their biosignature on exit, but after last night's events, they might. She toyed with the idea of sneaking back into her own office. It would give her an opportunity to clean up and change into some of the spare clothes she kept there. She could feign innocence and create a plausible reason for being there at this hour; she was infamous for her long hours and all-nighters. However, Andreia had no idea which of the many storerooms she was in. For her to wander around aimlessly on the executive floor dressed as a worker wasn't advisable. Her only option was to leave the building and hope they didn't double-check her.

Andreia decided to wait until the morning rush began, so she could blend with the crowd. Several thousand people worked in the vast building, and she had better hopes of escaping as one of the masses than alone in the night. Sitting down on a pile of small rugs, she pulled the cap down over her eyes and checked that she hadn't bled through the gloves. Exhausted, Andreia closed her eyes.

❖

"Paladin, to Jubinor. Come in."

"Jubinor here."

"How does it look at your end?" Roshan asked as she set the night-vision visor to compensate for the light of dawn. It was still dark enough to complete their mission, but too bright for full setting on the visor.

"They're marching a second bunch of our people into the shuttle."

"What type of shuttle?"

"A new sort of transport shuttle. I haven't seen this particular model before."

"Try to move in closer. I've dispatched two units of four to the power node station at the far north side of the compound. We need them to take out the force field before anything else can happen. Get back to me when you're in place. Paladin out."

Roshan looked at the sixteen men and women on both sides of her, ready to act on her command. They were part of what was left of her resistance cell, together with the eight she'd sent north and the twenty accompanying Jubinor. They were divided into units of four, which made it easier to move them up when required.

"Units five and six, I need you up by the tree line to lay down cover fire."

"Affirmative, ma'am." A young woman, a rookie, had proven herself strong during their last, disastrous mission. Without hesitation she now took control of the units Roshan sent to the tree line. Roshan felt a pang of remorse sear through her as she saw the group of young people ascend the ridge. She'd sent so many people toward an uncertain fate over the years; she ought to be numb by now. Roshan wasn't certain if it was good or bad that she wasn't.

"Jubinor to Paladin. Come in."

The communicator broke through her thoughts, and she clutched it and responded.

"We're in position. We have a good angle from here." Jubinor said over the slight static.

"Remember, we're not here to rescue anyone, just sabotage them." They didn't have the manpower to do that, and nowhere to place anyone they rescued at this point. They were here to take out whatever propulsion systems necessary to keep the Onotharians from deporting their comrades in arms to the asteroid prisons. It would at least slow things down.

"Got it, Paladin. Just give the word." Jubinor sounded confident, and it strengthened Roshan to know he was leading the other team.

"As soon as units five and six are in position with a clear field of fire and the north team has taken out the station," Roshan promised. "Over and out."

She reset her visor to binocular mode and scanned the tree line for her team. So far she saw nothing to suggest anyone had entered from the woods covering the ridge. Roshan shivered from the crisp air of dawn, despite her full combat gear. Wearing padded black coveralls, reinforced to withstand plasma-pulse fire and piercing objects, she knew the shudders didn't come merely from the cold air. Her thoughts returned to the last call she'd received from Andreia. Breathless and with a disturbing urgency, Andreia had breathed fear. Fear of what? Her own safety...or something else? Twenty years ago, Roshan would've been able to say for certain, just from listening to Andreia's voice. Today, she didn't know Andreia well; in fact, she was little more than a stranger.

"Units five and six, we're in position, Paladin."

"Excellent." Roshan scanned the tree line again. "I can't see you, though."

"You're not supposed to, ma'am." The young woman was a little short of breath, but sounded confident.

Roshan had to smile. "Good point. Remember your orders. No more, no less. Wait for my command." The rookies were always worrisome—some trigger-happy, some too hesitant. The young woman in charge of the tree line unit was obviously neither.

"Units one and two to Paladin."

"Go ahead."

"Node station out of commission, ma'am."

Blaring alarms from the compound beneath them confirmed the report. "I can tell," Roshan yelled into her communicator. They couldn't wait any longer. "Paladin to all units. Commence operations!"

A range of voices confirmed her command, and within a second, plasma-pulse fire singed the air before striking the shuttle in front of the main structure. Loud explosions caused enough havoc for Roshan to motion her own team on. They ran, hiding behind the smoke generated by continuous fire from the tree-line units. They all wore sensor scramblers, illegally smuggled to Gantharat by one of Roshan's ships and sewn into their coveralls to deflect any of the Onotharian soldiers' sensors. This was one of the few instances that Roshan's rebels were better equipped than the enemy.

The air filled with the typical smell of plasma-singed metal. The Onotharian soldiers returned fire, but apparently the smoke affected their aim since Roshan didn't receive any information of casualties.

She ran across a clearing, her team taking up position behind her, and threw herself on the ground, just outside the barricades. Together with Timis, who huddled next to her, she mounted an over-the-shoulder cannon and armed it with a series of five nano-reduced plasma charges. They were the most accurate of the high-yield explosive projectiles available to the resistance, and Roshan hoped to take out the propulsion systems of the three shuttles.

"Paladin to Jubinor," she yelled into the communicator to compensate for the fighting going on in front of them. "Come in!"

"Jubinor here."

"Keep the smoke screens going! We can't let them know exactly where our cannon's located."

"I hear you, Paladin. Laying down additional fire."

"Good. I'll launch within fifteen seconds. Over and out."

Roshan pushed her visor up and blinked hard to clear her eyes of smoke. She flipped open the small screen attached to the cannon and punched in the search for her first target. The built-in sensor rapidly found a shuttle and homed in on its rear. Roshan knew the risk of accidentally killing some of their own people was great, but she wouldn't allow the shuttles to take off if she could help it.

"All hands!" Roshan called out into her communicator. "Firing first charge!" She punched in the command and hid her face in the crease of her arm when the projectile hit its target. She looked up, but the thick smoke made it impossible to see anything.

"Paladin. A direct hit! Good job." Jubinor's voice crackled over the comm system.

"One down, two to go," Roshan muttered and reset the screen. "All hands! Round two!"

One after another, the small but deadly cannon destroyed the rear end of every shuttle, during which time they took heavy fire.

After she ceased firing, Roshan flipped down her visor, grateful to feel clear oxygen clean out her lungs. She coughed a few times and was about to turn to the young man next to her, wanting to commend him on assisting her, when she felt him jerk, then slump to his side against her.

"Hey, you all right? Timis?" Frantically, Roshan tore her gloves off and felt for the pulse on his neck just below the visor. She thought she could feel faint and rapid pulsations, but wasn't sure; she was so high on adrenalin since firing the cannon that her fingers trembled against Timis's clammy, pale skin. When she withdrew her hand, it was covered in blue blood. He'd taken a hit to the side of his neck and was hemorrhaging badly. "Man down! I need help here!" she called out, and got the attention of the woman next to Timis. "He's been hit. It's bad."

"Damn," the woman cursed. "Gods of Gantharat, not another one."

"I have to keep the fire off us so you can drag him up the slope. We're not going to make it otherwise." Roshan hardened her heart and didn't let doubt or worry infuse her voice. Routine set in and she fed off it, striving for composure.

"Yes, ma'am. Don't worry. I've got him," the woman said. Roshan had gone so far into battle mode that she didn't have space left in her brain for her team member's name. Sliding backward, the woman dragged Timis's listless body with her.

Roshan felt her upper lip curl into a feral grin as she pulled the plasma-pulse rifle from her shoulder and pressed the sensor to turn it on, its hum reassuring. Flipping her visor open with her free hand, she got up on one knee and raised the weapon to her shoulder. She pressed her eye to the sight, where a small screen outlined the individual firing on her team, seeing him through the smoke whereas a humanoid eye couldn't.

She pressed the release sensor repeatedly, taking out one Onotharian after another. Her hands seemed guided by someone else, someone with perfect aim and no hesitation. Roshan could only pray that most of the Gantharian rebels in the compound were well hidden, and she made a point of shooting only at the people in her sight who were positioned in a firing pose.

"Jubinor to Paladin. Confirming mission accomplished."

"Affirmative, Jubinor. Keep going. I've got you covered. All teams, fall back. Fall back!"

The first rays of the sun were beginning to glimmer between the trees, and soon she and her team would be completely visible. Roshan fired until a hand on her shoulder made her jump.

"Come on, Paladin," Jubinor said close to her ear. "You've destroyed or injured most of them. Let's get out of here."

Only then did Roshan notice that hardly any enemy response was coming from the compound.

"Damn," she whispered and looked up at Jubinor. "If they're all gone...we can save—"

"No." Jubinor shook his head emphatically. "We did what we came here for. We destroyed their communication nodes, their transporters, and most of their unit, just like Boyoda told us to do. Let's go."

Roshan stumbled on unsteady legs before she found her footing and rushed up the slope with Jubinor, chasing after her team as they hurried back to the hidden hovercraft. Roshan took the driver's seat in the sixteen-seater one and checked to make sure the rest of her team boarded the seven four-seat ones.

"All set?" she asked the rebels in her hovercraft as she pressed the wheel back against her. "How's Timis? Is he in a lot of pain?"

"No, ma'am," the woman tending to the young man said quietly. "He's not in pain."

The gentle voice made pain erupt in Roshan's chest. "He's dead." It wasn't a question, and nobody answered.

❖

Roshan fell from, rather than dismounted, her hoverbike and dragged herself up the wide stairs to her mansion—tired, hurting, and feeling utter loss. Since nobody knew Timis's true identity, all they could do was secretly leave his body at one of the major hospitals in Ganath and hope that his family would look for him there when they realized he was missing. Roshan hated this callous method of returning a young hero to his loved ones, but they had no choice. There could be no records of names and addresses anywhere, in case they were compromised.

"Good morning, ma'am," Wellter said as he opened the door. "You have a visitor. I showed her into the study."

"What? Now?" All Roshan wanted was to take a hydro shower and crash on the bed. "Damn, this'll have to be quick." She reached deep for a fragment of strength and strode toward her study. Pushing the doors open, she spotted a slumped figure in white coveralls on the couch.

At the sight of Roshan, Andreia sat up, her back ramrod straight. "You're back! Thank the Gods..." She moved as if to rise, then moaned and slumped against the backrest.

"Andreia?" Roshan could hardly connect the stunningly perfect woman she knew and the pale and dirty creature before her. "What's happened?" She walked to the couch and knelt before Andreia, reaching for one of her gloved hands.

Andreia yanked it back with a whimper. "I'm sorry. I know it was dangerous to come here." She cradled her hand with the other, and now Roshan saw the white gloves were bloodstained.

"You're hurt!" This realization, on top of the rest of the previous night's events, shook Roshan out of her daze.

"Yes." Andreia leaned forward with a pained expression on her face. "But that's nothing."

"How can it be nothing?" Roshan tried to tell herself she was overreacting, but as she began to peel off Andreia's left glove, seeing only more and more dried blood, her stomach nearly revolted.

"It gets worse." Andreia regarded her hand, seemingly indifferent. "I may have blown my cover."

CHAPTER ELEVEN

Andreia stared at Roshan, noticing for the first time the desolation and concern in her eyes. *For me?* Leaning closer, she forgot about her own troubles for a moment.

Roshan pulled her other glove off. "Gods, what have you done?"

"I had to get out of the building...the hard way," Andreia murmured. She knew she must look terrible. Her hair felt like it was sticking out in all directions, and dirt smudged her arms.

"Tell me." Roshan spoke curtly, but she was obviously distressed. "What happened last night?"

"I had to break into my father's office to get the information you needed." Her tongue felt uncooperative, and Andreia heard herself slur. "That set off the alarm, as my father obviously was at the chairman's function."

"How...how could you risk yourself like that?" Roshan looked stricken where she knelt in front of Andreia.

"I had to." They couldn't continue to fight for Gantharat's freedom with so many of the key members of the resistance missing. This was the only way she'd known how to obtain the information. Andreia examined her hands. The throbbing pain made them seem as if they belonged to someone else. "This," she murmured and held up her hands, "is a small price to pay for the safe return of our people." She looked up, suddenly alarmed. "Please tell me you were successful."

"We were. We stopped the Onotharians from transporting our people. For now. It won't take them long to call for backup transport shuttles. The ones they'd intended to use were new, huge and impressive."

"The latest model." Andreia frowned. "I didn't think it had even been tested yet. They've kept everything very close regarding this operation." She yawned and felt her cheeks warm. "I'm sorry. I'm so tired."

"We have to start by fixing your hands. I have a derma fuser upstairs. Come on."

"What if the staff—"

"Wellter will keep them away from us. Nobody knows you're here but him. He's supposed to keep it that way."

"Okay." Andreia stood on wobbly legs, feeling ridiculous as she balanced in her high-heeled boots.

"Come." When Roshan put her arm around Andreia's shoulders, Andreia gasped, stunned by the gentleness of the touch.

Roshan flinched. "Did I hurt you? Are you injured anywhere else?"

"No. No, I'm fine."

"Really?" Roshan took Andreia's chin and tipped her head back. "You're being honest now, right? When we were younger, you never did volunteer information. I remember carrying you home after your new shoes blistered your feet, just because you wouldn't tell me."

Andreia knew she was blushing again. She remembered very well how she'd tried to act brave when her feet began to burn, but also how the situation had backfired when she finally couldn't walk at all. Roshan had scolded her, but also held and comforted her. After she carried Andreia home, she used a home med-kit derma fuser on Andreia's heels and toes.

"I promise. Just my hands. Sure, my knees sting from crawling so far, but my hands are a mess."

"You crawled—Wait. You can tell me while we get you sorted out."

Roshan kept her arm around Andreia as she guided her through the house. It felt so familiar and oddly *right* that Andreia had to remind herself not to feel too comfortable and safe. Roshan and she were on the same side in this political and military conflict, but that was it. They'd mistakenly assumed they were enemies, and while they weren't, they weren't friends either. *Or anything more than that...*

When they reached a blackwood door at the far end of the upstairs corridor and Roshan pushed it open, Andreia realized they were in her private suite. Blue silk-draped walls held three-dimensional art, and the furniture looked as if it came from a multitude of cultures. Roshan gently nudged Andreia toward a door to the right, and they entered what had to be Roshan's bedroom.

Andreia was too tired to blush, but felt uneasy. Or was the tingling sensation in her stomach something else? It wasn't entirely unpleasant.

"I have everything we need here. Let me go get the med-kit."

"Sounds familiar." Andreia tried to smile, but instead she fumbled for support when Roshan let go, then cried out when she leaned too much on her hand as she grabbed for the bedpost. "Oh—"

"Here. I'm sorry. Come here." Roshan pulled Andreia close and helped her sit on the bed. "Now, don't move. I'll be back in a second." Andreia felt utterly foolish and suddenly lightheaded.

When Roshan returned with a bag, which folded out into four sections, she took out a small, cylinder-shaped instrument, placed it within reach, and regarded Andreia with soft eyes. "I may have to hurt you a bit when I take off the bandages and the other glove."

"Just do it." Andreia knew she sounded weak, but she was a coward when it came to these things. As Roshan began to peel off the remaining glove, Andreia's hand stung badly, and she groaned despite her best efforts.

"How did it happen?" Roshan asked.

Andreia spoke in a low voice, determined not to moan again, as she related last night's events. "I sat in the storage room until I heard people moving outside. I had to chance it, so I opened the door and managed to mingle with a large work force that came early this morning to repair the solar cells on the roof. It turned out they had their own machinery and several group badges, so I stole one, merged with the crowd, and used it to leave the building. I had to use the stolen badge because I couldn't use my fingerprints or biosignature. The guards didn't look at me twice or double-check my identity."

Roshan looked up, clearly startled. "But that means—"

"—that I'm officially still there. Kind of."

"And with no way to get back in to log out as yourself."

Andreia stared down at the deep slashes along her palms. "Oh. They look awful."

"Yes. They certainly do." Roshan reached for the derma fuser. "I'm setting this to cleansing mode first. All right like this?" Holding Andreia's left hand in hers, Roshan began to move the fuser along the wound. Coagulated blood and dirt disappeared from her skin, absorbed by the recycling part of the fuser and turned into a source of energy, leaving the wound fully visible. "There. Setting it to deep-tissue fuse now."

The wound began to close from the inside, and the initial tingle became a burning sensation, just below pain. When Roshan glanced at her with concern, Andreia realized she must've whimpered.

"Are you all right?"

"Yes. Yes, I'm fine." Andreia watched Roshan fuse the cut, but was more enthralled with how careful she was, and how her gentle touch sent tremors along her own arm. Roshan reset the derma fuser to fuse and closed the wound, leaving only a faint red line that Andreia knew would pale within a few weeks.

"Thank you. I can see you've done this before," Andreia said, and wiggled her fingers cautiously.

"I've had a lot of chances." Roshan's voice was hollow, her eyes a dull, dark blue.

"I'd think so." Andreia didn't like how Roshan stared unseeingly over her shoulder, as if lost in awful memories. "Ro?"

"Yes. What?"

"What happened last night? Something went wrong, didn't it?"

"We met our objectives. We destroyed the shuttles. Nobody was transported off the planet from that compound." As she rattled off the defensive words, Roshan seemed to close a door in Andreia's face.

"But?" Andreia persisted.

"What are you getting at? Isn't it enough that we did what we were supposed to?" Roshan's eyes launched daggers.

Breathless from the danger oozing off Roshan and from a long-forgotten excitement, Andreia refused to be intimidated. Instead, she touched Roshan's arm, trying to convey her understanding and sympathy. "You did well. That's not the issue. I can see that something went wrong. Did your team suffer casualties?"

Roshan swallowed repeatedly, the anger simmering in her eyes. "Yes. Like on so many other missions. That's not unusual."

"Who? Who died, Ro?"

"What do you care?" Roshan began treating Andreia's other hand.

The fuser stung worse on this one, and Andreia clenched her

teeth. She wasn't sure what was wrong, but Roshan was less careful, seemingly intent on shutting her up by inflicting pain. Or perhaps she was too distraught to perform the procedure correctly.

"Ow!" Andreia finally winced and pulled her hand back when the pain became more than merely annoying. "Roshan!"

Roshan jerked and dropped the fuser on the bed. "Oh, Gods, I'm sorry," she gasped. "I'm obviously going out of my mind. What was I thinking using the derma fuser with that setting? Let me see…"

Andreia looked down on her hand and saw an angry red welt swell next to the half closed gash. "You hurt me," she whispered.

"Not on purpose." Roshan's eyes filled with unexpected tears. "Andreia, listen to me. I could never hurt you deliberately. I was angry, yes, and not paying attention. Please, let me see what I did."

Slowly, Andreia extended her hand, jumping when Roshan cupped her palms around it. "I'll fix this. The right way." Roshan sounded strange. Defeated.

After she changed the settings on the derma fuser, the pain went away almost immediately as she began to move the instrument in a slow circle above the wound. Soon the gash was reduced to a fine line, and Roshan let go. "There."

"Roshan. Tell me. Who did you lose tonight?" Andreia knew she had to ask again, to show herself, and Roshan, that she cared and wouldn't be intimidated.

Roshan got up and put the fuser back into the med-kit bag, avoiding Andreia's eyes as she spoke. "Nobody I knew very well. His call sign was Timis. He was our youngest team member, little more than a child, really. Barely twenty years old, and so eager. Nice kid, too. He took a direct hit to his neck."

"I'm sorry."

"So am I, but what good will that do? We had to more or less dump his body at a hospital and hope they can identify him and inform his family. He'd been…to his brother's…goddamned…wedding…" Roshan's voice didn't carry all the way through her last sentence. She broke down into sobs and pulled back. "That's supposed to be a happy day, isn't it?" Roshan spoke through the tears with resentment and anger in her voice. "And now his brother will always remember that his happiest day is also the anniversary of when his brother disappeared… when they lost him forever…"

Andreia wasn't going to let Roshan blame herself. She walked over to her, her heart pounding in her chest and her mouth dry, and tentatively touched Roshan's shoulder. "Ro, don't. It wasn't your fault. You can't protect everybody all the time. It's dangerous every time we stand up to the Onotharians. I bet this boy knew that, having grown up knowing nothing of freedom."

Roshan didn't push her away, but glared at her with a hard expression. "Nice. But it's not true. I'm the team leader now. I should've anticipated—"

"I don't buy that. You're not perfect, and neither am I. I got you the information and tactical data last night, but I risked everything. I wasn't as fortunate as I normally am. This may be my last day of freedom. For all I know, they've figured it out by now and are waiting for me at home or at work, ready to arrest me. And," Andreia shuddered, "I'm not sure I could resist their measures of persuasion."

"I won't let that happen." Roshan's face changed from stone-carved to worried determination. "I'll hide you forever before I allow anyone to harm you!"

Andreia felt something inside her melt. Roshan stood so tall and proud, despite her disheveled appearance and wild white-blond hair. There was something of a tormented deity in her stance, of a goddess who'd stopped seeing or believing in her worshippers and now moved on without them. *That's it. She seems so lost, so...abandoned.* With her hands still on Roshan's arms, she shook her gently. "I believe you." Not thinking of any consequences, Andreia pulled Roshan closer, intending to give her a reassuring hug.

Roshan's hands went up, and Andreia would never know if the gesture was meant to stop her, because they pulled her into a fierce embrace instead. Andreia gasped, feeling small fires where their bodies met. As if transported back through time, she imagined the young, vibrant Roshan held her, tangled her fingers in her hair, and pulled her in for a kiss.

The older Roshan, with her full lips, curvy and obviously experienced, barely resembled the dynamic young woman who'd loved life with abandon. This Roshan, war-weary from the years she'd led a double life and fought for her homeworld's freedom, kissed her as if she were the last woman on Gantharat.

Probing, not allowing Andreia any time to catch her breath, Roshan towered over her, bending her back over her arm. Andreia never would have guessed such passion existed behind Roshan's normal mask of disdain. The tiny fires on Andreia's skin threatened to ignite all of her own desires, which scared her more than Roshan's surprising advances. Still, as she returned the kiss, Andreia hoped for Roshan to be a little tender. Tears rose in her eyes, and she mourned for what they nearly had twenty-five years ago, but lost, and could never have again. She sobbed into the kiss, murmuring against Roshan's lips. "Please, dearest Ro, don't do this. I can't stand it. It's…" *Too much.*

Roshan kept kissing her for a few scorching moments and cupped Andreia's cheek with one hand while she stroked her back with the other. Slowly Roshan released her lips and looked at her with eyes so dark blue they seemed black. Sunlight shone through the large window where thin curtains hid them from the world, engulfing Roshan from behind and painting her an aura of gold. Andreia blinked against the brightness. "Ro?" she whispered. *Oh, Roshan.*

"I'm sorry." Roshan's voice was hardly recognizable. "I have no idea what got into me. I never…act like this. Ever." Abruptly, she let go of Andreia and stepped back, wincing as she bumped into a cabinet behind her.

"I realize that." Andreia ran a hand through her hair and became tangled in her half-undone hairdo. She yanked her hand to free it. "Ow." Her scalp burned at her attempt to straighten out her hair.

"What are you doing?" Roshan reached out with an exasperated sigh. "Here. Let me."

"No! I don't want you to." Andreia feared what her own treacherous body might do if Roshan kept touching her. Her skin burned, and her nipples ached with need. The few trysts she'd allowed herself through the years had been unfulfilling, quick, and some even physically uncomfortable. None had ever taken her breath away…like Roshan's kiss had.

And now, when she ought to back away from the glorious woman before her, Roshan's hands were already in her hair, untangling the pins and combing out the wild curls with her fingers. "Your hair always had a mind of its own. And you still keep it long. Amazing." Roshan half smiled. "I like how it looks. It suits you."

"Eh. Thanks." Andreia wondered how Roshan could switch this easily. Hadn't the kiss affected her at all? "Now what?"

"We took care of your hands. Now we need to shower. Both of us. And sleep. It's barely daybreak and we must wait until there's a morning rush at headquarters to smuggle you back in and then officially sign you out. As far as I can tell, that's the only way for you to keep going. It's well worth the risk to do this, to keep Boyoda in play."

Was there genuine kindness in Roshan's voice? Andreia wasn't certain. She was so tired that her knees were giving in. "Just point me in the direction of the shower. I'll worry about the rest later."

"Okay. Here. Let's go." Roshan walked in front of Andreia into the spacious bathroom. Marble, gold, and glass dominated it, and Andreia stood in the middle of the room, swaying. She wanted to tell Roshan that she could manage, that Roshan could leave. *I need to gather my thoughts and figure out how to handle everything, including her.* Instead, to her dismay, her knees finally collapsed after her ordeal in the ventilation shaft. With a startled intake of breath, she sank ungracefully toward the floor.

Roshan lunged forward and managed to catch her. "Damn it! Are you all right?"

"Stupid knees," Andreia muttered and clung to Roshan. "All that crawling. It's nothing. Really."

Roshan doubted it. "Come here." She didn't ask permission, but simply unbuttoned the white coveralls and pulled them off Andreia's shoulders. Underneath, Andreia wore the same clothes she'd had on at the chairman's function. "We better get you out of these and into the shower before you fall again."

"I won't fall," Andreia muttered and took a step back. "For the Gods of Gantharat, I'm not a child!"

Surprised by the heated tone behind Andreia's annoyed words, Roshan let go. "I never meant to suggest you were."

"Well, you always were good at taking over." Muttering, Andreia pushed her coveralls down and stepped out of them, then unbuttoned the caftan and tugged fruitlessly at it. "If you want to help, then untangle my hair from whatever it's stuck to."

Suddenly not tired at all, Roshan obediently moved in behind Andreia and loosened the long, black strands caught in the ornamental stones at the neckline of the caftan. "There." She remained where she was as the thin garment slid down Andreia's body. Static electricity made her red shirt cling to Andreia like a second skin. Without looking back at Roshan, Andreia unbuttoned it and let it fall to the floor as well.

She tried to unfasten her black pants, but Roshan could see her fingers trembling and the button remained closed. "Let me." She reached around Andreia's waist from behind and unbuttoned the pants. Andreia's skin was like satin against Roshan's hands when she lowered them along slender legs, all the way to Andreia's small, pretty feet.

Kneeling, Roshan couldn't stop herself from exploring the way Andreia felt against her hands. The angry passion vanished, and in its place a tender, almost reverent feeling emerged.

"Ro?" Andreia turned within Roshan's arms and looked down at her with huge, golden eyes.

"Shh." Roshan gazed up, astonished at how anyone could be so beautiful. Dark, long curls framed Andreia's triangular face, which, despite her age, held a youthful, wondering expression. Roshan stood, slowly, and smoothed down the unruly tresses that insisted on falling over Andreia's eyes. It was suddenly so important to make up for the harsh caresses a few minutes earlier. They didn't have room for any confused anger, masked as passion.

Roshan had no idea why she cared how Andreia felt. They were in this last battle for the planet they loved together, but that was probably it. Once Gantharat was liberated, whether it took one year or ten, would they move along with their lives, their separate lives?

Roshan placed two fingers under Andreia's chin. Right now, they needed to trust each other, if only to stay alive and carry on the struggle. *We're pawns in our own fight. We have designated duties, and we don't have a choice but to stick to them, if we want to keep our honor and win.* Roshan's pragmatic inner voice couldn't calm the urgency of her feelings.

She looked down at Andreia under half-closed eyelids. "We should've been friends. We *were* friends. True friends." The words were over Roshan's lips before she realized what she was going to say. *H'rea deasav'h!* Too frank.

"The occupation destroyed many families, and even more relationships," Andreia said calmly. "The Onotharian families that had lived here for generations, who considered themselves Gantharians, if not by race, then by allegiance, are now part of a hated people. Not to mention the mixed families. Both camps consider them traitors."

"Guess we'd fit into that category if we hadn't..." Roshan hesitated, unable to speak because of the lump in her throat.

"If we hadn't hated each other first." Andreia leaned her cheek into Roshan's hand for a moment. Then she straightened her back and folded her arms in front of her. She was dressed only in her underwear, thin-linen panties and camisole. "I despised you for so many years. I know better now, but the negative feelings...they're almost engraved in my heart. Probably because what I considered your betrayal and collaboration hurt me so much."

"And now? Do you realize that I've had to live not only with your anger and resentment, but also hatred from my own people? Only three people, not counting you, know my true allegiance." Roshan shrugged. "To all other Gantharians, I'm what you said, a collaborator. A traitor."

"They'll find out the truth. You'll become a national hero, while I become a renowned traitor to *my* people. My fall from grace will make a resounding thud, I imagine."

The crooked grin on Andreia's face tugged at Roshan's heart. "Your people, *here*, will know the truth and understand."

Andreia began to shiver, perhaps from being undressed, but Roshan thought it was more from how she imagined the Gantharian people would react to her double existence.

"I'm not so sure," Andreia said. In fact, I'm sure the opposite will happen. People in both camps will see me as a traitor. I know this, and I've accepted it."

Roshan ached because of the pain behind Andreia's wry grin. "Not much I can say to convince you, is there?" she asked. Roshan wished there was. She wanted to erase the desolation and calm acceptance of what Andreia saw as her fate.

"No. Not really." Andreia rubbed her own arms. "I better go take that shower—"

"Yes."

"You wouldn't happen to have hydro-technology?"

"I do."

"That'll help me get warm again." Andreia headed for the shower stall, but turned back quickly. "Oh. Right. Do you have any clothes I can borrow? Something that isn't impossibly huge on me?"

"I'm sure I can find something." Roshan curled her hands into tight fists. Andreia looked so alluring, so innocent, as she stood almost naked in front of her. *If she doesn't go now, I'll have to kiss her again.* Roshan forced herself to breathe evenly and look confident.

"You need a shower too, I think," Andreia said over her shoulder as she pulled the camisole over her head.

Don't! Don't... Roshan squeezed her eyes closed at the hot images of sliding her hands over a soap-lathered Andreia. She could hear soft moans, as clearly as if—

"You all right, Ro?" Andreia sounded concerned. "You're making odd noises."

"I'll...I'll go see about the clothes. I can shower later." *Ice cold. Later.*

When Andreia nodded and stuck her thumbs inside her panties, Roshan fled the bathroom and rushed into the adjoining room where her clothes hung on a revolving rack. She kept some as patterns in a fabric recycler she'd bought on Corma, a few years ago. Roshan cursed out loud when she realized she hadn't asked Andreia's size. She'd have to guess. Booting the computer she envisioned the dark beautiful woman currently in her shower. Andreia was shorter than herself, but not small. Curvaceous without being overweight. "Non-woven briefs, size Medium-C, white," she instructed the computer. "Thin-linen camisole, Medium-D, white." Roshan hesitated. "Leather-like pants, Medium-B, red. Thin-linen collar shirt, Medium-D, white."

The computer hummed as it processed the order. It would take about ten minutes, and in the meantime, Roshan found some clothes for herself. She wasn't going to wait for Andreia to come out dripping wet; she was going to take an ionic-resonance shower, which lasted about ten seconds. Time-saving and at a safe distance.

Roshan knew she'd be back before Andreia got out, ready to face her with new resolve. She had to contain these new impulses, or old, whichever way you looked at it. She had had a minor lapse when vulnerable, but cleaning up and getting some rest would take care of that.

❖

Andreia sat up in the strange bed, uncertain for a moment what woke her and where she was. Instead of the dark gray, metal-plated ceiling, with lighter gray walls, like the ones in her apartment, she saw umbra-colored, organic velvet wall hangings, and a ceiling made from the same blackwood as the doors. She rose, and her feet sank into plush, dark blue carpet; the whole area around the bed was soft and pliant. "Mattress-rest floors. A customary Gantharian detail I've missed." Andreia reveled in the cushioned feeling under her feet as she tiptoed around the room, looking out the window. Rested, she now took time to survey the surroundings, impressed with Roshan's estate.

Roshan. Oh, stars! Andreia's breath caught as she remembered the heated, almost desperate kiss they'd shared. She could still feel Roshan towering over her, a magnificent warrior, determined to claim her... The word "prey" came to mind, and Andreia reached for the window frame and held on, lightheaded. She gazed down her abdomen and saw how her small nipples had hardened, clearly outlined by the thin-linen fabric. Wearing one of Roshan's large shirts didn't help, for its silky smoothness reminded her of Roshan. And her faint scent—dark and musky—was still there, unless it was Andreia's imagination. Over on the chair by the old-fashioned dresser lay her clothes, freshly replicated from a buffer pattern in Roshan's fabric recycler.

The guest room was located at the far end of the private part of Roshan's mansion. Andreia checked the time and realized she'd slept four of the five hours they'd agreed on. The hydro shower had left her lethargic, and she had very vague memories of Roshan showing her to the room. Andreia frowned, trying to remember, but all she was sure of was that Roshan had seemed cold and distant, almost hostile. Still, her hands had been tender as they guided her there, and the contradiction had only confused Andreia further. Now, when she was rested and more able to judge her own reactions, as well as try to interpret Roshan's, she was convinced that Roshan regretted letting her guard down earlier.

"How she must hate having shown such weakness," Andreia muttered as she reached for her clothes. "Kissing *me*, of all people. And like that."

The kiss had left Andreia breathless and filled with a reluctant, yet overwhelming, desire. When Roshan had bent Andreia over her arm, their lips meeting with such ferocity, Andreia could think only of how she wanted the craziness never to stop.

Andreia tugged at her clothes with jagged movements, groaning when the fabric caressed her heated skin, which seemed to have a memory of its own. Her skin sensed long, slender fingers pulling her close, as gentle as they were assertive.

"You're also awake, I see." Roshan's husky voice interrupted the communication Andreia had with her own skin.

"Ro!" *No, no. No squeaky voice like that.* Andreia cleared her throat. "You're up." *Oh, brilliant. Not much better.*

"Yes." Was there a humorous gleam in Roshan's eyes at Andreia's obvious discomfort?

"I…" Andreia forced herself to get a grip on her scrambling brain, and her only alternative was to slip into her role as Andreia M'Aldovar, spokesperson extraordinaire for the Onotharian master. "I slept fine, how about you?" she asked, her voice cool and detached, her smile thin.

Her transformation had more than the desired effect on Roshan, whose smile faded away, and whose amused expression vanished as if it had never existed.

"Fine," Roshan said curtly. "You hungry?"

"Not really," Andreia said as the thought of food made her stomach churn. "I guess it would be smart to eat something, though. I'll probably need my strength when I return to headquarters."

"You mean 'we?'"

Andreia had begun walking, but stopped at Roshan's short question. "No, I didn't mean we, but, well, if you insist on joining me, we'd better get our stories straight. I just don't understand why you would go."

"Officially? Or privately?" Roshan inched from the door frame as Andreia walked toward her.

Andreia couldn't judge if Roshan's words were taunting. Confused, she jutted her chin out and raised it in a good imitation of how her mother made an entrance. Le'Tinia could do that: walk into a room of strangers and within fifteen minutes become the uncrowned queen, indisputably the most charismatic person there. Andreia knew she could never play it like her mother. She didn't have the flare for such strategies, and normally she couldn't be bothered. Right now, however, the role seemed the appropriate, and only possible, course of action. And judging from Roshan's taken-aback look, she wasn't completely incompetent at it.

"Officially. That's the only version we have, isn't it?" Andreia smoothed the new pants around her thighs. "Why would you go with me to the headquarters where you've never set foot before, as far as I know?"

"We're getting reacquainted. You're very proudly going to show me around, and I'm going to shake hands with your parents." Roshan spoke smoothly, but her eyes were dull, as if the blue had washed out. "We'll make sure the guards are so taken with us when we enter, they won't notice that you don't actually submit your fingerprint. They'll be too busy adding me to their system to bother with a famous person like you."

The plan was simple, and in its simplicity, it sounded both easy and hard. "It's a big risk."

Roshan shrugged. "It's that, or they nail you when you go through the gates...or find out somehow that you never left. Either way, that scenario puts Boyoda, the most hunted resistance member on the planet, in jeopardy. If anyone even begins to suspect that you aren't who and what you seem to be..." Another quick jerk of Roshan's shoulders finished the sentence.

"So, it's a matter of looking east when you want to go west, you mean?" Andreia wrinkled her nose at the old Gantharian saying. "Well, there's the not-so-small matter to consider that if I get caught, with you in tow, you'll be compromised right there with me." Andreia gasped as the words strummed a foreign, rarely used string inside her. The tone, sorrowful and ominous, resounded in her head. The thought of Roshan dragged away to the prison compounds, only to be thrown into an asteroid prison and forgotten by most, tormented her. *I'd never forget you.*

Roshan moved away from the door frame and let the wall support itself. "All right. Let's go have something to eat, then." She looked at Andreia with sharp, arctic eyes.

"Very well," Andreia said. "I think I can manage something light." She suspected that her voice sounded as hollow as her heart and stomach felt.

❖

"Ms. M'Aldovar," the security guard beamed. "Good to see you again."

"You too. I haven't seen you in ages." Andreia returned the young Onotharian's smile.

Roshan wanted to groan impatiently at the sight of the starstruck guard. Andreia looked as if she basked in his adulation. *How much of that's part of her act?*

Andreia wore the new clothes with a casual elegance that Roshan never could've emulated, even if she'd wanted to. Despite the fact that Andreia was a bit shorter than the average Onotharian woman, her legs were long and shapely. She moved with calm, confident steps, and there was no way anyone could tell Andreia was wracked with a case of bad nerves. *How is it I can tell? She seems fine at first glance.*

"This is my very close friend, Ms. O'Landha. I thought I'd give her the grand tour."

"Certainly, ma'am. I'll issue her a temporary pass."

"Thank you."

Roshan had to go through a series of hand and retina scans before the guard was satisfied. She growled inside at the slow procedure and the fact that she was smiling and accommodating an Onotharian. Only the fact that Andreia stood so near, her body close to Roshan's while she pressed her hand to a scanning sensor, made it possible for Roshan to stick to the plan.

Once she was cleared, they walked through the medium-sized of the three detectors, and Andreia held Roshan's hand, giving her longing, loving glances. Roshan knew the overtures were all part of their scheme to get Andreia inside. *She's like a magician. Redirect the audience's attention by creating a diversion.*

Andreia stuck her small, narrow hand in Roshan's, telling herself that she was merely playacting, with no other motive than to make sure the guards were looking at anything but her own hand.

When they passed the scanning device, Roshan did something unexpected, even from her own point of view. She pulled Andreia close and kissed her cheek. The silken feel of Andreia's skin against her lips made Roshan linger.

"Mm," Roshan hummed against Andreia and rubbed her cheek gently with her own. "So sweet of you to show me around."

"Roshan?" Andreia sounded breathless.

Roshan was uncertain if Andreia was acting too, or if she was as taken aback as she sounded.

The guard and his colleague stared at them, more than likely stunned at the sight of the romantic overtures involving the famous Andreia M'Aldovar. Roshan would bet her last credit that they'd never seen Andreia act anything but appropriately.

Roshan placed her palm on the scanner, allowing it to enter her biosignature and handprint. She closed her eyes briefly, suddenly afraid that her data would exist in a file somewhere, without her knowledge. Half-expecting alarms to go off, Roshan squeezed Andreia's hand harder.

"Don't worry," Andreia whispered in her ear. "You'll be fine."

How did she know? Roshan sent Andreia what she hoped was a tender look. "Thank you, *henshes.*" She brushed her lips over Andreia's forehead and nudged her to move past the identification equipment. It would probably not begin to howl since Andreia was already logged in, but Roshan wasn't sure. It also might go into lockdown, which would jeopardize both of them.

No sounds, no alarms disturbed the peace. Andreia was safely inside, and Roshan was just about to remove her hand from their gentle grip when a familiar voice resounded from behind.

"*Henshes*, what are you up to?" Le'Tinia M'Aldovar rounded the people entering behind Andreia and Roshan. Roshan looked at the older woman with curiosity and, she hoped, well-hidden hatred. This was the woman she'd known only as the mother of her best friend all those years ago. Together with her husband, Valax, she had befriended Roshan's parents and ultimately betrayed them. Beautiful, in a cold and distant way, unlike Andreia's warm coloring, Le'Tinia now smiled broadly.

"Roshan O'Landha, this is a pleasant surprise." She glanced approvingly at her daughter. "Andreia told me you two had finally put whatever squabble you had aside and become friends again."

Squabble? Roshan was ready to throttle Le'Tinia with her bare hands. It took some nerve to call the death of her mother, and the wrongful arrest of her father, cause for a squabble. The pain, never healed and always simmering just beneath her skin, rose and was as fresh as it had been when Roshan had found out the fate of her parents, one only a few lunar months after the other. She had idolized her mother and worshipped her father. The fact that her best friend's parents were a crucial part of the group responsible for killing them had nearly destroyed her.

Now she forced down the fury brewing inside and smiled toward Le'Tinia. "Twenty-five years is a long time to hold a grudge," she said, hoping her voice was light and casual. "Andreia offered to show me around the premises. I've always been impressed with this building and how our interim government conducts politics." *So impressed that I'd readily take my unit in here and blast you all to hell.*

"Mother, Roshan and I have to go—"

"But since you're going to show her around your office, you can't miss out on re-introducing Roshan to your father. He's meeting with some of the ministers in his conference room in a little while."

"What ministers?" Andreia asked, still holding Roshan's hand as if to forestall a surprise attack against her mother.

"We have six of the North Onotharat ministers present. They came early yesterday, to see Chairman M'Ocresta off and to begin preparations."

Roshan struggled to keep her expression impassive, to not reveal how extraordinary this piece of information was. It struck her as a sign of Le'Tinia's arrogance that she shared it so nonchalantly with them.

Le'Tinia shook her head. "We almost had to cancel the whole meeting. Someone broke into your father's office last night."

"Father's room? Who could do such a thing? This building is supposed to be impenetrable," Andreia said, and Roshan had to hand it to her; she sounded genuinely baffled.

"The person, or perhaps there was more than one, we don't know, managed to disable the feed to the security sensors. They were still operational, but somehow this individual had managed to load a virus into the software. Every single picture frame is garbled beyond recognition. Our head of security isn't very optimistic."

"What about fingerprints?"

"None. The smudges on the keyboard indicate the perpetrator wore gloves."

"I see. I wonder what they were after, specifically. It could be any number of things, of course. Father's files are pretty extensive." Andreia glanced at Roshan. "Perhaps we'd better come back another day—"

"I'd like to take the opportunity to say hello to your father, Andreia," Roshan interrupted sweetly with a broad smile. "I wasn't able to greet your parents last night."

"You were so eager to dance with our daughter." Le'Tinia beamed and appeared happy to change the subject as well. "I can't tell you how much this delights me. We've wanted Andreia to—"

"Mother. I'll go see Father now. We're off to dinner after that, so we can't stay too long," Andreia said.

Le'Tinia looked as if she was about to pout, which was a hilarious thought. Andreia's mother was a high-ranking politician and advisor, and here she wasn't even able to control her own child. *It must infuriate her.* This possibility pleased Roshan, but from the small tremors in Andreia's hand, she could guess how the charade took a toll on her ally.

Roshan acted quickly at this small sign of distress from Andreia. Removing her hand from Andreia's grip, she encircled her waist. Andreia jerked, but played along. Roshan pulled her closer and made Andreia lean into her as she slid a hand up and down her arm.

"It was nice meeting you again, Le'Tinia," Roshan said, deliberately using the woman's first name to make her realize Roshan considered them equals. Such a move was bound to throw the conceited Onotharian off, and it no doubt mystified Andreia's mother how Roshan could find the strength and guts to adopt such an attitude.

"Very well," Le'Tinia said, then pasted a smile on her narrow lips. "Until next time, then."

"Next time." Roshan nodded. *Perhaps not next time, but at one point, I'll let you know just what the consequences are for what you and your people collectively did to my parents.* Roshan pulled Andreia along with her, and the farther they got from Le'Tinia, the stronger Andreia's steps seemed. Roshan wondered why Andreia would be so apprehensive, afraid even, of her mother.

Surely Andreia must realize that her position among the Gantharians was far more positive than negative. The Gantharians generally hated every single Onotharian, but it had always baffled Roshan how many of her countrymen actually admired and liked Andreia. True, Andreia had never officially condoned the aggressive tactics carried out by her people. Andreia somehow came across as the voice of reason, whether she recognized it or not.

Andreia's office was a display of blue crystalline glass, blackened aluminum, and old-fashioned brass. On her wall hung three-dimensional diplomas, and Roshan let her eyes glide over the many titles. The third diploma made her flinch. "You finished medical school?" She pivoted and looked at Andreia. "I never knew that."

"Not many do, and I never got to practice. Life, politics got in my way. I'm sure you realize that."

Roshan listened to the polite words and raised a questioning eyebrow. Andreia gestured toward the ceiling and placed a fingertip on her lips. Roshan thought quickly and raised her left arm as she pressed a sensor on her chronometer. "I do. I sometimes regret going into business rather than finishing medical school, but as you say, that's life." Roshan conversed casually while she scanned the room for surveillance equipment. She found two transmitters in each corner of the room and held up two fingers, while directing Andreia's attention to the devices' location. Andreia nodded with a grim look on her face.

"One day, perhaps," she murmured and walked over to Roshan. "Who knows?"

"Who knows?" Roshan realized they had to keep up the charade for the ones listening in on their conversation. "Maybe now, when we've found each other again, we can plan for such a future."

Andreia's head snapped up. "Roshan—"

Roshan placed a fingertip on Andreia's lips. "I know, I know, time's not on our side, but a person can dream, can't she?"

It took a few more moments before Andreia caught on. "Yes. Yes, of course they can," she said with pale lips.

Andreia's look, rigid and defeated, disturbed Roshan more than she would admit. There were no tears in Andreia's golden eyes, just very subtle signs of distress, but they were obvious to Roshan.

Forgetting that she had decided to stay aloof and not be the least personal with her former friend, Roshan hugged Andreia's stooped shoulders. "There," she said, infusing as much concern into her voice as possible. "I know you're hoping to live your dream, but we don't live in a perfect world—none of us do. We just have to make the most of what we have. I've gone by that rule for years now, and I'm not leading such a shabby life, am I?" Roshan swallowed and hoped Andreia would understand and read between the lines.

Andreia stood, still rigid, in Roshan's light embrace. "No, of course not. You've done very well for yourself." Andreia sounded almost forlorn, even if her eyes signaled that she understood. "I'm impressed with your success."

"Thanks. And yours is unprecedented, of course." Roshan winked, trying to lighten the mood. If Andreia didn't get it together, she might say something to tip off the ones listening to her true frame of mind.

"So I understand." Andreia smiled wryly and a faint light twinkled in her eyes. "The latest popularity polls have me in first place among those that count."

This comment wasn't lost on Roshan, who tossed her head back and laughed aloud, admiring Andreia's aplomb. She knew her friend was inspired by the moment, and as false as Andreia's statement might be, it stirred some very true feelings inside her. For the first time, she acknowledged to herself how important Andreia's, not merely Boyoda's, survival was to her. She watched as Andreia wrinkled her nose and made a funny face toward the surveillance equipment, finding this expression unbearably cute. *Cute?*

Oh, Gods. Roshan acted instinctively and pulled Andreia into her arms. The listeners should think this was what the two of them were up to, but that wasn't why she acted this way. Roshan wasn't sure if she'd been able to convey her true attitude to Andreia, because her vision was blurred when she brushed her lips over Andreia's.

Roshan felt a small sigh against her mouth when Andreia parted her lips. Sweet, intoxicatingly delicious, the tip of Andreia's tongue met her own, shyly to begin with. Soon Andreia's touch grew bolder and the kiss deepened. Roshan tried to keep her mind on the fact that they were being monitored, but all she could feel was how well Andreia fit in her arms. A little fuller, more rounded in all the right places, Andreia cushioned her own toned frame.

Roshan gently cupped Andreia's flushed face and pulled back a little to examine her expression.

"No," Andreia murmured, "don't let go..." She rose on her toes and pressed her lips to Roshan's again.

Drunk on the euphoria that filled her at the hungry caress, Roshan ran her hands beneath Andreia's jacket. The shirt underneath was thin and Andreia's skin hot to the touch. Greedily, wanting to savor everything at once, Roshan spread her fingers wide and moved them up and down Andreia's back. "I won't. I won't let you go, I promise..." The words startled Roshan back into reality. *I promise? Where did that come from?*

Andreia seemed to sense the withdrawal and pulled back, looking as if she'd sobered up. Her golden eyes darkened to a dull brown, like a light had turned off inside her soul. *Or is it my overactive imagination?* Roshan sighed in exasperation at her own choice of words. It used to be so easy to interpret Andreia's expressions; usually they were so obvious they didn't need any interpretation at all. Andreia would make herself so transparent to Roshan, without being even remotely predictable or boring. She was just so honest, the person Roshan had trusted most of all, next to her parents.

As soon as the image of Jin-Jin and Mikael entered her mind, Roshan pulled back completely, carefully arranging her features to hide how it hurt her physically to let go of Andreia.

"This isn't the time or place for this," Andreia said, laughing nervously. "Let me just look up a few things, and then we'll go see Father. He's meeting with the ministers soon, which means he'll be busy all afternoon, and perhaps the evening as well."

Roshan saw no trace of their kisses, other than Andreia's swollen lips. "Fine. I'll just make myself comfortable."

Andreia nodded curtly and walked over to her desk. Sitting down she seemed to grip her handheld computer tightly. Then she yanked a drawer open with uncoordinated movements and busied herself with its contents.

The sunlight coming from the window accentuated the highlights in Andreia's hair, making the wild, barely tamed curls come alive. Roshan wanted to run her hands through their rich masses. She had never felt the silky texture against her body, and right now, it seemed impossible that she ever would. Andreia's presence fulfilled a need in her, in a way Roshan would never have guessed possible. A maverick of sorts, she considered herself a true individualist, but somehow she doubted that fact now. Her body was apparently readying itself for Andreia's close proximity. It hurt Roshan to tear her thoughts away from Andreia, who was beautiful both inside and out.

Andreia raised her eyes toward Roshan. She blinked slowly, as if her thoughts had been elsewhere, on matters other than her computer, and she was only now waking up to reality. Her lips parted, and the pink tip of her tongue darted out to moisten them. Roshan almost groaned aloud, but managed to cough instead, and Andreia blushed faintly.

Alarms blared inside Roshan's head. Sliding her hand into her jacket pocket, she pulled out a handheld computer similar to the one Andreia was working on and brought up a document of her latest business transaction with one of the southern counties of Gantharat.

She needed the distraction badly, or she feared her eyes would give her away.

CHAPTER TWELVE

"Cloaking systems at one hundred percent, ma'am." The ensign at ops tapped on her computer console. "Shields at one hundred percent also."

"Excellent." Rae regarded the streaming information that scrolled down the small computer screen attached to the command chair's armrest. She had been very comfortable in this chair, supervising the *Gallant's* high-speed journey to Gantharian space during the last five days.

"ETA to the Gantharian asteroid belt, four hours, Admiral," the strawberry blond woman at the helm chimed in. "It's been a smooth ride so far. Any last-minute changes, ma'am?" Lt. Commander Leanne D'Artansis asked, looking back over her shoulder. She was, despite her small frame, one of the best pilots in the Fleet. With Commander Owena Grey, she'd lived and worked on Gamma VI under Commodore de Vies's command until Rae's father had approached them. It had taken them only a few hours to travel from the space station to Corma, which was also Leanne's home planet.

Fortunately, Leanne was well trained on the new high-velocity ships, having used the state-of-the-art simulators on Gamma VI. She arrived anticipating the mission and worried about her return to Corma. Rae knew that Leanne and Owena had visited Leanne's mothers not long ago, and Owena had hinted that the relationship was a bit strained.

"No changes," Rae now said. "Steady as she goes."

"Yes, ma'am."

"The weapons' arrays are charged and ready, Admiral," Commander Grey reported. "We've made repairs to the rear cannons. They're operating within normal parameters."

"Good. Thank you, Commander." Rae nodded toward the black-haired woman who stood with tall, lethal grace to her right. "Anything else I need to know about? The troops?"

"Marine units are gearing up. Their commanding officers are due in your office in an hour."

"Good." Rae liked the two female and one male officer that headed up the marines on this mission. Seasoned officers, having patrolled the border and dealt with well-equipped pirates in illegal high-speed tachyon-drive vessels, they were the best for this operation.

But do I know what to expect? It was time-consuming to sift through the massive amount of intel from Gantharat for any gold nuggets. Kellen had tried to gain more information from her sources on Gantharat, but had learned little.

"New specs for the cloaked approach, Admiral." Kellen interrupted her thoughts, as if she knew her wife was thinking about her. "The asteroid belt is in a constant state of flux, moving in a spiral pattern. I've estimated how we can enter it, which will provide ample shielding for us until we're ready to engage the enemy."

"Very well. Submit your calculations to Lieutenant Commander D'Artansis. Commander, adjust your course accordingly. We'll need time to survey the situation planet-side before we approach the resistance."

"Yes, ma'am." After a brief pause D'Artansis continued, "Course adjusted, ma'am. The ride may get a bit bumpy."

"Thanks for the warning." Rae glanced over at Kellen. "It usually is."

Kellen was stunningly beautiful in her SC Fleet uniform: black leather-like jacket, blue trousers tucked into knee-high black boots, and the shining new insignia of a lieutenant commander. Rae remembered their previous danger-filled mission to Gantharat, conducted in two altered pirate ships. They had run into both Onotharians and pirates during their journey, and in the end, Rae had barely escaped alive. Kellen had watched over her every minute she could possibly be away from the bridge. Rae grimaced. The pain in her neck, from irreparable damage done by an alien weapon, bothered her every now and then. If she closed her eyes, she could still see the face of the cruel Onotharian man, an officer in the OECS, and often woke up from nightmares about him, sweating profusely. Just before Kellen had killed him and saved Rae's life, she had identified him as Trax M'Aldovar, but somehow it didn't matter that he was dead. M'Aldovar's deeds had scarred her.

The ensign at ops interrupted Rae's thoughts. "We have an incoming encrypted message, Admiral."

"Patch it through to my office, Ensign. Lieutenant Commander O'Dal, join me. Commander Grey, you have the bridge."

Three "yes, ma'ams" in unison followed Rae as she strode over to the door leading into her office with Kellen right behind her. She rarely used it as an escape from the bridge. Through the narrow, tall windows, Rae could see the thin streaks of the stars they passed, but the room was impersonal, and since this wasn't normally her ship, she hadn't bothered to decorate it the way she used to when she was a captain aboard her own vessel.

"We'll probably need this information to be able to join the fun," Rae murmured.

Kellen took a seat across from Rae as she sat down at her aluplexi desk and watched the spinning SC insignia fade. A stream of unintelligible text flooded the screen, and Rae turned it toward Kellen. "A resistance encryption?"

"Yes." Kellen used the small keyboard to punch in a few commands, and one by one, the lines on the screen turned into Premoni, the official language of the Supreme Constellations.

"Read it out loud to me, please," Rae said, and rubbed her temples.

"Very well." Kellen pulled the screen closer. "Gantharian resistance to Supreme Constellations. Paladin, second in command of resistance cell 0011, requesting assistance. Confirm more than 6,500 resistance members, predominately senior officers, captured two weeks ago. One mission successfully completed. Forestalled shipment of prisoners to asteroid prisons. Reports of two thousand prisoner transports in progress. Onotharians in possession of new fleet of vessels, capable of transporting 750 individuals each. Specs included. Request you use encrypted messages sent on rotating frequencies, according to resistance movement protocols. End of message."

"That's not very detailed," Rae sighed. "Seems like they really need us, though."

"You need to get me to the surface to make contact with Paladin. I can easily find a transmitter and configure it to fit the resistance's specifications. Once I make contact—"

"No," Rae interrupted, and ran her fingertip along the encrypted message on the computer screen. "It's too dangerous for you to go down there alone. You're wanted by the OECS, among other things. If you're captured alone, we might never hear from you again. We stay together."

"You knew this mission would be dangerous," Kellen said, frowning. "So what do you suggest?"

Rae knew what she intended to do, which, given the circumstances, was just as dangerous. No way was she giving the Onotharians an opportunity to imprison the last Protector of the Realm. Kellen would be the second-best catch, from a propaganda point of view, after Armeo M'Aido O'Saral. The thought of Kellen, defiant and not intending to reveal any information, in the OECS's hands, made her furious. Kellen would withstand torture for days on end without ever giving them anything.

Rae tapped her fingernails on the desk as she met Kellen's eyes with determination. "I'll put together an away team consisting of you, Leanne, Owena, and me, and we'll use Ensign Hammad's medical skills with the derma fuser to turn us into Gantharians. It'll be a superficial transformation, but it's a good way to avoid detection at this stage."

"We'll be targeted for identification if anyone becomes even remotely suspicious," Kellen objected.

"I know. We'll have to be inconspicuous and not take unnecessary chances."

"Should you go with us?" Kellen asked. "You're in charge of this mission. If something happened to you—"

"I'm going." Rae looked steadily at Kellen. "You're my wife, my responsibility, not to mention you're the Protector of the Realm. I will *not* sit idly by and let you put yourself at risk alone."

"And if anything goes awry?"

Rae smiled. "Then we call in the marines."

❖

Kellen stood by the door to the small, state-of-the-art infirmary and regarded her wife with amazement. Rae's usually calm, gray eyes were now brilliant blue, and her skin reflected the fake Gantharian blood cells by shimmering in the faintest of blue. Her red hair, unheard of among true Gantharians, was now black, with violet highlights, and with her thin lips and command presence, she was spectacular.

"I could walk right by my mother and she wouldn't recognize me," Leanne D'Artansis said, not without glee. Her hair was white-blond and her eyes crystal blue. The freckles on her nose were now almost invisible and the tinge to her skin similar to Rae's. Leanne turned to look at Owena, her eyes widening. "Oh, and you look beautiful!"

Owena, tall and muscular, had natural black hair and blue eyes. Ensign Hammad had saturated her colors and also given her chiseled face an even stronger look.

"Owena, you look like the guardswomen that used to work as palace officers," Kellen said. "I'm not so sure you can get by with that true Gantharian warrior look. The Onotharians may think you're one of the few that got away."

"I will deal with them if that happens," Owena said with absolute confidence in her voice. The tactical chief had always carried herself with assurance, but only after she'd met Leanne and let the young Cormanian into her heart did she gain the calm self-esteem she now oozed.

"I bet you will." Leanne grinned and swatted Owena's arm. "And if you don't, I will."

"Here are civilian clothes, produced from Gantharian patterns. They'll hold your weapons without being obvious." Ensign Hammad brought them four piles of garments, and they quickly changed clothes, and then Kellen checked her appearance. She wore dark blue leather-like trousers and a white wool-lace sweater, and over it a long black caftan made of a thick sort of silk that farmers produced in the southern hemisphere. It withstood rain and even snow, and still allowed the skin to breathe. She felt quite at ease wearing the traditional clothes of her homeworld and rolled her shoulders to test their comfort. The other three dressed in similar clothes, but not completely alike.

"Admiral, I must scan you for any deficiency in the inoculations you went through during the preparation for this mission," Ensign Hammad said, and pulled out a small tubular device. Two dark blue lights glimmered at one end, and it emitted a soft hum.

Rae looked sharply at her. "Any reason to suspect that we may run into foreign agents we can't handle?"

"No, but we prepared with less time than usual, and regulations dictate that I make sure you're sufficiently protected." Hammad began to run the scanner up and down Rae's body and looked pleased. "You're clear, ma'am."

"Good." Rae oversaw the procedure with the other three, and Kellen knew she wouldn't let any of them deploy to Gantharat unless things were done by the book.

"You're all ready, Admiral."

"Excellent." Rae tugged her communicator. "Jacelon to shuttle bay. What's the status of our assault craft?"

Kellen had personally made sure the two vessels awaiting them in the shuttle bay were handling at peak efficiency. She wasn't worried and nodded, pleased, when the ensign in charge of ships' maintenance affirmed that they were ready for action.

"Very well. Let's go, then." Rae gestured for them to gear up and move out.

Kellen shouldered her large security carrier and stepped into the narrow corridor. She walked behind Rae, easily keeping up with her wife's brisk stride. They reached a ladder of steps welded into the bulkhead, where they climbed down two levels, and two turns later they entered the vast body of the destroyer that held its fleet of assault craft as well as six midsize transporter vessels. It smelled of metal and was hot, despite the large open area in the middle.

The crewman responsible for maintenance saluted them. "They're ready for you, Admiral."

"Good, Chief. We'll try to bring them back in the same shape."

"Appreciate that, ma'am." The master chief checked that the stop-blocks were locked in place, then allowed the four women to climb the steps to the cockpits.

Kellen slid into the pilot's seat, the chair encasing her body like a tight fist. She pulled the shoulder straps down over her chest and connected them with the short strap between her legs. The chair was one of the new prototypes, now being tested in action. If they had to eject in space, or into hostile environment, a force-field bubble immediately formed to keep the pilot and the navigator safe. It would stay intact even under plasma-pulse fire.

"O'Dal to bridge. Beginning quick-check." They were in too much of a hurry to perform a disaster-check.

"Bridge here. Affirmative," the captain of the *Gallant* responded.

Kellen went through the procedure, her mind now focused on

making sure the assault craft was ready for the demands they would place on it. When she was done, she switched the screen over to eyewear mode. Closing her visor, she saw data appear at the left side of her field of vision and along the bottom. "You all set, Rae?" Kellen asked into her mike.

"Yes. Let's go."

"O'Dal to bridge. Ready to commence takeoff." Kellen flipped a few manual switches, recalibrating their sound system. There was some static, and then another voice came through.

"D'Artansis to bridge. Ready."

Kellen had to smile at the eagerness in her friend's voice. No matter how dangerous the circumstances, Leanne always sounded as if she was going treasure hunting with her best friends. *In a way she is. The lost treasure of Gantharian freedom.*

"Bridge to assault-craft teams. You're cleared for takeoff. Return safely."

"Affirmative. We're off. O'Dal out." Kellen punched in the commands for automated takeoff, and the sleek vessel hovered for a few seconds before it plunged down the center chute, which launched it into space. Immediately they were surrounded by rocks and space debris of all sizes—some as large as the mountains behind her Gantharian estate, some hardly bigger than a fist.

"Computer, set to evasive pattern delta-zero-zero-one. Maximum shields."

The computer confirmed the precautions.

"Good. That'll save us from denting the prototype's features," Rae commented dryly from the navigator's seat. "We don't want to return and let everyone know we scratched the boat."

Kellen was now more used to her wife's slightly warped sense of humor, and also to the fact that the more trouble Rae was in, the more frequent and sharp her sarcastic comments became. "Doing my best to not damage your ride, Admiral." Kellen tried to reciprocate and was rewarded by a light chuckle.

"Much obliged."

They flew along a precalculated trajectory until they approached the window of opportunity they needed to reach Gantharat's atmosphere on a path that hid them from Onotharian sensors. Kellen engaged the cloaking device newly constructed for these smaller vessels, which were made from the specs taken from the Onotharian ships in custody, but altered enough that the Onotharians would be unable to break the code and decloak them.

"Trajectory for the Merealian Mountains laid in." Rae's voice came through distinctly across the comm system. "We've got a clear path."

Kellen was grateful for the computer system, which made her job of navigating among the space debris so much easier. The small nuggets around them might seem harmless, but if a ship hit them at high speed, they could eat away at the shielding little by little and jeopardize an entire mission that had no margin for error.

They planned to set down using coordinates from Paladin, and Kellen couldn't wait to get on the ground and familiarize herself with the situation at hand. If she could actually see and listen to her friend, everything would become more tangible, more real. The thought of Paladin and the way she'd come through for Kellen after her father's death made Kellen vow again to do everything she could to help.

"How long have you known this Paladin?" Rae asked, unknowingly tapping into Kellen's thoughts.

"Since I was eighteen. She took me under her wing when I joined my father's resistance cell after he died. I had to wait until Tereya and I joined the academy so my absence from the farm wouldn't cause concern." Kellen leaned back farther into her seat, as if trying to get closer to Rae. "I owe her so much. She saved my life several times when I was a rookie. And she brought my father's dead body to the farm, instead of merely dumping it anonymously at a hospital."

"Darling." Just one word, but uttered with such tenderness and love, it helped clean old wounds every time they talked about haunting matters of the past.

"Thank you," Kellen murmured. "So you see, not only do I owe her, but this is my ultimate duty—keeping Armeo and his heritage safe."

"I understand. And when you can help Paladin and her crew by doing so…"

For the first time Kellen knew in her heart that Rae understood where she was coming from. Rae always tried her best to understand her, but Kellen knew that her alien world's customs and unwritten rules, which focused so much on honor and tradition, were difficult to grasp.

"Submitting new course. The others are on track behind us." Rae sounded official again, but her soft words earlier made Kellen feel they also understood one another on a personal level. *She's in this for practically the same reasons I am.* Fighting for the freedom of her people was just a start, Kellen realized. She knew that if the SC didn't confront the Onotharian oppression, it would spread to other worlds. The Onotharian Empire was eyeing several less-developed planets, rich in natural resources. They needed to be stopped by any means necessary. *Or am I no better than them to think that way?*

Kellen watched the computer screen to the left of her field of vision and saw it would soon be time for a little hands-on flying. When they hit the Gantharian atmosphere, they'd be in for a rough ride, and she preferred to handle that part of the trip herself.

"O'Dal to D'Artansis. Switch to manual override in eighty seconds."

"Affirmative."

"Stay low and close to my tail. Less turbulence, smaller risk of detection."

"Read you, O'Dal."

"Here we go. O'Dal out." Kellen gripped the controls with years of confidence and prepared to enter the atmosphere. A white blanket of clouds waited for her below. Kellen felt her lips pull into a broad and, she guessed, feral grin as she pierced the cumulus clouds. Turbulence rocked the assault craft, and she pulled and pushed the levers, her body one with the ship. This was her true element, just as she was one with the Ruby Red Gan'thet suit during fights to the death. As Kellen indulged in the feeling of riding the element of air like a maesha saddled for the first time, she glimpsed the green and maroon formations of the Merealian Mountains in the distance. Soon she'd be home.

CHAPTER THIRTEEN

"M s. O'Landha is here to see you, ma'am," Rix M'Isitor, Andreia's assistant, announced, and stepped back from the doorway to let Roshan pass him. Both women had spent four days maintaining appearances, while preparing for the expected SC assistance.

As Roshan approached her desk, Andreia felt a stab of anticipation. Dressed entirely in black, Roshan possessed a darkish beauty, emphasized by her hair, almost silver when illuminated by the muted ceiling lights in the old Center Hall building.

Andreia stared greedily at Roshan's toned body. The form-fitted clothes left very little to the imagination. Remembering how the softness of Roshan's lips felt on her own, Andreia gripped the desk so hard she was afraid she might dent it. "How did you know where to find me?"

"Nice to see you, too." Roshan shrugged, a nonchalant twitch of her right shoulder, which stretched the silky fabric over her breasts and made Andreia forget the slightly sarcastic words. "I tried to page you, but there was only a forwarding message at your office. I figured that you might have had to conduct your…business elsewhere, since your offices were compromised last week." With a glance back at the open door, Roshan walked closer to the desk. "I felt like seeing you. It wasn't very difficult to figure out where the new provisional Onotharian offices were located. This was a logical choice. Not many structures in Ganath can host the Onotharian administrative workforce." She leaned closer and brushed her lips over Andreia's forehead. "Hello, you."

Though she knew Roshan was acting for the one-man audience able to hear and see them through the open door, Andreia realized the small caress left an exciting tingle on her skin. Very little went on in her office that Rix M'Isitor didn't report back to his father. *I bet the little weasel would report the size of my underwear if he figured it out!*

Andreia knew she had to play along, to justify Roshan's bold presence inside enemy headquarters. "Hello back," she murmured, and hooked her hand gently around Roshan's neck. "Sorry I was rude. I've missed you." It was startlingly true, and Andreia pressed her lips against Roshan's, shocked at the sudden revelation. It felt like more than four days since she'd seen Roshan, and it occurred to her only now how empty those days had been.

The kiss lasted a little longer than Andreia had planned, which she blamed on the way Roshan responded to it. She towered over Andreia and filled her hands with curls, murmuring inaudible words into her mouth. Eventually she pulled back and left Andreia breathless, speechless, for a few seconds.

"Anything important going on, or can you get out of here for today?" Roshan asked, looking pointedly at Andreia.

"Of course. Let me just clear my schedule for the next few hours."

"I may need you longer than that," Roshan said, and Andreia envisioned Rix sharpening his hearing.

"Oh, yes?" she replied, trying to sound playful. She was curious now, and hopeful that there had been a new development in their plans.

"Oh, yes." There was nothing teasing in the way Roshan spoke.

"Just a minute, then." Andreia walked out to her assistant where he sat by his desk. When Andreia informed him of her altered plans, being his usual pompous self, Rix nodded approvingly.

"Very well, ma'am. If you stay in regular touch with me, I'll make sure you don't miss a thing at this end. Ms. O'Landha is an important contact. Enjoy yourself."

Andreia wanted to smack the impertinent brat. She would've assumed that the rank of an assistant was not one the son of an Onotharian dignitary would accept, but this appeared to be a coveted job, judging from how Rix acted around her. Andreia had always suspected that Dixmon M'Isitor placed people he trusted implicitly in positions like these, to stretch his tentacles everywhere. The fact that Rix didn't seem to suspect anything about Boyoda, as far as she could tell, was reassuring.

"Thank you. Take the afternoon off. I won't need you anymore today."

"Are you sure you don't need me to—"

"Yes. I'm sure," Andreia snapped, annoyed at his patronizing tone. "That'll be all."

"Of course…ma'am." Andreia didn't miss the slight delay in the way he spoke and wondered if Rix himself knew how such rudeness gave him away. He wasn't very mature, or clever, after all.

"Everything set, Andreia?" Roshan asked, and joined them.

"Yes. Let's go."

They entered the elevator that took them down six floors, the door opening to the large obsidian glass hall. This impressive structure had once been a symbol of the proud Gantharian sovereignty. It was close to heresy for the Onotharians to claim the beautiful building as a mere backup facility. Andreia knew Roshan must feel the same way, yet she looked at Andreia with nothing but an appreciative light in her eyes. The fact that nobody was so close that they had to pretend anymore made Andreia's palms tingle. She wanted to take Roshan's hand, feel the warmth of the assertive touch against her, but it was impossible for her to escalate the pretence to that level in public. *And yet I had no problem kissing her in private just now.*

"We have to move fast," Roshan said, and even if there was nothing hostile in her words, there was no kindness either. This was obviously just business. "I've received information that gives me new hope. We might have the answers to some of our immediate problems."

"And what makes you think that?" Andreia spoke in staccato, a part of her exasperatingly disappointed by the abrupt change in Roshan's demeanor.

As they walked down the wide stairs outside the building, she held her head high and kept the regal pose her mother had groomed her to use.

"Our mountain camp received a brief transmission on an encrypted subspace band that said that two SC vessels will set down close by," Roshan said. "Granted, this could be a trap, but we don't believe it is, since the message carried a genuine SC signature tag." She pointed across the square in front of the building. "My hovercraft is over there. We can change at the mansion. Can you make up some lie why you have to be away for a while, perhaps a few days?"

"Yes. I'm supposed to go on a planet-wide tour soon. I can tell everyone that I need time to polish my speeches, and that I'm staying with my…good friend in the meantime." Andreia jumped into the hovercraft and felt herself blush faintly at how she stumbled over the last words. "Well, we can't waste any time. We have to set plans into motion. I sincerely hope whoever's here to help us has more than two vessels." Andreia meant it as a joke, but felt rather humorless. So much rode on freeing their missing resistance fighters.

"If it's who I hope it is, we'll have an advantage over the Onotharians—" Roshan stopped in mid-sentence, her eyes dark and brooding. "Damn it, it bothers me to talk about them, about your heritage, about people *like you*, with such hatred. You're Onotharian, but you're nothing like *them*. You're not a heartless, slaughtering—"

"—neither are your regular Onotharians, who just want to live with their families and see their children grow up to be happy, contributing citizens! Instead, the Onotharian chairmen make laws that say they have to join the armed forces, go to alien worlds, and carry out the politicians' greedy plans there. And perhaps they'll break their parents' hearts by never coming back." Andreia became breathless, gasping for air.

Her face pale, with a faint blue tinge to her cheeks, Roshan stared at Andreia as if seeing her for the first time. "I know. I know all these things. But I've experienced so much. Too much." She punched in commands to the autopilot steering, and the hovercraft left the square with a low hum. It soon lined up along one of the busiest land-air corridors five meters above ground.

Andreia averted her eyes and looked out the windows, unable to witness the torment on Roshan's face. "I know," she whispered. "So have I. I have to live with the fact that I stem from a greedy, callous species, whose most senior and high-ranking citizens want to conquer every world that may be even remotely beneficial. They don't hesitate to use their young men and women as laser-fodder, if that's what it takes."

"Such greed takes on a life of its own after a while." Roshan's voice was now calm, thoughtful. "That's the danger of a society set on expanding at all cost, no *matter* the cost. The growth and hunger for power becomes a purpose in itself."

Andreia looked at Roshan, but couldn't make out her expression. *There was a time when I knew that face as well as I did my own.* Andreia remembered when she could look at Roshan forever, when she sat at her computer, studying. "And it's addictive. I don't mean the greed," Andreia explained. "I mean the power. Greed is a way to monetary wealth, which in turn leads to power."

"Which leads back to increased prosperity." Roshan smiled wryly. "You come from an ancient culture, with a long history of dominance. It's engrained this ultimate goal in its offspring for centuries. It's not going to be easy for the SC, or any other union of worlds, to stymie a way of life that's embedded in the majority of its population. Most of them may be regular people, but they're also not hard to rally if the Onotharian propaganda machine powers up."

Andreia shook her head, saddened by the gloomy prospect of everlasting war between neighbors. "I know, but we can't sit idly by. The SC's decision to intervene is a step in the right direction. Without them, Gantharat would eventually be lost. The resistance is already on the verge of being wiped out."

Roshan didn't speak at first. She looked down at her laced fingers, and Andreia wondered what was going through her head. When Roshan suddenly extended a trembling hand, she jumped. "We've come so far. We've worked from opposite sides, but toward the same goal, Gantharat's freedom."

Andreia took Roshan's hand, which was ice cold.

"Some days I can hardly remember what it was like when my only worry was if I was going to flunk a test because I didn't focus on it enough."

"You? Not focus enough?" Andreia tried to joke.

"You were my main focus back then. Surely you knew that?" It was clear Roshan wasn't joking. Her eyes didn't waver, and she sounded as if the thought of the old days pained her.

"I thought so at the time. I mean, I guessed, since it was mutual. We were best friends, who could've been…more."

"Could've been? Those are truthful words." Roshan laughed, but with absolutely no joy. "Yes, I suppose that cargo ship left the docking bay a long time ago."

A sharp twinge of pain caused Andreia's heart to flutter without moving any blood through her veins. It was hard to breathe, yet nothing had changed, really. Roshan was lost to her, and it had happened twenty-five years ago. The Onotharian rulers had a lot on their conscience, and in the great scheme of things a broken heart was a very minor thing.

❖

"Lock and load!" Three hours later, Roshan led her team of twenty rebels across a small field. She raised her plasma-pulse rifle to her shoulder and pressed the safety unlocking sensor. "Fire only on my mark!"

To her left, Andreia held a borrowed firearm, a small handheld weapon, but just as lethal, in a two-handed grip. Roshan was relieved her team seemed to accept their story that Andreia was the sole survivor of her resistance cell during the Onotharian raid. Only Jubinor had regarded her with dark, suspicious eyes, pointing out the fact that Andreia was obviously a Gantharian/Onotharian hybrid.

"Stay sharp, people!" Roshan, Andreia, and the rest of the team were aiming their weapons at the far end of the canyon, behind the northern part of the Merealian Mountains, where two small vessels hovered ten meters up in the air, whirling debris around them.

"Don't let them any closer than that." Roshan was fairly sure these were, indeed, Supreme Constellations craft, but she'd been around too long to take anything at face value. "They're landing."

The two small craft landed on the green field, and their propulsion systems powered down with a muted whine of the power nacelles. Nothing happened for another few seconds, but then Roshan saw the hatch open on the craft closest to her and her team.

A tall, slender figure climbed from the vessel and stood still for a moment, as if judging her surroundings. The woman pulled off her helmet, disentangling her long blond hair that folded out into the wind.

Roshan smiled and shouldered her rifle. "I knew it," she said. She had to laugh, or the sheer poignancy of the moment would make her cry. "Hold your fire, everyone. These are friends."

"What? Who is it?" Andreia squinted toward the tall woman.

"It is her. Our only remaining Protector of the Realm has returned to Gantharat. Who would ever have thought that possible?"

"Kellen of the O'Dals? Here?" Andreia said with obvious disbelief. She raised the binoculars to her eyes. "Oh, Gods, it *is* her. I recognize her from the SC transmission when they introduced the prince."

"I don't recognize the other woman. She looks Gantharian." Roshan began walking to the ships, and Andreia kept an even pace with her.

"Paladin."

Kellen sounded so familiar when she spoke while regarding Roshan with calm blue eyes. "May I introduce Admiral Rae Jacelon? My wife."

"Wife?" Roshan blinked, momentarily amazed because the woman next to Kellen looked entirely Gantharian. "Good job on the makeover. We're thrilled to have you here, Admiral."

"Thank you. We thought it best to rendezvous with you on a smaller scale. We've brought troops."

"We'll need them." Roshan saw how curiously the two women regarded Andreia. The rest of her team was waiting ten meters behind them. "This is O'Daybo."

Even Roshan would never have recognized Andreia the way she looked at the moment. If Rae Jacelon had managed to alter her features that much using derma-fuser technology, Andreia had pulled off a complete transformation merely using hair dye, colored lenses, and makeup. The hour they'd spent at Roshan's mansion, quickly preparing to join the other rebels in the mountains, had paid off. It was a gamble, but if anyone recognized her as Andreia M'Aldovar, everything would be over. As disciplined as the rebels were, a lot of them were trigger-happy. Now they saw a reddish blond woman with pale skin and blue eyes. Even if nothing could be done about Andreia's height, she looked Gantharian enough to be a convincing hybrid. That also explained her Onotharian biosignatures setting off their scanners.

Two other women, looking just as Gantharian as Rae and Kellen, joined them from the other spacecraft. Introductions were made, and then Roshan suggested they return to the base camp. "It's only half an hour ride on the hoverbikes from here through a secret tunnel in the southern mountain that the Onotharians don't know anything about."

"We have to work fast. Our assault craft can stay on low-energy cloaking for only four hours." Kellen directed her firm gaze at the men and women keeping their distance. "Can some of your people remain behind to make sure they're safe?"

"Certainly. We'll be back here in time for you to return to your main vessel," Roshan assured them. Walking toward the rebel team members, she could feel a new energy and spring in her step. Her team would of course recognize the Protector, and Roshan hoped her presence would inspire them to believe in the future. The massive attack against so many of their leaders had damaged the ideals of the younger members.

"Paladin?" Andreia was walking a little way behind her, and Roshan now shortened her stride to wait for her.

"Yes?"

"How on earth are we going to be able to ensure the Protector's safety?"

"She doesn't expect us to do anything that she can't do herself."

"But if something happens to her…The prince—"

"Don't get me wrong," Roshan said quickly. "I'll do anything to keep her alive. I'll die trying. But she's a Protector, a warrior like neither of us has ever been or can ever hope to be. It's in her blood."

"I know from the file we keep on her that she's formidable in every way. Not to be underestimated. But she looks…incredible."

"She does and she is." Roshan watched Kellen's movements as the young rebels gathered around her, eyes shining and obviously awed when Kellen extended her hand to each of them, a gesture Roshan recognized from her father's way of greeting people. *She must've picked up this foreign tradition among the SC citizens.* Roshan knew that her father's homeworld, Earth, was the SC center, and Kellen had taken the prince there to keep him safe.

"All right, people, let's move out. Everyone, pair up so our guests have enough bikes at their disposal." Four bikes were freed up, and everyone drove to the tunnel system hidden in the bedrock, Roshan spearheading the convoy.

Dark, damp walls surrounded them as they sped through the narrow tunnel. Andreia sat behind Roshan on her hoverbike, and it didn't matter that she tried to keep her mind on their high-powered visitors; all she could think of was Andreia's arms around her waist.

Roshan stopped just inside the entrance on the south side of the mountain. On more than one occasion this precaution had prevented them from being discovered. If they lost their tunnel system, they'd lose their current advantage of escaping into thin air.

"Anything?" she asked Andreia.

"Let me switch to long-range scanning, just to be safe," Andreia said, and adjusted the scanner. "I don't see any Onotharian biosignatures other than my own. The only life signs are wildlife and the team members back at camp."

"Good. Let's move on, then." Roshan raised her hand and pushed her fist forward twice. "Team, double-cradle formation once we clear the tunnels," she said into the comm system embedded in their helmets. "Let's go."

Once they were out of the tunnel, the rebels took up formation around their visitors. Driving fast, they crossed the large meadows that led to a narrow pass between two rock formations. There, two rebels guarded the camp entrance, and, unwilling to stop and create another opportunity for a potential attack, Roshan signaled the guards by voice and hand gestures. The closest guard acknowledged with the correct signal, which assured Roshan that everything was calm in the camp.

As they entered the plain in front of the humble structures outlining their facility, Roshan saw Doc and Jubinor standing in front of the main building, their faces serious. She pulled up to the two men and shut off the propulsion.

"Good to see you all back, Paladin."

"Thanks, Jubinor. We've brought guests."

Kellen and Rae dismounted their hoverbike and joined Roshan and Andreia.

"Gods of Gantharat," Doc exclaimed. "Protector…"

Jubinor looked at Kellen and showed no expression. "When you set out to find backup, you don't mess around, do you, Paladin?" Then he walked closer and placed both hands on Kellen's shoulders. "Protector. I knew you only by your call name, but you were the bravest kid I'd ever come across. When you disappeared I was afraid you'd been killed."

"It's good to see you again, Jubinor," Kellen said. "I left because of Armeo. We were constantly in danger."

"I realize that now." Jubinor let go of her and wiped at his eyes. "Damn it, Protector, it's good to have you here. We haven't had much good news lately."

"So I understand," Kellen said. "Let's see if we can help change that. The SC is getting ready to engage the Onotharians, and our first priority is to free our people who risk ending up in the asteroid prisons."

"The senior rebels are crucial to the SC's involvement," Rae

Jacelon said. "We need their knowledge, their expertise."

"And you are?" Jubinor asked. "I don't remember ever seeing you before."

"You haven't. I'm Admiral Rae Jacelon, of the SC Fleet. Kellen is my wife."

Jubinor barely smiled. "Welcome to our homeworld. I pray the SC *involvement* will help us toward our ultimate goal, freedom."

Roshan had heard enough. She knew Jubinor was tired, and a lot of their cell's administrative work had fallen on his shoulders, but she couldn't allow him to border on insolence like this.

"Jubinor, I'm sure you appreciate that without Admiral Jacelon's connections, they wouldn't be here, and the SC would still be negotiating and discussing their involvement."

"Of course." Jubinor's shoulders slumped briefly. "I didn't mean to sound unappreciative—"

"And you didn't. You're fighting damn near unbeatable odds. I hope we can help alleviate some of the stress and strain." Rae motioned toward the building. "Should we go inside?"

"Of course." Roshan let them all enter ahead of her and Andreia. When they were alone outside, she took her by the hand. "You're frowning. What's on your mind?"

"I'm afraid I'm jeopardizing my identity by being here. I know the mask is good and that nobody has recognized me. Yet—"

"I understand that your identity as Boyoda—"

"No," Andreia interrupted harshly, her eyes like molten lava. "I'm not all that concerned that anybody will recognize me as Boyoda, but as Andreia M'Aldovar. Especially with our Protector and Admiral Jacelon present."

"Why? Why would that be worse?"

Andreia tugged at the sleeves of her jacket and straightened her back, as if she expected to be chastised any moment. "Trax led the OECS team that engaged the covert SC operation six lunar months ago. If they find out that I'm his sister—"

"Was that when he was killed?" Roshan asked, forcing her voice to sound soft.

"Yes." Dark emotions flickered over Andreia's face, and she paled. "Trax nearly killed Admiral Jacelon. She was still a commodore then, and as you know…Kellen O'Dal is a Gan'thet master."

"Of course, he didn't stand a chance." Roshan could have applauded Kellen's skills right then and there, but she knew how Andreia had once idolized her brother.

"She won."

Roshan pulled Andreia behind the corner of the building, out of sight of the rebels guarding the camp. "You understand he left her no choice, don't you?" She examined Andreia's face for any sign of how she felt.

"Naturally. He was the enemy. She had to protect her wife."

The words didn't ring true. Something in the way Andreia spoke triggered an alarm inside Roshan. "He knew the dangers when he entered the OECS," she tried. Roshan hated to criticize a member of Andreia's family, but the thought of Trax M'Aldovar made her skin crawl with disgust.

He'd been tremendously handsome and charismatic when they were young, and before the occupation, Roshan hadn't known what to think of him. Brilliance paired with an evil wit made him a dangerous, devilish man. He'd once offered to bed her, merely as a bodily indulgence, and Roshan had politely declined, since she wasn't interested in casual physical affairs. The truth was that her heart had pounded hard enough to break its restraints every time she looked at Andreia. Wisely, for Andreia's sake, Roshan had never made it clear that he didn't have anything to offer compared to his sister, who possessed something beyond physical beauty.

"My mother accepts me because of my popularity and whatever political power comes from that. She adored Trax and admired his unscrupulous aggressiveness. I don't think it actually mattered to her that it surpassed his political ambitions. The fact that Mother praised him and regarded his deeds as signs of great patriotism didn't exactly motivate him any less." Andreia tilted her head to the side, her eyes narrow slits. "And now you want to know if I can conceal my grief over my brother's destiny so I don't tip the Protector and her wife off to who I am." It wasn't a question. Andreia's eyes, unfamiliarly pale blue from her lenses, still revealed nothing.

"Yes, pretty much," Roshan confessed. "We can't risk a confrontation, as you yourself said. I need to know that you'll put the circumstances of Trax's death aside, for now."

"I can't believe you think you have to ask me that."

"I have to. I'm sorry if you can't see why, but you just have to get used to it. Keeping Boyoda safe is a duty I agreed on when Vespes asked me to become the liaison. I'll take every precaution to fulfill that duty."

"Very well. Consider the topic of Trax closed. One day when we're old and this is merely a memory, I'll bring it up and…settle it."

Roshan didn't like the way Andreia spoke regarding Trax, but was grateful that they had a consensus for now. She knew they needed to join the others and not waste any more time, but it was equally important that Andreia, as a major player in the plans they were about to forge, be prepared. "You ready to get back inside?"

"Don't worry about me." Andreia pulled back, freeing herself from Roshan's hold.

"But I do." The words were out before Roshan realized how they could be interpreted. "I do worry about you. All the time we're apart."

Andreia stood motionless, her back pressed against the rough wall. "I should…I mean I need to ask you why, but there's no time. We have to go inside."

"Yes. We do." Roshan couldn't move at first, and when she did, she stepped closer again, capturing Andreia between her arms, pressing her palms against the wall. "To make sure you don't forget what I just said." She bent down and took Andreia's lips with her mouth, demanded them without deepening the kiss, but also without any doubt. She spread her fingers wide apart, to cover as much of Andreia's back as possible. Roshan needed to feel Andreia close to her, chest to chest, heart to heart. She slid one hand up over Andreia's shoulder, up to her neck, and felt her rapid, tell-tale pulse. Roshan shivered at how fast Andreia's heart beat.

With a low whimper, Andreia relaxed against Roshan and parted her lips. Roshan was tempted to accept the silent invitation, but knew this wasn't the time or place to increase the intimacy. She wasn't ready for it, and the kiss wasn't meant as that kind of caress, merely a reminder that she would be here for Andreia, but was also watching closely every word and gesture. The kiss ended their discussion—for now.

CHAPTER FOURTEEN

K ellen stood rigid and proud by the far wall in the mountain base mission room. Observing the sixty or so that remained of the rebels she'd once belonged to, she noticed the new faces, young individuals. They were all regarding her with reverence and something resembling adoration. Aware of the extraordinary historical moment, Kellen was grateful to feel Rae's calm presence to her left. She wondered if any of the rebels realized her wife's true position.

"You've got quite a devoted following," Rae whispered, and raised a teasing eyebrow. "But where's Paladin?"

Kellen gazed around the room. "There," she replied as Paladin and O'Daybo entered. "And as for my 'fan club,' they're young and impressionable. They require leadership and, I suppose, a sign that things are finally about to improve."

"You represent that sign to them. Just remember, you're a myth come alive for them."

Kellen knew this was probably true. She'd grown up with the knowledge of who her father was and who she'd become. To her friends in school, a Protector of the Realm was like something out of a fairy tale. They spoke of protectors, of their heroic deeds and the eradication of one line of protectors after another during the occupation, and not once could Kellen breathe a word about her family.

"You forget something," Kellen said to Rae, reciprocating with a raised eyebrow of her own. "You are also, by marriage, a Protector. My duties are also yours."

Rae put her arm around Kellen's shoulder and squeezed her quickly. "Why do you think I'm here?" she murmured. "Armeo is the son of our hearts. This is his world, his heritage. And yours." She glanced at the barred window overlooking the plains. "It's breathtakingly beautiful, and for me it's an honor to help rip it out of the Onotharians' greedy claws."

Impressed with how bloodthirsty Rae sounded, Kellen again blessed the day she'd fled into SC space and into the arms, literally, of this woman. Never once had Rae backed away from the duties and hardship it meant to love Kellen, who'd turned out to be politically volatile. Kellen's heart overflowed, and the emotions still seemed so new, even after more than six lunar months of marriage to Rae. She would never get used to seeing a universe of emotions in Rae's eyes, no matter how long they were together.

She would sometimes wake up in the night, gasping from nightmares in which Armeo was lost to her and she was withering away in an Onotharian asteroid prison. During the chilling aftermath of such dreams, Rae always held her close, understood without a doubt why Kellen clung to her, shivering and sobbing. *I've never been allowed to think it was all right to act so weakly. Or that I'd grow so much stronger from it.*

Tapping into that strength, Kellen squared her shoulders even further and raised her hand to silence the murmur among the groups. "We don't have much time and there is a lot to discuss. We have more than 6,000 resistance fighters incarcerated planet wide. Without their expertise and aid, we can't hope for a successful intervention by the SC. This leaves us little choice." Kellen walked over to talk to Paladin and Jubinor who stood by a golden-glass map reader that showed the asteroid belt in great detail. "I don't see any other way. If what your intel says is true, we need to move a few people on the inside, and provide them with technology to communicate through the force field."

"What you suggest is suicide!" Jubinor growled. "Haven't we lost enough people?"

"Far too many," Kellen said. She couldn't allow herself to get upset. "And if we don't do anything, we won't be able to save the ones already shipped to the Kovos prison. That's more than eight hundred of your senior men and women!"

"And you say we could afford to let more go voluntarily?" Jubinor asked, with poison in his voice.

Paladin intervened. "We can't *afford* to lose a single member more. Jubinor, I know…I know how this has hurt us all. But the Protector is right. We need some volunteers to go in with the plans and organize our people."

"Just like that? And with what?" Jubinor spat.

"I have a fleet of ships that will convert into war-capable vessels with very few modifications, and you brought a destroyer, correct?" Paladin asked Kellen. "How many assault craft?"

"Twenty-two."

"Twenty-two against the entire Onotharian armada?" Jubinor asked.

"Not their entire armada. Most of them are gathered at the SC border, anticipating an attack any day now. They have only a few ships deployed here, with skeleton crews, according to our spy beacons."

"How detailed are your plans, Protector?" O'Daybo asked, rising from her chair as if to intercede between Jubinor and Kellen.

"Very detailed. I have several backup plans, but according to my calculations—"

"Which you've conducted in an alien setting, knowing close to nothing about the true situation here." Jubinor spoke slowly, with emphasis.

"I disagree," Kellen said calmly. "I know enough to make estimates, and if you think about it, Jubinor, you'll admit that no plans, devised on site or not, are set in stone. There must always be room for improvisation."

"We know that, Protector," O'Daybo began. "We're grateful that you're here and—"

"You suddenly speak for all of us? You've never been here before. All we have is your word that your cell's been wiped out—it's interesting that *you're* still here, O'Daybo. The only survivor." Jubinor's face was now darkening to a blue-red tint.

Kellen was about to say something when Paladin spoke up.

"Enough! Jubinor, I know it's been horrible lately, and I think most people here will be more sympathetic to your frame of mind if they realize that your partner is among the missing."

"Paladin, no..." Jubinor's face distorted. "Please."

"I know, my friend." Paladin walked up to her teammate. "We'll get Berentar and the others back. Just give the Protector's plan a chance. Can you concede that she may envision the opportunities more clearly since she hasn't been tormented with day-to-day struggles the same way we have lately?"

"I suppose."

"And as for O'Daybo, I want to repeat what I said this morning. I know O'Daybo personally, including her true name and who she is. She's beyond reproach. I won't tolerate any more whispers or speculations."

Kellen watched with keen interest how O'Daybo's expression softened as Paladin placed an arm around her shoulders. *Yes, they know each other. Well.*

Rae also glared at Jubinor. "Fine. Seems we've reached an agreement." Kellen knew that Rae was not uncaring, but rather that she believed everyone should leave their personal problems at the door in order to get the job done. "Now we have to figure out who the lucky four will be."

"Do we vote or volunteer?" O'Daybo asked.

"We consider who has the necessary skills to make this mission successful," Kellen said. "We need people from both the SC and Gantharat. One from each to infiltrate Kovos, and the same for the smaller, but higher-security facility on Vaksses. Paladin, which ones from your team would you recommend for this assignment? Remember, they have to be seasoned rebels, and I understand that this requirement limits your choices." *I hope you won't choose Jubinor. He's far too unstable right now.*

Paladin regarded the assembled rebels in her team for a moment.

Kellen, who stood next to her, would have liked to know what went on inside Paladin's head. After so many years she was still an enigma. With her sharply chiseled face and piercing eyes, she seemed relentless and dangerous. She moved with a slow grace, yet could change pace with lightning speed when required. Her voice could boom as well as growl in a frightening, low register.

Kellen wondered if Paladin ever found the time and opportunity to be the woman she was when she'd single-handedly lifted Bondar O'Dal's lifeless body from the back of a hovercraft and carried him into the farmhouse. She had spoken about Bondar's courage with pride and tried to console the sixteen-year-old Kellen. At the time, Kellen had hidden Tereya, ever concerned for her foster sister's safety. Kellen remembered staring at Paladin with eyes burning from restrained tears and trying to emulate the woman's strength and poise.

"Bury him privately, here on the farm, child," Paladin had suggested. "Make no fuss and people won't suspect anything. You breed maeshas, right? Tell people he was thrown and killed instantly. Here." Paladin had handed over a small digital document. "This is a death certificate, forged by our doctor, in case anyone suspects anything."

Kellen had thanked Paladin, kneeling by her father's battered body lying on the bed. Staring at Bondar's wounds, visible through the black coveralls, all she could think of at that time was how she'd be able to care for, and protect, Tereya. It was daunting to realize that at sixteen years of age, she was the only living Protector, destined to guard the only remaining O'Saral Royale.

"Commander? You all right?"

Kellen snapped back into the present and blinked at Commander Grey's tone. "Yes. Can you repeat what you just said?"

Owena—tall, dark, and almost as lethal as Kellen—frowned slightly. "I should be one of the volunteers from the SC. I resemble the Gantharians and could quite easily fool the Onotharians for the time being. My physical strength isn't like theirs, but I'm skilled in hand-to-hand combat."

"You are. I agree. I'll be the other one." Kellen glanced at Rae and wasn't surprised at the fine lines around her narrow lips. Rae wasn't happy, but would never argue in front of anyone else.

"And from our side—" Paladin began.

"I will go," O'Daybo said, sounding larger than her size. Tiny, the woman still oozed strength and determination.

"I'm not sure that's a good idea," Paladin stated.

"I have information regarding these places that can be useful," O'Daybo insisted. "I should be one of the two chosen. I also am familiar with the Onotharian way of thinking, since I'm a Gantharian-Onotharian hybrid."

"Very well." It was obvious to Kellen that Paladin wasn't happy. "And the second from our team?"

"I should be the one," the camp doctor, referred to only as Doc, said. "It's only logical to assume that the people on Kovos need medical assistance."

"Makes sense," Paladin murmured darkly. "So, now we have to review the plans, with everyone in place. We'll practice until we all know them by heart. We can't make a mistake."

"Affirmative," Doc said, and sat down at a long table. "Do I team up with you, Protector?"

"Yes, I agree that you're needed on Kovos," Kellen said, and continued the briefing. "You look strong and resilient, and so am I. We can pose as husband and wife, if necessary." Kellen drew her breath at the sight of Rae, who listened next to them. *How does that feel for her to hear? She looks unfazed.* "Commander Grey will team up with O'Daybo and use their combined tactical skills at Vaksses." She continued to unveil her plan for rescuing the captured rebels and thus reinforcing the teams the SC so desperately required for a full-scale attack.

❖

"Mother. Please, don't do this. I've told you I can't have any bodyguards with me right now. I'm a grown woman and I need my privacy." Andreia sighed and rapped her fingernails against the table holding the communication equipment. The mountain communication room was at her disposal, and she fought to stay calm as she listened to her mother's tirades. Andreia had managed to call her on a rerouted voice comm link that would be virtually impossible to trace, according to Roshan.

"Privacy? That's a new one," Le'Tinia huffed. "What could possibly be so…Oh. I see. You're away with Roshan O'Landha, aren't you?" Her voice changed from annoyed to immensely pleased in seconds.

"Eh, yes. I am." Andreia thought it better to stick to at least some truth. "I'll be gone for a few days. We're going…hiking." She groaned inwardly at her reply, but her mother seemed to swallow it unreservedly.

"Very well. There's a lot going on at the moment," Le'Tinia said, "but you can always catch up when you get back. This is far more important for you to pursue. O'Landha has built herself an empire, and if she hadn't been so elusive and reluctant to give interviews or make public appearances, someone would have snapped her up by now. She always was a bit aloof as a girl, wasn't she? And now she controls the majority of the import-export business in this hemisphere."

"Have you been running a dossier on her, Mother?" Andreia was appalled. "It's Roshan, for goodness sake. I've known her for decades!"

"It's never wrong to be methodical. She's a catch, that's true, but you can't be too careful. We want you with just the right person. It's about time."

"Don't push me, Mother," Andreia said warningly.

"I'm not pushing. I know what's best for my girl."

Le'Tinia's audacity and blatant conviction that she had her daughter pegged once and for all infuriated Andreia. "Just like you knew what was best for Trax?" she snapped.

Without the advantage of a video call, Andreia still knew her mother had paled and was now breathing in short little gasps, like she always did when her son was mentioned. He rarely was, these days. It was sad, but also a welcome change from all the praises at dinnertime she'd had to sit through.

"Trax was different," Le'Tinia said sorrowfully. "Trax wasn't strong enough, even if he seemed invincible until the end. If that woman hadn't committed a crime against us that way—"

"We've been over this a thousand times. We'll never agree, Mother. It was a mistake for me to bring it up. Let's leave it at that." Andreia leaned against the wall, slumped and tired.

"As you wish." Clearly Le'Tinia could have dived further into this subject, but relented with a pout in her voice. "I certainly wouldn't want to spoil a romantic getaway for you."

"You're not."

"You seem quite taken with this woman."

"I've always liked Roshan, Mother."

Le'Tinia laughed. "Liked? You were always infatuated with her. And it didn't take long for that look in your eyes to reappear."

"I'm sure you're correct, Mother."

"Of course I am. When I think about how the two of you danced—"

"Wait. Someone wants to use the communicator," Andreia lied, and stood up from her chair. "Give Father my best."

"I will. And cultivate this relationship. You could do worse, you know."

Andreia said good-bye, relieved to draw a deep breath and

terminate the conversation. She held on with both hands to the backrest of the chair in the communication room.

"So you like me, huh?" Roshan's alto voice rumbled, and Andreia turned so quickly, she had to cling to the chair so she wouldn't fall over.

"Ro!" *How much did she overhear?*

"Yes." Roshan glided toward her with a mix of the leisurely feline and cold-minded predator. "Your mother says you have a *look* in your eyes when you see me." Roshan walked up to Andreia and cornered her against the wall, between two of the tables. "Let's see if I can't get you to look at me that way now."

"Please." Her throat dry, it was hard to say the words. "Ro?"

Roshan placed a hand against the side of Andreia's neck and caressed it in slow circles. "How about that?" she murmured. "You're so damn soft. It's as if there were no bones, just wiry muscles under your skin. And that caramel skin, that olive tint, makes me want to stay up until whatever ungodly hour to touch you, and have you touch me." Roshan placed two fingers under Andreia's chin. "And you'd touch me so sweetly, wouldn't you? With your small, gentle hands against my skin?"

It was impossible to breathe. Andreia's world shrank until it consisted of the bright blue eyes of the woman towering over her. Standing next to the Protector, Roshan had seemed like a slightly older version of Kellen O'Dal. The resemblance was uncanny, and Andreia had found herself shifting her gaze between the two striking women who seemed cut from the same mineral ore. They were both lethal in the most literal way, yet they also seemed capable of great affection. The way the Protector had taken Admiral Jacelon's hand when they left the mission room for some privacy spoke volumes and reminded Andreia of how Roshan's tenderness could surface unexpectedly. "Roshan?" Andreia breathed. "Please. Why are you acting this way?"

"You were quick to *volunteer*." Roshan slid her hands languidly around Andreia's neck, followed the neckline of her black shirt, and stopped at the first fastener.

"I *am* the best one for that particular assignment." Out of breath, barely able to focus on her own words, Andreia tried to move away, but found it impossible. Her legs had stopped functioning, and she couldn't tear her eyes from Roshan's.

"Yes. That may well be true, but did you expect me to merely send you on your way without any chance of finding out?"

Confusion battled with a dark, heavy feeling that spread throughout Andreia's system. "What? Finding out what?"

"You know as well as I do that this mission is beyond dangerous. The Protector's plan is brilliant and daring, but risky. And as she said, we can't make any mistakes." Just as slowly as before, Roshan moved along the fabric in Andreia's shirt, and suddenly it gave way. Roshan had unfastened the first clasp. "You're leaving tonight, and I don't know if I'll ever see you again," Roshan continued, and now her voice was husky with emotions, vibrating as if her insides were trembling in unison with Andreia's.

"You're reading my mind," Andreia whispered. It was all she had thought of in her breaks from cramming the information she needed to concentrate on. Andreia looked up at Roshan, drinking in the image of the tall, stunning woman, so incredibly beautiful despite her obvious fatigue and distress. She also noticed something else in her eyes, something she'd glimpsed before, all those years ago, but never seen as fully exposed as now.

"I'm worried. It was clever of you to ask if you could borrow a derma fuser and claim mixed heritage as a problem. I think they all bought it. I know that Commander D'Artansis will use their derma fuser to make you look like a real Gantharian, but it's still only superficial. Your physical strength doesn't even come close to ours." Roshan's voice sank to a low, husky murmur. "And you're so small. I mean, I know you're strong, but you seem fragile."

"I wasn't fragile when I took out that OECS officer who nearly got to you in the forest." Andreia tried a smile. "And trust me, I'm not the shy, awkward kid you used to know. I can handle myself."

"I know all this!" Roshan said with a growl. "I know it. But to me, you're small, you're vulnerable, and you're going straight into enemy territory. You'll allow *them* to imprison you."

"We'll be able to talk over the earpieces that the Protector and the admiral brought. They're even more advanced than our latest equipment." Andreia jerked and looked down. Her shirt was now open to her waist, and her white lace-linen camisole wasn't opaque enough to cover her entirely.

"I know that too." Roshan's words came out slowly, as if the sight of Andreia made her mind come to a full stop. "Gods, Andreia…" She pushed the top of the black coveralls off Andreia's shoulders and left it around her elbows, making it impossible for Andreia to move her arms.

"Ro, please. You can't just—"

"I can. I have to." Despite the harsh words, spoken with obvious pain, there was nothing harsh or painful in the way Roshan caressed up and down Andreia's arms. "You're like pure Cormanian silk. And you smell so good." Lowering her head, Roshan kissed Andreia's forehead, brushed her lips along her cheek, avoiding her lips, and found the pulse point on her neck.

Andreia moaned and tried again to move her arms. If she had first intended to push Roshan away, now she wanted the opposite: to wrap her arms around Roshan's neck and cling to this amazing feeling of being so utterly alive. *Oh, Gods, she's making me want her so much. How can she do that with one glance, one touch?*

"I want to touch you too." Andreia whimpered the words against Roshan's cheek. When at first she didn't seem to respond, Andreia did what she could to calm her own rampaging emotions by placing kisses on the part of Roshan's face she could reach.

"Don't touch me." More pain. "If you touch me…" Roshan quickly cupped Andreia's face, forestalling any more kisses. "If you kiss me, you may be in for more than you're ready for."

"No, I don't think so," Andreia said. "I think we've been ready for a long time." Memories of heated looks and lingering touches flickered through her mind. Andreia's legs trembled, and her blood seemed to rush toward her lower abdomen. She had never been this sexually aroused before, not even close. Now that she was, she wasn't certain how to act. Assuming Roshan was the more experienced of the two, she waited while smoldering inside.

"Ready for this?" Roshan cupped a hand over Andreia's left breast, holding it gently. "Ready for me to touch you like this?" She slid her other hand around Andreia's back and firmly grabbed hold of her bottom. Pressing Andreia up against the wall of the semidark communication room, Roshan parted Andreia's lips and explored her mouth thoroughly.

It was more than Andreia could ever have expected. She'd been kissed before, but never in this all-consuming way. Their tongues intertwined and caressed each other, over and over, and Andreia forgot to breathe, as if oxygen was no longer necessary.

Sweat ran down between Andreia's breasts and along her back. She yanked her arms free of their constraints and flung them around Roshan's neck. Pulling Roshan closer, she instinctively raised one leg and hooked it around Roshan's thigh.

Groaning and trembling all over, Roshan slipped her hand around Andreia's thigh and pulled it up. Andreia hooked it around Roshan's hip.

"If we had time and a better place than this bloody communication room, I'd show you—" Greedy, passionate kisses revealed exactly what Roshan had in mind.

Opening her mouth, Andreia allowed the heat of her desire to spread through her veins. She filled her hands with the fabric of Roshan's coveralls and tugged at it. The way Roshan tasted, the way she smelled all contributed to Andreia's rapid loss of control. She knew she wouldn't see Roshan for a while, and a small voice inside her head asked, *"What if I never see her again?"* Desperate for the sensations Roshan created with her mouth and hands, Andreia grabbed hold of Roshan's left hand and placed it on one of her breasts. "Touch me. Gods, Ro, you have to touch me," she whimpered. "I'm burning up."

"Yes, you are." Roshan cupped Andreia's breast with far more tenderness than her voice relayed. Gently, she moved her hand in small circles, and Andreia moaned when her nipple puckered almost painfully.

"You're so beautiful. You were cute when we were younger, and you're stunning now," Roshan said. "If I could have my way, I'd push everything off this desk and lay your naked body on it. I'd delve into every part of you to make up for all those years when I hated you."

Andreia hardly heard the words. Her brain was in pure reaction mode, and she never wanted this moment to end. When it ended, they would have to return to the room where some of the rebels still waited for them. They would have to face reality, and reality dictated being parted from Roshan—for how long was written only in the stars. Instead, Andreia gasped aloud when Roshan left her mouth and kissed her way down her neck. "Yes, yes."

Roshan caressed Andreia frantically, her hands greedy against her. When Andreia's shirt came undone and Roshan's touch was no longer on fabric, but on skin, Andreia whimpered quietly, her head tipped back. "Ro, oh, Gods, Ro!"

Roshan jerked, her hands still around Andreia's breasts. "Gods, this is insane!" she groaned as she leaned forward and kept tasting Andreia's skin. "For the love of the stars, I never meant for it to go this far. This is insanity." There was agony in her voice as she pushed Andreia closer against the wall. "We should stop!"

Roshan broke free, and the sudden gush of cold air where her hot lips had just devoured her made Andreia sob and reach out.

"No." Roshan backed off. She regarded Andreia with flaming eyes, her mouth pressing into a thin line. The silence between them grew, only interrupted by their rapid breathing, and that too mellowed after a while. Roshan made a dismissive gesture with her left hand. "Straighten your clothes and make yourself presentable. We have work to do."

"Ro—"

"For skies and stars, remember to call me Paladin, *O'Daybo*."

Andreia was astonished and hurt beyond words at how Roshan could switch from volcano to iceberg within seconds. The abrupt shift stung, and more than that, the stinging pierced her heart, left it to convulse alone and bleed. Her hands cold, Andreia tugged at her shirt and coveralls, pulling them up into something that could resemble tidy. She avoided looking at Roshan until she was done. Only then did she meet the ice blue gaze of the woman who'd held her in the most intense embrace Andreia had ever known. "There. I'm ready to go back."

A muscle to the left of Roshan's lips twitched. "Andreia, I—"

"O'Daybo." Andreia pushed past Roshan and strode to the door. When she reached it, she looked over her shoulder, wondering if the shadows flickering over Roshan's face mirrored her own pain. She told herself she didn't care, but knew that was untrue. "Come on, then, Paladin. We can't keep the Protector waiting."

She left the room and didn't stop a second time to check if Roshan was following her.

CHAPTER FIFTEEN

The rain on Gantharat didn't just pour, it gushed from the gray skies, drenching everything completely. Owena and Andreia pressed against the wall of the dark gray concrete loading terminal as Owena scanned the premises.

"I read four guards on this side. This is it."

Andreia nodded. "Yes. This is our chance to get to Vaksses." She pulled the black fine-mesh hood down over her face, covering everything but her eyes. They needed to get inside and change into the gear the Onotharians issued the prisoners before they embarked to the smaller facility. Vaksses held members of the resistance who had just been rounded up and was meant to sustain up to a thousand prisoners before transport to the larger Kovos.

Checking her own scanner, Andreia punched in a few commands. "Let's go. We have two minutes before the codes reset themselves." She was deeply grateful for the SC device that allowed them to bypass the Onotharian seal on the doors. If it worked correctly, they would have disengaged the sensors and the alarm system for a few minutes. "O'Daybo to Paladin. We're moving in."

"Proceed with caution. We have you on sensors."

As Paladin's voice echoed through her eardrum from the tiny humanoid membrane earpiece, Andreia refused to listen to any special nuances in Roshan's voice.

"Affirmative. O'Daybo out."

With Owena right behind her, Andreia raced along the side of the building, making sure she was close to the wall the entire time. The concrete chafed the side of her coveralls-clad arm with a faint scraping sound. She could vaguely discern the outlines of the two closest guards through the dense curtain of rain. Part of her wouldn't mind making sure these guards never bothered a Gantharian citizen again, but Andreia knew if she killed any of them, the Onotharians would lock down the facility and most likely delay the transport to Vaksses.

When Andreia and Owena reached the double doors, Owena used her scanner again. "No guards on the inside. Just like Boyoda's intel stated, this holding terminal is almost entirely automated once the prisoners are inside. The Onotharians guard it from the outside."

"A blessing for us," Andreia said. "Not so great for the ones who figured that system out—they didn't count on the scramblers we brought with us."

"See, they work fine." Owena chuckled as she pulled the lever. The doors hissed open without any resistance, and no alarm klaxons blared through the dusk.

"Good." Andreia let go of the breath lodged in her lungs and followed Owena. SC technology came in very handy.

Inside, they ran through a long corridor leading to another set of double doors. Andreia scanned as she ran, and when everything read clear, she pushed one of the doors into its wall pocket.

Owena passed her and stopped just inside the threshold. "Look what's here."

Andreia stepped around her partner and stared at the long rows of coarse shirts and pants, stretching all the way through the long room, with an equally long counter running through the center of the room. No Onotharians were in sight, and Andreia guessed they were present only when a new prison transport arrived.

Owena's voice was crisp. "This is where they hand out the uniforms. That way they homogenize the prisoners. Strip them of some of their personality." "It's easier to erase a person's sense of self this way. Damn Onotharians." She uttered the words in a quiet, decidedly lethal tone of voice. "Find some that fit you."

Andreia didn't dare ponder the Onotharian philosophy behind the uncomfortable, yet no doubt durable, clothes. She picked a set that looked her size and pushed her coveralls off her shoulders and down her legs. A set of recycling computers would take care of their clothes and headwear. Andreia and Owena dressed in the ill-fitting shirts and pants, which were scratchy; Andreia feared that the unforgiving threads in the seams would soon abrade her skin. *And some people have lived for years in these clothes. Perhaps even decades if they're still alive.*

"We've just got a few seconds to go through the next door."

Andreia tossed her boots into the recycling computer and stuck her feet into the black, rubbery shoes provided by the Onotharians.

Owena looked grim. "You ready?"

"Let's go."

Owena picked up two small bags where she'd stashed their equipment. The material was easy to shape around her waist and attach with a belt. Also, it was made of an organic component that made it difficult, but not impossible, to be detected by scanners. They couldn't risk bringing weapons, so their hand-to-hand combat skills were all they had.

After they rushed through the next set of doors, which led into a narrow corridor with a low ceiling, Andreia fought the urge to bow her head and hurried down the hallway. All this time she scanned with the SC-issue mini-scanner that was shorter and thinner than her index finger, but accurate. The readings indicated a large crowd of Gantharian biosignatures farther ahead. Soon they'd be among the other prisoners, with no chance of getting out.

❖

"Get in line! If you give me any trouble, I'll shoot. Fucking Gantharian trash!" The tall, burly Onotharian's voice boomed within the large holding station as he spat in Kellen's direction. Kellen in turn made a production of clinging to Doc, her "husband," as she stuck to her role. She'd been bumped into by people and shoved from one end of the vast room to the other. The fabric of the clothes she and Doc had stolen in a storage room made her skin itch. Sweat ran down her back, making her irritated skin burn.

Earlier, Roshan, Jubinor, and Rae had created an effective diversion, designed to trick the Onotharians into believing someone was trying to spring a few of the prisoners. Now the Onotharians were patting each others' backs for managing to deter the resistance's attack. Instead, Doc and Kellen had broken into the huge building, temporarily housing more than four thousand detainees, soon due for transport to Kovos. The prisoners had all gone through a screening of sorts, to determine if they were high-ranking or important enough to qualify for the Vaksses asteroid. The rest, the regular resistance fighters, were all packed away like this and herded into vast transporters bound for the Kovos asteroid where, rumor had it, every prisoner had to fend for himself. Because the prison had a minimal number of guards, and nobody to keep order, Kellen could only guess what conditions were like up there. *I'll find out soon enough.*

A young woman to Kellen's left howled, "No, no, oh Gods, no!" She bent over and clutched at the wall with one hand and wrapped the other arm around herself.

"We have to help her." Kellen tugged at Doc, who was busy keeping them both safe and on their feet. The crowd moved in waves, and soon they would send the woman almost toppling over again.

Several times, the Onotharian guards had engaged a particularly cruel way of keeping the rebels in check. If an uproar seemed to be brewing, or the prisoners were merely scuffling somewhere, the guards sent an electrical shock through the metal alloy floor. It hurt enough to make most of the prisoners cry out, and it had already happened three times since Kellen and Doc had entered the room.

"Come," Kellen insisted. "She's about to collapse."

Doc pulled the young woman with them down to a kneeling position. "This way we won't fall so far if we're knocked over. I hope they don't zap us again." He held the young woman steadily by the shoulders, examining her closely with his firm gaze. "I'm a doctor—"

"It's too late. I've bled since I was captured. I'm going to lose my baby!"

Kellen's heart stopped for a few seconds before it began to thunder. "You're pregnant?"

"I am, I was...I'm losing it!"

"Don't jump to conclusions. Let me do what I can for you." Doc pulled a small pouch from under his armpit. Opening it, he produced a new sort of tricorder, a device given to him by Admiral Jacelon. Kellen watched him handle the advanced medical scanner almost lovingly as he ran it across the woman's body. He let it hover a centimeter from her abdomen, then examined the readings.

"Well?" Kellen was impatient and nervous. Her arm was behind the woman, and she stroked a thin, almost skinny, shoulder.

"Ma'am?" Doc asked the young woman. "What's your name?"

Obviously a seasoned resistance member, despite her age, she looked up at them with suspicious eyes. "Sarambol." Obviously her call sign.

Clever girl. Kellen held Sarambol tighter when the slender body shook under her touch.

"Oh, please." Sarambol now expressed barely more than resigned pain. Her blue-black hair, cut in a short, almost childlike hairdo, lay matted against her scalp, and sweat beaded on her pale blue forehead.

"Good news, for now, Sarambol," Doc said, and put the scanner back. "Your child is alive and well." He felt the still-flat stomach. "However, this environment isn't exactly helping."

"That's an understatement." Kellen felt elbows hit her in the head repeatedly, but couldn't become angry, knowing they belonged to people who'd fought for their freedom for so many years. "Let's get her over there, in the corner."

An elderly woman, far too old, Kellen thought, to be an active rebel, occupied part of the floor space in the corner. She tried to move out of their way as Doc and Kellen half dragged, half carried Sarambol there.

"No, no. Stay where you are. You'll get trampled if you move out there." Kellen pulled the older woman closer. "This young woman is pregnant and not feeling well. We're afraid she may lose her child if they knock her around any more."

"I'll keep an eye on her," the woman said, and wrapped an arm around Sarambol's shoulder. "I've seen her in here before. I was by the other wall a couple of days ago, and it took me a full day to move to this corner. I tried to walk along the walls, but I kept falling—"

"You hurt?" Doc asked and produced the scanner again.

The woman watched his ministrations with keen eyes. "That's some impressive equipment," she murmured. "It looks like a deep-tissue scanner, but it must also have an analytical chip, since you can get blood value, oxygen reads, and tissue cellular pressure and metabolic data."

Doc's head snapped up. "You a doctor?"

"No, I'm not." The woman smiled wryly. "That would've been the more useful occupation right now, but I am...used to be, an engineer. I'm too old to bother with call signs anymore. My name is Mandira O'Pedge. I used to teach and work out of the Tamanor Laboratories at the Iriosi Institute."

"And you've been in the resistance since day one. Your call sign is Berope." Kellen spoke softly, suddenly realizing who this woman was. "You're an icon to most rebels. We wouldn't have the technical development that we've had, despite the Onotharians, if it wasn't for you."

"Who are you? How do you know about me?" Mandira squinted at Kellen with clouded, light blue eyes.

"Call me Kellen. I doubt if you've heard of me, but I've been privy to this type of information. It's an honor to meet you, Professor O'Pedge."

"Professor..." The forlorn tone of voice in Mandira's voice soon changed into angry exasperation. "I won't have much use for the title once we're on Kovos. I won't last long. From what I've heard, people turn into animals quickly once they're left to their own devices up there. They fight to the death for scraps of food."

Doc shook his head. "Don't believe the worst. After all, it's mostly Gantharian rebels, or other dissidents, up there. They're on our side."

"They're on their own side," Mandira said, now calm. "Who can blame them? If they're strong enough to make it, they've been forgotten up there for years on end. Why would they care about us? We're just more people to fight over food with."

"True," Kellen said, "but a lot can happen when new groups of less-worn-down people arrive."

"Look around," Mandira said, her voice still kind. "Do these people seem *less* indoctrinated?"

Kellen did as suggested. Surveying the crowd, she automatically wrapped her arms closer around Sarambol's slumped form. The people nearest them stayed away from their corner only because Doc stood guard. "Why aren't they forming leaderships, establishing a chain of command?" she murmured. These rebels hadn't been imprisoned more than a few weeks, and they already acted on instinct, like chained animals.

"Every time a leader emerges, the Onotharians pinpoint who he or she is and drag the person off for interrogation, or worse. This way, they confuse the crowd and rule by terror. Some of the ones they've returned are barely recognizable."

"Damn. And how have people managed to sleep?" Doc asked. "Oh, Gods. On the floor in here?"

"Yes. There are latrines to the left, but no way to wash up. I've been waiting for diseases to strike, but so far we've been lucky." Mandira stroked Sarambol's head as the young woman pressed her face against her neck. "There, now. Don't listen too much to an old woman. Focus on staying well for that child's sake, little one. New life is new hope."

Kellen watched Sarambol raise her head and look up at Mandira. It was obvious that Mandira O'Pedge had once been a devastatingly beautiful woman, but life and time had plowed furrows into her forehead and whitened her hair.

A loud horn blared through the noisy crowd, creating instant silence. Four double doors opened at the far end of the room, and two long lines of Onotharian soldiers streamed into the hall.

"All stand. All stand!"

The ones who'd been sitting along the walls, exhausted and empty-eyed, now tried to get on their feet. They stumbled as the soldiers pushed them around and shoved them in the back with their plasma-pulse rifles. Eventually, the large group of at least eight hundred rebels, and other undesirable Gantharians, stood pressed tightly together in the center of the room, surrounded by armed men and women.

Kellen and Doc supported Sarambol and Mandira and tried to stay at the outer perimeter of the crowd.

"You will be transported to Kovos within an hour. The transport will take approximately one hour. I cannot answer for the consequences if any of you behave in the same despicable manner as you all did when you committed treason against Gantharat's new leaders."

"They're not *our* bloody leaders!" a hate-filled voice responded from the center of the crowd.

"Who said that?" the Onotharian leader said and raised his rifle. "Surrender yourself!"

There was only silence.

"Surrender, or I will fire randomly, and others will pay the ultimate price for your insolence!"

A new, shorter silence ensued before a young man pushed his way toward the Onotharian leader. "I don't recognize the new rulers. I don't recognize the joke you claim as courts of law. I don't recognize your presumed superiority."

Only when the person spoke did Kellen realize it was a young woman, barely twenty. "No," she murmured. "Don't antagonize them. They'll start firing." It would be disastrous if the guard fired aimlessly into the crowd.

"You shut up!" A guard shoved the barrel of his weapon into the girl's stomach, making her grunt.

Another soldier yanked her forward. "Kneel," he barked, and tore at the girl's short blond hair. "I said, kneel!"

Suddenly the young girl looked so much like a young Roshan, even like herself—the proud stance, the vibrant personality, everything. Kellen gasped for air, and with nothing else to hold on to, she hugged Sarambol, tucking her in under her chin. "Don't say anything more," Kellen whispered, and tried to will the young woman to not speak. "Just keep your mouth shut. Don't tempt fate."

The girl knelt, and Kellen guessed it was because of the heavy hands on her shoulders, pressing her down into the cold concrete. The leader grabbed a fistful of blond strands and dragged the girl's head up and back. "Good. Good," he chanted. "I could be persuaded to forget about your temporary misjudgment, but I need you to promise me something in return."

The girl looked as if she wanted to spit into his face. "What are you talking about?" she asked, her voice balancing submissive spitefulness as she spoke.

"Courtesy of my commanding officer, I have a standing order to make the call if I deem a rebel too far gone to ever be rehabilitated."

Kellen watched in terror as the girl struggled to get on her feet. "Well, then, my master, I'd better put on my best submissive face. Like this." She produced an ugly grimace. "You know what, enemy of mine, I just can't do it. I can't kneel voluntarily to the people who killed my parents, my siblings, my relatives, and just about everyone I cared about."

She's got nothing to lose! Damn, it, kid. Don't. Kellen gazed in horror as the girl leaped at her attacker, hands raised with broken nails ready. She dug the fingers of her left hand into the Onotharian captain's cheek and flexed them before she let go.

One of the other soldiers tried to grab her, but the girl was too quick. She pulled free again and sprang to her feet in one fluid movement. Twirling, the girl kicked out one leg in an easily recognizable combat movement. *She's a Gan'thet trainee! She has to be!* The girl's leg hit the captain on his chin and sent him flying backward, his eyes rolled up in his head.

"Damn, we have to stop her. She'll delay the transport," Kellen hissed at Doc. "And she'll get herself killed."

The soldiers seemed suddenly confused and panicky since the Onotharian captain was out cold from a kick delivered by a girl half his size and less than half his weight.

"Get her," the soldier next in command huffed.

Kellen let Mandira take care of Sarambol and forced her way through the crowd. The Onotharians shoved in from all sides, which would soon create a stampede if they kept it up.

Elbows hit Kellen's ribs, pummeling her as she slowly advanced through the detainees. She gasped in pain when someone jerked her hair to keep her upright, which was the only reason she didn't retaliate with a kick of her own. She ducked under an Onotharian's weapon, closed her hands around the girl's arm, and dragged her down and backward. When the girl didn't seem to want to move of her own volition, Kellen pinned her arms down and hissed in her ear, "Come with me and help us win this fight on a broader scale. You can still do a lot, but not this way."

"Stay away from me, you—"

"Fine. I would if I had the time. You're interfering with our plans," Kellen yelled over the deafening noise in the hall. "Come on, now. We can use you."

The girl stayed rigid for a few moments, and just as Kellen thought she'd lost her window of opportunity with her, the young woman let herself go limp in Kellen's hands and pretended to faint. Kellen hoped it was pretence.

As Kellen dragged the girl through the crowd, she wondered if it was her imagination, or whether the rebels actually closed the path after them, making it virtually impossible for the Onotharians to pursue.

As she reached Doc and Mandira just inside the outer perimeter of people, Kellen gasped, "She played hard to get," and let the limp body carefully slump to the floor. She watched in amused dismay as the girl immediately sat up and blinked. "Thought it was too much to hope for," Kellen murmured. "It would be easier if you slept through our mission, in fact."

"What mission?" the girl asked, her voice steady.

Kellen shared a quick glance with Doc. They'd avoided something that could've ended in a cold-blooded execution in front of an audience. Kellen couldn't let anything so ghastly happen. It would've had a devastating effect on the captured Gantharians, and something told her that she just might find this slightly annoying rebel useful once they arrived at Kovos.

"All stand! All stand! Start moving out in three lines. Get on with it. Move!" an Onotharian voice boomed.

Kellen pulled Sarambol along and saw how Doc helped Mandira remain on her feet. "Help him, kid," she told the girl, and nodded in Doc's direction.

"Sure. Why not?" The girl walked easily to Mandira's other side and wrapped an arm around her waist. "By the way, I don't like being called kid. My call sign is Ayahliss."

"Move, you vermin, move!" The Onotharian voices echoed continuously.

Phase two of their operation had begun. They were on their way to Kovos.

CHAPTER SIXTEEN

Roshan strode across the dusty plain, heading toward the low, camouflaged building that sat almost tucked into the mountain behind it. It had been her home away from home for twenty-five years, and she'd always been amazed how the Onotharians had almost compromised it only once.

Now, all she could think of was how Andreia had pressed against her yesterday evening. The heat emanating from Andreia's body had taken Roshan's breath away, as well as almost all of her common sense. She tried to tell herself she'd been right to break away, but every fiber in her body insisted she was wrong. *I shouldn't have spoken to her the way I did. Now she's in that place and I may never see her again.*

The torment rode her, and Roshan yanked open the door to the mission building with such force that the woman on the inside nearly stumbled.

"Everything all right?" Rae Jacelon asked. "Any news of their whereabouts yet?"

"Not that I know of. I was on my way to the communication room."

"I'll go with you."

As the two women walked along the narrow corridor, Roshan struggled to break the sudden silence. "Did you manage to catch some sleep?" Jacelon had slept in Berentar's room, while Jubinor had taken the first night's watch.

"It took me a while. I slept maybe two hours." The throaty voice didn't encourage any follow-up questions.

"Me too." She wanted to convey her fears, but knew this was neither the time nor the place for personal concerns. Besides, Roshan was sure Jacelon already knew everything about worrying about a loved one. *Loved? Oh, Gods.* Not even remotely ready to pursue the route her thoughts were taking her, Roshan motioned for Rae to enter the communication room ahead of her.

Jubinor sat with three other rebels, slumped back in their chairs. He had dark blue circles under his eyes and rubbed his temples as he leaned forward to punch in a command.

"You look like hell," Roshan stated with a wry smile, and walked up to him. "Any news?"

"We made brief contact with Commander Grey, but there was a lot of static, which is normal when in transit. The bulkhead of a spaceship, especially an Onotharian vessel, is designed to disturb unauthorized communications. They're right to be paranoid since we're on their ass constantly."

"And the other team?" Jacelon asked.

Jubinor shook his head. "Nothing. Their ship was probably due to take off later."

"Fine. Now go get some sleep," Roshan said. "We'll take over." Two more young rebels showed up just as she finished speaking and relieved their counterparts. Jubinor seemed grateful to get out of the room and left after a brief nod to the ones who'd worked with him during the night.

Roshan and Jacelon took over the controls at the main communication console, and Jacelon pulled a small black device from an inner pocket in her coveralls. "Jacelon to the bridge. Report."

"Good to hear from you, Admiral," the commander in charge replied calmly. "How are things progressing planet-side?"

"According to plan A, so far. I trust you're keeping a low profile?"

"Very low. We've set down on a copper-steel asteroid, to conserve energy. The metals embedded in the asteroid also help our cloaking system. Our engineer found that he can tap into the energy buried in the center, which will keep us going until we engage."

"Excellent. Remain on yellow alert until we're ready."

"Yes, ma'am."

"Jacelon out." She turned to Roshan, who was reviewing the few notes that Jubinor had made throughout the night. "You heard. Everything's fine on board my vessel."

"Yes. Now it's high time for me to ready my ships. I've devised a method that I'll test now." Roshan pulled a small metal box from behind the computer console and flipped open the lid. After she punched in a few commands, it lit up, a red light flickering over its small screen. "It's searching to connect to the mainframe. There." The red light became a steady blue. "We're hooked up." When Roshan placed four fingertips on a small sensor, the device used another red flickering beam to scan her, and then a blue diode lit up next to the sensor. "Excellent."

"What happens now?" Jacelon asked, following Roshan's actions with interest.

"I use my voice pattern to identify myself. We'll see if this works like it did during our previous tests." Her heart picking up speed, Roshan cleared her voice and hated her sudden bout of nerves. *Please, let this prove I can deliver when it matters.* "Paladin to O'Landha Armada. Enter armament codes. I repeat. Paladin to O'Landha Armada. Enter armament codes."

The screen was blank for several seconds before it began to fill with bright green lines against the black background. Ship after ship in her company, all with handpicked Gantharians onboard, reported back to her with the correct code. Now they'd mount their weapon arrays, install the dormant shield enhancements, and ready the smaller vessels some of them kept behind holographic walls in their shuttle bays.

"The same lines will turn blue once they've completed the installations."

"How long will it take?" Jacelon asked, looking quite impressed.

"Approximately four hours, depending on the ship's size. I also own two hangar-sized vessels, which might take longer. My captains are very experienced and secretly trained at a private…eh, I guess you'd call it a space-mercenary camp."

Jacelon's eyebrows rose. "Like the one on Orsos Prime?"

With reluctant admiration, Roshan nodded. "Yes. I take it that the SC knows of its existence."

"We monitor it. As long as they don't harm soft targets, we won't interfere. If this changes, the Supreme Constellations cannot sit back and watch anything that barbaric. You ought to understand, given the resistance's attitude."

"I do. My crews have trained there, several times, and the captains reported nothing untoward going on." Roshan opened her mouth to continue, but was interrupted by faint static coming through the communication system.

"…to base camp. Come in. Paladin?"

Roshan stared at Jacelon as they heard the voice. "We hear you, Kellen," Roshan said. "The admiral is sitting here next to me. Give us your report quickly. The sound quality's poor. You're barely coming through."

"We've arrived at Kovos, and they're herding us through long glass tunnels after docking. Many are wounded, and some look as if they haven't slept or eaten in a long time. They're in pretty bad shape, Paladin. I'm not certain how we'll be able to mobilize enough manpower. The Onotharians have already managed to grind our fellow rebels' fighting spirit to dust."

Roshan watched Jacelon with a worried frown.

"It's Rae, Kellen. Have you made contact with anyone?"

"Yes. I haven't determined who the most senior resistance member is, but I have talked with a young girl, call sign Ayahliss. She's obviously a Gan'thet trainee, and volatile, but she might be useful. We also have a famous engineer, Professor Mandira O'Pedge."

"I know her. We've met." Roshan noted the names and entered them into the computer. "Anyone else?"

"No. Well, only a poor pregnant woman. We have to handle her with care or she may lose the child." There was a brief silence. "But not if I can help it."

"They incarcerate pregnant women?" Jacelon closed her eyes, only to open them and look at Roshan with a hardening expression on her face. "This probably isn't news for you, but for me…it is."

"Have to go. I'll contact you as soon as it's safe and I have more news. Have you heard from the Vaksses team?"

"Jubinor spoke to Grey, but only briefly. Hopefully we'll have heard more when you make contact next time. Paladin out."

The static lingered for a moment before the connection was broken.

"I hope the Onotharians can't scan for messages like this," Roshan said wryly, out of earshot from the junior rebels. "If they do, we'll have them on our doorstep within the hour."

"They won't. Our engineers have invented a crystal-coded rotating frequency scrambler for this purpose. The Onotharians will consider it space dust, or solar flares, and ironically our scrambler is built on the same principle as their own cloaking device."

Roshan had to laugh. It was all so insidious. "The scheming and calculating of warfare," she mused. "Don't you ever get tired of it, Admiral?"

"Call me Rae." Rae shook her head. "I'd be lying if I said yes. But that doesn't mean that I like this particular situation. Having Kellen in such a dangerous environment, voluntarily captured, bothers me a great deal. If they see through her disguise...recognize her as the Protector..." She became quiet before looking straight at Roshan again. "But I don't have to tell you how that feels, do I? The way you look at O'Daybo speaks volumes. No wonder you could vouch for her. You know her personally." There was nothing inquisitive in the way Rae spoke, yet Roshan felt her cheeks become warm.

"Goodness, you look exactly like Kellen when she's feeling awkward. I'm sorry. I didn't mean to put you on the spot." She glanced over at the young rebels. "And in public, so to speak."

"It's all right," Roshan murmured. "I've always had strong feelings for O'Daybo, and I hate the fact that she's where she is. If I could have prevented her from going, I would have. But I don't outrank her, so..." Roshan shrugged. "And she's perfectly capable of taking care of herself, despite the fact that she's fairly small."

"She seems very knowledgeable. Well read."

"She is. When we were young, she was the one who never missed an exam, was always on time, and kept me afloat at the university—" Roshan broke off, knowing she was being far too open. Granted, Rae was a high-ranking SC officer, but so much danger surrounded them, it was wiser to remain tight-lipped. Angry at herself, Roshan fought to stay friendly. It wasn't Rae's fault that she instilled such openness in the ones she spoke to. "Anyway. She's definitely able to perform. I just want that to be clear."

"Very clear." Rae spoke softly. "And between us, I also understand that you can't share everything with me. Some things are hard to explain, and some are private. That's the part of warfare I hate the most, how it splits families, and friends, apart. I can enjoy the tactics on paper, in a way, because it's like a game of chess. But I loathe the idea of civilians ending up hurt, homeless, or worse, dead. My father, who's also an admiral, incidentally, says it's my greatest strength and my biggest weakness, that I can't just disregard the issue of collateral damage when I plan an operation. But I am who I am, and Kellen is who she is. I inherited her title, through our marriage, so it will be interesting to learn of Gantharat's reaction when they're free and we can tell them that they now have two Protectors."

Roshan knew she must look utterly foolish, sitting next to Rae, slack-jawed, stunned beyond words. "Protector. We didn't realize... Oh, damn the stars!" She wanted to rise from the chair and bow but knew this would tip the other rebels off. "Protector," she murmured, "I wish I'd known, or studied the old teachings better. The Protectors are mythical, fairy-tale people for many of us. We can hardly recall the times when they joined the O'Saral Royales in the Twin Lunar Parade through Ganath's streets. They rode massive maeshas, and it was a festive, happy time..." Roshan's voice faded, and she had to blink away tears.

"Blue tears. You're so like Kellen. She stands tall and proud, as you do, and it's clear that you've had a profound effect on her, ever since you took her father's body home. She told me about it in detail, coming here, so I'd understand without a shadow of a doubt why she trusted you." Rae smiled and shrugged. "I confess that I tried to warn her that people can sometimes change, but Kellen was completely unfazed. 'Not Paladin. Never,' she said. And apparently she was right."

"And apparently she picked the best spouse she could ever hope to find. Or perhaps you picked her?"

Rae smiled crookedly. "Let's just say that she found me, fired on me, and then I proposed to her—all within a few days."

Roshan wondered if she would ever become so bold, so decisive, qualities that seemed to define the true essence of Rae Jacelon. Uncompromising when it came to her duties, but ready to move heaven and earth to save the ones she loved. "I hope we—"

"Commander Grey to base camp. Commander Grey to base camp. Come in."

"Grey, this is Paladin," Roshan said quickly, and adjusted the sound quality. "Your admiral is here with me. Go ahead."

"O'Daybo and I are being placed in the cargo bay of an Onotharian vessel and are leaving for Vaksses in an hour, or less. Everything has gone according to plan."

"What's your physical status, Owena?" Rae asked.

"O'Daybo sustained a minor cut when a few of the guards tried to squeeze too many of us into the lift that took us up into the spacecraft.

I've looked at the injury. It's minimal, but the fact that O'Daybo is a Gantharian/Onotharian hybrid makes her blood red. We have to avoid any more incidents, or the guards may become suspicious."

"Read you, Owena. How long before your arrival at Vaksses?" Rae checked her chronometer.

"I've learned from O'Daybo and some of the other senior leaders here that Vaksses is located in the outer ring orbiting Gantharat. Approximately three hours, transport speed."

Roshan knew the Onotharian transport vessels were meant to carry as many bodies as possible, rather than move rapidly. She wanted to speak to Andreia, but refrained from asking for her. "Very well," Roshan managed. "Get back to us as soon as you have something new to report. Paladin out."

"Will do. Grey out."

Roshan sat still, her thoughts whirling so wildly, it was impossible to sort them, never mind speak intelligibly.

"I suppose they won't report in before the vessels have landed," Rae said, and stood. "I have matters to attend to on board my ship, so I'll borrow one of your hoverbikes and—"

Roshan flinched. "I can't allow you to go without a security detail. You'll have to take four guards with you. More, if you like, but no less than that."

Rae made a wry face, then nodded regally. "If you insist."

Roshan sighed. "Another pigheaded one," she murmured.

"Excuse me?" Rae lifted an eyebrow.

"Nothing." *Ah. So clever of you, Paladin.* "Let's go get you sorted then. We need to hook up a secure link between our communications center and your bridge."

"Agreed. I'll get right on it with my engineers." Rae stood up. "Ready?"

"Ready."

The moment they stepped out into the sunshine, Roshan knew that something had changed between Rae Jacelon and herself. It had been a long time since she'd made any new friends; she simply hadn't had time to indulge in anything personal. Roshan could hardly believe how easy it had been to talk to Rae, and she wanted to do it again. She just hoped that they'd live long enough.

CHAPTER SEVENTEEN

Cold rock walls with metal ore veins surrounded Kellen and Doc as the guards herded them into an enormous room chiseled out by prisoners on Kovos who'd come here before them. While they were being pushed by the guards and bounced off each other, Kellen and Doc tried to keep the pregnant woman, Sarambol, away from the worst of the shuffling. Ayahliss finally seemed to realize that Kellen and Doc weren't her enemies and had taken a protective stance, probably ready to attack anyone who dared threaten them.

Kellen looked at the fifth member of their little group, Mandira O'Pedge, who seemed tired and pale as she leaned against the rough wall. As if Ayahliss had read Kellen's mind, she moved up and placed a strong shoulder under Mandira's arm. "Here. Lean on me."

"Thank you, child." Mandira closed her eyes briefly. "This is what I get for being too stubborn. I had to check on those security systems myself, didn't I? And I had to do it the exact night the Onotharians launched their worst attack ever on us."

"Don't give up," Kellen murmured. "We need your skills up here. Let Ayahliss take care of you, and conserve your energy."

"Kellen! Guards, two o'clock, coming this way." Doc pushed her behind him. He was a tall, gangly man, and she tried to make herself inconspicuous. Knowing she was a celebrity by now, she'd used the derma fuser to alter her features. Still, she didn't want any of the guards to come close enough to examine her too carefully. The pouch of medical instruments Doc carried was another reason for them to keep a low profile.

"All clear," Doc murmured. "From what I know of this place, we'll go through a scanner when we enter the facility, and that'll be the last we see of any guards. Then, we're all on our own."

"Wonderful." Mandira shook her head. "I can't help but wonder how the ones who've been here for years have found a way to exist."

"We'll know soon enough. They're moving us in now. Stay close," Kellen said. "Sarambol, make sure you're between Doc and me."

Sarambol clung to Kellen's hand, white-faced and trembling. "I'm not usually such a coward," she sighed, her voice trembling. "Ever since I found out I was pregnant…well, things have changed."

"We understand." Kellen didn't elaborate, but she knew exactly what Sarambol meant. From the day Tereya O'Saral had told Kellen that she and Zax M'Aido were expecting a child, Kellen's duties had doubled, and her life had never been the same. *Armeo. How I miss you.* She deliberately pushed the thought of the beloved son of her heart away. Thinking of him would distract her and make her lose her edge.

They followed the crowd to a narrow gate where a blinking arch lined the rock wall. This was going to take some engineering, since they depended on Doc's small pouch of instruments for their continued success.

"Let me go through first, with Sarambol and Mandira." Kellen squeezed Sarambol's shoulders. "When I pinch you, throw yourself to the floor and cry out, as if in pain. I'll tend to you, and in the meantime, Doc will slide the pouch around the arch. I'll try to reach it, but if I can't, Mandira and Ayahliss, you have to try."

The other women nodded, and then they were almost there. Kellen held Sarambol's shoulders firmly as the crowd pressed against them. Kellen didn't even attempt to remain standing. Instead, she kept her head down and tugged Sarambol with her, fearful of losing her grip on her. When they were just under the arch, she squeezed Sarambol's shoulder tight.

To her relief, Sarambol sank to the floor with a cry. "Oh, it hurts! Please, help me. It hurts!" Either Sarambol was a professional actress or the pain was real. Kellen opted for the latter as she flung herself to her knees next to the girl and saw the sweat bead on her upper lip. "Stop, stop!" Kellen called out. "She needs help to get up."

The crowd kept pushing, trying to get away from the guards. The six guards manning the arch stepped together and formed an effective wall. "Fucking idiots! Halt!" the closest guard yelled. "Get her out of there!"

"I'm trying to!" It wasn't hard to sound desperate. Kellen kept her eyes on Doc, who stood to her far left, and saw him toss the small, flat pouch through the crack between the metal arch and the rough rock wall. It landed just inside, but Kellen couldn't reach it.

"Ow! Please, make the pain stop!" Sarambol cried, and at the same time, Mandira knelt next to them, close to the pouch.

"There, there, girl. Here, let's get you up and out of this bottleneck." Mandira placed her arm under Sarambol's and made a sweeping motion with the other one. When she moved, the pouch was gone.

Relieved, Kellen nodded to Mandira and Ayahliss. They half carried, half dragged Sarambol out of the three-meter-long tunnel behind the arch and stumbled into an equally crowded corridor, badly lit by small diode lights.

As Doc joined them, Mandira handed him the pouch. "You better hang on to this, Doc. I have a feeling you're going to need it."

They stood in the mayhem consisting of hundreds of Gantharians all trying to come to terms with the fact that they had arrived at Kovos, the notorious, hellish place that from now on was their prison.

❖

"Duck!" Andreia tugged at Owena, just before the Onotharian guard behind the human woman swung his weapon at them in outrage. "It wasn't her fault." She knew reasoning with him probably wouldn't work. A pair of young rebels had tried to protect an older man who'd stumbled into the guards when leaving the ship on Vaksses, and now utter mayhem had erupted.

"Back off! Back off!" the guard yelled, and flipped a switch on his rifle, aiming at them.

Andreia grew cold and tugged at Owena, who merely stood still, staring at the line of Onotharians taking up position. "Don't. Come on!" Andreia hissed. "We can't afford to cause any trouble. Not yet."

"Fine." Owena glanced darkly at the guards who now dragged the older man off to a corner. "They're going to hurt him."

"I know." It sickened Andreia to imagine the cruelty the guards subjected "offenders" like him to. Swallowing against the rising bile, she kept walking through the long corridors leading to the inner sections of the Vaksses asteroid. Once used as a military hospital, it was still a high-tech facility and boasted a clean environment compared to Kovos. Andreia had seen pictures of Kovos and shuddered to think of Kellen and Doc, stuck in such a horrible place.

Owena looked down at the small digital ticket the guards had given them when they disembarked from the transporter. "I think we're in the right corridor, judging from the sign there." She pointed at the wall next to a door.

Realizing Owena didn't read Gantharian or Onotharian, Andreia checked the sign and nodded. "You're correct. This is our room." She peered inside. "Ours and almost twenty more individuals'." Walking inside, they saw cramped bunk beds, narrow tables and stools, and two small cabinets, all in a twenty-five-square-meter room. "Let's hope the ventilation is working," Andreia muttered. *And that our neighbors are ready to help when we need it.*

As she sat down on one of the lower bunk beds, Owena remained standing, scanning the room with her cool glance. "I assume these bunks will soon be occupied. We better make sure we get this one, closest to the door."

"Good thinking." They would need to be able to vacate quickly, in order to set their plan in motion.

More people stumbled inside, some shoved by impatient guards. Unlike Kovos, this prison had guards on the inside patrolling each corridor constantly, and it would be impossible to overpower them. *I'll have to keep up the faith that the Protector's plan will work. That, or Onotharat's only popular person on Gantharat will turn out to be missing, imprisoned by mysterious circumstances.*

A man passed, half carrying another man with a bandaged head. Owena stepped up to them and helped to lay the almost unconscious man on the bunk bed next to Andreia. "He's in a bad way." Owena pressed her fingertips against the injured man's neck. "His pulse is thin and fast. What happened to him?"

"Berentar took a bad fall from the roof of a building when the Onotharians attacked." The younger man next to him shook his head. "I've taken care of him, but I got this when I asked for medical attention for him." He showed a bad contusion to the side of his head, apparently from the butt of a plasma-pulse rifle.

"Berentar?" Andreia rose quickly and approached them. "Are you a member of Paladin's and Berentar's cell?"

"Yes. I'm Eosomas." He stopped, suddenly looking even younger as he frowned. "They were going to send me to Kovos, but I managed to sneak along with Berentar, so he'd have someone he knew to take care of him. Do you have any news of my resistance cell?"

"We'll talk about this later," Owena hushed them, motioning with her chin at the new prisoners that entered the room.

Andreia knew they had to keep a very low profile. Eosomas was probably who he said he was, but they had to confirm this with Roshan before they continued their operation. They were under time pressure, since they had to coordinate with the Protector and Doc on Kovos. In the meantime, Andreia knew it would be wise to try and single out which one in their room was an Onotharian agent. She knew their methods, had even been forced to condone some of them herself, to keep her secret identity intact.

She glanced around the room, examined the faces of the eight men and six women, not counting Berentar and Eosomas. They all looked scared, some injured, and others merely fatigued.

Andreia sighed. *So. Which one of you is the traitor?*

CHAPTER EIGHTEEN

Kellen moved quickly through the crowd on Kovos, clutching disposable bottles of water and food rations against her chest. Her hair was in complete disarray, and her scalp stung from where a woman had yanked it, trying to get to the food dispenser. Annoyed, Kellen couldn't muster any anger toward people who had to fight for their food once a day. She doubted there was quite enough for everyone; in fact, she wondered if the Onotharians didn't estimate how many rations they needed, then downsize.

Around her, people pushed and shoved to get closer to the dispenser. Kellen could tell which prisoners had been on Kovos the longest. They were undernourished and pale, with tattered outfits hanging from their bony frame. *We need to get out of here and take them to SC medical facilities.*

Admiral Ewan Jacelon, Kellen's father-in-law, had arranged for the medical planners among his staff to deploy three of the SC's medical ships to the border. As soon as the SC forces were able to go forward, they would be ready to join the convoy.

Kellen ducked into the cave—there was no other word for the "room" she, Doc, Sarambol, and Ayahliss occupied with twenty other prisoners. Knowing full well that her food supplies wouldn't be enough for all of them, she sat down as inconspicuously as possible and handed out the rations. They had no real beds; instead they slept on mattresses laid out on the floor with one blanket each. Kellen had learned of a black market of sorts for blankets, and she'd traded the camisole she'd worn under her prison shirt for a second blanket for Sarambol. The woman now huddled under the covers, pale and reluctant to eat.

"I'm really nauseous," she moaned, "but I guess it's normal?"

"It is," Doc agreed, and held out half a ration bar. "But you still have to eat. You can't sustain the child merely on water."

Sarambol took the bar and nibbled it before swallowing hard. "Oh, that tastes awful. But anything for my baby." She smiled bravely and nibbled another piece.

"I imagine it's madness out there," Doc said, and sat down next to Kellen.

"Yes, it is. We have to wait until everything calms down, then reconnoiter. As far as I can tell, the only surveillance equipment is around the major gates, where we came in. I suppose their philosophy is, 'Out of sight, out of mind.'" She shrugged. "An Earth saying."

"I understand." Doc took a sip of water, then carefully closed his bottle and placed it inside his waistband. "So, when the new prisoners settle down, we need to figure out who's the leader in here."

"Yes," Kellen agreed. "Someone usually takes charge in places like these, and since most of the prisoners here are resistance members, or dissidents, I'm hoping that they still live by some sort of code of honor."

"There's always hope." Kellen turned to the young girl next to her. "Ayahliss, can you tell me how you came to train in Gan'thet?"

Ayahliss took a mouthful of her bar and chewed energetically. She resembled a power nacelle all by herself and seemed to be able to go full force all day. "The monks of the Quasatira Loy taught me."

Kellen stared at Ayahliss. "There's no way you could have… You're too young!"

"Are you calling me a liar?" Ayahliss stopped chewing and got to her knees. "I never lie!"

Groaning inwardly at Ayahliss's volatile nature, Kellen held up her hand. "No, I'm not accusing you of anything. I'm merely suggesting that you may have been tricked into believing—"

"I wasn't tricked. The monks took me in as a baby, when they found me on their Journey. I grew up with them, and they taught me everything I know. I have knowledge in six subjects that equal the degrees and diplomas at the University of Ganath, according to Ramnes Hegor."

Kellen tried to sort through what Ayahliss was telling them. "They were on a journey? Where to?"

"They were hunted down, one by one, during the occupation, and the holy place Quasatira Loy was leveled." Ayahliss's voice sank an octave and was barely more than a whisper. "Only twelve of them survived by hiding among ordinary people, and when they found their way back to each other, they prayed together for days. Eventually the Gods of Gantharat gave them a sign that they needed to relocate. Ramnes Dymor had a vision of an abandoned temple inside a cave." The girl fidgeted and her distress was obvious. "I was one of a total of ten children of various ages who the monks took in during the years just after the occupation. They wandered for four years, during which time they located me and the other children, before they found the cave."

"Where?" Doc said, as they all listened to Ayahliss's story.

"On the peninsula of Davost, inside the last part of the Merealian Mountains, they found an abandoned ancient temple, originally only a myth among the local people. The monks knew there had to be more truth to it and found the entrance. It was perfect, easy to defend if necessary." Ayahliss drank some water. "So, that's where I grew up."

"What 'degrees' do you have?" Mandira asked. "I mean, what did Ramnes Hegor teach you?"

Ayahliss smiled. "Oh, it wasn't just him. They all possessed different skills, and I learn easily, it seems. I have the knowledge equal to a degree in astronomy, herbal healing, mathematics, pottery, martial arts, and literature."

Mandira looked stunned and not doubtful at all. "Amazing," she said. "And you say it as if it were nothing."

"Oh, I don't mean it's nothing." Ayahliss grinned. "It was damn hard work, and a lot of tests, but I had very little else to do in the valley, and inside the old temple."

"And how did you end up in the resistance?"

"I grew up. It was time for me to leave, Ramnes Hegor said. I didn't want to, not really, but once I went out into the world and saw the injustices of the Onotharians, I knew I had to help do something about the situation." Ayahliss's face darkened. "I was naïve. I wasn't prepared for reality on the outside. Every new friend I made in my resistance cell was either captured or killed."

And so your fury grew almost out of control. Kellen knew all too well how it felt to lose a loved one. *There was a time when I thought it was because of me, of my failure, that Father and Tereya died.*

"I was at base camp with my cell leaders when the Onotharians struck. They killed the XO right before our eyes, and my cell leader... I'm not sure, but I think they took her to another holding place. That or she's dead."

"She's probably on her way to Vaksses," Doc murmured. "So, now we know." He looked at Kellen with an eyebrow raised. "We have quite an eclectic group here to start working with."

"Yes." Kellen glanced into the corridor. "I think it's calmed down enough for us to begin. Ayahliss, can I count on you to keep Mandira and Sarambol safe?"

"Certainly." Ayahliss looked as if she was ready to take on the entire Onotharian force. "No harm will come to them. I give you my word."

Kellen wanted to smile at the solemn way the girl spoke, but knew it was wise not to do so. She rose and tucked her water bottle into her waistband as Doc had just done. If she lost it, she'd have nothing to drink until tomorrow.

The roughly carved, winding corridors were still full of people. Some stood in groups, discussing loudly their fate and their accommodations. Very few seemed to consider this a good time to gather their forces and come up with a plan. *How did the Onotharians break them so quickly? How could brave and patriotic rebels become so quarrelsome, small-minded, and scared?*

As they moved to the right of the tunnel leading to the arch in the asteroid, the walls became darker, grimier. This was obviously the older part of the prison, and here they found fewer people standing around in agitated groups. Instead, the inhabitants moved slowly and glanced at Kellen and Doc with very little interest, as if newcomers were a common sight, something they really couldn't bother with.

"What's with these people?" Kellen asked. "Granted, some of them have been here for years, and it's understandable that—"

"Hey! You two! Get in here!" a male voice hissed from one of the small caves. "Hurry! Don't let anyone see you."

Mystified, Kellen glanced at Doc, who shrugged. It was up to her. "Stay focused," she said to him before she ducked and entered the cave. Inside, she examined what had obviously been someone's home for a long time. "Who are you?" she asked, making sure she stood with her back against the wall, near the exit.

"Who I am matters little." The man spoke Gantharian with a faint accent. "I spotted you two earlier and noticed you aren't afraid and panicked like the other newcomers." He stepped into the faint light from the diode lamp next to Kellen. Long, blond hair, kept in a rugged ponytail, ran down his skeletal back, and it was impossible to judge his age. He had blue eyes, like most Gantharians, and boasted a semi-long beard. It was impossible to judge the color of his skin in the muted light. Looking closer, Kellen saw the man's eyes were clear and intelligent despite his obviously worn state.

"It's who you are and what you're doing here that's important. I've been here long enough to distinguish friend from foe. You seem... neither, and that's impossible. You're probably here on a mission." The man scratched his beard. "What mission, I ask myself? Can you be the answer to my prayers, or are you just another set of bad news?"

Kellen decided this might just be the opening she and Doc were looking for. A man who appeared to have been incarcerated here for years couldn't be on the Onotharians' good side. "We *are* here to help," she said cautiously. "My name is Kellen. This is Doc."

"Those your call signs? You resistance?"

"Yes. We are." Kellen didn't elaborate. "It seems you've been here a long time, sir."

The courtesy wasn't wasted on the man. "Too long. I've been on Kovos since right after they attacked and the occupation began."

Doc stepped closer. "Would you mind if I give you a quick medical scan?"

"Want to make sure that I'm Gantharian?" The man chuckled. "You're going to be disappointed. I'm not."

"No?" Doc frowned and turned to Kellen, his eyes darkening.

"Scan him anyway. We need to know if you have any illness that impairs you after such a long time in captivity."

"Fine." The man shrugged. "Go ahead, young man."

Doc scanned the old man's skinny frame. "You have bronchitis, several digestive tract parasites, and rheumatoid arthritis. These things are easily cured, normally, so I take it the prisoners on Kovos don't get much medical attention."

"Only if what we have is contagious enough to pose a danger to the guards who randomly patrol the corridors. They only come a few times during every lunar cycle, except when there's a drill to educate new guards." He shrugged, only to grimace at what had to be pain from the movement. "Besides, one has only to use common sense around here to realize that these diseases are unavoidable. We have no medical scanners, derma fusers, or any other medical instruments. It's been too long since I used them, and I'm sure I wouldn't even recognize the new technology of today."

"You're a physician?" Doc scanned the man again, and now he looked at Kellen with an odd expression on his face. "Gods of Gantharat—"

"What is it? What's wrong?" Kellen's heart began racing, because Doc looked as if he'd been hit by a plasma-pulse rifle. She half raised her hands in a defensive gan'thet position.

"He's human, Kellen. A human physician! Do you realize what that means?"

Kellen frowned and looked at the man. "What's your name?" she asked again.

"I think your friend here has already figured that out. I was the only human on Gantharat, before I was imprisoned."

"Your name is Mikael O'Landha," Doc whispered, a catch in his voice. "You must realize your daughter thinks you're dead."

Kellen tried to follow the unexpected thread of conversation. "Please explain what you're talking about, Doc. How can you know who this is?"

"Paladin's true identity is Roshan O'Landha. This…" He placed a gentle hand on his shoulder. "…is Mikael O'Landha, her father. Paladin thinks he's been dead for decades. It was what she was told."

Mikael O'Landha stood rigid in the center of the small cave. "Roshan? You know Roshan?"

"Yes. She's a resistance leader."

"I heard from other resistance fighters that she's a collaborator." Mikael's voice became cold. "She's trading with them."

"You think of your daughter that badly?" Doc said. "That's just a front. She uses every credit she makes, more or less, to organize and outfit the resistance. She's the reason Kellen is here."

Doc raised questioning eyes to Kellen, who guessed what he was asking. She nodded, knowing they had to convince this patriarch of the Kovos asteroid prison of their true intent. Kellen guessed he pulled a lot of weight around the ones who'd been here a long time, and they needed this break.

"Your daughter is solely responsible for bringing back our last surviving Protector of the Realm, Kellen O'Dal," Doc said.

"What lies are these?" Mikael sighed, obviously getting fed up with their preposterous statements.

"These are no lies, Dr. O'Landha." Kellen walked closer and took both his hands in hers. "I am the last of the O'Dals. My father was Bondar O'Dal, resistance leader and Protector of the Realm before me. When he died, during an ambush, your daughter brought him home to me, so I could bury him. I was then responsible for Princess Tereya O'Saral." Kellen filled the apparently stunned Mikael in on Armeo's existence.

He let go of her hands and fumbled for a stool, which wobbled precariously as he sat down, listening to how Kellen's and Armeo's flight to Supreme Constellations space had been the turning point in the SC's ongoing debate about whether or not to engage the Onotharians.

"And now, with all these senior rebel fighters in custody, the Onotharians have struck a blow that we need to mitigate," Kellen said. "Sir, do you realize how important it is that we unite our people, here, and on Vaksses?"

"Protector…" Mikael wiped his forehead. "I've heard of this other prison. How do you propose we communicate with Vaksses?" He was in no way scornful; he merely asked a question.

"We have communication devices inserted." Kellen didn't reveal where they were located, since she still had some misgivings. She wanted to trust Paladin's father, wanted to think he was their way to success, but he had been incarcerated for decades, and who knew what the Onotharians had subjected him to? Still, her instincts told her he was a man of strength, and she hoped she'd turn out to be right. "Are you willing to help us organize our fighters?"

"I have nothing to lose," Mikael said, not even hesitating. "My daughter has obviously risked her life in the resistance for the duration of my imprisonment. My wife is long gone, and if there's even a remote chance for me to see Roshan again…" His voice broke, but he appeared beyond tears. He rose from the stool with new strength. "I know just who we should talk to. Corgan and Bellish live two caves down this corridor. They are our leaders, something newcomers usually find out quickly."

"And you think they'll listen to us?" Kellen asked. "We don't have a lot of time."

"They won't listen to you, but they'll hear me out," Mikael said confidently. "We're the same age. They knew me before we were captured, and...they knew Jin-Jin."

Kellen didn't have to ask who Jin-Jin was. The love and reverence with which Mikael spoke her name indicated she was his wife. Thoughts of Rae rushed through her mind, and Kellen deliberately transformed the piercing longing for her own wife into strength, a Gan'thet technique crucial to the success of a mission. The consequences of failure were catastrophic, not only for the people of Gantharat, but also for her personally. "Very well. Lead the way." Kellen motioned to the opening.

Mikael walked over to a shelf chiseled in the wall above his bed and put on a tattered caftan, obviously fashioned from a blanket. "Come with me, it's just down the corridor."

He led them away from the prying eyes of the Onotharian surveillance equipment farther up the tunnel. After they had walked for a few minutes, Kellen began to realize how big the prison actually was. Chiseled-out corridors stretched far into the asteroid, and the floor was covered with gravital plating. Kellen felt Doc touch her arm.

"We can't tell Paladin about this yet," he said gravely. "She needs to focus on her assignment, and if we tell her about Mikael, she's likely to lose her edge."

Kellen knew Doc was right, but it still pained her. "Yes, I agree. We don't know how she'll react and far too many lives depend on all of us staying sharp. But we'll have to let her know as soon as the mission is completed. It's inhumane not to."

"I agree. It bothers me to have to lie, but I also think she deserves meeting him face to face the first time."

They kept walking in silence and passed many other prisoners, who glanced at them suspiciously. Every now and then, people poked their heads out of the low entrances to their caves. Clearly, it was calmer in the old part, but its inhabitants didn't take anything for granted.

"Is it just me, or is it getting darker?" Doc blinked at the fading light diodes.

"It's getting darker."

"This half of the asteroid, the old part, uses old technology. When a diode goes out, they don't exactly rush in here to change it. And some of the ones that are still functional are fading. We've found a way to create light on our own, but we use it sparingly."

"How?" Kellen tried to envisage how anyone could find auxiliary power in this hellhole.

"Oh, you'd be surprised. The water bottles. One of our engineers found that if you used some of the newer diodes to slowly melt the material, it later could be broken off in smaller pieces and ground into a powder. This powder, in turn, acts almost like an old-fashioned fuse when you set fire to it."

"You can produce fire up here? How is that possible?" Doc asked, sounding just as incredulous as Kellen.

Mikael laughed, a husky, short sound. "It took us a while, but when we realized how, it was like child's play." He bent down and picked something off the corridor floor. "Like so." He slapped his hands together and produced a big spark that lit up his grinning face. "See? Two asteroid rocks together. Bang, there's your spark. The trick is to learn how to direct the spark toward the powder, then jump back when it begins to sizzle. It also takes a lot of powder to keep a steady light."

"Can't you merely set fire to the bottles the way they are?" Doc was obviously intrigued by the process behind the prisoners' discovery.

"No. We tried. There's something in the very slow melting of the bottles that changes the molecular basis of the material, according to the scientific group. It limits the potential toxic fumes as well."

"And the guards don't know about this?" Kellen asked.

"If they do, they don't care. We've been producing powder and using it for more than fifteen lunar years. Here we are." Mikael stopped by an entrance and waved at them to stand next to him. "Let them see your faces." He ducked his head and leaned into the small opening. "Hello? Corgan? Bellish? I've brought company."

"What company? You never see anyone, you old fool," a deep voice said. A man with the same tattered look as Mikael showed up, a broad smile on his face. It faded when he saw Mikael wasn't joking. "Who are they? Why did you bring newcomers here?" He spat the word "newcomers," making it clear that he didn't care for strangers.

"Listen to me, Corgan. This is important. Trust our long friendship and let us in, and we'll explain everything."

Corgan stood motionless outside his cave, studying the three of them, apparently indecisive.

"Oh, come on! Who's the fool now?" a female voice sighed behind him. With white haired and stunning violet eyes, she tugged at Corgan's sleeve. "We can't stand around here attracting attention."

"Fine. Come in, then." Corgan stepped aside, and Kellen knew he wouldn't risk turning his back on them for a second.

Inside, Mikael kissed Bellish on both cheeks. "It's been too long, dear one."

"It wouldn't have to be as long as this if you ever got out of that cave of yours." She cupped his cheek. "You're too lonely, I keep telling you."

"But not anymore. As you can tell, I've brought guests."

"Guests?" Bellish eyed Kellen and Doc under raised eyebrows. "They look like any other newcomers to me. What's so special about them?"

"This, my dearest friend," Mikael said, his voice suddenly trembling as he circled Bellish's shoulders with his arm, "is Kellen O'Dal, the sole remaining Protector of the Realm."

CHAPTER NINETEEN

When Berentar groaned and opened his eyes, Andreia leaned over him and pressed a damp cloth to his forehead, trying to alleviate the fever that seared his body. Gantharians were naturally warm, but their temperature could run extremely high, if not treated. Obviously the Onotharians weren't going to medicate their prisoners here at Vaksses, unless they had a use for them. *Aren't they going to interrogate him, a resistance leader? Why aren't they doing anything?*

Andreia suspected they were monitored, both by surveillance equipment installed in the former military hospital and by infiltrators. This was a downside to having autonomous cells and incognito rebels; it was damn near impossible to judge initially if you were dealing with an enemy. Right now, their room was empty except for Berentar, Owena, Eosomas, and herself. Everyone else was at the supply station stocking up on food and necessities.

"Berentar," she whispered. "Please lie still. You're injured and running a fever."

"Who...?" Berentar rasped, his throat sounding as if it was dry. It was a good thing he was awake; at least they could get some water into him.

"Eosomas is right here. He brought us water and nutrition bars. Let us help you drink some." Owena, on the other side of the bed, slipped her arm under the muscular man's shoulders and lifted him carefully. Andreia held the water bottle to his parched lips, and he drank thirstily, but when the water went down the wrong way, he began to convulse and cough spasmodically.

"Careful," Eosomas said, though smiling broadly. "It's great to see you awake, sir. I've been so worried."

"Who are...these people? Where are we?" Berentar managed to ask before coughing again.

"These are friends," Eosomas whispered almost inaudibly, with no lip movement. "They're in contact somehow with our cell. There's some good news. Paladin made it and Doc too." Andreia saw how Berentar's eyes darted between them, but that he hesitated to ask further.

"Jubinor is all right," she murmured.

"Thank the gods." Berentar sighed and slumped back onto Owena's side. "But...I don't understand...How the hell can you communicate with them?"

"We can't discuss it in detail, but if you have any misgivings, we can prove our identity to you later. Merely think of something only they would know, and we'll ask them to confirm it."

Berentar nodded. "Fair enough."

"Another team is deployed to Kovos, to coincide with our plan to liberate these two prisons. It's daring, but important if we're going to help the Supreme Constellations intervene. War's coming and they need us, or they'll be going in blind."

"Are you telling me...that you came here voluntarily to try to rescue us?" Berentar coughed and glanced between them. "It's a suicide mission!"

"You'd think so," Owena said, "but we have a plan devised by an excellent tactician."

"Who are you talking about? A miracle worker?"

"Almost," Andreia filled in. They needed to inform Berentar of the situation before the other prisoners came back. Most of them were probably what they seemed, but she was sure at least one of them was an OESC spy. "Listen, you probably saw the transmission from the SC, regarding Prince Armeo?"

"Yes."

"Well, our Protector of the Realm, Kellen O'Dal, has returned, and she didn't come alone or empty-handed." Andreia continued to tell Berentar of the last few days' events.

When she had finished, Owena placed the pale man back on his pillow. His cheeks were blue tinted from the fever, and the white in his eyes contained streaks of blue as well. "This is amazing news," he whispered. "I just don't know how I can contribute when I'm this way. I can't move because of the pain. As pathetic as that sounds, I can't help it." He looked at them with a disgusted expression.

"Don't worry. We just need you to tell us which ones you and

Eosomas know we can trust among the prisoners. We need all the intel you can give us to report back to Paladin."

Eosomas regarded Andreia with new hope in his eyes. "I'll help in every way that I can. I've recognized several people here, from joint missions. I can report back to Berentar, and he can confirm their call signs."

"Good." Andreia sat back on her heels just as some of their roommates returned. "Hello. Got your food all right?" she asked, to distract them from looking at Berentar.

"Yeah, a bloody mess out there," a man said grumpily. "I managed to get my hands on a lot of bottles of water."

"That may mean someone else goes without." Owena nailed the man with her dark blue glare.

He had the decency to look ashamed and blinked down at the bottles in his arms. "What if we keep them in this room, as common property?" he asked.

"Better idea." Owena nodded. "Why not put the entire surplus over on that shelf?" She pointed to the wall behind him.

"Sure. Why not? At least it stays in this room. We'll all share."

Andreia exchanged a glance with Owena as she leaned closer to whisper her suggestion. "Well, let's use the process of elimination. We let Eosomas vouch for people he can say for sure are resistance fighters, and they in turn can give us more faces, and so on. That way we have a reasonably accurate way of knowing that there'll be no impostors when we take action."

Owena looked impressed. "I can't think of a better way. Why don't I take him for a walk around the block, in a manner of speaking?"

"Yes, do that. We need ten to twelve to begin with, and if they can point out five or ten each, and they do the same, then we'll have a good foundation for what we need to do."

More people entered the room, and Owena and Eosomas rose to leave. Andreia met Owena's eyes, suddenly disturbed. *Granted, Berentar is a resistance senior leader, but he's also unable to move. I hope I can defend the two of us if it's necessary.* She wasn't sure if any of her misgivings showed on her face, but Owena smiled faintly before waving discreetly.

❖

"All set?"

Rae looked up as Paladin walked in. "Yes. My teams are ready at a moment's notice. And you?" She sat by one of the tables in the mission room with several handheld computers spread out in front of her.

"I've received positive confirmation from all my captains. My ships are armed and my people are on standby. All I have to do is give the command and they'll rendezvous with your vessel." Paladin pulled up a chair and sat down, rolling her shoulders with a small grimace of pain. "Any more all-nighters and I'll go into hibernation once I finally get to sleep. How are you doing?"

"Once I'm in battle mode, I don't need much sleep. Once I'm out of it...I'm unconscious for days." Rae leaned back in her chair. "Things will probably change. After all, we *are* getting older."

"So true. I hear that age shouldn't matter, but that's a damn lie sometimes."

"I agree. Although when it comes to warfare, more years usually mean more experience." Rae half smiled briefly. "Any more news from Vaksses or Kovos?"

"Not yet. Phase 3 of the plan shouldn't be rushed, and I hope O'Daybo and Kellen realize this. Granted, we don't have a lot of time, but if this phase fails, then we'll..." Paladin's voice faded, and her expression turned solemn, with no trace of jest in her eyes and voice.

"Don't even think about it. Both teams have several backup plans, and they're resourceful. I don't know O'Daybo and Doc as well as you do, but I know Kellen and Owena. Kellen's plans are well thought out. The SC Fleet's senior tacticians scrutinized them and changed only a few minor details."

"She's sharp. She always was."

"And she hasn't changed when it comes to that."

"Has she changed in other ways?" Paladin asked, crossing her legs.

"Yes, I'd say so. I'm sure you realize that as a Protector of the Realm, Kellen is trained in every combat skill known to humanoids, and then some. Her main goal is to keep Prince Armeo safe and, also, to regain the throne and his rightful position."

"Thus giving the Gantharians back their prince, their monarchy. We have a right to our own royal family, as much as he has a right to his kingdom. During the reign of the O'Saral Royales, we benefitted from living in a democracy. They were our symbol of freedom, of the rights of the people."

Rae listened, surprised at how adamant Paladin sounded. "I read up on your history when Kellen came into my life, and it surprised me to find how progressive the O'Sarals were. They seem to have had a great social conscience."

"They did. We had public elections, in which we voted for our chancellor every five solar years. Our natural resources made this a rich world, and we took our wealth for granted. The Onotharians rattled their weapons, but we never quite believed they'd actually attack us. We had a large community of Onotharians living here, in harmony with the rest of us for the most part, and to think some of them planned the occupation all along..." Paladin's face hardened. "They betrayed us and sold us out to an enemy that's been raping Gantharat—with no repercussions from any other nation."

"Yes, I realize that." Rae spoke in a factual manner, to show she was sincere. "But that's about to change, Paladin. And as for Kellen, don't get me wrong. Kellen is, under certain circumstances, as lethal and goal-oriented as they come. But she has a family now, people who care and depend on her, and that has made all the difference. She'll walk through fire for Armeo and, she insists, for me as well. She did during our previous mission to this planet, and I know she'd do it again. So, the people of Gantharat will regain their monarchy, their Protector, but they, you, will also have to accept that their Protector is also mine." Rae met Paladin's eyes firmly. "I'm not sure how they'll react."

"The Protectors were always family people, since the title is passed on to their children and spouses. Nobody will think twice about the Protector being married. Are you two going to have children?"

Rae realized the question wasn't as intrusive as it might appear. The Gantharians depended on the Protectors to keep their royal family safe, even if it now consisted of only a young boy, and they would want to know if Kellen would provide continuity. "We haven't talked about it. We both lead dangerous lives, and we have Armeo to think of. I guess we'll consider this issue when this conflict ends."

"I didn't mean to pry," Paladin said, sounding as if she were chastising herself. "It's none of my business."

"Don't worry about it." Rae shrugged. "This isn't exactly a normal situation. We have to trust each other with all sorts of information, or we'll fail in this mission."

"You're right." Paladin smiled. "I never thought I'd say so, but this isn't the time for secrets." She glanced down at her laced fingers before she gazed steadily into Rae's eyes. "My name is Roshan O'Landha. Some of the Gantharian people consider me a collaborator and almost a traitor, and that's been my cover for decades." Paladin/Roshan seemed to hold her breath.

"Thank you, Roshan. I appreciate your candor, but I'll stick to your call sign for now. I look forward to being able to use your name freely, when you can clear it."

"Thank you. I hope that day comes soon."

"From your lips to…"

"…the ears of the Gods of Gantharat." Paladin smiled. "My father used that expression. He said it was part of an ancient Earth saying. I always wanted to travel to Earth. He was born in an area called Scandinavian Alliance."

"I've been there many times. It's beautiful." Rae hesitated, then placed her hand on top of Paladin's, who glanced at their joined hands, then changed their touch into a handshake.

"I promise I won't give up on my dream to see that part of my heritage."

"Good, I—"

"Ma'am? A transmission's coming through." A young rebel stood in the doorway. "It's the Kovos team."

"On our way." Paladin rose, and with Rae right behind her, she wove through the large tables and walked to the communication center. They sat down and Paladin punched in a few commands. "Paladin to Doc, come in."

"Doc here. We're doing all right. Can you answer a few questions to help prove our identity?"

"Yes, go ahead." Paladin raised a curious eyebrow at Rae.

Doc fired off a set of questions, all containing elements of whereabouts, schedule, and tactical information, and Paladin rattled off the answers readily. After a brief pause, Doc came back, his voice slightly garbled. "I think we're in the clear. We have the most senior resistance fighters onboard here, and they'll help us rally as many as we need to continue our mission."

"And Kellen?" Rae kept her voice light, but her fingers trembled inside her closed fists.

"Kellen's doing well. She's making preparations as we speak."

"Preparations?" Paladin leaned closer to the communicator. "For what?"

"Our new friends handed over a crew manifest of sorts as soon as you answered their questions correctly. Kellen is going through it."

"Are you telling me that they've kept a log of the prisoners? I mean, all these years?" Paladin fidgeted with her hands for a moment, then stood up, restlessly rocking back and forth. "That…list can't fall into enemy hands or be destroyed. That's imperative, Doc." Her voice turned into a whisper before she cleared her throat. "Any names you can give us yet, of the people you're in contact with?"

After a brief silence, Doc returned. "Corgan and Bellish O'Gesta, from Mogeth. That's it for now. They're the leaders of Kovos and have been here, more or less, since day one."

"Any other names?" Paladin asked, and entered the O'Gestas into the encoded database. She kept punching in commands, and soon another screen began blinking.

"Not yet. Here's Kellen now, by the way."

Rae's head snapped up. "Kellen. Rae here."

"We are making progress, Rae. We're on schedule and have several new opportunities. I'll be planet-side soon."

Rae wondered if Kellen was deliberately reassuring her. In fact, she was sure her wife was being overly optimistic. "Good to hear. Do they provide enough basic supplies?" *Please, don't let the bastards starve you.*

"We have enough rations to survive for a week. Don't worry, Rae. We'll be back long before we need more. Trust me."

Rae trusted Kellen with *her* life, that wasn't the issue. *I need to believe in your ability to get yourself out of this alive.* Refusing to acknowledge the cold fist around her heart, Rae kept her voice steady. "I do. Keep up the good work. So far, so good."

"I will. We'll report further in a few hours, when we know more. Kellen out."

"The names are confirmed." Paladin looked up from the blinking screen. "Bellish and Corgan O'Gesta went missing the second year of the occupation. They were protesters who worked out in the open, supported by what could have become a people's movement, but the Onotharians struck it down in a completely ruthless manner. Bellish and Corgan were presumed dead after ten years. Obviously they're not." Her fingertips slid along the command keyboard. "My father went missing and was presumed dead after only a few months. I know the same conditions don't apply, but…I guess hope is futile in this case."

"But it's only natural to hope," Rae said. "Statistically, both Kellen and I should be dead, but we're not. We were both lucky and had enough help to make it through impossible odds when we were on a mission here last time."

"So you just never know."

"No. You never know." Rae hesitated before reaching out. It was important that Paladin remain strong and not too reflective. She took Paladin's hand. "What we should do, we must do, is to remain focused. Don't lose focus, Roshan."

It was as if the use of her real name snapped Paladin out of her weary mood. Straightening, she entered a few new commands. "There. I've entered the updated information about Corgan and Bellish. I hope to be able to do the same for many of the others listed here."

Rae leaned back in her chair. "So do I." She willed her fear to melt a bit. "So do I, Paladin."

❖

"We have four hundred people already, Berentar," Andreia whispered in the semiconscious rebel leader's ear. "We're going to contact Gantharat in a few minutes. I know they'll be glad to hear that you're still here, so hang on."

Berentar was slipping in and out of consciousness, and it infuriated Andreia that they weren't able to do more for him than to make him as comfortable as possible. She looked up at Owena, who stood by Eosomas on the other side of the bed. "We have to carry on," she murmured, out of earshot of the rest of the inhabitants in their room. "We need about two hundred more. Continue the way you're doing, Eosomas. I have faith in you. Don't walk anywhere without Owena, though. Consider her your bodyguard, because we can't afford to lose you."

"All right, O'Daybo. I'm on it." Eosomas looked tired, but the fire in his eyes never wavered.

"Good." Andreia glanced at Owena. "I'm going to venture out before you two leave again. I'll contact the base and get the coordinates for the Protector and Doc. We need to communicate directly with them in a few hours."

"I know. We'll sit with Berentar until you come back." Owena pulled up a stool and motioned for Eosomas to do the same. "Rest while you can, kid. You'll need it."

Andreia walked a few doors down the busy corridor before she found a small storage room, most likely once containing cleaning equipment. She slipped inside and hoped the Onotharians didn't keep surveillance equipment in the cleaning closets.

"O'Daybo to Paladin. Come in."

A few seconds of vibrations and static in her left ear preceded Roshan's calm voice. "Paladin here. Admiral Jacelon's present too."

"We've made progress. Four hundred individuals are with us, and we expect to have two hundred more within an hour. We're going by word-of-mouth and testimonials to verify dependability. This is the only way, since we don't have much time."

"We understand." Roshan sounded matter-of-fact, but something in her tone of voice made Andreia close her eyes.

"I also have news regarding your cell leader. Berentar is alive, but hanging on by a thread. I hope we haven't come too late to save him."

"Damn," Roshan said. "I'll let Jubinor know."

"I need the relay coordinates to allow us to contact the Protector and Doc."

"Use '*henshes*,' the Onotharian word for 'darling' and either 'Kellen' or 'Doc' to open communication."

Oh, great. Andreia rolled her eyes in the dark, dusty closet. "Affirmative. Will report back as soon as we're ready to commence operations."

"Good." Roshan seemed reluctant to sign off. "Please use caution, O'Daybo. I…we need you to come back in one piece."

With a sudden urge to swallow repeatedly, Andreia slumped against the wall. "I understand, Paladin. A great many things need explaining." *Will she understand what I mean?*

"I look forward to your…clarification."

Was there a hint of longing in Roshan's voice? Andreia pushed herself off the wall and slipped back into her Boyoda personality. "Very well. I will report as soon as we've established contact and are ready to engage."

"May the Gods of Gantharat be with you, O'Daybo."

"And with you."

Pushing through the crowds in the corridor, Andreia knew this was the calm before the pandemonium. In a few hours they would test the Protector's plan, and no matter the outcome, everything would change.

CHAPTER TWENTY

A ll hands, this is Admiral Jacelon. Battle stations! Secure the bulkheads." The alarms blared through the SC vessel *Gallant*. "Ready assault craft!"

Rae took her seat at the center of the *Gallant's* bridge, her eyes focused on the large view screen. They were in cloak mode, and she had to get as close to Kovos as possible. "Take us in, Lieutenant Commander D'Artansis."

"Aye, ma'am," Leanne replied smartly, and steered the *Gallant* through an elegant flight path. "ETA in fifteen minutes, Admiral."

"Very good. And the *Iktysos*?" The lead vessel in Paladin's armada was heading up her fleet of nine ships.

"She's right behind us."

Rae knew the traders were as lethal now as any warship. "So, we've commenced our operation." Rae stood up, to emphasize the importance of her words. "There's no turning back now. As soon as Kellen or O'Daybo gives the word, we'll move in."

"Yes, ma'am. We're ready." The tactical officer behind Rae sounded calm and on top of things, as expected.

"Cloaking aside, Admiral, I'm still concerned about the small armada of vessels located 60,000 kilometers from our present location. They seem to be conducting drills, and I'm not sure to what extent they're armed, but—" The operations ensign frowned slightly as she pulled up schematics on the smaller screen in front of them.

"But we need to monitor them. Stay on it, Ensign." Rae examined the position of the Onotharian ships. They were small training assault craft, possibly armed only with blanks, but it was wise to keep track of them, since their own position was vulnerable. She opened the scrambled communication channel to *Iktysos*, hiding in the asteroid belt just behind them. "Jacelon to Paladin."

"Read you loud and clear, Admiral. Go ahead."

"My long-range sensor has you in position."

"Confirmed. We are ready to engage as soon as the *Gallant* decloaks."

"Excellent. Now we wait."

"Not my strong suit, but I copy that."

Rae had to smile at how alike Kellen and Paladin were. Forged by the struggle against the occupation, they'd developed similar traits, and the way they spoke with similar accents was almost eerie. Kellen might mature into someone resembling Paladin and, no doubt, even more formidable than she was now, at only thirty-three.

"Major Egordash to Admiral Jacelon. My marines are on standby and getting eager, ma'am."

Rae half smiled at the gruff voice of the seasoned officer. "Acknowledged, Major. Keep them motivated." She rose and examined the field of asteroids before her. "They'll get their chance to fight today."

❖

"This is it!" Kellen called out to the vast crowd gathered behind her in the narrow corridor. Her voice carried easily, echoing above their heads. "I am Kellen O'Dal, your Protector of the Realm, and I've come home to help you escape this hellhole. It is time for all of Gantharat's proud fighters to return home and continue the struggle against our oppressors. Once this is accomplished, Prince Armeo O'Saral can assume the throne and commence his rightful path as leader of our free world."

Stunned silence followed her booming voice. Kellen knew there were doubters amongst the weathered rebels, but she didn't avert her eyes. Instead she let her gaze fall on every face within sight, challenging them to try her.

"The Protectors were all killed!" a man called out.

"I hid, with the prince, for several years."

"How do we know you're not lying?" A woman closer to Kellen glowered at her.

"She's telling the truth. I recognize her from the broadcasts a few lunar-months ago. Don't you?" Another woman, younger, elbowed those around her. They looked like "newbies," as Bellish referred to those who'd arrived less than two years ago.

"You've seen her?"

"And the prince?"

"Where is he?"

"Where are his parents?"

"Dead?"

The questions rained down on Kellen and didn't give her any opportunity to answer.

Bellish hollered over the many raised voices, "I vouch for her. I dare anyone here to question my allegiance!" She'd climbed up on Corgan's back and now was a head taller than everyone else. "We have an unprecedented opportunity for freedom, with backup from the outside. We've never had this good a chance to outsmart and overpower the Onotharians. Hear out this woman, our Protector. She brings information of new allies, of real hope."

The crowd stilled, and Kellen took a deep breath before she continued. "I bring good news, which most of you may be unaware of. The Supreme Constellations battleships are waiting by the Onotharian borders. They need to know that our freedom fighters are rescued and back on duty, ready to assist when they launch their attack on our oppressors. They will apply the same principles we've always followed: to cause as little collateral damage as possible. We will *not* become like our tyrants. If we do, we might as well surrender. And I know you all, I'm one of you, and as a Gantharian Protector of the Realm, and also as a rebel fighter, I will never give up!"

Seconds of dead silence passed until a few people at the front began to clap. Soon the corridors thundered with cheers, foot-stomping, and more applause. "Protector! Protector! Protector!" the crowd chanted in unison. Kellen felt her eyes begin to tear up, but forced the emotions back: she had no time for sentimental reactions now. Granted, they weren't within sight of the few pieces of surveillance equipment, but soon enough the guards would know something was up. She raised her hands for silence, and eventually the ever-growing group of rebels quieted.

"I need your trust, since we're working with a team on Vaksses. I can contact them, and you must act only on my mark. Understood?" Kellen let her eyes scan the faces of the ones closest to her. "Corgan and

Bellish will help you form two groups, which they will lead, so make sure your teams are equally strong. We have the element of surprise on our side, but we have no weapons."

"Is that right? Are we to serve as laser-fodder?" a man in the first row asked, not sarcastically, but matter-of-factly, as if he found the idea reasonable. Dressed in extremely tattered clothes, he had obviously been a prisoner for a very long time.

"No, sir," Kellen replied, shaking her head. "No one is to sacrifice himself. We'll have plenty of backup fire to divert the guards. Believe me. We'll get out of this place." She raised an eyebrow. "Unless anyone wants to stay?"

A resounding "no" echoed through the corridors.

"You convinced them, and that's just what we needed," Bellish murmured in Kellen's ear. "Your status and charisma rallied them. Good job, Protector."

"Call me Kellen, Bellish. We're all equals here." Kellen steadied a slightly wobbly Mikael, who stared at the crowd with moist eyes. "I need you on Bellish's team, Mikael. Are you up for it?"

"Yes. Yes, of course. I want off this godforsaken asteroid right now."

"Well, you may have to wait a bit longer," Kellen said with a faint smile, "but you'll see your daughter soon."

"I pray you're right, Kellen."

Bellish and Corgan moved with impressive speed through the tunnels, with a group of other elders whom the others prisoners trusted completely. Quickly they divided the incarcerated rebels into two enormous teams. Everyone carefully avoided the security equipment near the exit tunnel, and Bellish told Kellen they could reach every part of the asteroid prison anyway, since it was built around a circular, multi-level corridor. "There's just one more thing we need to take care of," Bellish said, her face serious. "The prisoners on the minus three."

"What?" Kellen didn't understand. "What's the minus three?"

"The cells there are locked. And as far as I know, sixteen people are there right now, on death by starvation."

"Oh, Gods." Kellen hadn't forgotten about the cruel punishment, but somehow hadn't thought to ask. "We need to rescue them and possibly carry them out of here when it's time."

"How do we break the doors down?" Corgan joined them, his

expression worried. "We've tried before, but the guards punished all of us."

Kellen thought about his words. "You mean, when you opened the doors, the guards entered the prison?"

"Yes."

Kellen smiled broadly. "Then that's just what we need to do. I had a different set of plans to get their attention, but rescuing the starving prisoners will do even better."

"But, Protector, it'll put you in danger." Corgan shook his head. "I should go, and Doc—"

"Doc will go," Kellen assured him, "and so will I. We need twenty more, young and strong, who can carry the locked-up prisoners to safety. Give me two minutes to collaborate with the Vaksses team."

"Very well, Protector."

"Doc, are you all set?" Kellen asked.

"Yes, and I'll help find twenty volunteers. Come on, Corgan, you can show me."

As the two men walked into the crowd, Kellen moved to the side and placed her left hand over her ear, to make it possible to hear the transmission. "*Henshes*, O'Daybo. Kellen to Vaksses team. Come in."

At first she heard only silence, not even static, but eventually a faint voice came through her earpiece, rerouted via the Merealian Mountain camp. "…to Kovos team. I repeat, O'Daybo to Kovos team."

"Kellen here. We're approximately forty-five minutes from achieving our first goal. How does it look at your end?" Kellen pressed her hand tighter to her ear to be able to hear, because of the poor quality of their connection.

"We have around six hundred people ready to go at a moment's notice." O'Daybo sounded sure. "One of Paladin's team members helped us. The message is out, and we've devised a new plan to get the guards' attention. Be sure to watch for infiltrators."

"Affirmative, O'Daybo. Is forty-five minutes doable for you?" Kellen had to admire her performance so far.

"Yes, I believe so. Let's signal each other in forty minutes and synchronize with Paladin and Jacelon."

"Affirmative," Kellen repeated. "I'll get my people in position. Kellen out."

"O'Daybo, over and out."

Kellen waited ten seconds. "Kellen to Jacelon."

"Jacelon here. Go ahead, Kellen." Rae sounded as if she was standing right next to her, and the underlying love in her wife's voice made her voice catch a little.

"I'm going to need MEDEVAC for at least sixteen, perhaps more, Gantharians once we commence operations, Admiral."

"People injured already?"

"No. These are prisoners sentenced to death by starvation, Rae." More emotion than she'd planned crept into Kellen's voice. *It could've been me.* "I don't know what state they're in. We'll carry them out, but they'll probably need medical attention immediately. Which ship will serve as a medical vessel?"

"One of Paladin's traders has the ability to provide for seventy-five injured people. All the other ships can take twenty-five with minor injuries, but from the way it sounds, we need to move Paladin's ship to the front. Good call, Kellen."

Kellen checked her chronometer, which she'd managed to smuggle in with Doc's medical equipment, along with a small set of tools, which she relied on now. "We have thirty-eight minutes to get in place before we contact Vaksses again. We'll also signal you when the time comes, so you can move into position."

"I'll take the fleet farther into the asteroid belt right away. We need to be as close as possible, but still avoid premature detection."

"Very well." Kellen squeezed her eyes shut. "Good luck, Rae. In half an hour, then."

"Half an hour. Rae out."

The silence in her ear ignited Kellen's battle mode. She turned to Corgan, who stood a few steps away. "Let's put our plans into action. We're going to need several bottles of your powder and rocks to ignite it. They'll give us another element of surprise."

Corgan looked at Kellen with something that resembled admiration, and nodded slowly. "Yes, Protector. I'm beginning to understand your plan."

"Good." Kellen placed her hand gently on the man's skinny shoulder. "It's time to finally get you and the others out of here."

❖

Andreia ran down the corridor toward the heavily guarded exit. Blinking lights and alarms accompanied her flight, and she suddenly recalled similar circumstances in the Onotharian Headquarters. But instead of being chased by the guards, she was now leading several hundred rebels, and for a moment she feared she might trip and fall, and ultimately be trampled to death.

"*Henshes*. O'Daybo to Kovos's team. O'Daybo to Jacelon! Move in! Move in!" she yelled, willing her earpiece to transmit her actions. "We're going to break out in less than five minutes."

"Jacelon here. Ships deployed. I repeat. Ships deployed!"

Andreia clutched a crude metal bar, broken off one of the beds, knowing they had less to work with than the Kovos team. They would have to use brute force to overpower the armed guards.

Owena ran next to her, with a grim expression and similarly armed. Her black hair fluttered behind her like the wings of a boyoda, and Andreia knew she would take out anyone standing in their way.

"Halt! Back off. I said, back off!" a guard yelled, panic in his eyes at the approaching crowds homing in on him from two directions. He fired at the ceiling, and smoke, as well as the smell of singed building material, filled Andreia's nostrils. Next to her Owena growled, and before the young man could aim properly, the commander was airborne.

"Argh!" Owena slammed into the guard. His plasma-pulse rifle went off again, spraying an arc of fire along the ceiling and down the wall behind him. Owena pivoted and kicked out her right leg, and the weapon clattered to the floor. Owena grabbed for it and pushed him down with her arm over his throat. "Stay still," she hissed. "Be a clever boy and just *lie there!*"

"Come on!" Andreia called, trying to project her voice over the noise. She let go of her bar and took the weapon from Owena. "I'll need this." Raising the heavy rifle, she aimed for the base of the arch that led into the exit tunnel. Noise at the far end of it indicated that the remaining guards were now on the move. Andreia fired twice, both shots accurate. The arch ignited in a cascade of sparks, and smoke billowed all around the exit.

Pleased, knowing the fire and smoke would confuse the approaching guards and also inhibit their vision, Andreia positioned herself between the enemy and the rebels behind her. Suddenly it was all so clear to her.

This is my fate. This is why I had to be Boyoda. I was meant to be here, this minute, this instant. Andreia made sure the rifle was ready, set to heavy stun. If she could avoid taking lives unnecessarily, she would.

Carelessly, with the cocky attitude of being in total command for so long, the Onotharians barged through the smoke and into the larger area just inside. Andreia let the plasma-pulse beam touch them all, making sure it knocked all six guards unconscious.

Suddenly, a distinct tremor under her feet made her stumble forward. A series of muted explosions created a traveling roar, as if a mythical monster had launched an attack against the asteroid.

"Jacelon." Andreia grinned. Their backup was right on time.

"Owena, Eosomas, hand the weapons you've secured to the less trigger-happy. Let's move out."

Andreia picked her way through the debris, which was all that remained of the arch, and proceeded into the tunnel. The small green light from her rifle lit the way, and she could vaguely make out the half-open metal doors in front of them. She kept her rifle raised and moved to the side, peering through the opening. She saw no one, but knew there were maintenance people who might well be armed. Prepared to take no risk, she stuck her rifle through the door and moved along the wall to avoid potential fire.

When it failed to come, she stepped through carefully. "Keep close and watch out," she said to Owena and Eosomas behind her. "How are we doing with the ones that can't walk? We need to evacuate Berentar."

"Two trustworthy rebels are carrying him. Last I saw, he wasn't doing too well, O'Daybo." Eosomas sounded worried, but his eyes were sharp. "I think—"

"Not so fast," a cold voice said next to them. "I knew you were up to something, but I didn't think you'd have this much power."

Andreia stared with dismay at the man from their room, the one who'd taken too many rations. He pointed a small, plump weapon at her, and she knew it would be all over for her if he fired. These illegal magma-blasters were common among criminals and easy to hide on one's body.

"Damn! I should've trusted my instincts about him," Owena growled. "I should've known."

"Now we know." Andreia lowered her rifle and bent over as if to place it on the floor. "How do you think you can hold hundreds of rebels at bay with one rifle?" She was deliberately scornful. "Some may be more than willing to sacrifice themselves, and then you'll probably be lynched."

"I can hold you long enough to move you back inside the door and lock it." The man, obviously an Onotharian in disguise, looked suspiciously confident, with a smug expression that made her wary. Andreia was now almost kneeling and knew she wouldn't get another chance. People might get hurt, but no way would she allow him to close the door on the rebels. It was made of an impenetrable metal alloy, and without knowing the codes, they might not be able to force it open.

Andreia gripped her weapon firmly, but instead of aiming at the Onotharian spy, she swung it against his now-stunned face. Hitting him hard, she made him drop his weapon before he could fire.

He cried out and fell to his knees, blood streaming down his face from his broken nose. As she'd anticipated, he hadn't worked alone. Weapons sounded in the crowd farther back, and screams revealed that they'd hit their targets. Andreia knew she couldn't do anything from her position other than make sure the door stayed open.

"Owena!" she yelled, and tossed herself forward, her rifled raised. "Keep an eye on this one."

"Sure thing." Owena stood with her weapon aimed at the Onotharian spy.

Andreia shot the control device on the outside panel, then gazed through the new smoke emanating from the door. Two metal chairs stood to the left, and she grabbed one. "We need to jam the doors!" Eosomas and another man seemed to understand her intentions and took the chairs from her, slamming them against the door to remove their legs.

"Shove them under the doors," Eosomas gasped. "If anyone locks them, we're doomed." He bent down and pushed a chair leg under the left door, kicking it to jam it securely. "There."

The loud, whistling sound of plasma-pulse fire still resounded within the tunnel behind them, but it had lessened, and Andreia could only hope there weren't too many casualties. *Why didn't I realize that if there were spies there must also be weapons stashed inside?* It wasn't productive to second-guess herself, and she tried to shake her regrets.

Loud cheers echoed from behind her, and the message soon

traveled to the front of the large group. "The infiltrators have been taken down," Eosomas said.

"How many dead? Injured?" Andreia dared hardly ask.

Eosomas turned to the men farther into the group, repeating the question. After a moment the reply came, which nearly drove Andreia to her knees. "Twenty-six wounded—of them, eight badly. Four dead."

"Gods of Gantharat," she whispered.

Owena stepped up to her side. "All right, people," she called, to drown out the murmur among the rebels. "We've come this far, and now it's time to move on. There are still more guards, possibly even more spies, to deal with, so stay sharp and on your guard."

"And then what?" a woman shouted from the back.

"We wait for the backup."

"Unless we're dead already," a man muttered, but quieted as people nearby glared at him.

Andreia walked toward the next exit, a barred door that was only half closed, and hoped they didn't encounter any more surprises.

"Right about now would be a good time to break through from the other side," Owena muttered as she walked next to Andreia. Her long decisive stride indicated that she was a martial arts master, and her eyes had become several shades darker since the fighting began.

"They're here. We felt them." Andreia carefully stuck her head out the door, but didn't see anyone. Frowning at the empty corridor, which seemed too good to be true, she motioned Owena to follow her and for Eosomas to keep the others behind them quiet.

Andreia and Owena crept out into the corridor, weapons raised, aimed at the ceiling. "Any risk of automated backup systems against fugitives?" Owena whispered.

"Not that I know of," Andreia said, and shook her head. "This facility was operated manually, with surveillance, and also with special facilities for…interrogation." She swallowed back the bile that rose at the thought of the atrocities her people had committed. "Since they consider the prisoners here high-ranking rebels, their methods to make them talk are…" Andreia couldn't finish.

"Atrocious?"

"Yes."

They moved down the corridor with a large crowd of rebels, surrounded by an eerie silence. They were almost at the door when a deafening roar sounded, and an unforeseen force lifted them like a giant's hand. Andreia lost all sense of what was up or down until her body slammed into the floor.

❖

Roshan moved past the row of marines who held twelve Onotharian guards at gunpoint. "Is this what's left of the entrance?" she asked Jacelon, who strode beside her. "That was quite some blast."

"Yes, but apparently necessary. The doors were made of a ceramic-grid armored alloy that required a four-spread plasma charge."

"I can smell it." Roshan hoisted her rifle and pushed through smoke and debris, eager to find Andreia. The smoke coming from behind the shattered doors still prevented them from seeing properly, and Roshan made sure her plasma-pulse rifle was set to heavy stun. She didn't want to accidentally kill one of their own.

"Over there," Jacelon said, advancing right behind her.

Roshan glanced over her shoulder. Four marines were taking up the rear. "What?"

"There." Jacelon pointed in a ninety-degree direction. "The side corridor. I thought I saw someone, or something, on the floor."

Roshan had completely missed the narrow corridor to their right. Noticing faint shadows on the floor about twenty meters inside, she wanted to rush forward and search for Andreia among the fallen bodies obscured by the smoke. Biting the inside of her cheek, Roshan harnessed her gut reaction and advanced in the cautious manner that had kept her alive the last twenty-five years. The ventilation system was still intact, and as the smoke began to evaporate, Roshan spied a reddish, curly head, belonging to a much-too-still form on the floor. *Andreia!*

Roshan dashed toward her, weapon still ready. As she came closer and the last of the smoke disappeared, she saw many more people slowly begin to move on the floor farther down the corridor. They pressed their hands to their heads and staggered to their feet, moaning.

"Cover me," Roshan said to Jacelon, who responded with a brief nod. Her face was serious and the steely gray in her eyes unwavering.

Using her shoulder-strap, Roshan pushed the rifle onto her back, throwing herself to her knees next to Andreia's still body. Next to her, Owena sat up, grimacing as she reached for her weapon. "Admiral?"

"You're safe, Commander. We'll have you out of here soon. How are you feeling?"

Roshan listened to Owena assure the admiral that she was fine. She leaned down and brushed Andreia's hair away from her pale face. Her eyes were closed, and it took Roshan a few heart-rending seconds to realize that Andreia was breathing. *Oh, Gods!* Roshan felt for Andreia's pulse, and to her relief it was strong and even. "Hey, you. Andr...O'Daybo? Can you open your eyes for me? It's Paladin." Struggling to maintain her composure, she leaned closer, her lips just above Andreia's ear, whispering. "Please, open your eyes. Andreia. It's Roshan. Come on!"

Andreia was still for another worrisome moment, and then she moaned and turned her head. "Ro?"

"Yes, it's me, Paladin," Roshan said, louder, and hoped Andreia would catch on despite being woozy after the blast. "Can you sit up? Are you injured?"

"Eh, no...I'm all right. I just...Oh!" Andreia sat up too quickly and slumped to one side. She leaned heavily against Roshan, who steadied her.

"Careful there. Not too fast." Roshan looked around. Most of the people were standing now, except two of the older ones. Some of Roshan's crew had arrived while she was leaning over Andreia and were now acting as medics.

Andreia finally stood, her knees sagging a bit, and she leaned against the wall, clutching her left elbow.

"I thought you said—" Roshan moved closer and reached for Andreia's injured arm.

"I'll be fine, Paladin." She looked at Roshan pensively, her eyes pale, no doubt from fatigue and pain, and she pulled out of reach. "I can manage."

Roshan tried to convey more than she could say at this time with her gaze. "I know you can," she said softly. "I...I was worried about you. Very."

Andreia stopped rubbing her elbow and tipped her head back, squinting up at Roshan. "Were you? I mean, were you really?"

"Yes." Though this was not the time or the place, it was the simple truth within a not-so-simple reality. "Yes. I was."

With her arms folded, Andreia nodded slowly, a thoughtful

expression on her face. "I'm glad you're here. All of you." Something caught her eyes. "Oh, look." Now a lot steadier on her legs, she brushed past Roshan. "Eosomas? Is he going to be all right?"

Roshan saw a man lying on a narrow stretcher carried by two of her crew. "Berentar!" She hurried to his side and stood next to Andreia, who'd taken the cell leader's hand in hers.

"Didn't I tell you, Berentar?" Andreia said, her voice trembling. "I said she'd come."

"Yes. You did." Berentar looked up, surprising Roshan with a steady gaze in his weathered face. "Jubinor?"

"Is back at base camp, working as our coordinator. Once you're on my vessel, you can contact him. We just need to have a doctor look at you first."

"Fine. Now, go and do your job, rebels."

"Yes, sir." Roshan smiled. "See you later."

As her crew members carried Berentar toward the exit, Roshan studied the situation. The rebels were moving out in a steady stream, and she realized that more of her ships must have docked at the asteroid. "Let's get out of here. I have to get the *Iktysos* ready for Kovos. We're using it as the hospital ship, and from what I've heard from Kellen, they need us desperately."

"I'd imagine so." Andreia looked ready to fall over. "I can't understand why I'm so tired."

"That plasma charge almost blasted you out into space. I mean, it hit you first, so you took the brunt of the impact. It was like having ten angry maeshas kick you."

"I think that sums it up." Andreia smiled faintly. "Still, I've been on physically more demanding missions than this. I just don't get it."

Roshan had her own ideas why this mission had been more taxing for Andreia, but couldn't risk talking about it here. "I have to get back to the bridge. I know you're supposed to…Hey!" Roshan caught Andreia when she staggered to the right. "I was just going to suggest we let our doctor look you over. Now I insist."

"All right."

Roshan had expected Andreia to argue, but when she didn't, Roshan was really worried.

CHAPTER TWENTY-ONE

Kellen moved lithely through the barely lit corridor of level minus three. The doors to the cells were black, with an irregular pattern of rust. The men and women Corgan and Bellish had chosen to assist them in their rescue attempt hurried behind her with all four bottles full of the special combustive powder tucked in their waistbands. Kellen hoped they wouldn't need them, but was fairly sure they might.

She stopped by the last door, unlike the other doors she'd seen on Kovos, and reached under her shirt. Pulling out the pouch Doc had lent her, she removed a small item encased in synthetic-humanoid tissue, which was the only way to get it past the security checkpoints. Kellen inserted the small item into the lock and pressed a sensor. A buzzing sound, followed by a faint click a while later, and the door opened an inch. "I've unlocked this one, Ayahliss. You remember how I showed you before?"

Ayahliss nodded. "I'll open the others while you start helping the poor devils out."

"Good. Hurry!"

"Like a flash." Ayahliss grinned and ran to the next door, the instrument clutched against her chest.

Kellen and Corgan pushed the door open and found the room pitch black and reeking of urine. "Hello," Kellen called, making sure her voice was gentle. "We've come to get you out. We won't hurt you."

"Hello?" a raspy, weak voice said from the far end.

"We need light in here. Cover your eyes." Corgan took a bottle from his belt. "Here we go." He clicked two small stones with his right hand, and Kellen had to admire how swiftly he set the powder on fire.

The room brightened, but at first Kellen couldn't see anyone. In one corner stood a bucket, most likely responsible for the horrible stench. Then she saw a small bundle of blankets in the corner, which she realized must be the prisoner's bed. "Bed" was too kind a word, for it was two or three blankets directly on the floor. Kellen hurried over to the corner and fell to her knees. "My name is Kellen. We have to hurry. Let me help you up."

"Kellen..." Corgan said warningly.

"I know." Kellen didn't look away. She peeled the blanket back, and what she saw brought instant tears to her eyes. A small woman, it was impossible to judge her age, trembled under the blanket, her eyes squeezed shut. Her long, blond hair was mashed to her head, and she was beyond thin. "Oh, Gods...Come here." Kellen didn't care if the woman smelled; she just wanted her out of there. She reached down and lifted her. "Corgan, one of the clean blankets?"

"Here." Corgan placed the blanket he'd carried slung across his shoulders over the woman. "I'm Corgan. Who are you, child?"

Child? Kellen looked at the almost-weightless burden in her arms. Now when Corgan held the bottle-lamp closer, she saw that this woman wasn't very old.

"I'm Eren," she whispered, her voice clearly unused for a long time.

"Come on then, Eren," Kellen said. "Some people will carry you upstairs. We're leaving."

Eren closed her eyes and nodded, apparently too stunned to say another word. Outside, Kellen handed her over to another woman, who tucked the blanket tenderly around her. "I've got you, dear."

"We need help!" voices called out, and Kellen saw Doc enter a room four doors down. She hurried over and ducked her head as she entered the room. Three other people were already in there, so she stopped just inside the door. "What's wrong, Doc?"

"We have a problem." Doc's voice was strained. "This is...a whole new version of Onotharian cruelty."

Kellen frowned, and as she pushed between the two men who'd entered the room first, she heard one of them murmur a Gantharian prayer. Kneeling next to Doc, Kellen looked at what had to be a preview of hell. "Doc—"

"I know. I know."

"Can you do anything?"

He ran his medical scanner over the shivering bundle on the blankets. "For her, perhaps. For the child, I don't know."

"I have...breastfed...him." The woman in the death cell was breathing fast and shallow. "I know...I have no nourishment to offer him. But fluid. At least."

"She's right." Doc scanned the baby again. "What's your name?"

"Illina."

"Illina, how old is your child?"

"I'm not...sure." Several breaths later she continued. "No sense of time. Maybe five days? A week?"

"You gave birth to him here, on your own. I can see from all the dried blood on your blankets. You're a brave woman. Let's get you out." Doc reached for the child, but the woman held on to her baby and stared at them with blue-rimmed eyes. "No."

A tall man stepped forward. "I can carry both of them. Hold on to your baby with one hand and me with the other, all right?"

The woman nodded slowly and raised her free arm, then clung to the man's neck. Another man tucked a clean blanket around them as they walked outside.

"We'd better hurry, even though we need to be careful with these people," Kellen said. "I'm sure the Onotharians monitor their death-cells so they know when their victims die. They probably have people on a waiting list for this sort of punishment."

"Yes, come on, before we have company we're not ready for."

They managed to get six more people out before they found a deceased older man, then two other corpses—of a boy and a young woman. They rolled the remains into blankets and put them on an unhinged door, carried by several individuals.

Altogether they had rescued twelve live individuals, plus one unexpected male infant. Kellen gave orders to ascend through the narrow circular staircase, and they reached the main level where most of the prisoners were waiting in complete silence. As the men and women who carried a precious burden walked through the crowd, a low hum began and stayed mellow, out of respect. Soon, Kellen recognized the words of a famous and popular hymn. She remembered writing it while in the Academy of Pilots and knew that nobody was aware that she had composed it.

The light in Your eyes
Brings glory to our soul.
We look with worship unto Them
Who keep us whole.
Our faith in our Gods
Is eternal and true.
Through prayers in the night
We will live anew.

Kellen sang in a low voice as she hurried to their vantage point just outside the monitored area. Detecting a faint rustling sound, she was afraid the guards were on their way. The hymn faded after the third verse, and then Kellen was sure she heard steps approaching from the tunnel.

"Light up!" Her voice boomed in the corridor, and she heard the clicking of hundreds of stones. The sparks ignited the powder, which illuminated the tunnel. Kellen held two bottles in her left hand, the walls of each bottle containing the steadily glowing powder.

The sound of clattering boots escalated, and Kellen tried to estimate how many guards approached. She knew that Kovos wasn't as heavily supervised as Vaksses, but the ones who worked here were heavily armed. She feared they would lose people at the front.

When the first guard appeared at the tunnel exit, just outside the detector arch, Kellen clutched the ignited bottles, but knew she had to get all of the Onotharians inside before they could launch their surprise attack.

The guards, obviously sure that the rebels posed no threat, stepped through the arch one after another until all eight were inside and stared at them.

"Now!" Kellen shouted, and suddenly burning bottles hit the guards from all directions. They backed up, but they had moved too far inside and couldn't reach the arch. Caught against a wall, they tried to raise their weapons and fire, but the bottles flew at them, several at a time. The flames spread and soon reached their boots, rose, and caught on their uniform pants. They stomped and tried to extinguish the flames with their hands.

"Come on! Disarm them!" Kellen ran forward, her right arm stretched out and her left in a fist with her elbow sticking out. She stepped through the flames, mindless of how they licked at her thin soles and pants, and yanked a weapon out of a guard's hands. He was young, merely a boy, and stared at her with eyes huge with fear. Kellen pushed him, and he landed on his back far away from the fire, where more rebels made sure he had no more weapons on him.

The bottles burned bright, but also fast once they'd crashed to the floor. The first line of rebels stomped out the remaining flames and moved forward to disarm the guards, several of whom managed to fire their weapons, and Kellen saw two of the rebels at the far left fall. Anger shot through her and she leapt forward, twirled in the air, and slammed the outside of her foot on the closest Onotharian's chin. She felt his neck crack, and when he slumped to the ground, she grabbed his weapon. The fire on the floor had burned out, but the remains of the powder were still melting the soles of her shoes. Taught to ignore pain while in battle, Kellen kept going. She fired at the base of the arch, and sparks rained through the air.

Tremors shook the floor, and at first Kellen was surprised that her gunfire could have such repercussions; then she realized that backup was arriving. Her heart hammered, and she pushed forward, grunting as two other guards slammed into her. Breathless, she used the plasma-pulse rifle to push them far enough away to hold them at gunpoint. Her blood simmered, igniting every cell in her body, until all she knew was the battle and the thirst for revenge. She acted purely by instinct when she used the back end of the rifle against the guards' temples, quickly, first one thud and then another. They fell to the floor, listless, perhaps dead, and at that moment, she didn't care.

"Kellen! We need to get through the outer chambers while the doors are open!" Doc shouted next to her. "Run!"

Still operating on instinct, Kellen jumped over the Onotharians' fallen bodies and dashed through the arch. The area beyond it was empty, but rebels smelling freedom filled it rapidly. Ahead of them loomed two large metal doors, one of them open a fraction. Kellen pushed through it with her weapon ready, set to kill. She'd gone into the fight with the same creed as the rest of the rebels, to avoid harming civilians, but the enemies here weren't soft targets…yet the face of the young Onotharian she'd spared and pushed out of the way said otherwise.

"Careful," Doc yelled as Kellen rushed toward another, larger door, which she surmised was the outer one. "I just felt the ship dock. They may blast their way in here. Don't get caught in the explosion."

"I won't," Kellen growled, adrenalin pumping and intent on seeing this mission through. Armeo's future and safety depended on it; it was her duty. Hearing faint scraping on the other side of the massive door, she ducked to the side. She couldn't contact their backup, but she could get out of the way.

"Stay away, everyone!" Doc yelled, and with Corgan's and Bellish's help, he kept the crowd under control. Kellen couldn't see Mikael, but hoped he was nearby. *He has to be. We can't lose him now.*

The blast echoed through the large cave and forced many of the older rebels to their knees, though by standing close to the wall, Kellen didn't feel the impact as much as some of the others did. Smoke billowed out for a moment, but ventilation and the cave's height made it disappear quickly.

Marines streamed through the hole in the door, lining up before the tattered crowd, weapons raised. Kellen surmised they looked more alien to the Gantharians than they realized, with their black survival outfits and elaborate headgear. Stepping forward she spoke to the closest one. "I'm Commander Kellen O'Dal. Protector of the Realm. Verify this with Admiral Jacelon."

"I don't have to, ma'am. I'd recognize you anywhere. Good to see you alive."

Doc stepped up and stood next to Kellen. "We have casualties that need to be evacuated first. Several of them—"

Several screams interrupted him, and the marine lieutenant aimed his weapon at the source of the noise.

"Don't even try!" someone yelled, and the crowd parted as a young woman pushed an Onotharian soldier in front of her, locking his arms behind him. "This one tried to get away. I think they have several emergency exits with shuttles waiting, just in case," Ayahliss said, and pushed the young man to his knees. Kellen recognized him as the guard she'd spared earlier who looked barely twenty years old.

"You're scaring him," Doc said calmly. "You can let go of him now, before you fracture his arms."

Ayahliss glared suspiciously at the pale boy. "All right," she muttered, and released him.

He slumped to the floor, clutching his left shoulder.

"I take that back," Doc said. "I think you, or someone else, broke his clavicle."

Ayahliss looked pleased, but Kellen sighed inwardly. The girl was dangerous, half-taught, diving into situations with more motivation than calculation.

The marine lieutenant called for medics, and people in civilian attire from Paladin's ships entered and spread out through the crowd with stretchers.

"Kellen." A hand on Kellen's shoulder made her jump and grip her weapon tighter. Rae stood next to her, her eyes glistening with unspoken emotions. "You pulled it off against such incredible odds."

"I had help."

"I realize that. These are quite some people, these rebels. I'm impressed with how they've kept a kind of command structure within the prisons. A survival thing, I suppose."

"This is Corgan and Bellish O'Gesta, the unofficial leaders among the rebels and other incarcerated people here. Corgan, Bellish, this is Admiral Rae Jacelon, of the SC. Rae is also my wife."

"Nice to meet you, especially under these circumstances." Rae pressed a hand to her chest and bowed slightly. "You won't be here much longer. Once the medics have carried the injured and sick onto their ship, the traders waiting outside will carry you home."

"Thank you, Admiral. We can never thank you enough."

"No need. This mission is purely Kellen's plan. Without her..." Rae shrugged.

Kellen felt a tug at her sleeve and turned to Ayahliss, who'd walked up to her. "Yes?"

"The old man over there, I thought you had some vested interest in his well-being. He looks like he's going to faint."

Kellen snapped her eyes to the right, where Mikael O'Landha was swaying while trying to remain on his feet. "Help me." She rushed over to him, with Ayahliss right behind her, and caught Mikael just as his knees collapsed. She lifted him with ease while Ayahliss guided his head, which seemed too heavy for him.

Bellish met them halfway, frowning. "Oh, Gods. How's he doing?"

"*He's* doing all right, thank you," Mikael said huskily, but with definite sarcasm. "I'm just a bit tired. I'm an old man, remember. And human. We aren't as strong as you Gantharians, you know."

"Human?" Rae came up to them.

"This is Mikael O'Landha," Kellen introduced. "We know his daughter," she added in a warning voice. They still had to be careful when they talked about people's real names.

Rae seemed speechless. "Yes, we do," she finally said. "We do. And I'm so glad to meet you, Mikael."

The man, obviously fatigued, nodded and barely smiled.

"We need a stretcher over here," Doc called out when he spotted the medics. "You need fluids and a nutritional infusion, Mikael."

"Very well," he whispered. "If you insist."

After Kellen placed Mikael carefully on a stretcher, she patted his arm reassuringly before they carried him away. "We'll see you soon."

❖

Kellen boarded the *Gallant* with Rae and entered the captain's quarters with a sigh of relief.

"Hello there." Rae ducked under Kellen's outstretched arm and stepped close. "You're back safe. Thank the stars," Rae said with a small catch in her voice. "I missed you." She embraced Kellen with warmth.

"I stink."

"Yes, you do, but I don't care. Honestly, I don't." Rae looked up at her. "I don't think you understand what you just pulled off here. I was facing a future without the woman I love more than anything, and to know she was in the same hellhole that we've both had nightmares about almost drove me crazy."

"But now I'm here." Kellen kissed Rae's lips, as always enthralled by their softness. "And so are you. Your timing was perfect."

"I rushed here from Vaksses, where we were successful too, by the way."

Kellen cupped Rae's cheeks and kissed her lingeringly. "I love you. Thank you for carrying out your part of the mission with such good judgment."

"You're welcome. Why don't you clean up and put on some fresh clothes?"

"I think I will." Kellen began to unfasten the coarse shirt, glad to get rid of the itchy garment.

"I'll be on the bridge. We should be able to leave within fifteen minutes. Paladin's transporter and carriers are swallowing all the prisoners faster than predicted."

"All right." Kellen began unfastening her pants while she walked toward the small bathroom. It would be wonderful to be clean again. Now that she'd had time to calm down, the foul smell from her clothes and her hair really bothered her. "See you in a minute."

In the bathroom she shed her last garment and entered the ionic-resonance shower, where the grime, soot, and sweat disappeared like magic, and small puffs of disinfectant made sure no superficial foreign bodies would bother her. She ached all over, but being back with Rae, fighting this battle side by side, was enough to re-energize her.

Now all they had to do to call this mission a success was deliver the rebels to their homes. Kellen hoped that as many of the resistance members as possible could return to fighting status right away. The Supreme Constellations forces would especially need their guidance around Ganath, the Onotharians' stronghold.

Kellen stretched and rolled her shoulders, first both and then one at a time, continuously, until the almost meditative exercise calmed her. She had to stay sharp while performing her duties, or she'd risk getting herself or, worse, someone else killed.

CHAPTER TWENTY-TWO

A s they stood close together in the small elevator onboard
the *Iktysos,* Andreia was mildly annoyed with Roshan,
who had insisted on asking the doctor why she was so affected by
her assignment. The doctor had assured them that it was a minor case
of smoke inhalation and stress. He handed her an alveoli-cleansing
inhaler, and told her to use it three times daily for the upcoming week,
to cure the smoke-inhalation damage. Now they were on their way to
Roshan's quarters.

"Did you have to sound like I was an insolent child, set on defying
the doctor and not knowing what was in my best interests?" Andreia
sighed. "I'm perfectly able to take care of myself."

"You're stubborn and you ignore your health sometimes." Roshan
pressed her lips together. "I had to be sure—"

"Of what? You can see that I'm tired, which is hardly a surprise. I
haven't had any sleep in days!"

"I needed to know if you were going to collapse again."

"I didn't collapse! I staggered, stumbled even, because, one, I'm
tired; two, I'd been blasted to hell only minutes before; and three, I'd
inhaled more smoke than if the Sororra tobacco industry had gone up
in flames!"

Roshan stared at her for a moment, then smiled slowly. "A slight
exaggeration?"

"Only slight." Andreia had to smile back as she slumped against
the elevator wall. "I really *am* tired. What I wouldn't give for some
misostena tea. I haven't had it in years…but I still remember how your
mother used to make it for us."

After a brief silence, Roshan's eyes softened. "Yes, she did, didn't
she? She learned to love it during her travels and imported it from the

SC. It's from Corma, I believe. Maybe Commander D'Artansis has some."

"Guess it would be a little too much to ask." Andreia grinned. "This is our floor."

The elevator door opened, and they stepped out into an elegant corridor with a thick black carpet, gold-plated ornaments along the ceiling, and smoky-glass stained-light fixtures.

"Wow, you do work hard at keeping up appearances, don't you?" Andreia noted. "And before you say it, so do I."

"I'm glad you realize that. Here are the quarters that I use while I travel. The captain has the more luxurious ones farther down, overlooking the bow."

Roshan opened the door and stepped back to let Andreia enter first. "Ensuite head is to your left."

"Thanks, I need it."

"So do I, but perhaps not quite so badly." Roshan walked over to a small bag sitting by the couch. "Here's your change of clothes. You need to remain O'Daybo a while yet."

"Yes, I agree. I have to return to the Onotharian HQ soon, though, and face my parents and the M'Isitors. If I stay away for more than the week I told my mother I'd be gone..." Andreia shrugged. "I'll have to really emphasize how good a catch you are, so they don't get suspicious that I was missing in action during the first SC attack."

Roshan's eyes darkened to blue-black, and Andreia wondered what she was thinking. "Will they do that? Suspect you?"

"I don't know. Think about it. They've kept things from me, vital information regarding their plans against the resistance. Why would they suddenly do that unless they were wary of my true allegiance?"

"I've thought about that too."

Andreia frowned. "You think I have cause to worry."

"I think you should be very careful when you go back."

"I promise." Andreia took the bag and headed toward the bathroom. "Is it all right if I take a nap when I'm done in there? I know I should eat, but I'm so tired." She glanced back over her shoulder. Roshan stood near the impressive blackwood desk ramrod straight, her eyes just as dark as before.

"Yes, of course. The bedroom is behind that door." She motioned to the right of the bathroom.

"Thanks." Andreia put the bag down next to the toilet and groaned when she glanced in the mirror. Her hair was completely disheveled, and she was so pale she looked almost jaundiced. As she studied the blue-black semicircles under her eyes that emphasized her fatigue, Andreia began to understand Roshan's concern better.

The ionic-resonance shower quickly removed the grime and sweat, and the smell of burned plasma and metallic alloy evaporated through the ventilation ducts. Andreia pulled a brush through her curly hair, enjoying how smooth and untangled it seemed, compared to the mess it had just been. After the ionic waves had bombarded her for five minutes, Andreia knew she was as clean as possible and stepped outside, but found no robe, which she was sure she'd packed, only a large demulcent-woven towel, which she wrapped around her. She walked out into Roshan's quarters and saw her sitting by her desk, dressed in a robe of a material similar to Andreia's towel, occupied with several handheld computers. Not wanting to disturb her, Andreia tiptoed into the small bedroom that held a narrow bed beneath a small, circular view port.

She sank down on the bed, grateful to be sitting. Her legs were heavy, and when she tried to fling them over the edge she barely made it. Tucking the towel around her, she curled up on her side and closed her eyes. The ship's propulsion system was on standby, roaring reassuringly far beneath her. "Mm."

❖

Checking on Andreia, Roshan was overwhelmed by mixed emotions. She was so used to controlling her feelings that being unable to focus on the documents in front of her unsettled her. She was supposed to overview the part of the Protector's plan called "Exodus," which entailed evacuating every incarcerated rebel under protection of the SC marines. Instead, with hunger stirring, Roshan watched how the faint light from the stars illuminated Andreia's golden skin. After two hours of deep sleep, she had a much healthier glow.

After entering the small bedroom, Roshan sat on the edge of the bed, her legs suddenly weak. Andreia could easily have been killed. She'd been directly in the line of fire, with Owena, but now, when they were both safe, Roshan trembled at what could have been. Exasperated at such unproductive reasoning, she straightened and was about to leave Andreia alone, when a faint moan made her hesitate.

"Andreia?" Roshan caressed Andreia's cheek as she frowned in her sleep and whimpered. "Hello, there. Wake up. You're dreaming."

"No," Andreia said. "I can't—"

"What can't you do? Look at me." As Roshan scooted closer, the towel covering Andreia slipped to the side, revealing a round, plump breast. Roshan's breath caught in her throat, and her hand moved of its own volition and held the breast gently, longingly. The warmth of it startled her, and, gasping, she let go and tried to pull the towel back up over Andreia, who'd shifted underneath and was half lying on it.

"Andreia, wake up. You'll get cold." Roshan let her hand slide along Andreia's arm, reveling in the feel of the warm, smooth skin. She leaned forward and placed a kiss on Andreia's shoulder. "Andreia?"

"Ro…"

"Yes."

"I dreamed." Andreia opened drowsy eyes and frowned at Roshan. "I dreamed I was lost. Couldn't find you."

Roshan's heart constricted at Andreia's bewilderment. "You're not lost. You're here. Safe. With me." The staccato sentence came out awkwardly, but Andreia's features softened and she smiled. White and glistening, her small teeth bit into her lower lip as she peeked up at Roshan through her eyelashes.

"I am." Andreia sat up, seemingly unaware that she was half naked. The towel now rested around her hips, and Andreia finally jerked a bit when she saw she was almost nude. "Oh."

"Oh." Roshan's mouth watered at the sight of Andreia's breasts with dark red nipples, so close. She wanted to touch Andreia so much that she moaned. Slowly, almost hypnotically, she raised her hand and touched a breast again, weighing it gently.

"Roshan," Andreia breathed. "Mm…?" Her voice quivered and her head fell back, revealing her slender neck.

"You're so damn beautiful. You're the bravest person I've ever met, and that together with your fantastic eyes…your body…" Roshan groaned and pulled Andreia to her. She couldn't have kept from kissing her if someone had paid her all of Gantharat's pure diamonite. Andreia's lips parted beneath Roshan's, and a low moan reverberated from one mouth to another. Roshan wasn't sure where it began or where it ended.

All she wanted was to keep tasting and feeling the woman she feared she'd lost. *Twice.*

"Ro," Andreia murmured through the kisses. "Ro, this is insane."

"I know." Roshan slid her tongue along Andreia's lower lip. "It's pure madness, but I can't resist you." Hot, deep kisses fueled, rather than satisfied, her rampaging emotions. Roshan's chest ached, her abdomen melted with desire, and all the lava seemed to pool between her unsteady legs. "Please, touch me." The words passed her lips before she realized what she had meant to say.

Andreia's hand hung between them, and Roshan stared at it, transfixed. Slowly, Andreia let her hand fall and gently tugged at the lapels of Roshan's robe. Roshan was eager, almost desperate, to feel Andreia's touch, and pulled at the loose knot of the belt.

"Oh..." Andreia stared at Roshan's naked chest under the robe, and then she didn't hesitate any more. Sliding both arms around Roshan, under the soft fabric of the garment, Andreia hugged her, followed by a heated kiss with a fierce battle of tongues and lips. Andreia groaned. "Gods, you feel so good. You always did."

"You never held me like this, back then," Roshan whispered against Andreia's lips. "You hugged me, as a friend, but—"

"—I wanted to do so much more." Andreia pushed the robe off Roshan's shoulders and stared at her with heavily lidded eyes. "Like this. I wanted to look at you, and touch you, *like this*." She caressed Roshan's breasts and gazed up at her. Nothing but sheer desire swam in Andreia's eyes.

"Yes." Roshan placed her hands over Andreia's and pressed harder against her heated skin. She was on fire, and the thought of the dangerous missions they'd both completed ignited even more passion. "Let me, Andreia. Please." At this point Roshan wasn't above begging. Her overwhelming lust urged her on, but her tenderness and unspoken feelings for Andreia made her stop and wait.

"Let you do what?" There was nothing coy in Andreia's voice, despite her words.

"Let me make love to you." Roshan's throat almost hurt for finally speaking the truth.

When Andreia parted her lips and ran her tongue along them, the moist line against the red fullness of the curvy mouth made Roshan cave in. She guided Andreia on her back and stroked the slight curve of her stomach, then wandered lower. Andreia's legs spread wide around Roshan's hips, as if she were trying to hold Roshan in place by hooking them around her.

"Oh, Gods, Ro…you feel so good…"

Roshan hovered over Andreia for a moment, as if suspended in time, considering her words, tasting them thoroughly. She found nothing but honesty and desire in Andreia's face. *She wants me.*

Roshan slipped her hand between Andreia's smooth, long thighs and, eventually, dipped between her swollen folds. She had dreamed of this all those years ago, then given up. To have it now was so unexpected, she couldn't believe it was actually happening.

Her fingers trembled as she explored the rich wetness and caressed sensitive tissues between Andreia's legs. Andreia's moans grew louder as Roshan teased the hooded, small ridge of nerves. She massaged it repeatedly and at the same time closed her watering mouth around one of Andreia's hard nipples, inspired to use both her tongue and teeth on it.

"Ro!" Andreia arched her back, pressing her breast farther into Roshan's mouth. "Ro…"

Roshan wanted to give Andreia the pleasure she so desired. What was more, she wanted to bury herself deep within Andreia's body, knowing if she did, she'd have no more pain, no more suffering, and no more war inside her heart.

Sliding two of her fingers inside Andreia, Roshan felt the incredibly wet velvet. The smooth tissues engulfed her, milked her fingers, and Roshan's own sex became wetter still.

A gentle nudge at her waist startled Roshan, as Andreia slid her hand out of Roshan and down her body. She anticipated the touch against her own naked skin, but nothing could have prepared her for the scorching pleasure Andreia's hand caused when it made contact. Shivering, Roshan had only one desire—to get between Andreia's thighs, enter her again, and unite them in the flesh.

"There, Ro," Andreia whispered hotly, and tugged the rest of Roshan's robe off. "I'm here. Feel me. I'm not going anywhere."

"I have to have you." Roshan didn't care if she sounded desperate or frantic. "Oh, Gods, Andreia. I need—I have to…" A red mist hung before her eyes and tinted Andreia's willing body in the same light of passion. Roshan rearranged the pillows to support Andreia, and despite her overwhelming lust, part of Roshan made sure she didn't lose touch with her heart.

"Come here," Andreia purred. Her eyes large and shiny, she gazed steadily up at her as Roshan settled between her legs. "That's it. Let me hold you…" She wrapped her legs around Roshan's hips again, and the feeling of Andreia's skin on hers nearly sent Roshan flying.

"Andreia!" Roshan pushed her hand between them and back into the abundant wetness between Andreia's legs. Finding the hard bundle of nerve endings, she ran two of her fingers up and down its little shaft.

Andreia bucked under Roshan's hand and flung her arms around her neck, then arched her back again and pressed her breasts into Roshan's. Nipples aching from the passionate embrace, Roshan growled deep in her throat. Pushing at the bed with her free hand, she managed to slip down along Andreia's sweat-soaked body. Roshan stopped when her chin touched the mound at the apex of Andreia's thighs and studied the arousing sight until it became too much for her.

Leaning down, Roshan slid her tongue along the entire length of Andreia's sex and inside the parted folds. She lapped eagerly at the wetness and, encouraged by Andreia's whimpers, increased the pressure and the intensity. The taste and the scent of the woman she'd wanted for more than two decades intoxicated her, and Roshan felt her own orgasm stir. She pressed one hand down to touch herself, and the other to enter Andreia.

"Ro, oh, for the love of the stars, Ro…" Andreia raised her hips, grinding her sex into Roshan's mouth.

Roshan sucked hard at the inner lips and the shafted clitoris, not unlike her own, but longer and larger. She milked it with her tongue, and suddenly Andreia exploded with a broken cry. Roshan kept caressing her, eased her through the orgasm with more patience than she knew she possessed. Finally Roshan heaved herself up and kissed Andreia's mouth. The long, exploring kiss shared the taste of Andreia's passion. Roshan was shivering, on the brink of release, but knew she needed direct touch to come.

As if Andreia had read her mind, she raised her knee and squeezed her leg between Roshan's. "Here, *henshes*, come against me." Andreia looked up at Roshan, supported above her by her arms, then pinched Roshan's nipples and rolled them between her fingers while Roshan rode her slender leg.

"Ah!" Roshan tumbled into a ravine of bliss and passion. "Andreia...Gods." Her body jerked and she coated Andreia's thigh.

"So sweet, so strong," Andreia sighed. "So beautiful." She pulled Roshan on top of her as her lover's arms buckled. "Here. Rest."

Roshan simply had no choice. She had to rest, since Andreia had drained her completely. Her head spun with unanswered questions and from the aftermath of the overpowering orgasm. *And now?* Roshan had hardly any energy left to consider the future. So much was uncertain, and they faced so many obstacles: the political situation, their personal history.

"Roshan? Please. Look at me?" Andreia's voice, breathless and yet so strong, urged Roshan to lift her head. "What are you thinking?"

"That I've wanted this for a long time," Roshan confessed cautiously. "I've always desired you."

"And that's it? Desire?"

"No. That's not all."

"Then...are you saying you care for me?"

Roshan bit her lower lip and wondered if it were possible to take this leap of faith in the middle of a war, in the middle of an assignment. Then again, what if she never had another chance to tell Andreia what was in her heart? What if something disastrous happened? "I care. I more than care." Roshan stared at Andreia in all her naked glory. "You're everything I could ask for. You're everything I would ever need."

Andreia drew a deep breath. "Oh, Gods, Ro. If you only knew how much I care. If I could make you see, for just a moment, what I felt all those years, whether I thought you were a collaborator or not. My heart's full of all these emotions, and I'm afraid—" She stopped talking.

"Of what? What are you afraid of?" Roshan touched Andreia's cheek. She still lay between her legs, but could feel the air cooling them, so she pulled the blankets up. "So?"

"I'm afraid that I'll allow myself to feel, only to have you recoil, get wounded in battle...even die. I don't think I could handle that."

"Me either." The admission was out before Roshan had time to second-guess the wisdom of lowering her guard. Still, Andreia had exposed herself, for Roshan to accept or discard. "I...I can't walk away again, Andreia. Not again."

Andreia's lips softened, as did her entire expression. Small tears formed at the corners of her eyes, yet she'd never looked stronger or more beautiful. Wordlessly, Andreia cupped Roshan's face with both hands. She stroked a thumb across Roshan's lower lip and smiled when Roshan kissed it.

"Is this your way of saying you feel the same way?" Roshan asked, her heart pounding.

"Yes," Andreia whispered. She was still caressing slowly, and Roshan guessed that Andreia was imprinting the memory of her face into her hands. A cold lump formed in the center of her stomach, and Roshan let her body align fully with Andreia's, kissing her forehead, then down her cheeks, to finally claim her mouth in the most bittersweet of kisses.

"We can't have come this far...only to..." Roshan whispered, trembling against Andreia.

"Shh, we'll be all right." It sounded as much a mantra as a convinced opinion.

"Yes. Yes, we have to." Roshan curled around Andreia, wrapping the towel closer. "We must be." *If not, I can't go on. I couldn't continue our fight to the end without her.* "We have a few minutes before we should contact Jacelon," Roshan murmured. "I just want to hold you until then."

"Good." Andreia turned her face into Roshan's neck. The tickle of her breath was proof enough of life, of being safe together right now, and made Roshan slowly relax.

We have this moment. She closed her eyes. *Am I greedy to want more? Much more...*

CHAPTER TWENTY-THREE

D'Artansis to senior crew. Enemy vessels approaching. Red alert." Alarms blared, and Jacelon turned from the view port in her small office onboard the *Gallant* and hurried toward the door leading onto the bridge.

"I have the conn, Commander," she informed Leanne, who rose from the command chair.

The captain of the *Gallant* had sustained injuries to his legs and was being treated in sickbay. Jacelon didn't expect him back on duty for forty-eight hours.

"On screen," Rae commanded, and took a seat. The large view screen lit up, and Jacelon saw a small armada of Onotharian vessels approaching them from orbit. "Shields."

"Shields at one hundred percent," Owena said from behind her. She'd returned to the *Gallant* only a few hours ago and insisted on resuming her duties on the bridge.

"Good. Start a comm link."

The ensign at operations punched in a command. "Channels are open, Admiral."

"This is Admiral Jacelon of the Supreme Constellations. We do not wish to engage you in battle. Stand down and keep your current distance."

The view screen flickered and a woman's face appeared. Black hair twisted into a hard bun emphasized an austere face with dark, almost black eyes under thin, equally dark eyebrows. "I am Captain Oeseta M'Axos. You are in the Onotharian sector during an ongoing conflict. I ask you to leave immediately."

"I beg to differ," Jacelon said in a friendly tone. "This is Gantharian space, and the Supreme Constellations doesn't acknowledge the

Onotharians' unlawful occupation of Gantharat. I don't want to engage you in battle, Captain, but I will, if you don't stand down."

Annoyance and something resembling surprise flickered across the captain's face. "You are trespassing and also engaged in an act of war against the Onotharian Empire by firing on our prison facilities—"

"Enough." Jacelon rose slowly and stood behind the small railing between her and the pilots' seats. "I have places to go, people to see, and I ask you again, for the last time, to *stand down*." She had learned to work with her voice early in her career and knew that people found it intimidating.

"I think not." If Oeseta M'Axos reacted the same way as most other people, she was obviously not about to show it. "You're far from home, Admiral. You'll regret the decision to go against the Onotharian sovereignty. M'Axos out."

The view screen turned black before the long-range sensors changed the image to an exterior view of M'Axos's ships.

"That went well," Jacelon murmured. "Commander Grey, take out their weapons and propulsion system. Those ships look impressive from a distance, but unless my memory plays tricks on me, those are old birds. All the new, powerful vessels, with cloaking ability and so on, are at the SC border. They've left the old ones back here, thinking they wouldn't need much defense on the home front."

"Firing, Admiral."

Blue-green streaks lit up the view screen, and they watched as parts of the ships were demolished, one after another.

"Incoming fire!"

Jacelon knew M'Axos was a capable opponent and was grateful that the Onotharian captain didn't have access to a better-equipped, state-of-the-art vessel. The bridge shook, and Jacelon gripped the railing to remain on her feet. "Report!"

"Shields down to eighty-two percent, Admiral." Owena rattled off the numbers. "Three casualties on deck three. No fatalities."

"Good. D'Artansis, make sure we're between Paladin's fleet and the Onotharians." The ships behind them were loaded to the top bulkheads with former prisoners, which meant they were vulnerable. One wrong hit and countless lives could be lost. *That can't happen. Not after we finally got them out.*

"Yes, ma'am." Leanne maneuvered the *Gallant* in an elegant dive, coming up with her side to the enemy, making sure they blocked their view.

"Eject distortion-buoys." Jacelon watched the small lights of the markers that would confuse any space torpedoes or plasma-pulse beams from the Onotharians, at least for a while. "Now, fire again, Commander Grey. Target their life support. They're close enough to Gantharat or, better yet, the deserted prisons, to save themselves."

"I'm sending you the coordinates, Commander," the young operations ensign said, sounding more assertive now.

"Firing all torpedoes. Direct hit. Seven ships without active life support. Two ships firing their plasma-pulse torpedoes."

Jacelon raised her voice. "All hands, brace for impact."

The *Gallant* bucked under their feet, and Jacelon felt her feet leave the floor when the inertial dampeners went offline. "Return fire! Status?" She pulled herself down to the railing and willed her body to stay upright.

"No casualties. Structural damage on deck four, the mess hall," the ops ensign replied.

"Anything we need to worry about?"

"I'm closing off the area. No crew members are present."

"Make sure. And get the inertial dampeners up and running."

The ops ensign looked up. "Yes, ma'am." Her fingers flew across the computer console. "Confirmed, Admiral. Engineering is working on the dampeners."

"Commander Grey, any signs of more trouble from this group?"

"No, we seem to have created enough havoc with them, ma'am."

"Excellent. No doubt, they've sent signals to what's left of the Onotharian fleet, so we'd better get out of here. Jacelon to Paladin."

"Paladin here. Nice work, Admiral."

"Thank you, but we need to debark. Are your ships ready to launch?"

"Yes. The last transport shuttle has just come home. We now have 37,000 former prisoners onboard my freighters. They're not very comfortable, but I understand it beats the hell out of where they came from."

"Good job, Paladin. We're about to pull out now. Are your other six vessels ready?" Jacelon listened for Paladin's tone, knowing how hard this must be for her, no matter what they had gained.

"Yes, they are. We're on track with the plans."

"It will be a big loss for you."

"It will be a tremendous triumph on the way to our ultimate victory," Paladin replied matter-of-factly. "It's a small price to pay."

Jacelon thought of the man who was resting in her sickbay to regain his strength. Mikael O'Landha had refused to transfer off the *Gallant* and onto one of Paladin's ships. He wanted to reunite with his daughter when he could face her standing on his own two feet. He was receiving nutrition and medical attention, mostly for the bedsores he'd contracted from sleeping on such a hard surface with an increasingly skinnier body, also for the other ailments that Doc had diagnosed earlier.

"Very well. I'll give the order to go. May your Gods be with you, Paladin."

"And with you. Paladin out."

Jacelon heard the elevator door at the back of the bridge hiss open. A familiar feeling of joy and relief told her who it was even before she turned around. "Lieutenant Commander O'Dal, you're just in time." She knew her voice probably sounded short and casual to anyone else but Kellen. Jacelon turned around and let her eyes declare what her voice couldn't under the circumstances. "Lieutenant Commander D'Artansis, take us toward the orbit coordinates above the Merealian Mountains. Engage flight pattern Alpha-Beta-4-4."

"Aye, Admiral. Flight pattern engaged. All we have to do is wait for the welcoming committee."

Jacelon walked across the bridge until she stood next to Kellen. She briefly let her hand touch her wife's elbow and received a raised eyebrow in return. "You're right, Leanne," Jacelon acknowledged. "And it'll probably be a very warm one. Plasma-scorching hot, in fact."

❖

Roshan stood on her bridge, allowing the captain to maneuver the large ship at his own discretion. She had enough space training to operate a smaller vessel, but these enormous ones, capable of carrying 120,000 cubic meters of goods, were beyond her capability. Behind her, four more ships of the same size lined up, then six smaller ones—a convoy of hope on a course to Gantharat.

"Paladin to engineering. Is everything prepared?"

"Engineering all set to go, ma'am," a concise voice replied.

"Good. Remain on standby."

"I see we're about to head home," Andreia said from behind as she came to stand next to Roshan. "I bet a lot of people will be celebrating in quite a few homes, in a day or two."

The thought of how the families and loved ones would react to having their missing family members home, without any warning, stung Roshan's heart. *I would've given my soul to experience this all those years ago, before I realized that all hope was gone.* Scattered memories of her mother surfaced: how she'd touch her with a firm, but gentle hand, when she explained something. Her father, his cheerful smile, the way he adored her mother...*No. No, too painful right now. Don't go there.*

Roshan forced herself, like countless times before, to focus on the task at hand. She had hated the endless missions for so long, and it had been nearly impossible to keep her hopes and motivation alive for more than two decades. In the beginning the anticipation of finding out what had happened to her father sustained her. One day he simply didn't come home from his work at the hospital, and she'd never managed to find out why. Potential scenarios had chased each other through her mind during sleepless nights, and they drove her nearly insane with worry and grief. *And now, the feelings are still there. Raw. Like a wound being ripped wide open.*

"Yes," Roshan finally managed to answer Andreia. "I imagine so."

A discreet touch on the inside of Roshan's arm startled her at first. She was trying so hard to focus on the space depicted on the view screen, to remain professional, but the mere touch, skin on skin, nearly made her lose control. "O'Daybo. Please," she said, aware that she sounded as breathless and begging as she felt.

"You'll be fine, *henshes*," Andreia whispered. "You have me to lean on, and you're not alone anymore." The simple words penetrated Roshan's defenses, and she placed her hand, palm on palm, with Andreia's.

"Thank you," she whispered back. Andreia's promise took some of the immediate sting away.

"Paladin! Enemy vessels, at least six of them, at our port bow."

The captain rose from his chair. "The *Gallant* is moving in between us and them, again, but we have to stay on our set trajectory. Our guests won't survive in our cargo holds for very long."

"Steady as she goes, for now, Captain," Paladin said, and let go of Andreia's hand. "We need to get them closer to inner orbit before we take action."

"Yes, ma'am. Maintaining course and speed."

The *Iktysos* followed the SC ship on a parallel course.

"They're gaining on us, Captain," a young man said from the operations station. "At this rate they'll be within firing distance in less than two minutes."

"Give me a fifteen-seconds-interval countdown." The middle-aged captain sat in his chair, looking grim and frowning.

Roshan walked closer to the screen, her eyes never wavering. The small armada of Onotharian ships looked more modern, and thus more lethal, than the ones that had attacked them just moments ago.

"One minute, thirty seconds until they're in range, Captain."

"Paladin to Jacelon. I suppose you see the new arrivals."

"Jacelon here. I do. We're prepared at our end. Good luck!"

"Thank you, so are we. Paladin out."

"One minute, fifteen seconds."

The seconds rushed by and Roshan counted every single one. She wanted to finish this; it was nerve-wracking to stand helplessly on the bridge, in relative safety, and merely watch, for now.

"Fifteen seconds," the operations crewman said.

"This is it," Roshan whispered. "They're on top of the convoy."

The *Iktysos* rocked and stomped underneath their feet, as proof of Roshan's words. The anticipated attack had begun.

❖

Kellen slid her visor down and scanned the information that streamed along her left field of vision, relayed from the *Gallant*. Normally a navigator handled the incoming data, but Kellen had opted to fly alone. Several of the SC navigators were wounded, and she'd flown solo when she trained in the Gantharian Academy of Pilots.

The data was in order and she opened communications. "Kellen to the *Gallant*. I'm ready to lead the assault craft team out of here. Are we concealed from the enemy?"

"Yes, the convoy has us in their shadow."

"Good. Kellen to D'Artansis. Everything set?"

"I'm ready to kick some Onotharian rears, if that's what you mean," Leanne replied cheerfully. "It's about time I get to come out and play with the big girls."

Kellen smiled, reluctantly, but who could resist Leanne's unwavering spirit? "Follow me, then."

Leanne was the leader of one squadron, and Kellen of the other. Flying on parallel courses out of *Gallant's* belly, they aligned themselves, as did the other twenty assault craft, ten on either side of Kellen and Leanne. Kellen checked her chronometer and synchronized it with the time given on her visor. "Fifteen seconds, D'Artansis. From now on, radio silence is in place."

"Understood. D'Artansis out."

They'd gone over the plan countless times while on their way to the Gantharat system, not knowing which scenario they'd end up in. Kellen trusted Leanne more than most people she knew, with the exception of Rae, and she now worried about the possibility of an overlooked flaw in her plan.

A yellow alert marker showed up on Kellen's visor, and when it snapped over into red, she pushed her stick forward, dove underneath the convoy, and slingshot her ship out to the other side. Before her, seven ships of varying sizes approached them, as if the Onotharians had scrambled to their closest launch site and merely taken what was currently available. One of the ships was the type of prison transport that had taken her to Kovos, and she knew it had minimal fire power, since the Onotharians considered themselves invincible within Gantharian space.

As soon as Kellen spotted Leanne's team, she pulled her assault craft into a steep climb, using the most elaborate of evasive patterns. She needed to get close enough to fire at the lead vessel, and unless she stayed away from their torpedoes, she wouldn't live to tell the tale.

Four of the ships from the convoy took up defensive positions, and Kellen knew that she and the other assault-craft pilots had to keep the Onotharians focused on them. "SC assault craft. Move into position. Delta maneuvers."

Like small beetles, the lethal vessels surrounded the enemy, moving in a constant, dizzying offensive pattern, designed and tried by Kellen during countless sessions in the simulators back on Earth. The Onotharians fired at them, but with poor result. *It may just work.* "All assault craft, fire at will, fire at will!"

Kellen pressed the sensor that spread a wide volley of plasma-pulse rounds against the Onotharians. Small explosions erupted, fires that were quickly extinguished by the vacuum in space. Light blue rays lit up the space between the Onotharians and the assault craft, and deep red ones steered toward the convoy.

The four smaller freighters in the convoy seemed to take the brunt of the attack, and Kellen pressed her lips into a fine line as she let her craft spew plasma charges over the rear of the largest Onotharian ship. The massive destroyer-class vessel veered to one side because of the explosions Kellen's rounds created on its lower decks. Debris slammed into her craft, and she knew she was being careless, moving in too close for the kill.

Kellen easily recognized her inner urge to retaliate, not only for what the Onotharians had done to the poor people imprisoned on Kovos and Vaksses, and several other asteroid prisons, still to be liberated, but also to her father and Tereya. She bared her teeth in a growl while telling herself it was necessary to fly in so low in a death spiral under the belly of the Onotharian ships. Focusing so hard that her jaw cracked and sweat poured along her temples inside her helmet, Kellen fired a new set of rounds, a wide spread of plasma charges into one of the ship's weapons' array.

The impact of the explosion knocked the controls out of Kellen's hand, and she spun wildly before her craft's automatic stabilizers kicked in. Only then did Kellen realize she was caught in the direct line of fire. She pushed the controls, but her assault craft responded too slowly as it turned around, obviously damaged due to its slow reaction, when a red beam seared through the cockpit, right before her eyes.

Kellen flung her arms up, covering her face, and moments later her seat ejected with an immense force that hurled her into space.

Kellen could feel the sizzling in the front of her space-survival suit and knew it had sustained damage as well. She carefully opened her eyes and realized she hadn't slowed down. Reaching down on both sides she tried to ignite the maneuvering thrusters, but they weren't operational. Unless she slammed into another object, she'd keep going into the ring of asteroids behind her.

❖

"Damn it! Kellen! What's she doing?" Jacelon stopped cold and watched the view screen in horror. The small, shiny assault craft came out from under the Onotharians' lead ship, spinning out of control. The small ship was headed straight into the field of fire. She couldn't order a cease fire from her end, since the other assault craft and the convoy as well would be obliterated, and Kellen would still be in danger.

Jacelon was still hoping Kellen's luck wouldn't run out, that she'd slip through between the ships, when a blast hit Kellen's craft and split it in two. The debris lit up very briefly, then scattered in all directions. "Kellen!" Jacelon gasped. *Not again! Déjà vu...* "Oh, God, no..." She quieted her pained murmur and turned to the ops ensign. "Life signs?"

The ensign didn't have to ask whose. "I still get a clear reading of the commander's biosignature. She's alive, ma'am, and the force field bubble is operational. However..." She punched in a few more commands, and Jacelon wanted to grab the young woman's arm and yell at her to hurry up. "Commander O'Dal's space suit is damaged and so are her thrusters. She won't be able to command the ejected chair."

Jacelon didn't have to hear anything more. If she'd had another ship available, she'd have gone after Kellen herself. However, this wasn't possible since all accessible ships were engaged in the ongoing space battle. "Jacelon to D'Artansis. Kellen's ejected and is on a collision course. We're sending you the coordinates now." The ensign nodded affirmatively behind her console. "Do you have them, Commander?"

"I do."

"Go after her, Leanne." Jacelon heard the catch in her own voice. No way would she lose Kellen now when they'd nearly completed their mission. *She's supposed to go home to Armeo with me, victorious after rescuing all these people.*

"I'll get her, ma'am."

"She doesn't have long. Her space suit's been compromised."

"I'm on it. D'Artansis out."

❖

Kellen struggled to tighten her harness, afraid she'd be knocked off the ejector seat if she hit something rear first. She found it increasingly difficult to breathe because the plasma splatter turned into miniscule droplets that corroded the pressurized suit and created small holes. Although her helmet, attached to the tank on the chair, and eventually the emergency tank at the back of her helmet, provided oxygen, she still couldn't breathe well because the pressure around her body was close to zero. The inner shielding of the suit kept her body from being sucked out through the small holes, but it didn't keep the pressure up.

Around her, ships of all sizes fired on each other, and Kellen couldn't help but admire the way her assault team handled themselves. She watched them press the Onotharians together into a cluster, and thus create an easier target.

Far away, one of the assault craft broke out of the pattern, and at first Kellen thought it had taken a hit. Then it turned toward her position, and she realized that the bridge had noticed her predicament and sent someone after her.

Just as relief flooded her, the suit ripped all along her abdomen and down her left leg, and she couldn't breathe the oxygen that spilled into her helmet. Her chest worked hard against the nothingness of space, trying to pull much-needed oxygen into her lungs, but her gasping only made things worse. Using the last of her energy, she grabbed the front of her suit and twisted it, trying to hold it together, even though she knew her attempt was futile. Her vision blurred, and she realized she was going to pass out any second. She stared at the dots far away that grew with every struggling heartbeat.

The last thing Kellen heard was a resounding bang, which made her lose her grip on the suit. After that, everything went black.

❖

The largest of the Onotharian ships slowly pushed the assault craft backward, thus gaining a clean line of fire against Paladin's four smaller freighters. As the *Gallant*'s captain slowly moved the ship into firing position, Jacelon watched on the view screen. The four other freighters were safely tucked away on the other side of the SC ship, and Jacelon clenched her fists as she watched the smaller ships take the brunt of the fire.

"Do we have communications with D'Artansis yet?" she asked the ops ensign.

"Not yet, ma'am. Too much interference from the plasma charges. I can only detect scattered static."

"How about the commander's biosignature?"

"Nothing for the last minute, Admiral. But it's probably just sensor disturbance."

Damn! "Keep trying." Icicles traveled from her chest to her hands, and Jacelon hid them as she folded her arms tightly. "Let me know when we're in position. D'Artansis and O'Dal had better be away from that mess by then." *I have no choice. I have to stick to the plan or risk all of our lives.*

"Yes, ma'am."

As the smaller Onotharian ships followed their lead vessel against Paladin's small freighters, the SC assault craft circled the enemy and approached from behind.

"Paladin to Jacelon. We're in position and can't wait any longer. I saw what happened to the commander." Paladin's voice was pained, and Jacelon knew she had to be completely devastated at the thought of losing their Protector just after they'd rediscovered her.

"I know. Stick to the plan, Paladin." Sounding brusque, she gave the orders that might kill the woman she loved more than life. "All hands, this is Admiral Jacelon. Commence Operation Space Storm."

A chorus of scattered voices confirmed her orders over the comm channels. Jacelon couldn't make herself sit down in the command chair; instead she gripped the metal bar in front of it and stared with burning eyes at the screen. The assault craft moved in closer, firing relentlessly at the same target. "Take us in, Lieutenant," she ordered the young man at the helm.

"Aye, ma'am."

"Commander Grey, prepare to fire on my mark."

"Ready, Admiral." Owena sounded emotionless, yet she had to be frantic, wondering where Leanne was. "Torpedoes and plasma-pulse chargers set to launch."

Jacelon calculated the seconds while glaring at the fierce battle on the screen. "Mark. Fire at will."

"Firing torpedoes. Now. Firing plasma-pulse charges. Now." Owena seemed totally professional.

The torpedoes raced toward the ships in the middle of the battle. The assault craft were now a short distance behind the center of the fight, which suited Jacelon fine. *That's right. Stay away, people.*

The impact of the weapons' array was beyond expectations. The space around the *Gallant* lit up in a blinding cascade of burning debris, which quickly turned into armor-piercing missiles heading their way.

"Report! Did we get them?" Jacelon called out, clutching the bar with ice-cold hands.

The ops ensign pulled herself back to her console with both arms. "Yes, the Onotharian ships are dead in the water, Admiral. What's left of them."

Jacelon slowly raised her head to the view screen, saw assault craft scurry to return to the *Gallant*, and hoped all were accounted for. Like blackened skeletons, scorched debris drifted in space between them and the incapacitated enemy ships. Jacelon didn't have to ask about Paladin's four freighters; they had been completely destroyed.

CHAPTER TWENTY-FOUR

"Come on, Kellen! Breathe!"

The voice, familiar, yet different in its intensity, hovered above Kellen, floating, fading, only to grow stronger. Small puffs of air gushed against her cheek.

"Open your eyes and take a deep breath."

A rubbery material covered Kellen's face, startling her enough that she opened her eyes. Masses of red-blond hair framed a pale face with dark green eyes.

"Leanne..." Kellen coughed into the oxygen mask. "Where are we?"

"On the backside of a small asteroid. I knew the blast would be bad, so it was my only option. I pulled you through the port airlock and dashed over here as fast as I could. You were pretty blue, I mean, bluer than usual, for a moment."

"You saved my life." Kellen sat up, drawing deep, cleansing breaths into the mask. She needed to get back in shape quickly.

Leanne shrugged and grinned. "Hey, I wouldn't want to face the Admiral if I hadn't."

"Do we have a comm channel?"

"Nope. The debris from the explosion is scattered all over the area, and I can't get through the static." Her face grew serious, and a shade paler. "Can you believe it, all those ships? Nothing's left of them."

Kellen nodded. "I know. But we didn't have much choice."

"True." Leanne sighed. "Well, if you're able to move, you can either pilot this thing or squeeze in behind the navigator."

Kellen grimaced at the thought of curling up in the small storage area, intended to hold med kits and survival gear, and glanced meaningfully at Leanne's small frame.

"I knew it," Leanne sighed, her eyes regaining their twinkle. "I'm about to get smashed."

"It'll only be for a minute, until we're back aboard the *Gallant*."

"Famous last words," Leanne muttered good-naturedly, and moved up through the small hatch, yelling to the navigator, "Hey, scoot over. I'm going into the back. Commander O'Dal's taking the pilot's seat."

Kellen couldn't hear what the navigator said, but entered the hatch as well and squeezed into the seat. As she adjusted it and its harness, she wasn't surprised that her hands trembled. The adrenalin rush from being alive had begun to fade when Kellen remembered the last thing she'd thought of before everything went black; countless images of Rae and a deep sorrow for leaving her, hurting her, lingered. She needed to get back to the *Gallant* quickly for more than one reason, but primarily she wanted to make sure Rae knew she was alive.

She completed the ignition sequence in record time, and the navigator seemed inspired by her urgency. Soon they sped in an intricate path between the asteroids. Kellen knew the danger wasn't over; the enemy could have more ships hidden, just waiting for a chance to attack.

They entered the area that had so recently been lit by multicolored streaks from the many weapons and was now a dead field of debris with only four visible assault craft, which seemed to be examining the wreckage. Kellen's head snapped up. Were they looking for her?

The computer couldn't identify the pilots in the small vessels, but Kellen tried the comm channels, hoping to get through. "O'Dal to SC assault craft. Do you read me?" She heard only static. "I have to get closer," she muttered, and piloted her ship in a low, wide angle that took them straight up to the starboard side of the nearest craft. It was dangerous to fly this close to someone among that much space rubble, but Kellen needed to make eye contact. The pilot, whom she thought she recognized as one of the two Imidestrian women, looked out the small right-hand window, her eyes huge. She pointed at Kellen and made an inquiring gesture with her arms and shoulders pushed up.

Kellen replied with one thumb up, an ancient Earth gesture that actually made sense to her. When the Imidestrian woman smiled brightly and looked relieved, Kellen drew a circle in the air in front of her and pointed at the other three vessels near them, gesturing for them to return to the *Gallant* together. The other woman nodded eagerly, and

Kellen guessed she wasn't all that thrilled to be among the debris of the destroyed ships. Half of the junk floating aimlessly around them came from Paladin's shattered freighters, after all.

Like five arrows, the assault craft sped toward the convoy, which was barely visible and about to enter low orbit above Gantharat's atmosphere.

❖

Rae trudged to the *Gallant's* main docking port, but she doubted that her dejection was visible to her crew. They still tiptoed around her, not meeting her eyes, since they knew Kellen and Leanne were missing. This meant that her crew also feared Owena, who dared anyone to pity her by hurling her steely, ice blue glare at anyone who tried.

It was impossible to reach the four pilots Rae had left behind to search the debris. She would've preferred to do it herself, to let the *Gallant* remain behind and scan every single grain of space dust. However, the surviving ex-prisoners needed to return planet-side. Now Rae had docked with the *Iktysos* and was about to meet Paladin. The remaining freighters had linked with each other and the *Iktysos* in a chain formation, which would make any potential transfers easy.

The door slid open to the airlock and Rae saw Paladin, with O'Daybo by her side. "Admiral, Rae," Paladin said, and merely stood there, studying Rae with warm, worried eyes, so blue, so like Kellen's. "Have you heard anything yet?"

"Nothing." Her throat hurt when she spoke, but Rae geared herself to do things by the book, as always. "How are your survivors faring?"

"Not too bad, considering they have to sit on the floor in the cargo space, and we don't have enough blankets. They're taking everything in stride, though, and my comrades have informed them that it's only a matter of hours. We're going to need your marines again. All according to…the Protector's plan."

"Yes, I know. They've had some rest and food, and they're ready to deploy to your vessels. Not counting the wounded, of course, I can offer you some fifty marines for each of your five ships." Rae sighed. "Speaking of ships. I'm sorry about your freighters. They were fine vessels—"

"But we saved even finer people," Paladin filled in. "Who knew the remote controls we installed four lunar-years ago would come in handy in a situation like that? But it took the skill of some of your pilots."

Rae's pilots had sat in the *Iktysos's* engineering bay, steering the four freighters, whose only cargo consisted of massive explosives, by remote control toward the Onotharian ships. Firing her torpedoes against the vessels hadn't been easy for Rae. It was, however, worth the destruction of a thousand ships to save thousands of rebels. She turned to the tall man behind her. "Major Egordash, deploy your teams."

"Yes, ma'am." He saluted and issued orders for the marines under his command to begin moving into position inside the docked ships.

"I'm glad we could help," Rae managed. "I—"

"Senior staff to the bridge. Senior staff to the bridge."

Rae flinched and began to run, and heard Paladin and Andreia follow. The red-alert alarms were quiet, which meant the Onotharians weren't on top of them yet. They had a window of opportunity before the Onotharians planet-side realized what kind of defeat they had just suffered.

Rushing onto the bridge, ignoring the smart "Admiral on the bridge" from the closest ensign, Rae encountered a dark-eyed Owena. "We have five incoming assault craft," she informed the stunned Rae. "There's no way to communicate with them because they're too polluted by radiation from one of the Onotharian ships. They'll have to go through decontamination procedures before they can enter our shuttle bay."

Rae wanted to tell Owena to screw the decontamination procedure, but she knew it was vital for everyone who might come in contact with the hull of the small vessels. "Hurry up, then."

"Already on it."

God. How hard it is to wonder who's in those ships? Chances are good that Leanne made it...but... Rae felt herself sway slightly, and only the gentle pressure of a palm against the small of her back made her able to square her shoulders. She glanced quickly behind her and saw the kind glow from O'Daybo's eyes.

Rae merely nodded and stared at the images provided by the short-range hull sensors. Automatically a sanitizing force field appeared in the shuttle bay opening. Inside of it, long metal hoses sprayed a misty substance over the assault craft, one after the other. Only when they were all treated would the inner shuttle bay doors open.

"I can't just wait here," Owena muttered. "Permission to leave the bridge, ma'am?"

"You and me both," Rae said huskily. "Lieutenant," she said to the man by the helm, who had the highest rank of the remaining senior crew. "You have the conn. Stay alert and page me if anything's amiss. Anything at all."

"Yes, Admiral."

Owena was already halfway to the elevator, and Rae, with Paladin and O'Daybo, barely entered behind her before the door closed. They rode in silence to the shuttle bay corridor and hurried toward the entrance, where they saw the last of the assault craft descend and power down.

Stopping just inside the door, Rae pressed a hand against her chest, knowing full well she didn't look like the together and collected admiral she was supposed to embody for the crew. She scanned the hatches of the ships that opened one after the other, producing people in flight suits, and tried to recognize them from how they walked, but they were all stiff and rigid from more than eight hours in the narrow seats.

A pilot emerging from the closest ship stood still just outside the hatch, gazing around the shuttle bay while unfastening her helmet. Long, blond hair flowed, floated a bit from static electricity, and landed on strong shoulders. The pilot's eyes, shimmering blue even at this distance, locked onto Rae, whose knees were about to give. "Kellen…" she whispered, her voice broken.

Kellen ran up to Rae and grabbed her with strong arms. Apparently not caring about creating a public display, she pulled Rae to her and buried her face in her neck.

"You." Rae could barely speak. "You. Did it. To me. Again. You—"

"I'm sorry." Kellen interrupted the pained words. "I'm sorry, Rae. I never meant to worry you that way again. I'm so sorry." Soft words spoken directly into Rae's ear.

"I thought you were dead. That you and Leanne were caught in the explosion…" Rae pulled away a little and stared up at Kellen. "Leanne?"

"She saved my life. There she is." Kellen motioned with her chin toward the small woman throwing herself into Owena's arms. Owena merely lifted her and carried her out the door, which reminded Rae that they themselves were embracing in front of the entire shuttle bay crew.

"Kellen. Let's go. Come on." Not about to let go entirely, Rae took Kellen by the hand and began to walk back to the elevator. "We have more work to do," she said as they entered it with their friends, who now included Paladin and O'Daybo. "But before that, we need to get you checked out at the infirmary."

"I'm fine—" Kellen began, but Rae stopped her with a glance. She nodded. "But if you think it's best, of course." She turned to Paladin. "Would you come with us? And you too, O'Daybo. We need to make sure that we're all in good shape before we finish this."

Paladin looked at them with apparent surprise, raising her eyebrows. "We have our own physician onboard the *Iktysos*," she reminded them. "I don't think it's necessary to—"

"But I do," Rae insisted. She had to take Paladin to the infirmary. Now that Kellen was safely back aboard the *Gallant*, this was all she could think of. She and Paladin had shared so much while waiting for the Kovos and Vaksses teams to get in touch. Rae felt a special connection, and she admitted to herself this might also be because Paladin reminded her of an older Kellen.

"All right, then." Paladin shrugged. "A joint venture to the doctor it is." She looked inquisitively at O'Daybo, who merely nodded and walked along with them.

The infirmary was overflowing all the way out into the corridor. Paladin stopped when she saw how many injured people waited for treatment. "You can't possibly expect your physician to pay any attention to me or O'Daybo, when seriously injured people need him."

"No, I wouldn't want to waste any of his time," Rae agreed, exchanging a look with Kellen. "But we still need to go inside. Trust me." *Don't argue, Paladin, just do it.*

Paladin shook her head, obviously impatient, and with an exasperated sigh she followed Kellen.

❖

Roshan wasn't amused. She had so much to do, and Jacelon and Kellen were acting strange, to say the least. She walked behind the

Protector into the infirmary, prepared to do the right thing, visit with the rebels and reassure them, which was most likely why they wanted her and O'Daybo to join them.

Stretchers and medical beds were lined up in long rows in the fairly spacious infirmary. Two physicians and eight assistants worked with the wounded, and Roshan saw people of all ages, seated or lying down, looking pale. She walked up to a young woman on a stretcher, who held a small bundle. "Oh, Gods! A baby?"

"My son. His name is Kellon." She pointed to Kellen. "The male version of your name, Protector. I named him after you."

"I'm deeply honored. How is your baby now, Illina?" Kellen asked, and Roshan realized Kellen had rescued this woman herself.

"The doctor says he'll need nutritional infusions and medication to calibrate his blood-balance. Other than that, he'll be fine."

She burst into tears and Kellen patted her shoulder. "We'll try to reunite you with your spouse as soon as possible. In the meantime, I believe you have a lot in common with the young girl over there. Her name is Sarambol. She's pregnant and was close to losing her child. She's doing much better, but she may need someone to talk to, if you think you have the strength?"

Illina looked over at Sarambol. "Do you think she'd like to sit here with me? I mean, there's even room to lie down if she's tired. I'd like the company."

"I'll ask her in a bit." Kellen smiled gently and pushed sweat-soaked tresses from Illina's face. "Just rest now."

They walked from bed to bed, moving toward the far corner where the patients requiring nutritional infusions were hooked up to different units. An older man sat sideways on his stretcher, a little slumped. His white hair reached his shoulders, and he sported an impressive beard. Painfully thin, he needed all the nutrition they could pump into him, Roshan thought. She was going to smile politely, but when he looked up something inside her completely halted.

Roshan stopped, making Andreia bump into her from behind and say, "Paladin, what—?"

"Who's that man?" Roshan asked, her voice barely carrying. "That old man, over there on the stretcher. Who is he?"

"Why don't you go over to him?" Kellen suggested, her voice low. "Just talk to him, Roshan."

The use of her own name should've sparked some sort of reaction, but all Roshan could think about was how the man's eyes never left her face. He even raised his hand halfway, hesitant and trembling. It was the same hand she'd held so many times. Older, wrinkled, with age spots and awful nails, but nevertheless the same hand that had caressed her long braid before her father went off to work at the hospital every morning.

"*Pappa...*" The old Earth word slipped over her lips. "Oh, Gods of Gantharat!"

"It's him, Roshan. He's recognized you." Rae placed a hand on her shoulder. "Why don't you go over to him? He's waited so long for this day."

"I...Yes. Of course." Roshan felt like she was moving in suspended animation as she rushed among the stretchers. She didn't take her eyes off Mikael O'Landha where he sat, shivering under a blanket. His broad face now consisted of hollow cheeks and deep-set eyes with blue-black circles underneath. But the eyes were the same, clear blue in a completely different shade than any Gantharian eyes. His teeth had seen better days, but his smile was the same—warm, if a bit tremulous.

"Child." His voice shook as much as his hand, but it was his voice.

"Pappa, I thought you were dead." It was hardly the most appropriate way to start a reunion of this magnitude, but it was the truth. "They...the Onotharians, said you died during transport. They said..." Roshan couldn't go on, couldn't find the words to explain any more. She took the last step forward and wrapped her strong arms around the mere shell of a man that was her father. "Oh, I've missed you all these years. I'm sorry, I'm so sorry."

"Whatever for, child?" Mikael asked, his face buried in her shoulder.

"I believed them. I gave up on you, didn't try to find you. I believed *them*."

"Then I'm sorry too, for my crime is worse." Mikael pulled back, and his eyes were tormented. "When prisoners arrived and called you a collaborator...there were moments when I believed them."

His words stung, but she could hardly blame him. She gazed down at the man who'd loved her mother with an undying passion, and who had worshipped Roshan and supported her in anything she wanted.

He'd always told people how proud he was that she wanted to be a doctor, like him.

"Everyone was supposed to buy into their lies, which was the point," she said. She looked Mikael over once more, stroking the white hair, smoothing it down. "We've lost so many years, and I…I just want to hold you, Pappa, and never let go."

"I can't believe I'm seeing you again, that I'm out of that hellish place and that I have, perhaps, a few more years with you." Mikael slumped more over to the side, and Roshan caught him in her arms. "Doctor!"

"No, no, I'm all right, Roshan. Just a little tired."

The SC military physician walked up to them, scanned Mikael, and frowned slightly. "Mr. O'Landha, I think you need to lie down for a bit. All this excitement has become a bit too much for you. Your… friend, here, can perhaps—"

"My daughter," Mikael whispered, then cleared his throat. "She's my daughter," he repeated in a stronger voice. "Though I hope my daughter is also my friend."

Roshan's tears spilled over and streamed down her cheeks, where they soaked the tall collar of her shirt. "Pappa, yes, yes, I am. I'm both those things." She helped Mikael get comfortable on the stretcher and bent down to kiss his wrinkled cheek. "Rest, now. I'll be back later, once we've completed our mission." It tore her apart to have to leave him, but she was immensely grateful to Rae for not keeping him from her. If something happened to her now, at least she'd held her father close and felt his loving arms around her once again.

"You'll be careful?" Mikael asked as his eyes began to close.

"I promise I'll be very careful. I'll be back soon."

As Roshan dried her tears with the back of her hand, she sensed, rather than felt, Andreia's presence just behind her. Gazing down at Mikael, she reached for Andreia's hand and vowed on everything she held sacred in life that "soon" wouldn't mean another two decades, this time.

❖

Andreia saw Roshan straighten her back as she spoke to Jubinor over the comm channel. "What's going on?"

"Apparently the entire Onotharian government is in an uproar, and they're conducting a planet-wide search for Andreia M'Aldovar," Roshan whispered to her. "Their propaganda machine is saying that the Supreme Constellations and the rebels have kidnapped you."

Andreia's heart began to race. "What else can you tell us?" she asked Jubinor, amazed at how calm she sounded.

"The news of Kovos and Vaksses is crossing the planet quickly. One of our junior rebels has listened into unauthorized civilian transmissions, and the Gantharians have new hope for the first time in years. People are also praying that their loved ones are among the prisoners saved."

Roshan placed a hand on Andreia's shoulder, squeezing it tight. "And the Onotharian government?"

"They're in session more or less around the clock. M'Isitor has broadcast twice and managed to turn this into a personal vendetta, calling it 'an act of cowards and misguided fools,' which is a total insult, and he knows it. He isn't trying to convince the Gantharians, because he knows that's a lost cause, but he's probably trying his best to keep the Onotharian civilian citizens in check."

"You mean there's been trouble in paradise when it comes to his own people?" Roshan squeezed Andreia's shoulder again. "I'd think they're as sick and tired of this situation as we are."

"Perhaps."

"How are you doing?" Andreia asked. "Is the camp secure? The first prisoners should be arriving any minute."

"We're as secure as we'll ever be."

"And more," Roshan said. "Our physicians have found that many of the prisoners, especially the ones at the Vaksses facility, have been tagged. Jacelon's engineers decoded the nano-tags, and for some reason, they've been divided into four different groups. The Onotharians evidently managed to get some information out of them about their expertise and so on, and tagged them for future reference. Fortunately the SC tech people showed our doctors how to neutralize the nano-tags fairly easily by merely setting the new medical scanners they gave us to a corrupting frequency."

"They won't have the time to check every person on the ships. Will we get more scanners to use planet-side?"

"Yes, they'll include more with every shipment of rebels, and also,

SC marines will stay in the camp until we know who can go home and who can't."

"I just hope that most of them can rejoin the fight," Jubinor sighed. "You can't blame them if they've had it, though."

"From what I understood on Vaksses," Andreia said, "there's a lot of fighting spirit left. The morale's high among many of the ones from Kovos too."

"Sounds good." Jubinor seemed to hesitate. "When are you two returning?"

"As soon as we can." Roshan looked into Andreia's eyes. "Something's come up that we need to take care of."

"All right. I'll keep the soup warm for you."

Roshan smiled faintly. "And, Jubinor, I made sure that Berentar is on the first transport. He needs medical attention, but should be all right, according to Doc and the SC physician."

There was a brief silence. "Thank you."

The simple words, uttered with such softness, stirred something in Andreia, and she leaned against Roshan. The many reunions were wonderful, but also emotionally draining. She knew Roshan couldn't stop thinking about Mikael, and that it was hurting her that she had to be away from her father so soon after they'd found each other again. It was somehow so right that Kellen had returned Roshan's father to her, since Roshan had done the same for Kellen, years earlier.

"Good job keeping the base camp safe, Jubinor. Over and out."

Roshan leaned her hip against the communication console. They'd borrowed the captain's quarters to talk to Jubinor, and now Andreia tried to wrap her brain around the fact that she was listed not only as missing, but also as a "victim" of the rebels' and the SC's actions.

"I need to go back. I have to make an appearance and—" She spoke quickly, but stopped when Roshan put a hand up.

"Wait! Not so fast. If you go back, as things are now, you'll of course show the world that the Onotharian leadership is way off base. But you'll be stuck there. They'll want to use every single bit of your goodwill to further their agenda. And let's face it, sweetheart, you're popular among your own people, but many younger Gantharians also think pretty highly of you." Roshan spoke passionately. "They'll use you, from the time you get up in the morning until you fall asleep at night, as their prize possession. Their salvation, even."

"But I can't stay away and let the Gantharian population think that the rebels are holding me captive or, worse, that they've killed me."

"Wait a minute…we need to think about this." Roshan rubbed her temples, and Andreia could almost see her mind whirl, turning the dilemma around, inspecting it from all angles. "If you return, the Onotharian propaganda machine will concoct a huge lie, saying you were held captive, but managed to escape a fate worse than death, or something similar. If you stay with us, they'll say you're dead and turn you into a martyr, which won't be difficult since you're so popular. Any suggestions?"

Andreia folded her arms in front of her. She could think of several ideas, and none of them appealed to her. Roshan was right. No matter what, it came down to the two versions she'd just described.

Placing one hand on Roshan's chest, Andreia pulled her closer with the other. "I don't think we have a choice," she said, her voice husky and deep with emotion. "I have to go back."

CHAPTER TWENTY-FIVE

A ndreia adjusted her clothes and made sure she looked just as wrinkled and dusty as someone who'd been hiking. She'd changed clothes at the base camp where she'd arrived only hours ago, among the returning rebels. She was amazed at how efficiently the SC marines had moved them with the transporter shuttles, which managed a couple of thousand at a time.

The vast majority of the rebels had ended up in the mountain camps, which had the largest camouflaged structures. The rest were dispersed at smaller, safe locations all over the northern hemisphere, where most of the rebels resided. It would take some time to return them to their loved ones, but Andreia knew that was Roshan's top priority, coupled with aiding the SC in their advance toward Onotharian territory.

It had been so hard to say good-bye to Roshan, not knowing when, or if, she'd ever see her again. They had stood inside the airlock, people passing by behind them, which made it impossible to exchange anything but pained looks and fake smiles.

"Is there any way I can talk you out of this?" Roshan had asked.

"No, *henshes*, there isn't. I have to return and make sure they don't use my absence to their advantage. We can't let any shadows fall on the rebels. Our situation is already vulnerable."

"Be careful among those people," Roshan said, squeezing Andreia's hand. "They may know more about you than you realize. Use your instincts. If you suspect anything—"

"I know. I'll get out of there."

"I wish there was another way."

"So do I." *I don't want to leave you. Ever.* Andreia looked down, studying her boots when Roshan's smoldering eyes became too painful to gaze into. "I...I haven't had a chance to tell you everything. I mean, about how...I feel." She stuttered and was aware of shuffling feet behind her where their fellow rebels were entering the large transporter."

"I know. Me either." Roshan's short words spoke volumes, and Andreia had to look at her again.

"*Henshes,*" she breathed. "Tell me we'll see each other again soon."

The brief delay before Roshan spoke told Andreia of her fear. "Of course we will, love." The term of endearment came over Roshan's lips in a rush, but Andreia knew she'd cherish the moment forever.

❖

"Ma'am? Your security badge, please?" A young Onotharian guard in the Onotharian headquarters smiled politely at her and startled her out of her reverie. He wasn't familiar and didn't recognize her, obviously. Andreia knew she looked different from her official image, hair a curly mess and no makeup.

"Oh, right. Yes." Andreia pulled the card up and slid it through the reader. The detector read her biosignature and pinged approval. The whole process with the detector brought back the feeling of dread that had momentarily spread through her when she entered the Vaksses asteroid prison. Andreia held her breath for a while as she began walking toward her parents' offices.

Her steps were heavy, but she forced herself to act casual when she stepped out of the elevator. The door to her father's office was half-open, and even from the elevator, Andreia could hear the raised voices. People were running down the corridor, seemingly in a frenzy. Armed guards stood next to the exits, the elevator included, their plasma-pulse weapons raised across their chests.

Andreia almost made it all the way to her father's office without any special attention from the guards. She turned a corner and suddenly found herself staring into the metal-plated chest of a tall Onotharian guard.

"Ms. M'Aldovar," he said. "Come with me." He pointed toward her father's office.

"No need for the muscles." Andreia sighed, but wasn't surprised when the guard escorted her conscientiously all the way to the door.

Peering inside, she saw her mother standing by the window, arms folded in a defensive posture.

"I don't care what you say, Valax. We can't leave the border unprotected. To bring back a large part of our fleet for this unfortunate event—"

"Unfortunate event? You're absolutely, unbelievably ignorant when you talk like that! We're losing control of the situation here. Vaksses and Kovos, our best and safest places to put those damn rebels, are empty. Even the prisoners on death row are gone! This unexpected guerilla warfare is highly disturbing, not to mention dangerous." Andreia's father rose and rounded the desk. He stood in front of his wife, hands on his hips as he challenged her. "We have to get more space vessels here to deter this surge of military activity."

"Where the hell did they come from?" Le'Tinia asked. "I've heard rumors of thousands of SC soldiers flooding the tunnels of Kovos, which is impossible, of course. More unbelievable yet, some say that the Protector has been sighted."

"Oh, Gods, that's all we need. If she's here and everyone finds out, the situation will stampede totally out of control."

Andreia decided it was time to go in. "I see that I'm just in time to find out what the hell's been going on as soon as I turn my back for a vacation." She strode into the office, casually dropping her bag onto the low couch.

"Andreia!" her parents gasped in unison and stared at her.

"What? Is something wrong?" Feigning innocence was easy after the years of lying through her teeth when it came to her parents. "You look like you're staring at an underworld spirit."

"We thought you were…Oh, dear child!" Le'Tinia rushed over to Andreia and embraced her. "We thought the rebels had taken you, or worse. How could you go away without your bodyguards?" Her eyes seemed honest enough, and Andreia realized that her mother had actually been worried.

"I had a great time with Roshan O'Landha. We hiked all over the Cortasero Mountains." The mountains were located not far from Ganath, but on the opposite side, compared to the base camp. "I just realized today, when I got back, that we've had an incident. I came right away, as I'm sure you can see, before changing."

"We appreciate that, *henshes*, since it's far more than an incident," Valax emphasized. "The rebels raided Vaksses and Kovos, with the aid of covert SC military assistance. We were sure, when you never checked in with us, that you'd been accidentally caught up in it and taken prisoner."

"We thought we'd get a ransom demand, or ultimatums from the rebels, but when we didn't hear anything from them either…we began to be afraid you were dead." As Le'Tinia stroked her forehead, for the first time Andreia saw her mother's true age. "I couldn't bear to lose another child to these people."

"You didn't." Andreia placed an awkward hand on her mother's shoulder. They'd never been inclined to hug or kiss, but the pain in Le'Tinia's voice resonated in Andreia. No matter what, these were still her parents, and the fact that they were on opposite sides of this struggle hurt Andreia more than ever. "I'm here now. Why not brief me on what's going on?"

Her father, who seemed more able to handle the situation as a professional, recapped the events. He spoke in a low tone where he stood next to his wife, by the window. "And so you see, we have to strike hard against the rebels, Andreia. If we don't ask for assistance from our homeworld, demand that they bring the cruisers and destroyers back from the SC border, we're going to be stuck here with outdated vessels which the SC ships can easily destroy."

"No ships available from Onotharat?" Andreia held her breath while she waited for the reply.

"No, they're betting everything on this upcoming battle with the SC. The entire balance of power is in jeopardy, and the chairmen aren't going to risk it. I tried to tell them about what's happening here, several times, but we've been so proficient at keeping the rebels at bay before, they're expecting us to merely round them up again and destroy them."

"That will be nearly impossible," Le'Tinia huffed. Waving a dismissive hand in the air, she seemed both tired and angry. "The rebels aren't fools. They won't allow themselves to be captured in the same way again. It doesn't take a genius to figure out that they'll regroup, start new cells with new strategies, and we won't be able to find them, unless we begin incarcerating people randomly."

"What?" Taken aback at her mother's words, Andreia said, "Surely that won't be efficient enough?" *Oh, Gods, no. Don't panic and lash out like that, Mother!*

"I know. It's not an option. Yet." Le'Tinia sat down on the chair closest to the window. "But we have to do *something*."

"Now that you're back, we could use a bit of goodwill." Valax laced his fingers and leaned against the desk. "You're popular, and people have been just as concerned about you as we have."

Because you used me in your damn propaganda. "Just tell me what to do. An official broadcast, perhaps?"

"Yes, that…and also something with more impact." Le'Tinia cocked her head, and Andreia knew from experience that her mother was hatching yet another of her chilling plans. "I know." Le'Tinia rose and let her finger slide down Andreia's cheek. "You have a small scratch here. We can extend it, make it worse."

"What are you talking about?" Andreia knew she should have used a derma fuser before she came back, but she'd run out of time.

"Just trust me. You're going to look the part, and *play* the part, of a woman who escaped the rebels' claws just in time before they tortured her to death." Le'Tinia moved Andreia's head back and forth, examining it. "You already look pale and uncomfortable. Excellent."

"But Mother, I don't think it will help the situation to pull off such a stunt—"

Le'Tinia's dark eyes became small slits of contempt. "This is how we'll do it. Unless you decide to let them gain territory because all you can think of is that woman you allied yourself with? She's taking you away from your duties far too much. It's not acceptable for her to have any power over you. No matter what she demands, you need to focus on the situation at hand."

Only a few days ago you were thrilled to hear Roshan was interested in me. How quickly you change your mind when it suits you, Mother. "I will. I am Onotharian first and foremost," Andreia lied, and felt a stake drill into her heart as she spoke. "What do you have in mind?"

"We give you a proper makeover and broadcast the news of the rebels' actions toward the planet's most known and beloved woman."

"When?" Andreia's mouth was so dry she could hardly speak.

Le'Tinia raised inquisitive eyebrows at her husband, who shrugged, obviously content to leave the decision to his wife. "Tonight," Le'Tinia said triumphantly. "I like the idea more and more. The rebels will lose some of their so-called halo and thus the support of many of their own people. Tonight we'll discredit them in the Gantharian public's eyes and reveal them as the lying, self-righteous bastards they are."

❖

Roshan stood in the communications room with Jubinor, Kellen, and Jacelon. They had reviewed the discussions among the different resistance cell leaders around the northern hemisphere. The Onotharians had captured two of the leaders, and their neighboring cells now planned how to liberate them.

The Protector stood next to Jacelon, her shoulders rigid. "We'll help as much as we can," she said. "We need to collaborate with the rebels in the cells geographically closest to them. We should set up a command center that deals with this immediately and—"

The sudden noise in Roshan's left ear made her flinch, and it took her a few seconds to realize it was her earpiece, the first one that she and Andreia had used. She had plugged it back in when she returned to earth with the faint hope that Andreia might find a way to communicate. When she hadn't heard anything for more than twelve hours, she assumed Andreia hadn't thought of it, or had been unable to get to her equipment.

"Boyoda to Paladin. Can you hear me?" It was almost physically painful to hear the beloved voice and know she was so far away.

"I'll be back in a minute," Roshan told the others. "I need to take care of something." She walked out of the room and continued outside. Everywhere she looked, she saw people. A city of tents lined the entire grass field that the low buildings surrounded. Roshan snuck in between the structure she just left and the one serving as the food center. It was almost dark, and she felt her way along the wall until she was sure she was out of earshot. "Andreia. I'm here."

"I don't have long, *henshes*. I've managed to scramble the audio surveillance for a while. You were right. They're going to use me to turn as many Gantharians against the SC and the resistance as they can. Not to mention the Onotharian population here. I…I can't go through with it." Her voice was unsteady, but Andreia still sounded fairly collected. "I just don't know how I'll get away. It's as if they suspect me of something, or, I don't know, they think I can be sacrificed for the Onotharian cause. I'm under constant surveillance." The last words gushed out, and Roshan thought she could detect a trace of panic.

"Andreia. Listen to me. Breathe. What are they going to make you do?"

Andreia told Roshan about her parents' plan and the impact it might have on everyone involved. "No matter how you look at it, it's going to hurt the resistance by tarnishing its noble attitude. If I'm on display as having been tortured and raped, that good reputation will crumble, and we'll lose the support of many of the nations in the SC."

Roshan pressed her palms against the wall behind her and leaned her head back. *Damn! I should never have let her go back there.* Andreia hadn't exaggerated. She was beyond famous all over the planet, a household name, and everything the Onotharians would like to portray themselves as: kind, fair, smart, and, not to mention, stunningly beautiful. If they made it look as if a resistance cell had kidnapped and violated her, no matter how unbelievable most people would think the allegation was, it would indeed dishonor their cause. *And Andreia, forever victimized in the eyes of everyone.*

"Andreia, love, we have to stop this. Are you at headquarters?"

"Yes, I'm waiting for the surgeon that'll perform the 'makeover.' I'm not sure how long that'll be. Perhaps a couple of hours from now."

"Didn't anyone see you enter the building unscathed?"

"If they did, they didn't recognize me, the way I looked. And even if they had recognized me, they wouldn't dare object."

Roshan clenched her hand. She didn't know what made her tremble, the cool evening air or the adrenalin that rushed through her veins. She formed a plan, daring and unorthodox, and her mind raced as she tried to figure out the pros and cons almost instantly. "Are you willing to step away from it all, Andreia?"

"You mean, tell my parents I won't do it and just walk out the door? I don't think I have a choice. They'd probably sedate me, have the surgeon do his job, and present me to the people of Gantharat while I was unconscious."

"But, if you could walk away, would you? I mean, forever? It's important for you to tell me the truth."

"Yes. In a heartbeat."

"Then I'll put things into motion. If we're going to succeed, I have to act fast. I'll contact you as soon as I know something. All right?" Roshan waited for Andreia to respond, but all she heard was someone breathing deeply, as if trying to stay calm. "Andreia?"

"Yes, Ro. I hear you. Yes."

"Good. Now, let me know if they speed things up. Let's hope they don't."

"Yes, let's do that."

"Andreia. It'll be all right." Roshan wasn't sure she'd be able to pull off her idea, but knew she'd die trying.

"Ro. I…" Andreia sounded as if she was choking.

"I know. I know, love. I'll be in touch later."

"Okay. Until then. Boyoda out."

Roshan followed Andreia's example and took a few deep breaths of the evening air before she returned to the communications room. She stopped just inside the door and watched Jubinor, Jacelon, and the Protector where they stood over by the communicator system, discussing transports.

The Protector looked up and saw her, her eyes immediately narrowing. "Paladin, what's wrong?"

"Something's happened. We need to assassinate Andreia M'Aldovar, then pin the blame on the Onotharians."

❖

"What the hell are you talking about? An assassination?" Rae was obviously deeply disturbed by Paladin's matter-of-fact statement.

"Before I get back to that, bear with me." Paladin looked seriously at them as everyone took a seat except Kellen, who was restless and remained on her feet. "I have something to tell you that can go no further. I trust you all to keep this secret."

"Of course," Rae said. "Go ahead."

"We have a serious situation that entails the resistance leader, Boyoda, and also O'Daybo."

Kellen suddenly understood and wondered how she'd missed it before. "Boyoda—O'Daybo. It's an anagram. She's the same person, isn't she? O'Daybo is Boyoda."

Rae and Doc stared at her, then back at Paladin.

"Yes. You're right. O'Daybo is Boyoda, but it's more complicated than you think. We told you that O'Daybo is a hybrid of Onotharian and Gantharian. That isn't true. She's an Onotharian."

"What?" Kellen rose, angry. "Are you telling me Boyoda is an enemy double agent?"

Paladin held her hands up with her palms outward. "No. She's not. O'Daybo was born and raised on this planet and considers herself a Gantharian in every respect other than genetic. She loves this world and its people, and her own race's atrocities infuriate and sicken her."

"And now she's in trouble?"

"Yes. Major trouble." Paladin took a deep breath. "This is going to be as big a surprise to you it was to me, almost. Boyoda, whom you know as O'Daybo, is one of the most famous people on this planet, Andreia M'Aldovar."

"Oh, my God!" Rae sighed. "She's even famous throughout the SC, and highly admired."

"She's also one of them! Andreia M'Aldovar is right in the middle of the Onotharian power structure," Kellen growled. "And she's the sister of the man who nearly killed you, Rae." Kellen's heart thundered as she pictured the disdainful, mocking man, Trax M'Aldovar, who had stood next to a fallen Rae, one boot firmly planted on her stomach as he triumphantly laughed and called her a coward. She also remembered, with grim satisfaction, how she'd snapped his neck with her Gan'thet rods. Kellen didn't regret taking his life.

"I understand." Rae walked over to Kellen and touched her arm. "But she's not him. She's the woman who's led the resistance for so many years. I've read that Boyoda is so mythic that some people question if it's really a living, breathing person. And to think we worked with her for days without realizing it! O'Daybo and Owena pulled off something amazing on Vaksses. No wonder O'Daybo knew so much about both prisons."

Doc spoke up for the first time. "And how is Boyoda in trouble, exactly?"

As Paladin continued to describe Andreia's current situation, the worry and anger were evident in her voice, and she blinked repeatedly, perhaps to avoid shedding the tears that had formed in the corners of her eyes.

"So, tell me if I understand this correctly," Rae said. "They intend to put their world-famous daughter on display, as a fake victim of renegade rebels, and accuse said rebels of molesting her? Are they insane?"

Paladin shrugged. "Your guess is as good as mine."

Rae let go of Kellen and sat down again, legs crossed at the ankles. "And what did you mean about an assassination?"

"Just what I said," Paladin said, her voice detached and her face austere in the harsh light. "Andreia M'Aldovar must die."

CHAPTER TWENTY-SIX

A ndreia sat at her office desk, two guards by her door. Her mother claimed they were for her protection, but Andreia knew this was a blatant lie. She was a captive, nothing else, and soon they'd force her to run a gauntlet for the good of the Onotharian occupation. Andreia had even tried to figure out if she could take the guards by surprise and run toward the ventilation shaft she'd used once before, but she knew it wouldn't work with this many people in the building.

Everyone was working around the clock to mitigate, and track, the results of the raid of the asteroid prisons. Le'Tinia had sounded so pleased when she poked her head in and let Andreia know that they'd pinpointed two rebel camps. Andreia found it almost impossible to hide her despair for the people involved, and her mother's glee really disturbed her.

"*Henshes*, here's the surgeon now." Le'Tinia walked in, and a man with dark hair followed. "He's going to alter you, then wrap your wounds. We'll slowly remove the bandages during our broadcast so your disfigurement will be much more dramatic, with a greater impact." She turned to the surgeon. "Dr. M'Ouvos, was it?"

"Yes, ma'am."

"And you know exactly what we want you to do?"

"Yes, my instructions are very detailed and clear."

"Very well. I'll leave you to it, then." Le'Tinia made a production of kissing Andreia on top of her head. "Now, don't worry. The procedure's fully reversible."

"I know, Mother."

The door closed behind Le'Tinia, and the doctor approached Andreia. To her surprise he didn't start right away, but glanced surreptitiously around the room. Approaching her quickly, he raised his hand to her.

Andreia blinked in surprise until she saw there were something written on his palm.

Is the room under surveillance? Audio? Visual?

She glanced quickly up at him. "Doc?"

"Shh. We don't have much time," Doc mouthed as he was gathering his instruments from his bag. "Act dismayed."

❖

Kellen moved along the main communication center where a large crowd stood waiting to watch the charade that the M'Aldovars had initiated. A lump of molten lava still burned in the pit of Kellen's stomach when she thought of Paladin's revelation. Their plan had many unknown variables, but she was going to do her part and more, if it meant reaching their objective.

The crowd began to cheer, and Kellen moved into position not far from where the five hovercraft had set down. The doors opened on the third one, and a distinguished man emerged, followed by an elegant woman. As they received both appreciative and negative shouts from the crowd, Kellen realized they must be Andreia's parents. They carried themselves as if they owned the world, which they did, in a way.

Kellen knew from Doc's whispered communication earlier, through their individual earpieces, that he and Andreia were in the second hovercraft. The door was still closed, and she saw Paladin casually approach it from the left. She had located herself where she could easily pull the driver out. Kellen eased closer, in case Paladin needed help.

Somewhere in the crowd, Owena hid, armed and outfitted with the latest technology. She had taken the assignment with her usual serene expression, and her only condition for going above and beyond was that they let Leanne in on it. Paladin had objected at first, not wanting too many people to know, but relented when she realized she had no choice. Kellen and Rae knew Leanne's capabilities, and Rae suggested the pilot be part of Owena's escape plan after she'd committed the deed.

Onotharian guards lined the open plaza in front of the communication central, and the "assassination team" mingled with the crowd. Obviously the M'Aldovars were more interested in reaching as many people as possible than keeping onlookers at bay. They apparently wanted the public to get as good a view of Andreia as possible and thus be properly outraged. *Their mistake, our gain.*

The doors of the first, fourth, and fifth hovercraft opened, and guards exited them. One opened the door to the second vehicle, and Doc stepped out and extended a hand into the hovercraft. A slender, pale hand, partially bandaged, took his, and a female figure slowly emerged, clinging to Doc as if he were a lifeline. Kellen had to concede it was good acting, and the crowd murmured in sympathy.

They walked a few steps from the hovercraft, Doc with his arm around Andreia's waist. When they reached the first of twelve steps, a disturbance to the left in the crowd stole everyone's attention from Andreia.

A woman, of obvious Onotharian descent, pushed forward, shoving screaming people away with her raised weapon. "Get the fuck out of my way!" she roared, and Kellen had to admire the perfect Onotharian accent. Completely unrecognizable, Owena began firing at the convoy of hovercraft.

"Our cue," Kellen muttered, and adjusted her body to move with the now-boiling mob, intent on getting Paladin into the hovercraft, no matter the cost. A man pushed Kellen to the side and found himself in an arm lock. "Move!" Kellen shoved him out of her way. She reached the hovercraft and saw Paladin pull out one guard, who was large, nearly twice her size. The crowd surrounded them now as everyone wanted to see what was going on, despite the danger. Kellen chalked it up to humanoid curiosity as she pressed forward, grabbed the other guard by the collar of his jacket, and yanked him out.

"She's hit! Oh, Gods, she's been hit! Get her out of here!"

"It's bad! Look at all that blood. She won't make it. Get her to the hospital! Get her out!"

Frantic voices came from the other side of the vehicles, and Paladin kicked the guard's legs out of the driver's seat. "Why don't you get in here? You'll get trampled with these fools stampeding this way," Paladin yelled to Kellen over the noise of the roaring mass of people. "Come on!"

Kellen hesitated for only a fraction of a second before she jumped in. *All right. Plan C.* She gazed at the driver lying on the ground outside, barely visible among the forest of legs around him. A short twinge of regret, a hope that he wouldn't be killed by the people around him, shot through her as she slammed the door. Annoyed at this sudden softness, she climbed across Paladin's knees to sit in the other seat. Kellen hadn't heard Doc return Andreia to the hovercraft, and she gazed out the windows in their direction.

Doc appeared immediately, carrying an unconscious Andreia, his chest as bloody as hers. She could see his lips move as he demanded that people move. He spoke Onotharian effortlessly, as many of the younger generations did since it was mandatory in school, and his demands eventually carried through to them. "Let me pass! Step away, people. She needs a hospital and I can't wait for any other transport."

There was no sign of Andreia's parents, and Kellen thought it was entirely possible that they were already back in their craft, to avoid getting hit. A roar made the crowd yell, and Kellen saw a tall woman, Owena, shoot straight up into the air from where she'd stood when she shot Andreia. Her visor was down and the thrusters on her back, so small they easily hid under a jacket, took her up to a two-thousand meter altitude. There, Rae and Leanne would be waiting in a cloaked shuttle, to meet her, if all went as planned.

The door slammed shut behind Kellen, and a fist hammered on the small door between the backseat and driver's seat. Kellen opened it and Doc leaned in. Paladin pushed the controls, and the hovercraft began to rise above the crowd. The powerful gush of air knocked over several people, and its ascent created more disturbance and confusion, Kellen surmised, because at first, none of the other vehicles seemed to move.

"How is she?" Paladin called out, her voice hollow.

"She's unconscious. I'm afraid she hit her head." Doc's voice was filled with dismay. "The crowd was so intrusive, they had me off balance just as Lieutenant Grey fired. I tried to catch Andreia, but wasn't quick enough. She fell onto the stairs."

"Gods, is it bad?" Paladin asked, her face ashen.

"I don't think so, but some of this blood actually *is* hers. Can you help me, Protector?"

Kellen moved in and helped place Andreia more comfortably on one of the seats. Slight, with rather fragile-looking wrists, she seemed so defenseless. When Doc took off the bandages, Kellen inhaled sharply, even though she knew none of the injuries to her face and neck were real. O'Daybo…Andreia, she corrected herself, looked as if she'd been through hell. Swellings, cuts, and bruises deformed her face and made it nearly unrecognizable.

"I'll get rid of that in a minute. I just have to fix the back of her head first," Doc muttered. "Can you hold it up?"

Cautiously, Kellen cradled Andreia's head while Doc parted the long black curls and moved the derma fuser over the broken skin.

"Thank the Gods," he said with relief, "she didn't fracture her skull, and no major blood vessels are damaged either."

"Damn it, they're after us now! Hang on back there!" Paladin shouted, and the hovercraft plunged, only to ascend again in an almost impossible ninety-degree curve.

Kellen held on with one hand and, with the other, carefully placed Andreia's head back onto the seat. While Paladin straightened up the hovercraft, Kellen watched Doc restore Andreia's almost elfin looks. The delicately shaped features weren't quite like O'Daybo's, and Kellen realized Andreia had also been wearing a disguise while on the Vaksses mission. Finally, Andreia looked as if she was merely sleeping, and Doc unbuttoned her blood-soaked shirt. He removed the pouch and was about to button the shirt again when Kellen stopped him.

"Why not dress her in this? I have an undershirt on too, so I'll be fine." Kellen pulled off her thick coat and removed her own shirt, which was made of retro-spun cotton and would make Andreia feel better when she woke up.

Kellen felt unexpectedly concerned at the sight of Andreia dressed in the too-big garment, looking almost childlike. Though she told herself that her sympathy was unwelcome, she couldn't keep from admiring and wanting to protect the brave woman. *Rae's fault. I'm getting too soft.*

Kellen climbed back into the co-driver's seat just in time to witness Paladin slide sideways between two houses. The hovercraft roared as she pushed it through air corridors. "We're going to set down soon and change to my own vehicle," Roshan called out. "You ready to move her, Doc?"

"Yes. You land this thing safely, and I'll look after Andreia."

Paladin's lips were a fine line as she slid down four air corridors and took off to the right. There, barely visible from above, a long, lean, black hovercraft stood parked beneath two honey-trees. The government craft sank to the ground with what sounded like a sigh of relief, and Paladin threw herself out the door, as Kellen did the same.

Not being sure how long they had before the Onotharians found their own vehicle on their short-range sensors, they helped Doc place Andreia inside the much more luxurious hovercraft. Paladin leaned down quickly and kissed Andreia's lips before she hurried up to the driver's seat. Somehow this action didn't surprise Kellen, but Doc looked like he'd swallowed something that choked him. He coughed, apparently to mask his surprise, then held on to the nearest handle when Paladin took her vehicle up into the air corridors above them.

If the government hovercraft had been fast, Paladin's moved like lightning. She pulled over into the corridor to the far left and picked up even more speed, leaving the slightly ill-reputed neighborhood behind them.

"We'll reach one of my tunnels in twenty minutes. At the estate, my butler has arranged for a transport to the *Iktysos*. Hopefully, Andreia should be conscious about then."

"Good plan."

As the hovercraft sped through the dark evening, cutting through the air like a sword, Kellen leaned back in her seat and thought of the potential consequences of their actions this past week. She was certain of one thing: the situation on Gantharat was going to change, one way or the other, and she would do everything she could to make it change for the better.

❖

Muffled voices hovered around Andreia's head. Her body ached, and the skin on her face felt prickly. She tried to move her hand to see what was wrong, but couldn't lift it. She merely listened to the voices, oddly calm as she tried to figure out how to wake up and where she was.

She didn't know if she dozed off again, or if the voices disappeared from one second to the next, but it was suddenly quiet. Worried, she moaned, then whimpered. Annoyed, and now almost frantic, Andreia moaned again, this time in a deeper tone, more of a growl.

"Careful, love. You must be pretty sore."

That voice! Andreia pried her eyes open by sheer will power.

Muted light spared her pupils as she squinted at the face above her own. *I knew it. That voice. Her voice.* Roshan's beautiful face, now frowning worriedly, came into focus.

"Hello," Andreia managed, her throat dry and stinging.

"Hello there." Roshan smiled and kissed Andreia's forehead. "You're awake."

"Almost. Where—?"

"On the *Iktysos*, hiding in the asteroid belt. We're out of your parents' reach, love."

She was too tired to feel anything but relief right then, though she knew she would miss her parents just a little. "I'm glad. Was anyone hurt?"

"Possibly the driver of your hovercraft." Roshan's face darkened. "Nobody got killed, except you. It's possible that your parents realize that the rebels extracted you, but everyone who was there, the illegal camera crews, the public, believe you're dead. They saw the blood from the pouch, and how you hit your head, which wasn't a part of our plan, and...they're certain an Onotharian killed you."

"Oh, Gods. How long have I been out?"

"We could've woken you earlier if you had been hit only by the heavy stun, but the head injury was an unforeseen factor. Doc and our SC physicians all said to let you wake up on your own. So to answer your question, eighteen lunar-hours."

"Oh. That long, huh?" Andreia sat up, slowly and grimacing. "Ow, I'm sore. What time is it?"

"It's late afternoon." Roshan steadied Andreia tenderly. "Can I get you something to drink? Eat?"

"No, not yet. I need the bathroom though." Andreia felt her cheeks warm.

"I'll help you." Without missing a beat, Roshan lifted Andreia effortlessly, carried her to the ensuite bathroom, and placed her on a chair next to the toilet, then stepped back. "You all right from here?" Roshan caressed Andreia's cheek quickly.

"Yes. Thank you." Andreia watched Roshan walk out of the bathroom, dressed entirely in black. She had the same barely visible limp that Andreia had noticed at the meeting of the Commercial Lobby, held at Roshan's mansion about a lunar month ago. It seemed so much further in the past. So much had happened, and the fact that Roshan was still limping made her realize how quickly time had passed.

She finished her business in the bathroom and carefully stood, trying her legs. To her delight, they seemed to work, and she padded across the floor, automatically glancing at herself in the mirror. She wore a knee-length shirt of a semi-transparent fabric and already knew she wore no underwear. *Did you undress me, Ro?*

When Andreia opened the door, Roshan wrapped an arm around her shoulders. "Hey, you, easy there! You have a minor concussion, according to Doc, so don't do anything too adventurous."

For some reason, Roshan's choice of words made Andreia laugh, then almost howl. At first, Roshan merely stared at her. "Oh, please, *henshes,* you do have a way with words sometimes." Andreia laughed again, realizing that, unless she kept laughing, she'd cry for all she'd lost…and that she was so grateful for all she'd gained.

Finally she quieted and walked back to the small alcove holding the bed. "I can never go back to being Andreia M'Aldovar," she said, merely stating a fact. "But who am I, then? I'm Boyoda, but Boyoda is a mythic figure, something I could never live up to."

"And you're also O'Daybo, which is a nice name, by the way."

"Very well, so that's my new last name?"

Roshan sat down next to Andreia and pulled her onto her lap, cupping one hand around Andreia's cheek and holding on to her waist with the other. "Sounds good to me. You've developed a new reputation for courage, and you're highly admired as O'Daybo. Why not use that as your real name, rather than your call sign? From now on maybe we'll be able to fight more directly. We can begin using our real names and standing up for who we are and what we believe in."

"All right. And what about a first name?"

"Keep your own. It's not that unusual, among Gantharians and Onotharians."

"Andreia O'Daybo." But I look so very Onotharian. People will recognize me.

"A derma fuser can make the transformation you and I managed with makeup and colored lenses permanent. Doc told me we'd have to let your skin rest a few days before he performs such a procedure again, but then it's up to you."

"That would solve a lot of problems," Andreia murmured, her eyes fastened on Roshan's face. "I really don't care how I appear, as long as you look at me that way."

"Yeah?" Roshan smiled and seemed a little embarrassed.

"Yes. Like that. Like you want me." Andreia raised her hands and tucked a few errant strands of short hair behind Roshan's ear.

"Oh, I'll always want you, love," Roshan said. "After all, I ached for you for more than twenty-five lunar years. Now that I have you close, and know that you care about me, how could I not want you?"

"And I want you too. I want you in my life, no matter what it entails." Andreia's throat seemed to swell and she had to cough. "I care…and I love you."

Roshan's eyes lit up, then filled with tears. They didn't spill, but emphasized her luminescent blue eyes until they looked like glittering stars across the vastness of space. "I love you too, Andreia. I can't remember when I didn't love you. For the longest time, I hung onto life, stayed alive, trying to hate you, wanting to show you that I could fight you and everyone else, no matter what. But it was love, pain too, but love that remained with me throughout the years." She kissed Andreia, and her tears spilled and fell onto Andreia's cheeks.

Her own eyes dry and feeling great joy, Andreia wrapped her arms around Roshan's neck and held her close. "I missed you so much, and I tried everything to forget you, since I hurt every time you entered my mind. When you came back into my life and turned out to be just the person I initially thought you were, everything came rushing back. And it didn't take me long to realize how I felt, but I'd denied it, because I thought you hated me."

"I did. Or I thought I did. But only because I loved you so much, I was drowning."

"And you're not drowning anymore?" Andreia asked.

"No." Roshan kissed her with so much tenderness that Andreia began to tremble against her. "On the contrary. You elate me."

Parting her lips under Roshan's, Andreia infused all her love into the kiss they shared. It was as if they'd signed an agreement to never mistrust or lose each other again. The kiss tasted of Roshan's tears, which made it all the more intimate.

"I love you," Roshan whispered against Andreia's lips.

"I love you," Andreia responded, and pressed her lips against the quickening pulse point on Roshan's neck. "And I want to show you just how much."

Roshan laughed, a thoroughly sexy sound in the depth of her throat. "You're convalescing, remember?"

"Oh, but I believe in proactive measures to sustain quality of life throughout the process of recuperation." Andreia wrinkled her nose and winked.

"Gods, if you look at me like that, I'll show you proactive…Do you have any idea how utterly beautiful you are?"

Andreia curled up on Roshan's lap, fatigue overwhelming her, but she was reluctant to let go. "I think you're the stunning one, but I won't argue with you. It makes you cranky."

"Cranky?" Roshan pressed her lips against Andreia's hair. "I'm never cranky."

Laughing at *that* exaggeration, Andreia closed her eyes. She felt Roshan settle in against the pillows, cradling her. For the first time in a long while, Andreia felt completely safe and that she could briefly let go of duties and obligations. So sure that Roshan would watch the universe for her, she allowed herself to drift off. Roshan's scent of soap and leather filled her senses, and the happy thought that they'd still be together when she woke up made it easy for Andreia to fall asleep.

EPILOGUE

The convoy of three ships steered through the vastness of space. It had been several days since they'd left Gantharat, and Rae stood in her office, as usual, contemplating the stars while she sorted her thoughts. She twisted and turned a keep-hot mug of Cormanian coffee between her fingers, occasionally sipping it absentmindedly.

"Are they for sale?"

Rae jumped at Kellen's sudden voice behind her. "What?" She turned around and placed the mug on her desk.

"Your thoughts."

Still not understanding, Rae placed a hand at the back of her head. "Say that again?"

"Are your thoughts for sale?" Kellen enunciated.

Rae felt a broad smile break out on her face. "You mean, as in 'a penny for them'?"

Kellen looked confused. "If that's the going rate," she said hesitatingly, with a faint smile. It transformed her face as it always did, and Rae knew now that they were on their way back toward SC space, Kellen had a lot to smile about.

"Actually, I was thinking of our arrangement with the resistance. It's something you can be very proud of, Kellen, and also another significant step toward Gantharat's freedom."

"It wasn't just my idea. You were the one who suggested Revos Prime."

"Only because you didn't know of its existence. You suggested that all the prisoners return with us to SC space." At first the idea hadn't sounded feasible, but when Kellen explained why it was not only impractical to leave them on Gantharat, but also impossible, Rae knew she had to find a way. So many of the rebels were in even worse condition than they'd anticipated. If the former prisoners remained in the different resistance base camps, valuable, able-bodied rebels would be tied down caring for their fellow resistance fighters, rather than fighting the Onotharians.

When Rae began to think of the situation as a Retrograde Operation for the Gantharians, she realized they could evacuate them to Revos Prime, which belonged to SC space, but was governed jointly by Earth, Corma, and Imidestria. Used mainly for military exercises and war games, it was also a beautiful spot for recreation and had a benevolent equatorial climate. *We get to "play" in the north and south and have R&R in between.* Rae smiled at the military saying as she sat down on the edge of her desk.

They had also thought it better to transport the rebels to Revos Prime before the Onotharians woke from their nightmare scenario regarding Andreia. Loading them all onto the six spaceships, they made sure their basic needs were met, but knew the trip would still be very rough on them. Roshan's medical personnel had worked around the clock, along with the SC medical officers.

"They'll thrive by the Credarian Ocean and under the care of our specialists. I just talked to Father, and he's issuing orders to establish a Medical Reception Station. I sent enough information for him to make the Revos Prime medical teams aware of the rebels' condition. Once they've healed, we'll retrain the ones with a clean bill of health and help them devise a new Gantharian Force."

"Excellent. You finally managed to reach Ewan? How's Armeo?"

"From his squeal in the background, he's beyond thrilled that we're coming home. Father also granted us a whole two-week leave. Very generous."

"It is," Kellen agreed readily.

Rae was grateful to her father, not only for granting her the expertise the rebels of all ages needed to help them recuperate, but also for keeping Armeo's spirits up the way he had. It made up for all the time she'd felt misunderstood and misjudged as a child and a young woman. *Perhaps he had to go through raising me to be ready for Armeo, Prince of Gantharat. Go figure.*

"...will stay and oversee it all." Kellen looked at her under raised eyebrows. "Rae?"

"Sorry. I was thinking about Armeo. What were you saying?"

"I think Revos Prime will be a good place for Andreia and Roshan to stay for a while. They need to be out of the public eye."

"Absolutely. Andreia will find her bearings as Andreia O'Daybo and get used to her altered appearance, and Roshan will see if she's been compromised. It's possible, since she was involved with Andreia openly before her assassination." Rae scowled. "It feels strange to even say it, though I know it was all for show."

"Yes." Kellen joined Rae, leaning her hip against the desk. "Owena pulled it off almost too well."

"When Leanne and I finally hauled her inside the shuttle, she was frantic with worry that she had actually killed Andreia. We had two Onotharian surveillance ships on our tail when we took off. Good thing Leanne was at the helm after all. I'm a good pilot, but not in her class, or yours."

Kellen smiled again and ran her fingers through Rae's hair. "True."

Rae laughed. It felt so good to be able to do so, for the first time in ages. She was exhausted now, yet excited about going home. A strange energy filled her with new strength.

"So Roshan and Andreia will be the spokespersons for the 37,000 Revos Prime rebels," Rae summed up. "It's a very good idea, in fact."

"It seemed logical," Kellen said.

"And tell me, why are we taking this volatile kid, Ayahliss, home with us to Earth?" Rae folded her arms and leaned back a bit so she could study Kellen's face. "Do you have *any* idea what my mother will have to say about that girl?"

"She needs guidance. Half trained in the art of Gan'thet, she has the physical skills, but not the mental training or sense of how to use it. I have to train her, it's my duty."

"And isn't it also that you see something of yourself in her?"

"Perhaps."

"Fair enough." Rae stretched. "I'm tired. How about we check on the bridge and hand the conn to Owena for the evening?"

"Good idea. I'm tired too."

Kellen sounded utterly astonished at Rae's suggestion, which made Rae burst out laughing again.

"I've missed your laughter," Kellen said, her smile going from faint to wide. "It's such a happy sound."

"Well, no wonder. You make me very happy, whether I'm laughing or not." Rae leaned in for a soft kiss. "You make me very, very happy. I love you, darling."

"I love you too." Kellen returned the kiss with so much passion that Rae began to question how tired she really felt.

The hum of the *Gallant's* powerful propulsion system vibrated steadily beneath them as they strolled back to their quarters. As Kellen undressed, illuminated only by the starlight coming from the view port, Rae watched with the same ache in her heart she'd felt all those months ago when she first saw this extraordinary woman. She loved her with every atom in her body, and always would.

When Kellen turned around, gloriously naked, Rae was already undressed, eager to hold her. Rae wanted to get back to Earth for several reasons, but this wasn't one of them, not at this moment. Out here, in the middle of outer space, they belonged to each other in every way, and she couldn't wait a second longer to make love to Kellen while blessed by the stars.

About the Author

Gun Brooke, a former NICU nurse, lives in an 1800s cottage in Sweden with her family and her beloved dog. In the calm and quiet countryside village, which dates back to the Viking era, she enjoys the closeness to nature and writes full time. Gun has won two Golden Crown Literary Awards for 2005 with her first novel, *Course of Action* and her first science fiction novel, *Protector of the Realm*. In 2006 she published her second romance, *Coffee Sonata*. Gun has also published three short stories in three different anthologies. Currently, Gun is working on her fifth novel, the romance *Sheridan's Fate*.

Books Available From Bold Strokes Books

More than Paradise by Jennifer Fulton. Two women battle danger, risk all, and find in one another an unexpected ally and an unforgettable love. (978-1-933110-69-1)

Flight Risk by Kim Baldwin. For Blayne Keller, being in the wrong place at the wrong time just might turn out to be the best thing that ever happened to her. (978-1-933110-68-4)

Rebel's Quest: Supreme Constellations Book Two by Gun Brooke. On a world torn by war, two women discover a love that defies all boundaries. (978-1-933110-67-7)

Punk and Zen by JD Glass. Angst, sex, love, rock. Trace, Candace, Francesca...Samantha. Losing control—and finding the truth within. BSB Victory Editions. (1-933110-66-X)

Stellium in Scorpio by Andrews & Austin. The passionate reuniting of two powerful women on the glitzy Las Vegas Strip where everything is an illusion and love is a gamble. (1-933110-65-1)

When Dreams Tremble by Radclyffe. Two women whose lives turned out far differently than they'd once imagined discover that sometimes the shape of the future can only be found in the past. (1-933110-64-3)

The Devil Unleashed by Ali Vali. As the heat of violence rises, so does the passion. A Casey Family crime saga. (1-933110-61-9)

Burning Dreams by Susan Smith. The chronicle of the challenges faced by a young drag king and an older woman who share a love "outside the bounds." (1-933110-62-7)

Fresh Tracks by Georgia Beers. Seven women, seven days. A lot can happen when old friends, lovers, and a new girl in town get together in the mountains. (1-933110-63-5)

The Empress and the Acolyte by Jane Fletcher. Jemeryl and Tevi fight to protect the very fabric of their world: time. Lyremouth Chronicles Book Three (1-933110-60-0)

First Instinct by JLee Meyer. When high-stakes security fraud leads to murder, one woman flees for her life while another risks her heart to protect her. (1-933110-59-7)

Erotic Interludes 4: Extreme Passions. Thirty of today's hottest erotica writers set the pages aflame with love, lust, and steamy liaisons. (1-933110-58-9)

Storms of Change by Radclyffe. In the continuing saga of the Provincetown Tales, duty and love are at odds as Reese and Tory face their greatest challenge. (1-933110-57-0)

Unexpected Ties by Gina L. Dartt. With death before dessert, Kate Shannon and Nikki Harris are swept up in another tale of danger and romance. (1-933110-56-2)

Sleep of Reason by Rose Beecham. While Detective Jude Devine searches for a lost boy, her rocky relationship with Dr. Mercy Westmoreland gets a lot harder. (1-933110-53-8)

Passion's Bright Fury by Radclyffe. Passion strikes without warning when a trauma surgeon and a filmmaker become reluctant allies. (1-933110-54-6)

Broken Wings by L-J Baker. When Rye Woods meets beautiful dryad Flora Withe, her libido, as hidden as her wings, reawakens along with her heart. (1-933110-55-4)

Combust the Sun by Andrews & Austin. A Richfield and Rivers mystery set in L.A. Murder among the stars. (1-933110-52-X)

Of Drag Kings and the Wheel of Fate by Susan Smith. A blind date in a drag club leads to an unlikely romance. (1-933110-51-1)

Tristaine Rises by Cate Culpepper. Brenna, Jesstin, and the Amazons of Tristaine face their greatest challenge for survival. (1-933110-50-3)

Too Close to Touch by Georgia Beers. Kylie O'Brien believes in true love and is willing to wait for it, even though Gretchen, her new boss, is off-limits. (1-933110-47-3)

100th Generation by Justine Saracen. Ancient curses, modern-day villains, and an intriguing woman lead archeologist Valerie Foret on the adventure of her life. (1-933110-48-1)

Battle for Tristaine by Cate Culpepper. While Brenna struggles to find her place in the clan, Tristaine is threatened with destruction. Second in the Tristaine series. (1-933110-49-X)

The Traitor and the Chalice by Jane Fletcher. Tevi and Jemeryl risk all in the race to uncover a traitor. The Lyremouth Chronicles Book Two. (1-933110-43-0)

Promising Hearts by Radclyffe. Dr. Vance Phelps arrives in New Hope, Montana, with no hope of happiness—until she meets Mae. (1-933110-44-9)

Carly's Sound by Ali Vali. Poppy Valente and Julia Johnson form a bond of friendship that becomes something far more. A poignant romance about love and renewal. (1-933110-45-7)

Unexpected Sparks by Gina L. Dartt. Kate Shannon's attraction to much younger Nikki Harris is complication enough without a fatal fire that Kate can't ignore. (1-933110-46-5)

Whitewater Rendezvous by Kim Baldwin. Two women on a wilderness kayak adventure discover that true love may be nothing at all like they imagined. (1-933110-38-4)

Erotic Interludes 3: Lessons in Love ed. by Radclyffe and Stacia Seaman. Sign on for a class in love…the best lesbian erotica writers take us to "school." (1-9331100-39-2)

Punk Like Me by JD Glass. Twenty-one-year-old Nina has a way with the girls, and she doesn't always play by the rules. (1-933110-40-6)

Coffee Sonata by Gun Brooke. Four women whose lives unexpectedly intersect in a small town by the sea share one thing in common—they all have secrets. (1-933110-41-4)

The Clinic: Tristaine Book One by Cate Culpepper. Brenna, a prison medic, finds herself drawn to Jesstin, a warrior reputed to be descended from ancient Amazons. (1-933110-42-2)

Forever Found by JLee Meyer. Can time, tragedy, and shattered trust destroy a love that seemed destined? Chance reunites childhood friends separated by tragedy. (1-933110-37-6)

Sword of the Guardian by Merry Shannon. Princess Shasta's bold new bodyguard has a secret that could change both of their lives: *He* is actually a *she*. (1-933110-36-8)

Wild Abandon by Ronica Black. Dr. Chandler Brogan and Officer Sarah Monroe are drawn together by their common obsessions—sex, speed, and danger. (1-933110-35-X)

Turn Back Time by Radclyffe. Pearce Rifkin and Wynter Thompson have nothing in common but a shared passion for surgery—and unexpected attraction. (1-933110-34-1)

Chance by Grace Lennox. A sexy, funny, touching story of two women who, in finding themselves, also find one another. (1-933110-31-7)

The Exile and the Sorcerer by Jane Fletcher. First in the Lyremouth Chronicles. Tevi and a shy young sorcerer face monsters, magic, and the challenge of loving. (1-933110-32-5)

A Matter of Trust by Radclyffe. When what should be just business turns into much more, two women struggle to trust the unexpected. (1-933110-33-3)

Sweet Creek by Lee Lynch. A celebration of the enduring nature of love, friendship, and community in the heart-warming lesbian community of Waterfall Falls. (1-933110-29-5)

The Devil Inside by Ali Vali. The head of a New Orleans crime organization falls for a woman who turns her world upside down. (1-933110-30-9)

Grave Silence by Rose Beecham. Detective Jude Devine's investigation of ritual murders is complicated by her torrid affair with pathologist Dr. Mercy Westmoreland. (1-933110-25-2)

Honor Reclaimed by Radclyffe. Secret Service Agent Cameron Roberts and Blair Powell close ranks to find the would-be assassins who nearly claimed Blair's life. (1-933110-18-X)

Honor Bound by Radclyffe. Secret Service Agent Cameron Roberts and Blair Powell face political intrigue, a clandestine threat to Blair's safety, and the seemingly irreconcilable differences that force them ever farther apart. (1-933110-20-1)

Innocent Hearts by Radclyffe. In a wild and unforgiving land, two women learn about love, passion, and the wonders of the heart. (1-933110-21-X)

The Temple at Landfall by Jane Fletcher. An imprinter, one of Celaeno's most revered servants of the Goddess, is also a prisoner to the faith—until a Ranger frees her by claiming her heart. The Celaeno series. (1-933110-27-9)

Protector of the Realm, Supreme Constellations Book One by Gun Brooke. A space adventure filled with suspense and a daring intergalactic romance. (1-933110-26-0)

Force of Nature by Kim Baldwin. From tornados to forest fires, the forces of nature conspire to bring Gable McCoy and Erin Richards close to danger, and closer to each other. (1-933110-23-6)

In Too Deep by Ronica Black. Undercover homicide cop Erin McKenzie tracks a femme fatale who just might be a real killer...with love and danger hot on her heels. (1-933110-17-1)

Stolen Moments: Erotic Interludes 2 by Stacia Seaman and Radclyffe, eds. Love on the run, in the office, in the shadows...Fast, furious, and almost too hot to handle. (1-933110-16-3)

Course of Action by Gun Brooke. Actress Carolyn Black desperately wants the starring role in an upcoming film produced by Annelie Peterson. Just how far will she go for the dream part of a lifetime? (1-933110-22-8)

Rangers at Roadsend by Jane Fletcher. Sergeant Chip Coppelli has learned to spot trouble coming, and that is exactly what she sees in her new recruit, Katryn Nagata. The Celaeno series. (1-933110-28-7)

Justice Served by Radclyffe. Lieutenant Rebecca Frye and her lover, Dr. Catherine Rawlings, embark on a deadly game of hide-and-seek with an underworld kingpin who traffics in human souls. (1-933110-15-5)

Distant Shores, Silent Thunder by Radclyffe. Dr. Tory King—along with the women who love her—is forced to examine the boundaries of love, friendship, and the ties that transcend time. (1-933110-08-2)

Hunter's Pursuit by Kim Baldwin. A raging blizzard, a mountain hideaway, and a killer-for-hire set a scene for disaster—or desire—when Katarzyna Demetrious rescues a beautiful stranger. (1-933110-09-0)

The Walls of Westernfort by Jane Fletcher. All Temple Guard Natasha Ionadis wants is to serve the Goddess—until she falls in love with one of the rebels she is sworn to destroy. The Celaeno series. (1-933110-24-4)

Change Of Pace: *Erotic Interludes* by Radclyffe. Twenty-five hot-wired encounters guaranteed to spark more than just your imagination. Erotica as you've always dreamed of it. (1-933110-07-4)

Honor Guards by Radclyffe. In a wild flight for their lives, the president's daughter and those who are sworn to protect her wage a desperate struggle for survival. (1-933110-01-5)

Fated Love by Radclyffe. Amidst the chaos and drama of a busy emergency room, two women must contend not only with the fragile nature of life, but also with the irresistible forces of fate. (1-933110-05-8)

Justice in the Shadows by Radclyffe. In a shadow world of secrets and lies, Detective Sergeant Rebecca Frye and her lover, Dr. Catherine Rawlings, join forces in the elusive search for justice. (1-933110-03-1)

shadowland by Radclyffe. In a world on the far edge of desire, two women are drawn together by power, passion, and dark pleasures. An erotic romance. (1-933110-11-2)

Love's Masquerade by Radclyffe. Plunged into the indistinguishable realms of fiction, fantasy, and hidden desires, Auden Frost is forced to question all she believes about the nature of love. (1-933110-14-7)

Love & Honor by Radclyffe. The president's daughter and her lover are faced with difficult choices as they battle a tangled web of Washington intrigue for...love and honor. (1-933110-10-4)

Beyond the Breakwater by Radclyffe. One Provincetown summer, three women learn the true meaning of love, friendship, and family. (1-933110-06-6)

Tomorrow's Promise by Radclyffe. One timeless summer, two very different women discover the power of passion to heal and the promise of hope that only love can bestow. (1-933110-12-0)

Love's Tender Warriors by Radclyffe. Two women who have accepted loneliness as a way of life learn that love is worth fighting for and a battle they cannot afford to lose. (1-933110-02-3)

Love's Melody Lost by Radclyffe. A secretive artist with a haunted past and a young woman escaping a life that has proved to be a lie find their destinies entwined. (1-933110-00-7)

Safe Harbor by Radclyffe. A mysterious newcomer, a reclusive doctor, and a troubled gay teenager learn about love, friendship, and trust during one tumultuous summer in Provincetown. (1-933110-13-9)

Above All, Honor by Radclyffe. Secret Service Agent Cameron Roberts fights her desire for the one woman she can't have—Blair Powell, the daughter of the president of the United States. (1-933110-04-X)